The Law of Magic

Tyler A Mann

To Mrs. Wilkens and Mrs. Maher. Thank you for making me
believe this dream could become a reality

CHAPTER ONE
New Lessons

Kyzyl realized he had over packed after the third trip from the ship to the docks. Each item had seemed reasonable when he considered it by itself. However, he recognized that, if it took him and three members of the ship's crew three trips to unload all his possessions, he could hardly expect to be able to carry everything he brought inland.

He went over his luggage, running his fingers through his thick black hair. There was an alchemy set that he'd used for years to test various samples he'd gathered from his father's estates. If he was going to the University Arcanum, they'd provide better equipment than a child's set of glass vials and crucibles. The small set of books he'd brought would be a drop in the ocean compared to their library.

His eyes fell on one particular book. <u>On Magical Theorem</u> was the book that got him interested in magic. It was a collection of essays done by a Lukoran scholar describing the mechanics of moving energy from one form to another, the foundation of arcane magic. He'd practically memorized the book in his childhood, so it was of no use to him now. But it was the book that made him want to come to this land and study at the same place as this scholar. Parting with it now felt very much like abandoning everything he'd learned up until this point. Was he prepared to do that after everything else he'd left behind?

Before he came to a decision, he noticed two of his silk robes were missing. He chuckled. No doubt they had been lifted by the crew members who assisted him. In a way, they had done for him that which he couldn't bring himself to do. Perhaps it was best to follow their example.

Most of the things he'd brought were a way of hedging his bet on the University Arcanum. If his admissions exam didn't go well, and he didn't get in, these things would allow him to continue his studies wherever he ended up. Now that he'd arrived in Tamerrel, the largest port city in the kingdom of Strophe, this fear he had been holding felt more like it was holding him back. That wouldn't do. "Success comes not to those who hesitate," his father would say. Very well then, no hesitation.

The sailor's theft had also given him an idea. He walked up to one of the dock workers and offered him a trade of a silk robe for his horse and cart. The man eagerly agreed despite the fact that the robe was half his size. Kyzyl could see everyone around him was wearing some combination of leather and homespun wool, low-class clothing compared to his tailored silk. Most of the dock workers had to lace their clothes to make them fit properly. He wondered idly how much tailored clothes might be worth in this part of the world as he made it back to the ship with the cart.

"Captain?" Kyzyl asked. The captain; tall, lean muscled, and imposing elf; finished yelling at his crew to "get a move on" and looked at Kyzyl. "Where could I find a pawn shop around here that will give me a decent price for my things?"

The crew members gave him a look like they didn't

appreciate hauling all his stuff off the ship just so he could pawn it. "Not down by the docks, but there's one not too far from here that will give you close to a fair price. Just don't look too desperate, mind you."

"That'll do. Tell your crew I hope the robes they stole suit them well." Kyzyl finished loading the cart and led the horse away as the captain gave the crew members an angry glare.

When Kyzyl got into the city proper, he was assaulted by its rancid smell. The docks had an off-putting odor, but it was pushed back by the breeze coming off the ocean. With the buildings blocking that, the smell nearly over took him. He soon missed the open-air nature of his father's estates, and he hoped the university would be more spaced out than this port city.

It took Kyzyl a few minutes to find the pawn shop the captain was talking about. It was barely more than a small warehouse with shelves. The sign outside didn't have any words, just a picture of a hand reaching for a coin purse, but he was certain this was it. The bell rang as Kyzyl walked through the door. The shopkeeper was middle aged and slender. His ears were slightly pointed, and there was fuzz on his face that suggested he'd skipped the last couple of days shaving.

Kyzyl had learned from the captain that elves didn't grow facial hair, and he wondered idly about this man's heritage. Were the elves on this continent hairier than their Techarian counterparts? Was this man something else entirely? He decided these were not polite questions to ask and resolved to drop the issue by the time the shopkeeper spoke.

"Why hello there, young sir. And what can I do for you this fine day?" The shopkeeper gave Kyzyl a hungry smile. It was only now that he saw the man's eyes and hungry grin that Kyzyl began to question the wisdom of entering a pawn shop wearing clothes that were clearly tailored and more expensive than half the things in the shop. Kyzyl looked around. Scratch that, most of the things in the shop.

"I'm looking to sell a few things. I recently came into town, and I seem to find myself overburdened. Is there a way you might be able to help?" Kyzyl said.

The shopkeeper pulled his grin tighter until it was almost off-putting. "Why of course! Here at the Copper Coin, we always aim to please. Now, which of those fine jewels you have there will we be looking at today?" The man gestured to Kyzyl's hands that bore three rings. Only half the number he usually wore, but he did have enough foresight to leave the rest in his coin purse.

"You misunderstand me. These rings are hardly a burden to me. The things that need to go are outside." Kyzyl gestured, and the man followed him to the door. "If you could help me to bring them inside, we can start discussing things."

"I'd be happy to assist." The man responded in an overly polite tone.

They spent a quarter of the next hour hauling everything into the shop as the owner's tone became one that Kyzyl could only describe as viciously polite. At one point, Kyzyl had accidentally jostled a young, dirty boy of about eight, or maybe he was twelve and merely malnourished.

After they had finished, the owner examined everything very carefully. "Well, everything here is just lovely. The clothes are of an exquisite make and the glass on this brewer's set is of very fine craftsmanship. Are we going to be selling today or pawning?"

"Selling." Kyzyl's hand went to his coin purse, but it wasn't on his belt.

He barely kept from cursing as he put his hands through each of his pockets. He tried to do so subtly, so the shopkeeper wouldn't notice. It was gone. Every coin he had brought with him, and his family's signet rings, had been stolen.

Kyzyl felt his stomach drop and his heart begin to pound. He was in an entirely new continent, a six month sea voyage away from anyone he knew. He only had one choice: milk this shopkeeper for everything he could and hope it would be enough.

"Oh? Gotten into some trouble down at the docks, have we?" The shopkeeper must have noticed Kyzyl's panicked look.

Kyzyl took in a long breath and let it out slowly. He gathered his composure and put on a mask of indifference. He snorted at the shopkeepers question. "Hardly. No, I'm headed inland, to the University Arcanum." There was still a slight edge to his voice, but he was hoping the man wouldn't notice.

"I see, I see, and you need money for the trip of course."

Kyzyl rolled his eyes. Part of bargaining was convincing the other party how much you simply didn't need whatever it was they were giving you, so Kyzyl tried to make it seem like he didn't just lose all of his money.

"I already told you. I'm trying to lighten my load. Now the clothes alone are worth at least twelve gold molas, giving you a fifty percent profit margin brings it down to six gold molas for me; the *alchemy* set," Kyzyl stressed the word to make it clear he was no brewer, "can be yours for the low price of nine silver lapi, allowing you to mark it up to two molas with room to spare; and the books are worth a whole platinum mark to the right seller, so you can have them for five gold, since you aren't quite the right seller." Kyzyl did a quick tally.

"Ten molas should be plenty. We are, if I'm not mistaken, in the Kingdom of Strophe, so that works out to," Kyzyl paused for dramatic flair and to give himself time to breathe, "twenty crowns and five nobles." He made his tone casual but firm. Making it clear that, though this wouldn't add much money to his purse, the price was nonnegotiable.

"I'll give you fifteen crowns because you entertained me, kid." The shopkeeper dropped the politeness and spoke frankly. "I couldn't make back twenty crowns in a year. Look around you. You've got dock workers, prostitutes and beggars. How many of them do you think want to buy books they can't read, clothes they can't work in and a set of glass vials for something they know nothing about? I might be able to sell it to one of the distilleries as a brewer's set, if I'm lucky. Everything else is just going to take up space."

Kyzyl had to take a moment to collect himself. He hadn't expected the shopkeeper to switch tones so effortlessly. When he'd collected himself, he said, "As generous as you think that offer is, sir, my offer is the one with which I am standing. You don't think I noticed your little spot here. I was thinking you might want to break into the big leagues and cater to some decent folk."

Kyzyl hoped the man didn't notice the white-knuckled fist he was hiding behind his back or the slight quiver in his leg. His father had tried to instill him with the confidence of nobility, but Kyzyl still had a hard time wearing it. "I assumed you were waiting for just the right buy to get you out of this slum and into the nicer part of town. I suppose I was mistaken. I'll go find a pawn shop worth my time." Kyzyl moved to take his stuff, but the man behind the counter stopped him.

"Fine. Twenty crowns. That's all you get, understand me? It's still going to be hell to find someone willing to buy any of this junk and I can't waste my time."

"Deal." Kyzyl took the money. "And you can have the horse and cart for another five."

The shopkeeper grimaced and took out another handful of coins. Kyzyl took his money, glad to have a lighter load and money in his pocket. Hopefully, this time, it'd stay there.

Once outside, Kyzyl spotted the captain of the ship

he'd just left. The man was moving through the crowd with an expert grace and, when he caught Kyzyl's eye, he gestured for Kyzyl to come toward him. "Sir, to what do I owe the pleasure?" Kyzyl thought back to the crew mates that stole his clothes. He hoped the captain hadn't just got done punishing them for the theft.

"I felt bad about my crew stepping out of line. I wanted to come--"

"Think nothing of it."

"Please, after the months you spent on my boat, I feel it's my responsibility to make sure you know what sort of gift you allowed them to steal off you."

"What do you mean?" Kyzyl stepped around the captain and gestured for him to follow. "It was just a couple sets of clothes. As you might have noticed, I have plenty." At least, he had plenty before he sold them. Now, he was down to five sets.

It was embarrassingly sparse for someone of his bloodline, but what choice did he have? He ran his thumb under the fingers with the three rings he had left. They were a safety net of sorts. When the twenty-five crowns he just got ran out, he'd need something to sell for the rest of his tuition.

"That's just it, my lord. The silks you wear are really rare here. The two sets of clothes you let them have would be worth as much as my ship to the right seller and at least a week of whoring and drinking to anyone on this side of town."

"Really? That is interesting." Kyzyl thought about the money he had just gotten from the pawn shop, the admissions exam at the university, and what living here might cost. It was nice to know he had an unexpected safety net. Still, the idea that something like silk was that rare on this side of the world seemed strange. Maybe he looked richer than he realized. Was it safe for him to dress like this?

"What did you get for your things, if you don't mind me asking? You seem to have lightened your load quite a bit." The captain gestured toward the one remaining backpack on Kyzyl's shoulders. The only things he had left were his last five sets of robes, including the ones he was wearing, and the two books he couldn't part with: <u>The Three Fundamental Laws of the Arcane</u>, and <u>On Magical Theorem</u>. Neither of them held any information he didn't already know, but when the time came, he couldn't part with them.

"Enough to get me through the Admissions Exam." He left off the word "hopefully."

The captain let out a long whistle. "If you're going inland with that kind of coin, you're going to want to leave it with the dwarves. You'll also want to get some good homespun. You'll look too rich on the road, you're liable to get your throat cut by a bandit."

"Is the King's Road really that dangerous? I was always under the impression that safe roads were the bones of civilization."

"No king has an army big enough to cover every step of the road." The captain waved his hand. "Regardless, it is best if your money is safe with the dwarves. They are experts in keeping your things safe." The captain pointed the way to the bank and said he had to get back to his crew. Kyzyl decided he had time, and headed to see what was so great about this bank.

The bank wasn't hard to find. There are few buildings in the world as ornate as the kind for storing valuables. After he walked in and saw the interior, he was even more convinced. Kyzyl had entered into a massive hall with an arched ceiling at least two stories high. It was held up by stone columns that were as wide as his shoulders, the floor was a shining marble, and each piece of furniture was carved from oak and varnished within an inch of its life.

He walked up to a line of tables that divided the

room and left the back quarter of it inaccessible from the main entrance. The dwarf behind the table was separated from Kyzyl by thick iron bars. When Kyzyl got to the table, he noticed something under the varnish. There were arcane runes etched into the wood. He suspected they were wards to keep the workers safe from more nefarious customers. "How can I help you, young sir?" the dwarf asked.

"I was told your bank could keep my money safe."

"No place safer than one of our banks."

"And there is more than one?"

"Got hundreds of them scattered throughout all of Lukor. From the base of the Holy Mountains to the seashore. In Strophe, Calcut, and Antorn."

"Only those three countries? What about the Unclaimed Hills, Hamlin, or the North Forest?"

"We only build banks in civilized places lad. Can't have no orc raider rushing the place. As for Hamlin and the North Forest, you ever try to run a bank in a place populated by monks or halflings?"

Kyzyl shook his head.

"Neither are big on worldly possessions. Not owning things by yourself doesn't lend itself to needing a place to keep things safe."

Kyzyl nodded. "And if I gave my money to you," he said, getting back to the matter at hand, "where would I be able to get it?"

"You ask a lot of questions boy. I'll explain this slowly, so you don't get confused. I take your money. I give you a Writ of Deposit. Then, wherever you go in all the land, excluding the wilderness, all you got to do to get your money is show someone at one of our other banks that Writ, and they'll give you whatever you need. It'll be taken out of your accounts, and everything will be settled."

Kyzyl nodded. "Anywhere in Strophe?"

"Anywhere in Lukor."

"Your bank isn't backed by the crown then?" Suddenly leaving anything in this place seemed like a risk. What would happen if this bank, or any of the others were robbed? How would they be able to return everyone's wealth without the assurance of the state?

"Backed by a crown that's barely a century old? Ha. The Bank of Dalthor is older than most of the existing governments in Lukor. Which means this bank is backed by the fact that no one would dream of trying to steal from us. Unless they found their thumbs to be a burden to them." He chuckled at his dark joke.

"Let me see your purse, so we can get started." Kyzyl sheepishly handed him the twenty-five crowns, feeling embarrassed at not having a purse for them. The dwarf didn't comment on it. He made a few notes in the ledger in front of him.

While he wrote, Kyzyl took a look at the runes in front of him. Arcane runes were still somewhat a mystery to him, but he could make out a few anti-kinetic glyphs. Those would stop any object over a certain momentum from passing over the table. He touched the iron bars and wondered if the spell was reinforced by them, the wood of the table, or both.

The dwarf looked up from his ledger. Kyzyl caught his eye. "Since you seem to be somewhat clueless, I'm guessing your house doesn't have a standing account with us."

Kyzyl was getting rather annoyed by his gruff directness. This dwarf's attitude was a stark contrast to the polite tone of the pawn shop owner. "Will that be a problem?"

"Not exactly, but there is a service fee for opening a new account."

"How much?"

"Three percent of your initial deposit."

"What? Why? By doing that you incentivize people

depositing as little as possible and coming back later to deposit the rest."

"Any deposit made within the same day is considered the same deposit. This way, people that come into money in an unsavory fashion, have to think about how to time putting it away. Gives them more time to be caught with it, and we don't have to bother with it."

"I guess that's reasonable." The clerk nodded, but before he could take the money, Kyzyl stopped him. "Taking out three percent would leave me with some change. Two and a half silver nobles." Strophe's monetary system being base 10 made it so much easier to do math.

The clerk nodded. "Would it be possible for me to get that out as coin. I have some business in the city I need tending to." The clerk sighed, making it seem like it was a difficult task, but Kyzyl couldn't guess why.

He walked to the back with Kyzyl's money. Kyzyl continued to examine the wards on the table. He didn't recognize any additional runes, but a thought did occur to him.

After several minutes, the clerk came out with a slip of parchment with intricate calligraphy, and two silver nobles and five copper pennies. "This is your Writ of Deposit. It's coded, enchanted, and sealed with the finest magic money can buy, so don't go thinking you'll be able to forge it."

Kyzyl put his hands up and tried to look innocent. He had thought of a number of ways while he was here to rob or otherwise cheat the bank, but merely as a thought experiment to keep him occupied.

"With this sort of magic," Kyzyl indicated the runes on his desk, "I doubt I'd be able to think of anything that could get through your defenses. If you have access to anti-kinetic wards for your desk, I'd bet the same ones are on your vaults. Probably anti-thermal ones too." Kyzyl paused. "Are there wards against summoning?"

The clerk let out a loud belly laugh. "Aye. There are. Like I said, our bank is protected by the finest magic money can buy. I doubt the Masters at the University could get around them. You sure know your stuff. Are you a mage?"

"I'm a mage in training." At least, Kyzyl hoped to be when he got to the University. Right now, he was technically just a noble who knew about magic.

"Well then, mister mage-in-training, after the fee and your piece back, your total deposit was twenty-four crowns. Do you have a seal?"

Kyzyl sighed internally. All his signet rings were in his coin purse. "I don't suppose my signature would be enough."

"Signatures can be forged. You don't have a house seal?" The clerk looked significantly at Kyzyl's robes.

Kyzyl rubbed the back of his neck as he thought, then an idea came to him. "Can I borrow some of your ink?" The clerk looked at him confused, but slid him the bottle. Kyzyl took out the rag he used to clean his pens, turned the ink bottle over on his thumb, and rubbed most of the ink on to the rag until there was the smallest film of ink.

The clerk handed him the parchment and pointed to a spot in the bottom right-hand corner. He didn't hide his skepticism, but Kyzyl was confident. "Press in the corner and the writ will do the rest." Kyzyl did so, and a swirl of red ink morphed itself into a perfect impression of his thumb print. The clerk looked surprised.

"Ink usually has trace metals in it. The spell you use to identify seals and signets checks the metals in the ring. You can use ink to trick it into taking an impression of anything."

"That may prove useful to us." The clerk gave Kyzyl a thankful nod, and Kyzyl took his writ and put it in a pouch he'd strapped to his chest with one of his remaining silk

sashes. Two and a half nobles and a writ for twenty-four
gold. It was all the money Kyzyl had left. He hoped it would
be enough for tuition. Once he took the exam, there was no
way to change his tuition, and he needed his money to last
years while he studied.

Kyzyl went about the central market square
looking at fine wares and chatting with many of the
merchants around, who were as diverse a group as he
could imagine. Most were human, of one sort or another,
but there were several dwarves selling finely made arms
and armor. There were also several short, stout halflings
selling everything from baked goods to jewelry, and a few
other wares that, based on the halflings' overall manner,
Kyzyl guessed weren't entirely legal.

Perhaps they were merely acquired in an unsavory
way. Kyzyl didn't bother with them. He didn't want to risk
breaking laws in an unfamiliar country.

After a bit of milling about, Kyzyl looked up at the
sun. He held up his hand and counted three fingers from
the base of the sun to the building nearest to the horizon.
He juggled some numbers in his head and estimated about
four hours before the sun was completely set. His stomach
was rumbling, he felt dirty, and he needed to find a caravan
going inland. He decided on the bath first and asked the
next person he saw where the bath houses were.

"A house just for you to take a bath? Yeah, it's right
over there next to the sleepin' mansion." The halfling
chuckled at his own joke and walked away.

No bath houses? Kyzyl thought. *Maybe this place
is a little barbaric.* Seeing that option out of reach, he
settled on washing twice when he got to the university and
set about on his secondary plan: finding something to eat.

He ended up in a quaint little inn at the edge of the
market district. It wasn't terribly large. The entire town
seemed to be packed so tightly that very few buildings
could boast even a medium footprint. However, it was
clean, quiet, and there was an exceptional lyrist playing by

the hearth.

He approached the bar and asked the woman standing behind it for something hot, and she came out quickly with a try laden with still warm bread, soup that Kyzyl guessed was a mix of potato and beef, a side of butter, and several jams.

"That'll be two iron mills," the barmaid said flatly. Kyzyl raised an eyebrow. He was used to hot meals being a bit more expensive than just the food, but that was a bit much. He pulled out a copper penny. His funds had dwindled considerably after buying several well-tailored sets of clothes and a new coin purse. The penny he held up was also about five times what the woman had asked for.

"I also need a travel sack with as much food that will keep on the road as this will afford me." He slid the coin over to her. The woman picked up the coin and walked briskly into the kitchen.

"We have some lovely apples that came in from the orchard this morning. Some juicy Empires, would you like some of 'em?" she called without looking back at him.

"That would be lovely, thank you," Kyzyl answered.

She returned just as Kyzyl was finishing his meal carrying a burlap sack that was full nearly to bursting. She handed it to a surprised looking Kyzyl. Apparently, a hot meal in an inn was quite the up-charge from travel food around here. He bowed graciously before heading back to the market square.

Finding merchants who were headed in land was easy enough, and after negotiations, he gave a Caravan Master two copper pennies, the last of his hard coin, and was told to put his things in the wagon. When he put the sack full of food next to his backpack in the wagon, a dwarf who was part of the caravan looked at him over his glasses. "Expectin' us not to feed ya?"

He hadn't been actually, but he didn't want to

offend the dwarf by saying so. He thought quickly and said, "I figured that it couldn't hurt for the group to have a bit of extra food along the way, in case of disaster."

The dwarf laughed heartily. "I pegged ye all wrong boy! I thought you were some high noble's son."

"What if I was?" Kyzyl responded, keeping his tone measured.

"Well, if ye were, I'd say yer right practical for yer lot. There's more sense in tha' thought ye had than I've seen in all the noblemen I've had to ferry around this damned overworld you people call home."

"You're not from the, ah, overworld, was it?"

"Nay lad, I'm here fer book keepin' purposes. I got a head fer numbers ya see, so I was recruited by Elidra there," he gestured toward a halfling woman ordering around a group of humans packing wagons, "and I've been gettin' dragged all over this part of the world ever since."

The woman came up to the hip of the man she was ordering around. Her face was rounder than a human's face, and she had a stout figure. Her hips were wide and her torso was narrow, reminding Kyzyl of a perfume bottle.

"I see. Where are you from originally?"

"Ye ever been as far as the Great Divide?"

"I've heard of it."

The dwarf let out another loud belly laugh. "Aye, I bet you have! It is, after all, the dividing line that separates half the continent from us."

"I'm not from around here."

"Aye. Then we both be strangers in this 're land." Kyzyl nodded, glad to have found common ground with someone. Strophe was even more different from his homeland than he'd expected, and he was feeling a little overwhelmed by this point. "Right then, if we be leavin', we be leavin'." The dwarf declared, and the wagons lurched forward as the horses began to march.

"We're actually leaving now? But it's going to be

dark soon. Is that wise?"

"Aye, bandits can't see as well in the dark, on account of them being mostly you overworldy types, no offense. We got our own kinda nasty in the mountains. If'n ye be wantin', since ye can't see well either, ye can ride in the wagon till ye get used to seein' in the dark."

"I think I'll manage." Kyzyl didn't want the other caravaners to think less of him for not being able to keep up.

"Aye, just don't go turnin' an ankle or nuthin' while ye walkin'"

"I'll be careful."

CHAPTER TWO
Learning More

The caravan trundled onward through the night. There were roughly five wagons in total and each wagon was heavy with exotic goods that had been shipped in from the port. The wagons were so full, in fact that the four occupants that would normally ride on the seats were forced to lead their horses from the ground.

That meant, in total, including the dwarf, the guards, Caravan Master Elidra, and the merchants, there was easily two score of people traveling on-foot through the dark woods that night. The shadows on the trees made Kyzyl uneasy and he stayed close to the dwarf while they walked. It was his first time being acquainted with a dwarf, and the man's stocky build and gruff composure set Kyzyl at ease.

Kyzyl and the dwarf, whose name he had learned was Baerûn, walked along together, each telling stories of their homeland. Baerûn asked where Kyzyl learned Aragoran, and Kyzyl told the story of how he'd taught himself to read it using a few books in his father's library. The rest he learned from the sailors he met on his six month journey here.

Baerûn had gone into an equally long story about

the time his father had an envoy of subterranean elves meet with him for a trade agreement when he ordered the wagons to stop. The men walking alongside the wagons dropped immediately but the horses stood firm. In fact, Kyzyl noticed, they didn't seem to be tired at all, even though he was sure they had to have, at the very least, been pulling carts for at least ten hours by this point. He didn't have much time to dwell on this strangeness before Baerûn sighed.

Kyzyl watched as the horses disappeared. He was impressed, recognizing this immediately as magic.

"Learned tha from me pa. We be usin' tha spell to pull mine-carts fer as long as I can remember."

Kyzyl was astounded by what he had just witnessed. The dwarf's casual use of a summoning spell with no sleep was one thing, but he had to maintain concentration on up to eight of them by Kyzyl's count. The land he was in was practically brimming with magic that would be a treasure in his homeland.

"That was amazing. What other spells do you know?"

"None. Me pa only taught me the one spell. It's a kind of legacy for me family. Father to son, mother to daughter, the spell survives because we need it. The carts in the mine my family works are too heavy for us to push, and real horses aren't built fer the mountains. We had to find a way to make it work, and we did. Tha's another reason Elidra has me on as her bookkeeper. I know tha spell like I know me own beard."

"But how? How can your mind handle the strain? I don't think you realize how exceptional this level of mastery is."

"Aye. I suppose I just gotten used to it. Been casting tha' spell since I was a boy. At first it was hard; I could barely keep one horse around fer a whole day. Eventually tha' got easier, and I moved on ta two. Kept going until I am where I am now. Took a century or two, mind you, but dwarves live as long as stones, so tha's no big deal fer us."

Kyzyl had more questions, like where he got the energy for such a huge casting, but a wave of fatigue washed over him at that moment and he staggered. Now that his body wasn't moving, it was demanding sleep, and Kyzyl had to focus on his breathing to stay awake. "I presume this means we are stopping for the night?"

"Only long enough for our men to get their rest. We try ta keep movin'. Gets us where we be goin' faster. If ye be tired, now is the time for restin'."

"I think I will do that." Kyzyl climbed into the back of the wagon. "Will they be able to walk when it's time for us to move again?" Kyzyl gestured at the guards that were already nodding off beside the carts.

"Aye, they just be a bit over dramatic. They'll be fine."

Kyzyl nodded, found a spot among some sacks, and covered himself with his cloak. He had barely stopped moving when he fell asleep.

When Kyzyl awoke, he heard yelling, the choral ring of weapons being drawn, and fearful screaming outside the wagon. He bolted up and looked around. The caravan was in chaos with black masses scuttling about. Kyzyl threw on his cloak and jumped out of the wagon in front of one of the masses. It was a giant spider that had been feeding on one of the caravan guards. It was the size of a large dog with eight onyx-colored eyes that quickly locked on to Kyzyl. His hand went instinctively to a sword that wasn't there.

"Thrice damn my father for demanding I leave my sword behind!" he shouted. He only knew one spell. He looked around for a moment. Power, focus, effect. The spell would act as the focus. He already had an effect in mind. But where to get the power? He spotted a small pile of embers. It would have to do. He took a calming breath, and pushed his mind into the focused state he used for spellcasting.

It was a state of mindfulness he had begun to call Wind-dance because he'd practiced it while following the wind as it shifted around in his father's courtyards. It pushed out all thoughts of the future or past. There was only the present moment.

***

The spider is scurrying toward him. Kyzyl chants and flexes his fingers, pulling the heat from the burning coals. He feels it wash over him. The energy travels down his arm, and then a bolt of burning arcane energy erupts from his hand and slams into the spider, sending it flying. When it lands, it scurries back into the forest from whence it, presumably, came. He lets go of the concentrated mindfulness and slips back into his normal state.

***

Kyzyl, rather proud of himself, began to round the wagon, and his face fell. Where he had thought he had solved the problem. The real problem, the carnage, lay before him. An entire swarm of spiders, each at least as large as the one he had scared back into the woods, were attacking the caravan.

After a moment of fear that stretched for ten, albeit rapid, heart beats, Kyzyl forced himself back into Wind-dance. Everything but the present moment fell away.

***

He moves quickly to the closest target. Kyzyl speaks the words and flexes his fingers again. This time he pulls the heat from his own limbs. Once more, fire erupts from his hands and blasts the eight-legged creature off an unconscious caravan driver. Kyzyl moves to him and checks him for injuries. Nothing fatal. He picks up the man's sword and swings it a couple times to get a feel for its balance. It isn't quite as well balanced as the one sitting in his room back home, but it will do.

Just then another spider launches itself at

Kyzyl, but Kyzyl's trained senses pick up on it. A moment later the creature is in half on the ground. Kyzyl surveys the rest of the battle. Baerûn had conjured a team of horses to beat back a few spiders while he crushes others with a massive hammer. Several of the halflings that made up the bulk of the mercantile force are throwing daggers at nearby spiders. Most of the men that were hired on as guards are brandishing spears or clubs.

Then Kyzyl sees something that makes his blood run cold. A spider twice as big as any of the others is descending slowly on one of the wagons. Kyzyl thinks about burning it, but it wasn't very likely to do much. He has to act fast before it traps everyone in a web, or worse, kills them with its venom.

Kyzyl blasts as many spiders as he can, but his limbs are going numb. He points the people he saves toward the monstrous spider. They all know exactly what to do. They encircle the beast while Kyzyl continues to rally more support. He dispatches the lesser spiders until he can't move his fingers anymore. The massive spider lands on an uncovered wagon.

Baerûn is at the front of the crowd. He chucks his hammer much further than Kyzyl would've thought possible. He watches as Baerûn's hammer cracks the spider's exoskeleton and the spearmen take aim at the creature's broken defenses. Tens of spears drive themselves into the gaping wound and the spider crumples with a shrill cry. Kyzyl hears a sound, spins, and cuts down the last living spider that has not fled into the forest already. The battle is over, and only most of the caravaners were injured. Kyzyl slips back out of his mindfulness state.

***

Kyzyl's mind started racing through the fear and adrenaline he had forced to the side while in Wind-dance. He took a knee and clutched his chest. He had read a few medical treatises on panic attacks. This rush of emotions

21

always felt similar to how they were described.

"What were those beasts?" One of the guards spoke through labored breaths.

"Aranae Gargantua," Kyzyl answered through deep breaths. "They are more commonly known as giant spiders, for reasons that, I assume, are obvious." Focusing on answering someone else's questions gave his mind something to do other than be overwhelmed by emotion.

"You've encountered them before?"

Kyzyl shook his head. "I've only read about them in my father's library. They're supposed to be incredibly rare and mostly solitary. I can't imagine how we came across so many at once."

"Probably some kinda nest. Tha big one could've been the mother." Baerûn interjected. He looked exhausted, and he was moving gingerly. Kyzyl saw blood on his shirt. There was a lot of it, but he hoped not all of it was Baerûn's.

Kyzyl nodded. "It could be hatching season for them. I'm not familiar with their mating habits, but the larger one did seem a bit protective." He looked around at the caravan. "Several of the men are unconscious, some women too. We should find a safer part of the forest and rest. I'll provide first aid to anyone who needs it. The guards that are still conscious should keep watch."

Baerûn agreed and they set about putting the still living but unconscious bodies on to the wagons. They found a few whose bodies had succumbed to their wounds or the spiders' venom. All of them were part of the caravan, and Baerûn explained that the caravan was the only family these people had.

The bodies were carried to the side of the road. A grave large enough for all of them was dug, and by the time the bodies were placed in, the sun had risen. Afterwards, there was a moment of meditative silence broken only by light sniffing from some of the still conscious caravaners.

During the silence Kyzyl had an idea, and when they got back to the site of the battle, he checked his backpack and nearly yelped in excitement. He had saved a few glass vials from his alchemy set, and now he was going to put one to use. He took the vial in one hand and broke off the tip of a fang in the other. It wasn't easy, after all it was literal bone, but he found the right leverage. It snapped and the venom began to drip into the vial.

"What are you doing?" one of the caravan drivers asked.

"I'm collecting a sample of their venom to bring to the university and study."

"Why?" The man sounded suspicious, like Kyzyl just said he was going to sell it to an assassin.

"I've heard that it has alchemical properties." Kyzyl put a stopper in the vial and went back to his backpack to grab a stick of wax. He lit the wick with a smaller version of the spell he had used on the spiders, and then he began to drip wax onto the seam of the vial. He put it into his backpack just as the wagon was pulling away. The caravan began moving forward, carrying the unconscious victims, and Kyzyl ran to the front where Baerûn was riding atop a number of barrels.

He winced with every bump, and Kyzyl saw that he was clutching his side. There was a deep red mark spreading over his loose cotton shirt.

"You're injured," Kyzyl said without any inflection. Remaining calm was an important part of providing medical care.

"Aye. There were quite a few of 'em, and one caught me off guard. Got me in the side 'ere." He gestured to his other side. Someone had wrapped it in a torn piece of cloth and Baerûn was keeping pressure on it.

"Have you had anyone look at it, or did you do that yourself?"

"Aye, I looked at it meself. I'm fine."

"I saw their fangs. A bite to the side with those things could be serious, not to mention their venom. When we stop, I'll look at it." Kyzyl could tell the bookkeeper was in pain, and he wanted to do something to help.

Baerûn gave him a dark look. "We dwarves are hardier than you give us credit fer boy. Toxins don't do much to ya when ye spent your entire life in caves and caverns surrounded by spiders. As fer the wound itself, I'll put some salve on it."

"OK. And what about the bandages you need? Sides don't take stitches well, but you're going to need to cover that wound so it doesn't get infected." Kyzyl gave a significant look at the scraps of cloth. "The bandages should also be boiled or somehow disinfected."

"And what makes ye such an expert on medicine, eh?" Baerûn gave Kyzyl a curious look out of the corner of his eye. Whatever tension the dwarf had about Kyzyl insisting on helping him, it seemed to have subsided by now.

"My father wanted me to join the local temple. Many of them are healers, so I made medicine a part of my studies so he'd think I was going through with his plan." Kyzyl shifted a bit. Talking about his parents made him nervous considering what he had done.

"Aye. Wanted ye to be a priest, did he?"

"Not exactly. Many of the healers where I come from are closer to mages or scholars than holy men. I've never really seen the correlation between gods or religion and medicine. Unless you're relying solely on miracles, why not ask someone who studies the world that made you sick in the first place?"

"I suppose that makes sense from a certain perspective, but ye can't deny that it makes sense to entrust the care of your body and soul to the same people nay?"

"I certainly can. It leads to the danger of a cleric

trying to cure a man's soul of an affliction when his body is what needs attending. For instance, if a priest tries to rid you of a demon to cure a cough, when all you really need is an herbal tea, the exorcism could further exacerbate the disease."

Baerûn shook his head. "Clerics know how physically draining exorcisms are. They know it better than anyone. A cleric wouldn't--"

They hit a bump and Baerûn shouted in pain. They were coming up on a clearing and he signaled down the line for the wagons to pull over off the road. Kyzyl decided to trust the Caravan Master rather than risk irritating him with further discussion. He could tell that his help was not being welcomed openly, and he didn't want to further alienate his new friend.

He helped the injured man off the wagon and told a nearby driver to fetch bandages and whatever salve Baerûn was talking about.

"I can wrap me own bandages boy. I've done it before," Baerûn protested as Kyzyl pulled his shirt off. The dwarf didn't fight the removal of his shirt. Kyzyl didn't know how much he'd be able to get away with by simply ignoring Baerûn's objections, but he was sure his help was needed. He didn't plan on accepting no for an answer.

"I'm sure you're perfectly able, but I want to be sure things are done correctly. The best way to do that is to do them myself." Kyzyl realized how his words sounded the moment they came out of his mouth.

Baerûn just chuckled. "Aye, boy. You an' I ain't so different after all, eh?" He slapped Kyzyl on the back while Kyzyl examined the wound. It was shallow and didn't appear to have pierced any organs. Perhaps Baerûn was right about how hardy dwarves were.

Kyzyl finished his examination just as the driver came back with bandages in a tin and a tightly closed jar. Kyzyl took these things, set them down on the seat of the wagon, and sent the driver to fetch a bowl of water, and a clean cloth. Meanwhile, Kyzyl looked through his backpack. He didn't have any disinfectants, only the wood alcohol he used to clean his pens.

"Does anyone in your caravan have iodine or potent alcohols?"

"I hardly think this is the time for drinkin', lad," Baerûn said.

"I need a disinfectant. Well distilled spirits will work until we get somewhere with a reputable doctor."

"The salve should do well enough. I've used it plenty of times without issue."

Kyzyl came back to Baerûn as the driver returned. Kyzyl took the cloth and shooed the driver away, not wanting anyone gawking at their Caravan Master as Kyzyl tended to him. Then he picked up the salve, pulled off the tight lid and sniffed. Then he took in a big whiff and smelled all the different, intermingling herbs: Catmint, Aloe, Comfrey, and... was that bilberry? He was suddenly very aware, both of how similar and different the people that surrounded him were from his people. He couldn't think of a single physician in his homeland that would use this kind of mixture. This salve was either genius, or it was madness.

"You said you used this salve before?" Kyzyl asked. He tried to keep the condescension out of his voice.

Baerûn heard it and gave him a look. "Aye. Spiders the size of horses ain't the only danger on these roads. That thing ye got in yer hands has saved my skin more times than I can count."

"This can counteract the venom of a spider? It doesn't seem to have anything anti-septic in it. Are there any side effects?"

"Aye. Nothin' I can't handle. That right there is a general healing salve made by a cleric I'd trust with me own first son. He's an expert healer."

"Very well, but promise me you'll tell me if you start feeling ill. I don't want you to die because neither of us knew what 'medicine' you were putting in your body."

Baerûn heard the condescension again and it seemed to rub him the wrong way. "I'd be willing to bet a wagon's worth of goods ye think we still use leeches don't ye?"

"You may not, but I doubt everyone has been caught up on that small fact. You're a traveler. Have you been to many small towns?"

"Have you?"

"Not far beyond my father's lands," Kyzyl admitted.

"And?"

"We never used leeches."

"Your people never used anything that was anything less than helpful in your entire history?" Kyzyl didn't look at Baerûn's face, but he heard the smile in his tone, and it softened Kyzyl's growing indignation.

Kyzyl paused for a moment and considered that question. "Mercury. Some people in the past believed mercury was the secret to immortality."

Kyzyl looked up to see Baerûn nodding, seeing that his point was made. "And how'd that work out for ya?"

"I see your point. Progress must be made with all people."

"My point is you'd do well to get off yer high horse before you make it to the college. I don't know much about the Masters, but I know they don't tolerate students who look down on people."

Kyzyl thought about Baerûn's words. He had spent his entire life on his father's estate and outlying fief. He was used to being one of, if not the, smartest person within a day's walk. But there was a difference between being smart and knowing what you were talking about. "Perhaps you're right. I'm sorry. I'm starting to sound like my father."

"Aye?"

"He didn't want to send me to the university

because he couldn't believe that your 'barbaric culture' could build anything that was half as good as the things in our lands."

"Maybe you can convince him otherwise by being twice as good as any mage he can find in your lands."

Kyzyl nodded at that. He was going to live in this land, with these customs. He couldn't very well go around insulting everyone at the college by telling them their "barbaric" customs were all wrong. He didn't trust religious figures and didn't think anyone else should either, but saying so loudly and often would surely alienate everyone around him and may even get him kicked out. He finished dressing Baerûn's wound and made his way to the closest fire. He took a bowl of what was in the pot and ate ravenously. He hadn't eaten in almost a full day. After four bowls of stew, Kyzyl thanked the cook graciously and found a large oak. He leaned against it, wrapped himself in his cloak, and fell into a deep, dreamless slumber.

CHAPTER THREE
Admission and Admiration

The rest of the trip was comparatively uneventful. Kyzyl spent most of it talking to Baerûn about the differences in their cultures. Kyzyl was careful to avoid the topic of faith in healing. He was still not entirely sold on Baerûn's assertions the so called "healing magic" assisted in the fight against disease and the mending of wounds.

They, instead, stuck to safer topics like Kyzyl's cultural emphasis on regular washings and the dwarf's rather layman understanding of magic. Baerûn even asked him one day if he had made a pact with an "otherworldly sort," and Kyzyl had to ask what he meant. As it turned out, some who have never known a mage think they get their powers from demons or fae creatures. This made Kyzyl laugh, and he was, apparently, lucky that Baerûn never really believed those stories.

"If my da saw you laugh like that, he'd have thought ye were mad as a hatter," Baerûn told Kyzyl.

"But your father taught you the spell with the horses. What makes that different from what I hope to do?"

"A difference of scale mostly. He thinks that one spell is all a body can handle, so anyone who can do more than that must have demon blood in his veins."

Kyzyl nodded, considering this. Demons didn't exist. He knew that for sure, but still the idea made him chuckle. "My family tree only seems to go back so far. Maybe there is a demon in there somewhere," he joked. Baerûn just shook his head. He looked uncomfortable, and Kyzyl was surprised the normally humorous dwarf didn't take to the joke.

When they did finally reach the town that surrounded and served the university, the caravan began unpacking their wagons. The wagons themselves unfolded into makeshift stalls that fit well into the market square, lining a space for the extra wares that was encircled by the stalls. It was all a rather ingenious set-up, and Kyzyl couldn't help but be impressed.

Baerûn and Elidra finished helping the merchants unfold their wagons, and Baerûn came to speak to Kyzyl. He held out his hand to the young man, and Kyzyl took it, matching the dwarf's sure grip with his own.

"Can't thank ya enough fer how ye handled the spiders back there." He indicated his side, where a wound that was only a week old had healed over very rapidly.

"I'm glad the salve worked out for you. I'd have hated to stop to bury you as well. Too much of a delay."

The dwarf grinned and gave Kyzyl's arm a light punch. He'd learned the dwarf's coarse humor well during their week together, and he was sad to think they'd never trade quips again.

"Don't get all sappy on me, boy," Baerûn said in response to Kyzyl's sad look. "You may not be used to 'em, but us caravaners know a thing or two about good-byes. No sense in drawin' 'em out gettin' all weepy. Go on now. There be Masters waiting for you to strut your stuff."

Kyzyl nodded. With one final good-bye to the rest of the caravan, he walked away from the town square and toward the gate of the University complex. He heard Baerûn shout something, but he was already to far away to make out the exact words. Besides, he was probably just shouting at a merchant.

Once he arrived at the open gates of the university, Kyzyl bit his thumb to ensure he wasn't dreaming. The shops around him sold glassware, herbs and medical supplies, tools for etching and engraving, and so many other things that magi would make regular use of. In addition to the shops, there were inns and tap-houses aplenty. Most of the students in the university were some level of wealthy, and Kyzyl suspected many of them took study breaks that involved heavy drinking.

Then there were the university buildings themselves. He could see a huge pyramid made of dark stone, a towering hall with stained glass, a nonagonal tower that was surrounded by a well-kept garden, and, at the center of it all, was the crown jewel of the University Arcanum: the Library of Arcane Theory. It was the largest repository of magical knowledge in the known world.

He shook himself out of his amazement. "Entrance exam first," he told himself. He looked around and found himself in the middle of a place he didn't recognize. He had read countless books about the university, but that was entirely different from being here. There had to be someone here who could point him in the right direction.

Kyzyl spun about, chose a tavern at random and walked in wearing his best nobleman's bearing. He held one of his hands in a tight fist behind his back. His anxiety was making him shake, but he was his father's son. He called out to the crowd at large and asked, or more accurately demanded, that any students of the university point him toward the place that held registration.

One rather annoyed looking patron pointed him toward the stone building that housed the temple to the Knower, the patron god of the university's clerics. Kyzyl nodded in thanks, walked out proudly. When he was out of sight of the inn, he laughed as the tension in his body released. It worked and he was deeply relieved.

Kyzyl walked down to the smallest of the great

stone buildings. At least the Masters had the sense to put those clerics in their places. Just walking into the building and seeing all the artwork and architecture annoyed him.

The building itself had an overhang that was held up by slate grey columns. Every window was stained glass and depicted its own unique fractal design. The parts of the walls that didn't hold stained glass windows were painted a deep blue that made Kyzyl feel like he was back on the ocean with the sailors.

Kyzyl assumed the religious leaders of this region had made the demand for the temple. What better uses could this building have been put to? The university had a hospital where the Master Physician taught medicine, they had a library and plenty of inns and boarding houses for the students.

As he walked up to the desk, he decided that, since there was nothing that this university needed that it didn't already have, the temple wasn't doing that much harm. There was a young man, younger than Kyzyl, at least, writing very carefully and meticulously in a log book. Above him were the words "Knowledge is Man's Greatest Tool. Desire For Knowledge is Man's Greatest Ambition."

Kyzyl felt himself agreeing with the sentiment. He found it ironic scrawled on the wall of a temple, but at least the clerics of this temple had their goals aligned with his. Kyzyl cleared his throat and the young man jumped. When Kyzyl heard him squeak, he realized that the young man was hardly more than a boy.

"Is this where I register for the entrance exam?" Kyzyl asked.

"Yes. You're just in time. The Masters are just finishing with their last contestant, so had you come just a few minutes later, I would've had to turn you away."

Kyzyl tried to smile through the fear of being so close to disaster. Being turned away would mean he'd have to wait another three months to try and register again. "Fate must be with me then."

The boy nodded. "Name."

"Shenta Kyzyl."

The clerk raised an eyebrow. "Where are you from?"

"Techarae." The university took students from all around the world, but foreign students were still rare.

"How'd you get here? I thought the mountains of the Great Divide were impassable."

"The world is round. There's always more than one way to get somewhere."

The boy gave a low whistle "Wow. Talk about the long way. Did you spend all that time learning Aragoran? I've never met a Techarian, so I'm surprised you don't have an accent."

Kyzyl chuckled. It was mostly from the mounting anxiety of his upcoming exam. "I was with a lot of sailors from this side of the world for about six months. I guess my speech patterns just adapted. Anyway, about the registration..."

"Oh!" The boy wrote furiously in the log book. "OK. You're all set. The man inside will tell you when it's time."

Kyzyl started to walk inside then paused. "Are you a student here? I thought I'd be one of the youngest."

The boy shook his head. "My family lives nearby. The Masters allow Bernard, the head of the accounts, to hire kids like me to help with the bookkeeping."

Kyzyl nodded. "So, this is a job for you? You get paid?"

"Yup, and I get to learn to read and write too."

"Thus, making you more educated and, by extension, a more skilled laborer. Making an apprenticeship more likely." The boy tapped his nose. His curiosity satisfied; Kyzyl walked through the door.

The waiting room was nearly bare, lit by a large, narrow window with a stained-glass moon. There were a few chairs and a man sitting behind a desk. He was old enough to be Kyzyl's father. When Kyzyl entered, he looked up. His faced was touched gently by time, there was the barest hint of lines on his face, and his greying hair and beard just made him look more distinguished. He stared at Kyzyl with a single raised eyebrow. When Kyzyl didn't immediately speak or walk out the door, the man gestured silently to the chairs in the room.

Kyzyl was filled with nervous energy, and elected to stand. As he waited, the man kept looking up at him, as if Kyzyl's presence was disturbing.

After an hour of quiet waiting, a man at least five years Kyzyl's senior walked out of the room connected to the waiting room. Kyzyl stood and looked at the man behind the desk. The man gestured him into the room and turned his attention to the man that had just entered.

Kyzyl walked into a dark room. The three glowing white orbs floating above a U-shaped table cast everything in the room in shadow. It was difficult for Kyzyl to guess at the size of the room; he couldn't tell if the walls he saw were just more shadow. The table was on a raised platform, so, even sitting at the table, the Masters were staring down at everything. The Masters wore black robes that made them look almost indistinguishable from the darkness in the rest of the room. Kyzyl was very grateful that the edge of the light stopped just before where he stood at the door, so the Masters couldn't see his initial reaction of awe at the entire spectacle.

His gaze fell on a second, round platform that was obviously where he was supposed to stand. He knew from some of the books he read that this platform was rigged to turn as the Head Master introduced each Master in turn. That way, when a Master was questioning you, you faced him head on. Kyzyl had read many stories of nerves colliding with motion sickness and making would-be students throw up all over the floor.

Kyzyl, for his part, was trying to still his anxiety by reminding himself how much preparation he'd done for this very moment. He was ready, he was sure of it. He had read every book he could get his hands on from cover to cover, and absorbed everything he possibly could about magic. All to not only impress, but astound, this group of nine men.

"Kyzyl Shenta. Please come forward." The Head Masters voice boomed in the silent room. Kyzyl almost didn't register that it was his name. He was used to his culture where your family name was given first. That, coupled with the surprise that the man had pronounced it correctly gave Kyzyl pause. He was prepared for his name to be butchered due to its root in a foreign tongue. The Head Master also doubled as the Master Diviner, so Kyzyl suspected he had some kind of clairaudient spell near the registration. But, then, why would he have reversed the order? He stepped on the platform as instructed and the Head Master continued.

"Here, on the twenty-first day of Seedling, I, Head Master Herman, do hereby invite Kyzyl Shenta to take the entrance exam for the University Arcanum. Kyzyl, do you accept my invitation?"

"I do, sir."

"Then I shall begin with the first question. What are the three Fundamental Laws of Arcane Theory?"

"The Law of the Triad, The Law of Conservation, and the Law of Equality."

"Explain them."

"According to the Law of the Triad, all spells must have three components: a source of power, a focus for that power, and an effect for that focus to enact. Power, focus, effect. The Law of Conservation states that energy cannot be created or destroyed, only moved from one place to another. The Law of Equality states that all forces applied by a spell must be balanced, in some way, by the caster."

The Head Master nodded, then turned to one of the other Masters sitting at the far end of the table. "Master

Abjurer." The platform rotated quickly, and Kyzyl came face to face with a tall, thin man with tired eyes and a hooked nose.

"Name and describe the three basic types of magical defense," he said.

"First is active defense, such as shields. These defenses require specific direction by the caster. Passive defenses generally require less focus, but cannot move with the same ease. Things like walls and spells that act like armor. Last is field defenses. They're more colloquially known as wards. These surround an area and provide near complete protection from very specific forces. I was actually exposed to a rather good example of this on my journey—" Kyzyl was cut off by a wave of the Master's hand.

The Master continued. "What is the first concern of the Abjurer?"

"Always be prepared, even for the unexpected."

The man slid back in his seat and the Head Master called out the next man on the list. "Master Artificer."

Kyzyl's platform spun to meet a rather stout looking dwarf wearing goggles and thick leather gloves. His beard was singed in several places and he was missing half an eyebrow.

The Master asked, "what sort of material would you use to make a sword?"

"Steel probably. There's a reason most weapons are made from steel. It's light, and holds an edge well enough. The forging process makes a great deal of difference though. My people use sand or glass while melting it, and closed-top forges."

"Oh? And why is that?"

Kyzyl smiled at the opportunity to demonstrate his people's ingenuity. "It's a technique that has been passed down through my people's blacksmiths for some time. Using sand and glass attracts possible impurities in the iron.

"Using a close-topped forge keeps heat in, since hot air tends to rise. The increased heat melts the iron ore fully, allowing more impurities to separate themselves based on their specific gravity. The closed top also releases heat slower, giving the forger more control over the temperature of the steel and allowing it to crystallize more favorably." He'd learned how to forge as part of his training as a swordsman.

"Very good."

Kyzyl expected more of a reaction, but he suspected the Master Artificer already knew the benefits of crucible steel.

"Master Conjurer," the Head Master announced, and Kyzyl's platform rotated again.

Master Enwin was a man of average build who had his hood up and covering his face and who, Kyzyl realized, had a dragon, about the size of a cat, sleeping on his shoulders.

"How would you contain a dangerous creature, like say, a demon?"

"Do the students here learn to summon such things?" Kyzyl asked.

The question caught him off guard because he knew the answer. The Master Conjurer shook his head. That meant this question was a trap.

"I wouldn't summon something like that. Any summoner with wit enough to study here knows you shouldn't summon anything you can't control."

The man nodded. "Assume then, that one of your peers had summoned one, and found himself incapable of controlling it. How would you contain it?"

"I would erect a magical containment field, and then look for a Master to banish it."

"You have the magic necessary to contain a supernatural power at your disposal?"

"Well... sir... I... uhm..."

The man waved the question aside and sat back.

"Master Enchanter," The Head Master announced.

The platform spun again and an old gnome with a few days worth of stubble practically jumped out of his seat. "What is the best way to break an enchantment?"

Kyzyl paused at the scope of the question. There were several answers he could give, but only one that he was sure of. "Pain. Real pain grounds the mind to the body in ways that other sensations simply don't.

"Most enchantment magic relies on controlling the subject's perception, but if that perception was grounded by a real sensation, the enchantment would break when the mind had a way of sorting out real from perceived."

"If you found yourself enchanted, how would you deliver this pain?"

"Assuming no one could do it for me?"

The small man nodded.

"If I were sure that it was an enchantment, I would probably try and break a bone. Not an important one mind you. I wouldn't want to limp everywhere I go for the rest of my life. Perhaps my pinky would do."

"Why not cause a minor bruise or something less severe than a broken bone?"

"Not all pain is created equal, Master. A broken bone, while easily set by a practiced physician, allows for a constant stream of sensations that keeps the mind grounded in reality.

"To put it simply, a broken bone serves a dual purpose in pulling one out of the current enchantment and preventing further enchantments." The tiny gnome started giggling, clapped, and sat back in his chair.

"Master Evoker," the Head Master announced.

The Master Evoker was a man named Sendrin. He had dark facial hair encircled his small mouth. His sharp eyes scrutinized Kyzyl's every detail. He was the only one of the Masters who seemed interested in looking at Kyzyl. He smiled warmly at Kyzyl.

"Name the four basic arcane energies." The man's voice was filled with encouragement and patience.

Kyzyl took in a breath of relief. He had begun to suspect the Masters were disappointed in him somehow, but the Master Evokers kind smile shed a new light on his viewpoint. Were the other Masters bored?

Kyzyl smiled back up at him. He seemed pleasant despite the fact that he looked like an evil sorcerer in his dark Master's robes. "Heat and light, kinetic, electrical, and chemical."

"I count five in that list."

"Heat and light are two sides of the same energy. That is why a fire is both hot and glows. This is also true of molten metals."

"True, but when one boils water, it does not glow."

"Just because we don't see it glow doesn't mean there is no light energy in it." The Master gave a satisfied smile as he sat back.

"Master Physician," The Head Master announced. His voice was straining to remain stately. Kyzyl looked back at him in time to catch a small cough. The Head Master took a drink of water as Kyzyl's platform finished rotating to face Master Telma.

It seemed appropriate to Kyzyl that Master Telma was the master who looked most like Death itself. The hood of his robes was pulled over his head and he spoke with a low baritone that begat absolute power. "How would you keep a man from dying?"

"Of what is this hypothetical man dying?"

The Master shrugged.

"Assuming you are asking for the secret to immortality, I will remind you, sir, that if I had eternity to study magic on my own, I would have little reason to travel half way around the world. Not, of course, that I am disappointed by this place so far."

The Master chuckled. "Very well then. What would you use to identify the cause of one's death?"

"Are there any obvious wounds on the remains?"

The Master shook his head.

"I would make a vertical incision down his breastbone and examine his internal organs."

"And what would you be looking for?" the Master Physician asked.

"Signs of disease, internal trauma, anything that would interrupt the natural rhythms of life. Though, to be perfectly honest, Master, I don't have sufficient medical training to perform an autopsy.

"I could, perhaps, make a few educated guesses if any of the internal organs seem to be discolored, but if I have access to one of your assistants, I would rather rely on their abilities than my own."

The Master Physician nodded and, since he never sat forward, continued leaning back in his chair.

"Master Transmutist"

"Why can you not simply resurrect the man in Master Telma's scenario?"

Kyzyl hoped the Masters didn't expect him to command that sort of power. "Because I am not a god?"

This got a chuckle out of the master to the far left, the Master Cleric. Kyzyl felt a hot welt form in his stomach when he saw the man. He was wearing a robe like the other masters, but Kyzyl could see the collar of priestly garb underneath.

Kyzyl quickly changed his answer. "Which is to say, it's because of the complexity that makes life work. It's the same reason my answer to Master Telma was so vague. Life is complex and there are many things that can end it or keep it from beginning."

This seemed to please the Master Transmutist and silence the Master Cleric. Kyzyl found it very pleasing to have seemingly one-upped the old fool.

"Where would you start if you were to try to recreate life?"

Kyzyl paused at the scope of the question. "Are you asking for recommended reading Master? Because that's as far as I've gotten on this particular issue.

"If you're asking for an Elixir of Life, I'd remind you that alchemists all over the world have been trying that since the dawn of humanity. If such a thing existed, I suspect we'd have it by now."

The Master Transmutist went quiet as he considered this. Kyzyl didn't realize his question was over until the Head Master spoke up again.

"Master Cleric." The Head Master announced. It was time to answer nonsense questions about arbitrary things.

"Name three basic logical fallacies."

This request took Kyzyl by surprise. He had known that the Master Cleric was also the man who ran the classes on rhetoric and logic, but it never occurred to Kyzyl that one of them might find that sort of thing important. He hesitated and the man raised an eyebrow.

"Uh... circular logic, ad hominem, and... straw man."

"What is the Universal Law of Magic?"

"To which Law of Arcane Theory are you referring?"

The Master shook his head. "I'm asking for the law that guides what spells we do and which we do not."

"Ability?"

The Master Cleric gave Kyzyl a curious look. "You believe a wizard should be allowed to perform any spell he is capable of? Say if it were one that would cause harm to a fellow student?"

"Ah, you're asking for a Universal Law of Ethics, then? I don't think I have one sir."

"You are from where, again?"

"Hanra. It's a small peninsula off the Techarian mainland."

"Is there a cultural system that defines magic-users and their place where you are from?"

"Most of them serve court positions. Noblemen hire them as doctors, engineers, or simply to help improve whatever farming is going on at the local level."

The Master Cleric nodded and sat back.

"Master Diviner," the Head Master announced himself. Kyzyl guessed Head Master Herman had the ability to read Kyzyl's every thought.

He didn't, however, get the sense of deep personal intrusion that he felt when his tutors probed his mind. Perhaps Head Master Herman had more respect for his privacy than teachers appointed by his father.

At the same time, perhaps the Master Diviner was more subtle with his mental intrusions. It had only just occurred to Kyzyl that, with an estate far from any bustling metropolis, his father's lands would not attract the best his people had to offer.

"Why do you desire to be a student here?"

Kyzyl paused, surprised by the personal nature of the question. "Am I still being tested?"

"An honest answer will be correct."

"Right. I want to learn magic at the school that has produced the best magi in the world."

"Magi?"

"Sorry sir, that is what my people call masters of the arcane. I believe your word for them is wizards, is that correct?"

"Yes, why do you want to be a wizard?"

"What do you mean?"

"Why do you want to learn magic?"

Kyzyl didn't expect this question at all. He wasn't sure what the Head Master was looking for. Mastering

magic had always been something he wanted to do.
Studying and satisfying his curiosity while attaining great
power and prestige seemed like an easy choice. He realized
he'd hesitated for too long. Any more time and it would
seem like he was lying.

"I'm sorry, sir. I guess I don't have a satisfying
answer to that question. Hopefully I can find one while I'm
here."

The Head Master nodded. "Please step down from
the platform as we discuss your tuition."

Kyzyl did and the Masters began to deliberate.
Kyzyl couldn't hear what they were saying. He looked a bit
more carefully at the air surrounding the platform upon
which the Masters were seated. He could see subtle
disturbances in the air, the telltale sign of some kind of
ward. He suspected the Masters preferred discussing their
students without eavesdroppers.

"Mister Shenta, please step forward," Master
Herman's voice shattered the previous silence.

It made Kyzyl jump. Kyzyl stepped back up on the
platform. "Your tuition has been set at ten crowns, due on
the first. You may settle your accounts with Bernard in the
Accounts Office."

"Thank you, Masters." Kyzyl bowed and walked out
the door. A ten crown tuition represented almost
everything he had left. He could definitely survive off the
remainder for the term, but once tuition became an issue
again, he didn't know what he'd do. He walked over to the
man behind the desk and asked him where Bernard or the
Accounts Office was.

"The Accounts Office is in the Enchantment
Building, but I'm Bernard. If you want to settle your
account now, I'll write you a receipt and take it over later."

"Do people usually have ten crowns in their purse
when they come to be tested?" Kyzyl asked surprised.

"They set it at ten crowns? One of them must like

you quite a bit. Most people bring as much money as they think they'll need. It's kind of like a game, like betting on your own intelligence."

"How much do people usually bring?"

"Anywhere between fifty and one hundred crowns. Depends on how they did last term."

Kyzyl thought back to his examination. None of the Masters seemed particularly impressed by him. He wondered if it might've been Head Master Herman. His only question did seem rather... odd.

"Do you have ten crowns?" Bernard asked. Kyzyl took out his Writ of Deposit. "Technically yes, but it's in this form."

Bernard sighed. "Lucky for you we have a deal with the branch of the bank in this city." He rummaged in the desk until he found a small piece of vellum. The writing on it was intricate and tidy. It read:

I, who have signed below, do hereby authorize the use of Bernard Ulimati of the University Arcanum Accounts office to use my accounts in payment of my tuition at said university.

It had a space for Kyzyl to sign his name. "Sign this and I can take your Writ to the bank and have them transfer your tuition from your account to ours."

"Will they tell you what my balance is?"

"Do you want them to?"

"No." Kyzyl didn't like the idea of anyone knowing how much of a bind he was in. If tuition did, in fact, normally go as high as fifty crowns, Kyzyl needed to find a generous source of income soon.

"They only tell us if you had the funds to cover it. As long as you do, they tell us were square and we both move on with our lives."

Kyzyl signed the paper. After he did so, he noticed Head Master Herman exiting the exam hall and caught up with him.

"Sir, I wanted to ask you about your question during my exam."

"Yes?" The Head Master's voice was slightly hoarse. Kyzyl hoped he could keep this conversation brief to give the man time to rest his voice.

"It's just, do you usually ask personal questions like that? I had assumed that my aptitude would be sufficient to gain admittance."

"You are correct. Normally we don't ask anything more personal than your name. You, however, are a special case Mister Shenta.

"You have come a long way to study here, that is clear. However, we did not receive any sort of letter from your country or crown announcing your arrival."

"That is true." Kyzyl understood the Head Master was implying he was no one of great importance like a diplomat in his country. He didn't want to mention the other reason they received no announcement was because no one else knew Kyzyl had already left.

"There are many places to learn magic in Techarae, and plenty of ways, I assume for you to be educated in your own country. I found it interesting, then, that you chose to come half way around the world to learn here. Thus, my question, as to why. Why study magic, and why do it here?"

"Because this place is the best. The other schools in my country teach lots of unnecessary things about philosophy and religion. I don't want to learn about spirits and ancestors.

"To them, magic is just a consequence of all that. They don't have magicians so much as sages. I want to learn how the world actually works. The physical laws that govern our existence. This place is different. Save for a few exceptions, you're all focused on the tangible cause and effect of magic."

"You're speaking of the Master Cleric." The Head

Master's voice was even in tone. It gave no indication of rebuke or condemnation.

"Why do you even have a Master Cleric? I thought this university was a center for arcane knowledge and understanding the physical world. What purpose does a man focused on the supernatural serve?"

The Head Master gave Kyzyl a dark look. "You will learn, in time, why we do many things Kyzyl. For now, you would do well to show all the Masters your deepest respect.

"As for the Master Cleric, I suspect you and he will get to know each other quite well. He has personally requested you for his class, Rhetoric and Logic."

Kyzyl hoped he looked properly chastised. He kept his head down, but couldn't keep the next words from spilling out of his mouth. "Learning logic from a man of faith. That would be true magic."

Master Herman was looking at him with a smirk. "I think you'll be rather surprised."

Something else occurred to Kyzyl just then. "You know a great deal about my people, but one of Bernard's errand boys seemed to be surprised at the idea that someone from that continent could make it here. How much do you know about my people?"

"More than you might expect." The Head Master smirked. "We don't get many students from so far away, but divination magic is largely about extrasensory perception, and many wizards specialize in it as a way of learning more about the world around them."

"Do all diviners want to learn about the world?"

"In a manner of speaking. There are some who use their magic for less... scrupulous acts. We, here at the university, try to push our students toward a path where knowledge is sought for its own sake, but that is not the only reason people desire knowledge."

Kyzyl considered this for a moment until the

Master continued. "You seem rather invested in learning as much as you can while you're here."

Kyzyl nodded his head vigorously.

"Perhaps taking a few classes in my field would benefit you."

With that, Head Master Herman walked away. As he did so, Kyzyl thought about everything he said. He'd had been selected to be in a class taught by his least favorite Master. A Master he had just been instructed to respect despite the fact he saw no reason for the Master Cleric's presence at a place like this. He could refuse the offer, but how would that look? If there was one thing he had learned from his father, it was that you should never slight your superiors, no matter how much you hate them.

Kyzyl decided that pretending to respect the Master Cleric would look largely the same as actually respecting him to any outside observer. Internally, he could still detest the man and what he represents, the intervention of religion in Kyzyl's education. Meanwhile, he'd play the part of the humble student, and quietly watch for opportunities to show the other Masters the value of leaving religious nonsense behind.

Kyzyl also thought about the Head Master's own invitation. He had said that divination magic was useful in learning about the world. Perhaps becoming a diviner would be prudent. He was, after all, curious about so many things, and having magic that could help him learn further did seem like the most logical way to satisfy his curiosity. Would he have enough money to pay tuition while he mastered it though?

Kyzyl started walking down the street. The sun was going to set soon, and Kyzyl wanted a place to sleep before it did. He went from inn to inn, there were several scattered around the university complex, until he finally settled on one that seemed small but not ratty, called the Noble Steed.

It was the perfect inn for a man from a noble family

that is ten-thousand miles away and who had most of his money stolen. He walked in and looked at the woman behind the bar. He approached her and looked at a bottle behind her to avoid making eye contact.

"Excuse me ma'am, are you the owner of this inn?" Out of the corner of his eye, he saw her trying to trace his gaze to see what he was looking at.

"Ha!" A voice came from the kitchen. In a moment, a skinny, bearded man wearing an apron emerged from the kitchen. "She wishes she was the one in charge. The name is Seth, and that there's my wife Joanne. What can I do for you?"

"I was hoping I could convince you to let me live in one of your rooms while I complete my studies here at the university."

"Somethin' wrong with the bunks in the Livery?"

"Those beds come with strings. If I stay there, I'll be expected to work as an intern for one of the Masters or a magical errand boy for some older student. I prefer my free time to be mine. It lets me pursue extracurricular study."

"Ay, I suppose you got the coin as well."

"I can give you two crowns for the first term." Three months of boarding was a lot to ask for from a place whose main income was renting out rooms for short terms. Kyzyl hoped the generous offer would offset the exceptional request.

The innkeeper's eyes lit up and he took Kyzyl's hand and shook it before Kyzyl could change his mind. "With that generous offer, I'll let you stay and have whatever's in the pot at any meal. I'll get the key to the attic room."

Seth came back and led Kyzyl up to a small room with a slanted ceiling. The room's only occupants were a bed and a slender flat-lidded chest. Kyzyl set his bag down on top of the chest and sat on the bed. It was cozy. It reminded him of when he was a child, hiding in the closet with a book to avoid his older brothers.

Kyzyl came downstairs a moment later to a wonderful smell. It was the allure of warm potato stew that Seth was warming up in the kitchen. Joanne filled a bowl and set it on the bar for him. The feeling of finally having a fresh, hot meal in the place he dreamed of for so long was overwhelming. Kyzyl started to tear up at it all. He was finally right where he belonged, and he had no intention of going anywhere.

CHAPTER FOUR
Books and Classes

The morning sun found Kyzyl already awake and wandering the university, marveling at everything he saw. There were several buildings that made up the university's complex. However, there were nine main buildings that stood out from the rest.

Each of these was built to house the lecture halls, studies, and labs that served each of the nine main subjects as well as any other amenities the students of that particular subject would need. They were each built in their own unique style, but each was built of a dark stone that was cut so smooth and perfect that not a hair's breadth of space existed between any two blocks.

The library, which also served as the divination building, was a perfectly round cylindrical tower. The evocation building was a perfect square pyramid. The Conjuration Building was a tower similar to the library, but square with a top that tapered into a point. It also seemed to be reinforced by two flying buttresses on each of the four sides. The Artificery was a squat building lined with chimneys that weren't putting out smoke, yet. The medical building, which doubled as a hospital where the university could treat all manner of patients, was a large building in roughly a cubed shape.

The final four were the temple where Kyzyl took his entrance exam, the Enchantment building that seemed to disappear when you were looking out of the corner of your eye, the transmutation building that seemed like it was carved to look like a blazing inferno, or perhaps it was transmuted from one, and the abjuration building that looked like a military outpost.

Each of these nine buildings had a campus surrounding it. The university hospital had enclosed its campus for privacy reasons and had used the extra space to erect different wings off the main buildings to serve as different, specialized wards. The other buildings had filled their campuses with gardens, specialized shops, and boarding for higher level students who didn't want to continue living with the new students.

It made the entire university complex a lot bigger than it needed to be, but everything seemed to be carefully constructed. Kyzyl noticed that, when the wind blew, it seemed to be directed down main streets and walkways, making the entire complex feel open and breezy.

After he'd finished his walk to familiarize himself with the campuses, Kyzyl decided that he'd spend the rest of the time until registration opened doing what he loved most, reading. He turned away from the abjuration campus he'd been heading toward, and back toward the divination campus that held the Library of Arcane Theory.

He went in to the towering building. The entrance room had two sets of double doors set in the back wall. Between them was a desk with an open ledger and a very tired looking human. Until he looked up at Kyzyl, he seemed like he had been sleeping with his head up.

"Name."

"Shenta Kyzyl."

The man looked through a log book. "Not here. Sorry I can't let you in if you're not in the books." The man sounded like he had been up all night.

Kyzyl wondered what a student had to do to get placed on the night shift. Was this a punishment of some sort? When Kyzyl didn't immediately leave, the man looked at him expectantly. "Are you waiting for something?"

"I forgot. I said that backwards. Try Kyzyl Shenta."

"You forgot to say your name in the right order?"

"Right is a relative term. Some people would argue that placing one's individual name ahead of the family name leads to less than orderly consequences."

"I presume you're a new student," he said around a yawn.

"Why do you say that? I think my argument is well reasoned." Kyzyl tried not to sound defensive.

"Your argument was fine, but it sounded like you were opening for a formal debate. Save that stuff for the classroom. Out here, you don't have anything to prove to anyone.

"Lots of first-term students get it in their head that they need to sound extra educated to make people believe they belong here." The man shrugged and leaned against the desk. "Whether you do or not is none of my business. I'm just here to get my studies done and hopefully get a court appointment at some cushy noble's estate."

Kyzyl looked down at his feet. He felt his face getting hot and he tried to stammer out an apology, but the man at the desk just laughed.

"Like I said, you aren't the first person to sound like that. Gods know you won't be the last. Just try to relax. Keep your head down, focus on your studies, and let your work speak for itself."

Kyzyl nodded. When he looked up, the man was paging through the ledger books again and found what he was looking for. "OK, go on in and read 'til your hearts content."

"Thank you. I didn't catch your name."

"Espen. Glad to meet you Kyzyl."

Kyzyl smiled, feeling as if his first impression with the library clerk was already being waved aside. "And I, you good sir." Kyzyl bowed low. Espen stood, grinned, and returned the bow in equal measure, letting his head dip below the desk.

With that, Kyzyl walked eagerly through the doors labeled "library" into a room packed with shelves, shelves filled with books, books filled with answers to ten times ten thousand questions. The place was dark and filled with the smell of leather and parchment. The air was still, and if it hadn't smelled fresh and clean, Kyzyl would've likened the place to a crypt or a mausoleum. He realized he had no source of light, so he went back outside and asked Espen for a lamp.

Espen handed him a rod of oak he called a sunrod. "Hit it against your hand," he explained. Kyzyl did so, and the stick started to glow with a soft red light. "The alchemists here learned a long time ago how to treat wood with a potion that converts kinetic energy into light energy.

"Will the stick burn?"

Espen shook his head. "There's hardly any thermal transference, so almost all of the energy gets converted into light. The heat that does get created isn't even enough to make the stick warm, let alone catch fire."

Kyzyl nodded. "Which makes it an ideal light source inside a place lined with books that are fragile."

Espen tapped his nose. "You got it. Master Diviners have had a ban on anything flammable in the library for generations. Pretty much ever since we've had these."

Kyzyl returned and was dumbfounded. The shadows that he'd now been able to extinguish had hidden the majority of the truth. Troves of literature as far as the eye could see stretched out before him. Not just ten times ten thousand, but perhaps more books than any mind could begin to comprehend. It felt as though the wealth of human knowledge had all been laid out before him, and it paralyzed him with indecision.

He picked an aisle at random and started walking. He looked at so many titles of books, but quickly understood how unorganized everything was. He moved to a different shelf and continued perusing. To his astonishment it seemed that the Library of Arcane Theory as a whole was largely an unorganized mess.

Some sections were in good condition on their own: organized and on well made shelves with lovingly refurbished spines. Other sections he found seemed to have been forgotten by the masses. He found a sailors travel log that was cracked and had several pages falling out of it. Another book appeared to be a catalog of a set of gods he'd never heard of, though that wasn't surprising, but the book had holes where some kind of insect had bored through it. It reminded Kyzyl of the only time he'd ever visited Chenta.

It was the closest major city in their providence, and a major seat of political power for the region. As he explored it, he discovered that, when you left the places where the wealthy and powerful lived, you would quickly end up in a place that was bustling with unsavory characters. One man even tried to sell Kyzyl a knife out of his cloak. Kyzyl was appalled by the indecency.

When he told his father about what happened, his father merely nodded. He warned Kyzyl to stay within the boundaries of the "safe" streets, but Kyzyl didn't like that solution. He felt that a place so close to a seat of power, even one in a minor providence, should have people that can enjoy organization and peace. Instead they were left aside where people could ignore them.

So too, did these books, the collective experiences of all the sentient races, deserve to be treated with respect. He decided that, rather than spend his time studying, he would endeavor to address this concern. The library as a whole was too vast for him to organize in a morning, but he could do his part to begin the process.

He chose a particularly disused shelf, took the books off and placed them in a pile. His exploration of the shelves gave him a pretty good idea what the newest organization system was like, and he began re-shelving books according to the closest approximation of that system he could.

Kyzyl had lost track of the time when Espen found him. "Have you just been sorting and reshelving books this entire time?"

"Sorry, it looked like this section was unorganized and I thought I may be able to help."

Espen shook his head, a look of surprise on his face. "It's fine." He looked at the books Kyzyl had rearranged. "Everything looks in order, but you didn't have to do that. We keep the books people need well organized so people can find them, but these books haven't been opened in so long that no one cares."

"How can you expect them to care if no one knows there's a problem?"

Espen put his hands up placatingly. "It's not as easy as all that. You saw how big this place is. Even with every student in the university working together it would take years to go through all these books. The fact that only one in every ten decide to work here means we have to prioritize the books people need."

"I understand. Still, I'd rather these books be findable by the people who can get something out of them." Kyzyl placed a one of the books he'd been holding in a stack. He'd wanted to keep books that needed major repairs out of the sorting so they could be turned over for copying or refurbishment.

"You really seem to care a lot about this sort of stuff. You should sign up for shifts here. You'd make a good scripturon. Who knows, maybe you could even work your way up to archivist. Speaking of which, the class sign-ups started about an hour ago."

"What? Why didn't you tell me?" Kyzyl abandoned his project without giving Espen a chance to respond. He ran through the shelves and out the now opens doors of the library. He hoped desperately that an hour wasn't long enough for the best classes to get taken.

He huffed and puffed as he sprinted through the university complex to the administration buildings that stood near the Enchantment building. Class sign-ups lasted all day, but Kyzyl didn't want to chance the classes he wanted being full before he could sign up for them.

He collected a list of entry-level classes and started reading. There were classes for all kinds of subjects: mathematics, biology, history, astronomy. All of these were in addition to all the introductory courses for each of the eight kinds of magic plus philosophy and rhetoric taught by the Master Cleric and his students. Most of these classes were taught by more senior students who had been hand-picked by the Masters.

Kyzyl quickly realized that there were too many classes for him to take even just one in each of the subjects he wanted to study. He'd have to choose what to focus on for now, and use his leisure time in the library to study on his own.

Both the Master Cleric and the Master Diviner had invited him to study in their fields, and Head Master Herman had mentioned that divination offered a wizard many ways of gaining yet more knowledge. However, Kyzyl had the more practical problem of needing to work out his finances.

For his idea to work, he'd need to focus on summoning this term, and hold off on practicing divination until he was sure he could pay next terms tuition. He also signed up for an introductory class in wards and protection spells. Knowing how to make a ward might help him learn how to circumvent them.

Then he looked down the list until he came to the class he had been dreading. Introduction to Rhetoric and Logic was at a time Kyzyl had hoped he'd fill by accident with another class. Unfortunately, he had no such luck. He signed up for the class, not wanting to offend one of the Masters in his first term.

"Rhetoric and Logic, eh? I guess we'll be in class together then." A voice from behind him said. Kyzyl turned toward the source of the voice. Standing behind him was a man with bright, almond-shaped eyes, a pixie face, and pointed ears. He stood with his arms crossed, leaning back on one foot, and a smirk on his face. "The name is Emrys." He put out his hand.

"Kyzyl." Kyzyl took it, and they shook.

"Kyzyl? That's one that I haven't heard. Where are you from?"

"Chenshu. It's a providence in Hanra."

"Hanra? That means 'river under heaven,' doesn't it?"

"I'm surprised you knew that," Kyzyl admitted. "I didn't expect many people here to know anything about Hanra, let alone be able to translate the name."

Emrys laughed. "I think you'll find I know a lot of things I shouldn't. Are you all done signing up for classes?"

Kyzyl looked at the class log. "I think so."

"Excellent." Emrys took Kyzyl's arm and started pulling him toward the door. "I'm meeting a friend at our favorite watering hole and I'm sure he'd love to meet one of the new pups."

"Pups? Are you making fun of me?"

"No more than I am anyone else. My apologies, you just wear your bewilderment so plainly. You look like you haven't spent a day outside of your father's castle. Or was it your mother's? I hear there are far-away lands that prefer a more matriarchal system."

"It was an estate not a castle. But it was my father's,

and, for your information, I spent a lot of time in the surrounding villages and traveling with him to meet other important figures in our providence."

"Oh me, oh my. Well color me impressed great Far Traveler." Emrys stepped in front of Kyzyl and open the door to the street while making a mock bow.

Kyzyl walked through the door. He was still trying to figure out if he should be insulted by this man's mockery. A quick survey of his feelings revealed he wasn't and he assumed that was for the best regardless of Emrys' intentions.

Emrys lead Kyzyl to a tavern called the Burning Forge, where he was introduced to a man named Donovan, who claimed he was studying Alteration magic, a subset of Transmutation that focused on altering one's body. He was a grizzled man at least ten years Kyzyl's senior. His hair and beard where a sandy blond and his eyes were emerald green. His broad shoulders and thick arms seemed a stark contrast to most of the students Kyzyl had seen around the university.

After introductions were made, Kyzyl told the men about a pirate ship called the Alosa that had robbed one of the three ships he had sailed on as it passed through the Pirate Isle. The two men were an excellent audience, with well-timed reactions to his tale.

"Sounds like you had quite the experience that day," Donovan proclaimed half-way through their fourth round. He was beginning to talk rather loudly and slur his speech. "I bet you were scared those damned pirates would do you in before you ever got to this place, eh?"

"Probably not," Emrys said. "I read about a weapon that pirates often encounter on Techarian ships. It's called the Thunderbuss or the Plunder-Buster. The sources I've read disagree. Anyway, it makes a loud noise like an explosion and sends out a projectile.

"They say no matter where you get hit with it, you're a dead man. No physician can heal you. Although I doubt pirates have access to the same level of medical expertise that we do, so I don't know how true that is."

"How do you know about that?" Kyzyl asked. His face had gotten pale and his voice was shaking.

"There are lots of pirate journals and the like in the library. I've read so many accounts of encounters with that weapon, though oddly enough, no one seems to give a description of it. Just the devastation it can cause."

Kyzyl relaxed visibly and Donovan gave him a questioning look. He thought about the wisdom of revealing what he knew of his people's secret to strangers. Then he decided Emrys had already said more than the small piece Kyzyl knew anyway.

"Techarae has a weapon that is only meant for us. It is kept secret from all outsiders so it can't be used against us. Merchants that can afford one keep it on their ship as protection against pirates, but it's mostly used to defend our coasts and borders from raiding parties."

"I hadn't realized it was meant to be a secret." Emrys said. "I'm sorry. If it's any consolation, I haven't found any Techarian accounts of the weapon. Just pirates that ran into it while raiding. The secret itself seems to be safe as long as your people don't mind others knowing the weapon exists."

"Probably better that they do," Donovan said. "The best kind of weapon is one you only have to use once. Then, after word spreads that you can kill a man with a single hit anywhere on his body, no one is going to come knocking down your door."

Kyzyl thought about this. It was possible that was another reason for the secret. If something is largely misunderstood, it tended to lead to fear, awe or both. If pirates spread word about the weapon to outsiders, perhaps that was what kept most non-Techarian people from raiding Hanra's coastline.

Just then a tall, regal looking elf with ears at least

two hand-span long walked in with a posse of other people. They all looked like students. The man wore green linen robes, and a bright red silk sash served as his belt. He walked with a confidence that bordered arrogance. Kyzyl also notice that his nails were painted black with blood red symbols etched into them. Kyzyl couldn't read them, but he guessed it was some sort of symbol of status. The elf strode right up to Kyzyl and stood in front of him with a sickeningly polite smile on his face.

"So," he said in a patronizingly slow and careful tone, "you're the one from far far-away. What was that place called again Tekee-something?"

"Techarae," Emrys corrected.

"Quiet half-breed!" the man spat. Emrys jumped from his seat and wobbled noticeably. Donovan grabbed his wrist to keep him from advancing on the newcomer.

The man in green turned back to Kyzyl and in an irritatingly polite and slow voice said, "what was your name?"

"My name is Kyzyl, and I would appreciate it if you wouldn't speak to me and my friend in such a way."

The man's smile faltered for just an instant. "Yes, well, my apologies. You see, Kyzyl, I wanted to make your acquaintance and offer my services to you. Knowing that you come from such a faraway land, I'm sure you could use help adjusting to our culture."

The man took a sidelong glance at Donovan and Emrys. "Associating with the wrong people could be bad for your reputation, and, as a fellow noble, I know how important reputation can be."

He offered his hand to Kyzyl. Kyzyl just looked at it. There was a moment where Kyzyl wanted to take it. The man was right that adjusting had been difficult for him.

Kyzyl looked at Emrys. His eyes were burning with hate. He didn't know very much about the two men at his table, but they had been kind to him so far. The richly-dyed

elf, on the other hand, seemed to have done something
very rude.

"I think I'm far enough from home that I can afford
to make a few mistakes. It's not as if anyone around here is
making their way to my father's estate anytime soon. I'll
stick with the friends I have, thank you."

The man pursed his lips and let his hand fall. "As
you wish," he said before walking away, nose in the air like
a true nobleman, and slamming the door behind him. The
rest of his posse had to open the door again to leave with
him.

"Who the hell was that?" Kyzyl asked.

"Siradyl. He's from one of the five royal houses of
Antorn," Emrys said with a scowl toward the door.

"Did you just say five royal houses?"

Emrys nodded. "Antorn is a confederacy. It has
five royal houses, each named after a species of dragon and
making up a fifth of their Royal Council: House Aurum of
the Golden Hoard, House Aegir of the Silver Smiths, House
Cyran of the Copper Legion, House Lorian of the Bronze
Heart, and the House of the Platinum Crown. The last isn't
quite a bloodline so much as it is a line of rulers that head
the Royal Council and are elected by the Council's
members."

"And he's from which house?"

"Aurum. They are second in command after the
Platinum Crown. They control the tax collectors and the
treasury, which makes them very good financiers." Emrys
seemed to know a lot about all sorts of places around the
world.

"He called you..." Kyzyl trailed off. He didn't want
to upset his new friend, but he was curious.

"Half-breed. Honestly, that's tame compared to
what he usually calls me. I assume he was trying to put on a
polite façade to try and pull you into his group of toadies."

Kyzyl opened his mouth to ask a follow-up

question, but he caught Donovan's eye and Donovan shook his head.

Emrys noticed and sighed. "It's fine. Go ahead and ask."

"It's just that... I didn't know that... you're half elf right?"

"And half human, yeah."

"You're the first half-elf person I've met. Though, looking back, I think I may have met another on my way here. I didn't know elves could... I mean humans and elves seem so different."

"Not that different. You don't have much experience with elves, do you?"

Kyzyl shook his head. "Most of the sentient races on Lukor don't exist in Techarae. Human seems to be the only one we have in common. I didn't meet an elf until I was sailing through the Pirate Isles."

"Interesting. So you don't have dwarves or halflings either?"

Another shake of the head. Kyzyl added, "I've read a lot about the other races: dwarves live in the mountains of the Great Divide and are particularly good craftsmen, halflings have a country called Hamlin where they have backwards ideas of property ownership, and elves are especially good at magic."

"You do sound like you read that out of a text book," Donovan said. "Firstly, high elves, like our friend," he gestured toward the front door, "are the ones who are skilled in magic. It's not based on their race. It's because Antorn uses magic for a lot of their infrastructure. That means becoming a wizard is an easy way to get a job there.

"The other kind of elf you'll run into in these parts are the wood elves. They tend to keep to themselves when they can. They're not too friendly with their highborn cousins, and they're killer with a bow if the rumors are true.

"Lastly, most of the dwarves that are craftsmen stay in the mountains. Any of the ones you meet on the surface are going to either bankers or bookkeepers. The Caravan Masters use a lot of dwarvish bookkeepers.

"What you said about the halflings is mostly correct. They like to use the 'a tool belongs to he who uses it' philosophy to justify taking whatever tickles their fancy."

Kyzyl sat quietly for a moment. He took in everything he'd just been told before speaking up again. When he did, his question was for Emrys. "Would it be inappropriate to ask about your parentage."

"Generally yes, but since you're new to the land, I'll let it slide this time." He winked at Kyzyl and gave a half grin before continuing.

"I don't know much about either of my parents. All I know is what my patron, the man who took me in, told me. My mother was an elf of some kind. I don't know if she was a high elf like our friend," he gestured toward the door the same way Donovan had, "or a wood elf. All I know is that one day some bastard noble's son decided he wanted something from her and he didn't much care what she had to say about it."

Emrys took a deep breath. Kyzyl didn't have much experience with the feelings of people outside his family, but he could tell this was becoming difficult for Emrys.

"After she became pregnant, she decided she didn't want a living reminder of what happened to her, so she took a poison. It didn't work as she intended, so she gave birth to me a little early and just left me in the woods. I have no idea how I survived. All I know is my patron found me wandering in his wood one day and took me to live in his house."

"How does your patron know all this?"

"I asked him that once, and he said the story is basically the same as all half-elves. We're all unwanted half-breeds."

"I don't know much about the rest of your kind," Donovan chimed in, "but I find your services rather useful. Thus, rendering you wanted, by my standards." He let his hand settle on Emrys' shoulder, but Emrys just looked at him.

Emrys seemed put off by the comment, and Kyzyl thought he was going to say something to Donovan. Before he did, however, his stoic expression cracked into a smile and they both laughed. It left Kyzyl feeling very confused about the whole exchange.

"If you actually thought in such a utilitarian way, I don't think we could be friends," Emrys said. "'Useful to me.' Honestly, if you aren't careful who you tell that joke to, someone might assume you actually think that way."

Kyzyl started to understand, but he stayed silent. This seemed to be a familiar exchange between the two, and he didn't want to interrupt it.

When Emrys finally pulled him back into the conversation, it was with the same question as Head Master Herman, "why here?" He still wasn't sure of his answer, so he just shrugged and said that the University Arcanum is the best in the world.

The three men began discussing everything from their plans at the university to women until the owner of the Burning Forge kicked them out. They stumbled back to the Noble Steed and headed up to Kyzyl's room, ignoring some of the odd looks from the two patrons at the bar.

"If you're trying to, *hic* to seduce us Kyzyl," Emrys began before Kyzyl pushed him over.

"I'm not sly you idiot. I have to make sure my two new friends don't stumble into a river and kill themselves. This term is going to be lonely enough for a foreigner like me. I don't need your deaths on my conscience."

By the time Kyzyl finished talking, Emrys was already sleeping. Donovan's and Kyzyl's eyes met and they both laughed until their consciousness succumbed to their drunkenness.

CHAPTER FIVE
Summoning and Speeches

The first term of classes didn't start until the beginning of the next month, so Kyzyl did everything he could to prepare for the classes he signed up for. He studied books like <u>Beginnings of Conjuration</u>, <u>Wards and Other Magical Protections</u>, and even a trite collection of philosophical books on the structure of arguments.

The last of which was difficult to get through because of it's lack of any real world applications. It continued using hypothetical conversations the author invented to demonstrate the author's mastery of the subject. It all felt so artificial.

When he wasn't reading in the library, Emrys and Donovan took him to the Burning Forge, the Mask of St. Leer, and the Cozy Pint. Kyzyl was grateful neither of them seemed to have particularly expensive taste. If his plan for getting more money didn't work out, he'd need to save his coin for tuition.

He did have some luck on the financial front when he was able to sell the vial of spider venom that he'd collected for two crowns. It was a fair price and he was grateful he was able to recover the money he'd spent on lodging. Still, by the time the term began, He was down a whole silver noble with fewer and fewer options.

The first class of his new term was Basics of Conjuration. He was lucky enough to sign up for the one class being taught by Master Enwin himself, and was excited to see what the Master of Conjuration had to teach. He was at the lecture hall ten minutes early with several sheets of paper, two pens, and a full bottle of ink.

Master Enwin arrived right on time and didn't greet the class before beginning.

"If any of you think you will get away with nonsense spells and foolish casting in this class, you are utterly mistaken." Master Enwin walked briskly to the raised dais at the front of the room.

With the help of the dais, he towered above his sitting students. His hood was down and his face was serious. His dragon was dozing around its master's shoulders.

"Welcome to the Basics of Conjuration. The first lesson you will learn is knowing your limits. If you think you want to learn to summon demons and fae, you may leave this class immediately."

After a pause, two students walked out of the class. Master Enwin looked at the class, smiled, and said, "there's always at least one."

Master Enwin leaned back against the desk and crossed his arms. "Right then. Conjuration, the art of calling. Usually when you conjure something, if it's living, you do so in hopes of making it a servant. That being said, you should never assume just because you can conjure something that it will serve you.

"Few creatures are friendly toward conjurers, most are not. If you cannot also dominate the creatures will, it will most likely try to kill you. This is because being pulled from one place, through reality, to another place is unpleasant, a fact you will most likely learn in your advanced classes as you begin to study teleportation magic."

He grinned.

"No, most creatures will be very disoriented and very aggressive after being pulled through the aether. That is why I recommend to those of you who will be seeking mastery over this subject that you take as many classes in Enchantment as your schedule allows. Those of you with any amount of wisdom will find it prudent to take at least a few.

"Remember, even wizards who specialize know plenty about the other disciplines taught at this university. Being a well-rounded scholar is better than being a prodigy in a single course or subject.

"I am, of course, getting ahead of myself. Most of you will learn the basics by summoning objects, and then move on to other things. That is what this class is for. I don't want something to go on a rampage in my classroom. Does anyone have a problem with that? No? Good."

Master Enwin rubbed the head of his tiny dragon. "I'm sure by now most of you have noticed my friend and are wondering 'how do I get my own pet dragon?' The answer is simple. You don't.

"In all actuality, this creature on my shoulder is not a dragon. It is a spirit I formed out of the aether that surrounds us. Thus, it is, for all practical purposes, an extension of my own will and not a creature in its own right.

"The distinction is important because, to this day, no one in the history of the world has been able to dominate a dragon. Many people have summoned dragons and have subsequently been eaten by said dragons. It goes without saying that if any of you even attempts summoning anything vaguely dragon-shaped, you will be told firmly to leave this university and never return."

Until the last line of his speech, Kyzyl had not been taking notes, but he decided that this final rule was worth writing down. When he looked back up, he saw that Master Enwin was writing with a piece of chalk on a board of slate mounted to the wall. He was writing and drawing diagrams that Kyzyl slowly began to recognize as instructions for a spell, and he quickly began copying it.

"All summoning spells have a subject and a call. The subject of this spell is an inanimate object of relatively small size. Anything you could hold in your hand should be sufficient.

"The call, of course, is the mechanism by which you bring the object to you. For this particular spell you must be familiar enough with the object to know it from other objects like it, for instance if you merely specify a particular book, you will most likely get any random copy of that book that exists in the given location. That is, assuming you can concentrate on the idea of that book effectively enough for the spell to manifest.

"Which brings me to the second part of the calling: the location. Usually, it's called the receiving location to distinguish it from the sending location. Much like the object, the more specific the location, the better. When we start learning about summoning living things, I'll tell you a story of the conjurer that got his pet owl stuck in a brick wall. It's an amusing story as well as serving as an object lesson in what happens when you aren't specific about your receiving locations.

"If you want something to land in your hand, you should know the precise distance your hand is from the ground and the angle of its orientation. If you want something to land in front of you, you must know the precise measurement of distance.

"You should also be ready to specify its height from the ground. If you make it zero it will get stuck in the dirt. Make it too high and whatever you summon will likely break as it falls to the ground.

"Your first assignment is to master this spell. I have already devised the test by which I will measure your mastery, so once you think you are ready, come see me. The test will be administered in front of your fellow classmates, so I hope none of you have stage fright.

"You may use the rest of this class and the latter half of each subsequent class as study time, but the best of you will find it not only prudent but wise to spend time outside of class studying it as well. The first of you that can perform this spell to my satisfaction will win a prize. The rest of you will earn a lesson. You may begin."

Kyzyl finished copying the diagrams and began his work, silently mouthing the words for the incantation and making gestures and signs with his hands. If magic was a language, spells were sentences where everything had to agree in tense, or all the energy the spell stored up would turn on the caster.

"Yes?" Kyzyl heard the Master Conjurer say. He looked up in time to see one of the students put her hand down.

"Um, what do we do if we don't know how to read glyphs yet?"

Master Enwin looked at the board and back at the young woman. "Right. You are signed up for Basics of Glyphs, yes?"

She nodded.

He wrote a list of titles on the board. "These are books in our library that you will be assigned to read in that class. They will also help you decipher this glyph. I'll help you copy it down from the board correctly, and you will have it deciphered into whatever instructions are best for you by the next class."

The woman nodded and Master Enwin moved to assist her and the other students who were confused.

Kyzyl took a deep breath and held it in his chest as he moved his concentration back on the spell before him. What to summon? He could summon one of the books he read from the library, but he assumed the Master Diviner kept those under wards to keep them safe from thieves.

He had a couple other ideas, but wanted to get right into the casting, and decided he'd land on the subject better if he was in his focused state. He let out the held breath, and his mind tipped into the presence and mindfulness he called Wind-Dance.

***

After a moment he is reading the glyph and practicing the motions. He notices the air in the room is kept warmer than he expects. The spell itself leaves its power source open to the caster. He makes necessary adjustments for the spell in his mind.

The spell still needs a subject. The answer comes to him easily now. His mind is on one singular object: his sword, locked away in his room at his father's estate. It is the only thing he regrets leaving behind.

He makes the hand motions and speaks the words. He pulls heat from the air around him, sending a draft downward as the chilled air sinks. He finishes the spell. Nothing.

Kyzyl looks over the glyph, practicing the hand motions again. He watches his hands carefully for any wrong movements. He tries again. Nothing.

He goes over the words of the spell again. He closes his eyes and pushes his attention fully into the words. He moves his lips, tongue and teeth carefully over each one, letting the sounds of the words and their meaning fill his whole attention. He tries a third time. His mind's eye sees every detail of his sword: the basket hilt, the flowing cross guard, and the long, slender blade. Still, nothing happens.

Kyzyl feels something shimmering at the edge of his consciousness. He tries to pour his attention on to it, but it's gone within the moment. Was that the spell trying to manifest?

***

A clock somewhere in the distance rang the time,

pulling Kyzyl out of Wind-Dance: fourth bell. It was time to leave, and no one had been able to summon anything more than a speck of dust. Kyzyl packed up his things. He kept the notes and diagrams in his hands. He started walking out of the class room while looking at the notes.

He was so enamored by the notes, he didn't notice Master Enwin until he crashed straight into him. "Hello, Kyzyl, right?"

"Yes sir."

"You seem to be quite engrossed in today's lesson. What was it you were trying to summon?"

"Something I had to leave at home. I've been feeling rather naked without it, so I thought this would be a good opportunity for me to get it back."

Kyzyl didn't think it was wise to tell one of the Masters that he was trying to summon something most people here only saw as a weapon. To him ti was a tool. It was mostly for self defense, but its sharp edge held all sorts of uses. Still, many people saw a sword as threatening, and Kyzyl didn't know how people in this land would react to such an object.

"I see. Many students would assume something so far away would be incredibly difficult."

"There's nothing in the spell that suggested there was a distance limit."

The Master nodded. "I'm impressed. I expect many of my students wouldn't have read the spell closely enough to notice something like that.

"You are, ultimately, correct. However, the way the spell works is by using the energy you put into it to bend space to place the object in your hand.

"The further your hand is from the object you're trying to place in it, the more energy you'll need to bend the space between. Merely something to consider."

Kyzyl grinned at the compliment. He hadn't expected to impress Master Enwin so quickly, but he was glad his dedication was being noticed. "Thank you for the advice Master Enwin. I will consider it." The Master Conjurer nodded and walked away.

Since it was about midday and Kyzyl didn't have a class that he had to rush to, he decided it was an appropriate time for lunch. He made his way down to the Noble Steed, greeted the barmaid who gave him a sly wink, and asked Seth for a bowl of whatever was hot. He happily obliged and got him a hearty bowl of potatoes which had been mashed and mixed with a bit of the left over broth from a beef stew.

The bowl was still steaming when Seth handed it to Kyzyl. He added a splash of milk he'd kept cool with a device made by one of the artificing students and told Kyzyl to mix it in to cool the potatoes. They were still warm and the added stew and milk made them creamy and meaty. It was easily the best meal Kyzyl had eaten since he left home.

"Just a little something I'm working on," the man explained.

"It's good. What do you call it?"

"Ain't really in the business of naming things. Figured I'd just call it what it is, mashed potatoes."

"That's sensible," Kyzyl commented. He was used to chefs who insisted on naming everything they made after themselves in some way. He ate three full bowls before he heard the clock tower chime sixth bell.

He had a class to get to and he was going to be late. He jumped up and ran out the door. He got halfway down the street before he had to catch his breath and started to slow down. While he was catching his breath, he remembered the class he was going to was Rhetoric and Logic. He groaned. This was going to be a new kind of challenge.

He entered the classroom to see most students already seated and the Master Cleric already speaking about Rhetoric.

"Welcome Mr. Shenta. I'm glad you could find the time to join us. Take a seat please."

Kyzyl did so, sitting next to Emrys who had saved him a seat, while trying to explain why he was late, but the Master Cleric simply raised his hand for silence.

"That's quite alright. Simply don't make a habit of it. As I was saying, mastery over Rhetoric is a kind of magic all its own. The ability to successfully defend or defeat a point can sway hearts and minds that, to even the most powerful enchantments, are impossible to crack.

"The best way to practice such abilities is to find someone who quite fervently disagrees with you on a topic and see how they might be swayed. It is, of course, inadvisable to try and antagonize them with an insistence that you are right. The best approach, I have found, is calm and logical. If you stay calm, they will as well."

The Master Cleric clapped his hands together. "Now, let's get down to the nitty gritty. Who can tell me the one most important rule, The Great Law of Magic?"

There was a silence as each student looked around the room for someone to answer the question.

"No one. You've all come so far in your educations and not one of you has stumbled upon the Law which keeps us from falling into chaos? I must say, that's a bit disappointing."

Emrys raised his hand. "Sir, it's just that. We don't know what law you're talking about. Are you talking about one of the laws of Transmutation? Galvin's Universal Law of Alchemy?"

"No, no. Nothing quite as mundane as all of those. I'm speaking about the one law that overrides them all. The law that guides all spellcasters: wizards, sorcerers, and clerics alike. The law that commands a man to do nothing when he holds power enough to shape the world to his whims. The law that governs each and every use of the magical arts."

Again, silence. Kyzyl wasn't sure if everyone was confused, or afraid of saying something stupid.

"Right. That's quite alright, we can start with the basics. This will also allow me to show you how deductive arguments work. The Law is thus, balance. In all things, we must maintain the equilibrium of the universe. Remember this if nothing else my young students. To light a candle is to cast a shadow. Anytime you change even the smallest scrap of the world, you change the world. You mustn't do so without knowing, fully, how the world will change."

Kyzyl could feel his frustration with the man's mere presence converging with his frustration over his philosophical nonsense. Before he could stop himself, his hand was in the air.

The Master Cleric called on him, and Kyzyl could feel ever eye in the room turn to him. He took a breath and tried to calm his anxious nerves. "How would one prove such an assertion?" Kyzyl asked. "Master," he added after realizing he'd neglected the Master Cleric's formal address.

The Master Cleric didn't seem to notice. "I'm glad you asked Kyzyl." He drew three dots in a triangle on the board and wrote out the words "Balance must be maintained" on the board. Next, he drew a line above it and wrote out three numbered lines.

1. Balance keeps us from chaos.

2. Chaos must be avoided.

3. Anything that keeps us from chaos must be maintained.

"This, dear students, is an argument. Specifically, it is a deductive argument. These are characterized by structure of going from large concepts to smaller ones. The numbered statements are premises and the final line is a conclusion. A deductive argument has two qualities that make it a good argument: validity and soundness."

He began writing more words on the board behind

him. "A deductive argument is valid if all the premises, when combined, lead necessarily to the conclusion. The argument is sound if it is both valid and all the premises, and by extension the conclusion, are true.

"In a deductive argument such as the one I have on the board, there are two lines of attack available to the opposing viewpoint. If you can prove the argument is invalid, then you can say that the conclusion has not been proven. It is then the responsibility of the arguer to add or modify their argument to make it valid.

"If the argument is valid, and I will teach you how to test these things as we learn together, you must argue against one or more of the premises to prove they are not true. First is this argument valid?"

Another round of silence.

The Master Cleric nodded. "It is, in fact, valid. A good logician will be careful to make any deductive argument valid, so it is not normally an effective line of attack. Thus, me must move on to soundness. Does anyone want to take a crack at one of these premises."

Kyzyl had a few ideas as to why the Master's argument was flawed. He raised his hand, and the Master nodded to him. The idea of going up against a religious authority brought back memories that Kyzyl had to push aside. He was shaking as he began to speak, but he hoped the Master Cleric and the other students didn't notice.

"Your argument claims that balance keeps us from chaos and chaos should be avoided. Both of these words are subjective, and we don't have an agreed upon system to test the existence or absence of either balance or chaos."

"Very good Mr. Shenta. There are entire classes taught by this university on definitions and how to spot a dubious one. For now, let's discuss these things as if we had a shared definition. What about the premises do you take issue with?"

"What about chaos makes it necessary to avoid it? The natural world is chaotic and seems to be doing just fine. Individuals may perish, but the system seems to maintain itself easily enough."

The Master Cleric nodded. He wrote more lines on the board.

    1. The natural world is a chaotic system

    2. Said system is able to maintain itself

    3. If a system can maintain itself within chaos, chaos need not be avoided

    ∴ Chaos doesn't need to be avoided

"Is this a fair representation of your argument Mr. Shenta?"

"I guess so. But I'm at a bit of a disadvantage here, Master. I don't yet know how to recognize validity and have to rely on you to construct valid arguments for me."

"This is true but, as I will try to instill in all of you, the best debates are ones where both sides are presented in the most favorable light. Only by considering the best of our opponents' arguments can we reach closer to finding fundamental truths. That, and not the defeat of our opponents is the goal of the Rhetorician."

The Master Cleric turned toward the board and spoke over his shoulder. "Plus, to represent your argument in an unfavorable light would be to commit a straw-man fallacy, and I do my best to avoid fallacious arguments."

The Master Cleric circled Kyzyl's first premise. He drew a line to a new argument. "The first problem I find with Mr. Shenta's argument is supposition that the natural world is simultaneously a self-sustaining system and chaotic in nature.

"He is correct that the natural order can introduce chaos into the lives of individuals, but the system itself is bounded by laws that keep order. Thus, it would be misrepresentative to call the system as a whole chaotic. I doubt the Head Master of this very university would disagree with me."

"What does the Head Master have to do with this discussion?" Kyzyl asked.

The Master Cleric turned back toward the class. He smiled and nodded. "Why, nothing at all Mr. Shenta. Or rather, I just failed to introduce him as an authority on the subject.

"Head Master Herman is, in fact, a studied naturalist, but in my failing to bring up that point I have committed a logical fallacy. Can you tell me which one?"

"Appeal to authority. You used his status as Head Master of the university to place him in high regard without establishing his credentials as they relate to our discussion."

The Master Cleric clapped his hands together once. "Excellent. That is exactly right. You truly know your way around a debate Mr. Shenta."

Kyzyl didn't like that he was being praised by the Master Cleric. He felt as if he was being spoon fed and being told he was doing a good job at chewing. Still, a piece of him reacted positively to the praise, and it eased his anxiety about objecting.

Their discussion continued, and Kyzyl was getting more and more frustrated at the easy and pleasant façade this priest was putting on. A distant bell chimed the end of their class period. The Master Cleric finished his statement, and students began to exit the lecture hall.

Kyzyl had to admit that the Master Cleric was a skilled speaker. That was likely what made him such a good marketing tool for whatever temple or church he belonged to. Still, the university was meant to be a place where Kyzyl could go to focus on the practical art of magic. He didn't want a bunch of nonsense philosophy and debate getting in the way of learning how the world actually worked.

"Mr. Shenta, may I speak with you for a moment?"

Emrys mouthed "good luck," and Kyzyl went up to

the Master Cleric. "Yes, sir?"

"Kyzyl, you were rather hostile during our debate today. This isn't uncommon for first-year students, but it seems to go deeper than frustration. Is there something you'd like to tell me?"

"May I speak freely Master?"

"All may do so in my class, if they are able to defend what they say."

"I don't agree with your position as a Master. This place is about learning real magic, not the kind of thing clerics try to pass off as magic. Not to mention the fact that you seem to maintain your status by teaching philosophy and rhetoric instead of actually teaching us something useful. At least the other Masters actually teach us how to do something. Your kind of magic is nothing more than ceremony and sorcery."

He knew he'd gone too far as the words came flooding out. He opened his mouth to apologize, but the Master Cleric held up his hand. "Expressing your viewpoints, however radical, is something I encourage in all my students. Kyzyl, do you know why I have a seat with the other Masters?"

"I had always assumed the church you belong to was afraid of real magic, so they demanded a seat to keep an eye on things around here."

"Your assumption is shared by many people, and not just students. Many people attend this university and become fully realized wizards without learning how my seat came to be filled by clerics instead of any other type of spellcaster.

"My seat originally belonged to a Master of a very different kind of magic. A magic that has since died out and only exists in the oldest legends. That magic was called Naming and it was the most respected form of magic taught by this university. People from all over the world would come here to learn under the Master Namer, who was more than once also one of the seven True Namers, if rumors are to be believed. That was when this place's reputation became what it is today.

"However, when the art of Naming became a thing of the past, the other eight Masters went looking for a new kind of magic to take the place of Naming. They heard rumors of a kind of faith-based magic and they invited many who practiced this magic to showcase their abilities. This was back when magicians dueled to prove their strength, and some who practiced this magic held their own against the best and brightest students of the university. One of them even won the tournament and won the right to be the new ninth Master.

"Since then, the seat I now hold has been granted to the best cleric this university can find, and we have earned a profound respect from many of the best wizards on this side of the world. Do you know why I am telling you this?"

"Because you think it will convince me that you deserve to be a Master?"

"So, you understand why I am here, and, most importantly, so you believe me when I tell you that despite what you think you know, my kind of magic is the most powerful magic available here."

"If that's the case, why are you not Head Master?"

"Because there is more to being the Head Master than magical might. It takes a leadership quality that I lack. I am perfectly happy where I am, teaching students how to use reason and logic. I also take the ones who have the kind of faith that is required for my kind of magic and teach them how to channel it. I don't want to be Head Master because that is not my place in this world."

The Master took a deep, calming breath, and let it out slowly. "I invited you to my class because I thought you would be interested in learning from me. If that is not the case, you have my permission to pursue other things."

"I…" Kyzyl couldn't begin to think of what to say. He thought back to their discussion. He thought about what the Master Cleric had said about rhetoric and how it could sway minds. "I will see you next class Master…"

"Jonah. My name is Jonah. Thank you, Kyzyl, I look forward to teaching you what I know."

"I still don't think I believe in all that talk about faith-based magic but since that's not what you're trying to teach me, I don't think it really matters."

Master Jonah nodded his head, and Kyzyl walked out of the classroom.

#

"You called him a sorcerer? That's a low blow," Emrys said in amazement.

"Said the man who was named after the greatest sorcerer of legend," Donovan countered.

Emrys made a lewd gesture at him. Kyzyl had just finished recounting what had happened between him and Master Jonah over a round of mead at the Noble Steed.

"Besides," Donovan continued, "clerics tend to not be a part of the elitism most of us great wizards arc. Granted, the fact that you meant it as an insult will not go unnoticed, but I'm sure he's been called worse. You're not the first person to have this opinion, you know."

"There are people here who don't believe in faith magic?" Kyzyl asked.

"There are some. There are a lot more people who have it in their heads that a wizard can do anything a cleric can do, but without the intervention of a god. It's kind of an independence thing. Most of us scholarly types like to do things our way and don't fancy some cosmic being making up a set of arbitrary rules to go along with the magic they promise."

"And what's your opinion?"

Donovan shrugged. "I've seen clerics do lots of things I haven't learned how to do yet. The way I see it, clerics and wizards are just two distinct kinds of spellcasters. To say one is better than the other is like saying a meat pie is better than a fruit pie. Anyone who says so is missing the bigger fact that they serve two different purposes."

"So, your argument is that, just because you don't know how to do everything they do, they must know more than you?" Kyzyl asked.

"Not more, they just know things I don't, and I can't overlook that."

"Don't you have faith-magic in your lands? What are they called? Kunashi?" Emrys asked.

"First of all, one day I would like for you to explain to me where you get all this knowledge about my homeland. I had to spend years learning just the basics of your culture and I was preparing to come here. The fact you have all this off-hand knowledge would be frustrating to me if we weren't already friends.

"Secondly, Kunashi aren't the same as clerics. Then again, maybe they are. I don't really know how their magic is supposed to work, but the Kunashi pray for the intervention of spirits, usually ancestral spirits, on behalf of people who come to their temples.

"Though such prayer usually come with some kind of price. Which is at least one reason I hold such distrust to those types of people. They always want something from you, and I would like to know what Master Jonah wants from me."

"It is possible, and don't take this the wrong way, that his intention is to teach you. That is his job after all. And seeing as how you've already told us of your staggeringly low tuition, I'll bet he thinks you're worth the effort."

Emrys sat back in his chair. "Of course, there is always the possibility he wants to steal your soul and offer it up to his dark god as a sacrifice."

"People believe in dark gods?" Kyzyl asked. He was pretty sure Emrys was joking. Most things he said were meant to be, on some level, humorous, but Kyzyl had only ever heard of benevolent gods before. Who would want to worship a god they knew was evil?

"People believe in lots of things," Emrys explained. "That's how their magic works. If enough people have faith in your god, real faith that can move mountains, then it creates energy like the kind we manipulate for spells. The god they worship acts as the focus, and the cleric chooses and prays for the desired effect. Power, focus, effect. Their magic isn't that different from ours."

"So, it's just down to faith. The god doesn't actually have to exist for this to work?" Kyzyl asked. Emrys and Donovan just shrugged. Kyzyl made a mental note to ask Master Jonah to clarify further.

Donovan set his mug down. "Right. No more talk of deep personal beliefs like how much you believe in god," he declared. "Did either of you see the dress Kahente was wearing today? My, what I wouldn't give to make that woman mine."

Emrys smiled but said nothing.

"Who is Kahente? Is she a student here?" Kyzyl asked.

"That's right," Donovan said stroking his chin. "You haven't been here long enough to be acquainted with the greater female population. You don't know that she's the most desirable woman in the Artificery."

"She's a wood elf. Probably one of the few here. They mostly keep to themselves, especially when it comes to high elves, but her father sent her here to learn how to enchant weapons. He is the largest seller of elvish-oak bows in the entire country," Emrys explained.

It was no secret that he was shy around women, especially elvish women. Still, if there was anything to be known about anything, Emrys would discover it.

"Is that why Donovan likes her? Her daddy's rich." Kyzyl gave Donovan a sidelong glance.

"I resent that notion. I like her for her abundant charm and incalculable wit."

"Was that why you were staring at her dress? Did it have something witty embroidered on it?"

Kyzyl and Emrys laughed as Donovan turned red in the face. When they had finally calmed down, Donovan posed the question to them.

"Well, c'mon you two. Since you're so eager to poke fun at me you must have given it quite a bit of thought. What is it that gets those young, boyish hearts beating?"

"I don't really know actually," Kyzyl admitted. "I guess I don't have enough experience to have a type really."

"Really?" Emrys asked. "You never had so much as a childhood crush?"

"Well, there were a few daughters of this farmer or that merchant that came to see my father, but they never stayed long enough for me to do anything about it. I did kiss one once, out by the stables."

The memory of the horse smell had overwritten any memory of what the kiss was like. "Other than that, I've mostly been studying and preparing for my admission here."

"Well," Donovan declared, "since you're finally here, you can take a break from studying and we can learn your type. Come now little cockerels. Father Rooster is about to show you where the hens are."

Donovan got up from the table and headed toward the door. Kyzyl and Emrys followed him out, but began questioning him immediately as to where they were going.

"The only place where little cockerels like you have a hope of catching a mate. You both have money, don't you?"

Kyzyl and Emrys looked at each other both wearing

their realization plain. They were headed to a brothel as their first excursion of the new term. Wonderful.

CHAPTER SIX
Lounging after Learning

Kyzyl and Emrys allowed Donovan to lead them to a grand house near the edge of the university complex. The university complex was nestled in the center of a town that Kyzyl assumed grew up around the constant influx of students learning to become full realized wizards. While nothing outside of the buildings the university itself built were associated with the institution, many of the businesses and shops were built near, or sometimes inside, the greater university complex.

This particular house had a large, heavy, and carved Redwood door. The ornate silver knocker made a loud bang as Donovan pounded against it. The door opened promptly onto a robust figure in a tight corset that made her prominent breast practically spill out. Her smile was shining and her hair was as red as flame. "I was wondering when I'd see you this term Donovan," she said without breaking her smile.

"Hello Matilda, I have a couple of boys looking to become men. Can your lovely ladies help them?"

"Excuse me," Emrys protested, "but I never said I was a virgin. Kyzyl was the only one who admitted anything."

"Emrys you can barely talk to a woman. Explain to me how you would seduce one." Donovan had a point, but that didn't stop Emrys from looking red in the face and glaring at him.

"Now, now gentlemen, there's no need for any of that in my house," Matilda said chidingly. "Emrys was it? My girls are no strangers to the shy types. I promise you we'll take good care of you."

Emrys blushed a deeper red.

"That must make you Kyzyl." Matilda presented her hand to Kyzyl and he bowed low, brushing his lips across her knuckles. "My, my, what an exotic gentleman we have here. Where are you from, love?"

Kyzyl felt very uncomfortable being described as "exotic." It made him feel like an animal in a menagerie or an attraction at a fair. He didn't know how the people around him would react if he voiced his objections, though, so he merely answered the woman's question. "A very long way away from here. Are you familiar with a place called Techarae?"

"I can't say that I am. You'll have to tell me all about it." Matilda stepped to one side and the three men entered the front room of the house.

"She seems nice." Emrys said.

"Of course, she's nice. She wouldn't make any money if she spat at everyone who came through the door," Donovan said.

They were led into a parlor with a small but well stocked bar in the corner. Milling about the parlor were a number of men and even more women. Every body type, hair color, and eye color were represented. There were women of each of the sentient races that populated Lukor from the small-statured halflings to the broad and muscular orcs.

Most of the men present appeared to be other clientele, but Kyzyl got the distinct impression that the couple of men chatting at a table in the corner were, in fact, a client and worker discussing prices. Each of the workers gave a friendly wave or a sultry smile and wink to the three men that just walked in, but several of them were already with clients whom they continued chatting with.

"Gentlemen," Matilda said as she stepped in the room, "please feel free to mill about and chat. If you find a girl to your tastes, please allow her to let me know and you two can take one of the upstairs rooms. Ladies, please make our guests feel welcome."

The girls all smiled and giggled at the trio of young men standing before them. Kyzyl felt his embarrassment grow, but didn't fully understand why. He'd felt self-conscious around people giving him attention before, but this was different. He didn't know what he was supposed to do.

As Matilda left, Donovan approached a very slim elvish woman and started talking to her. He gestured toward the bar and they both sat. Donovan didn't even have to ask before the woman behind the bar started pouring two drinks.

Kyzyl looked at Emrys and, from the look on his face, guessed he was just as clueless about what to do. It didn't take long, however, for a few girls to start approaching them. One practically skipped over to them in a way that made her seem especially friendly, and Kyzyl felt himself relax as she approached him.

She was human, with long blond hair, wide hips, and a lean physique that was accentuated by a skin tight dress with a slit that showed just a little too much thigh. Donovan had told him that this trip was about finding his type, and the woman who stood before him made his heart pound harder than anyone ever had before.

"Hey big guy. How about a dance?" she said with a smirk. She made a gesture and the barmaid pulled out a contraption from behind the bar. It could only be from the Artificery. She touched a few sigils and a sweet, slow song began to flow out of it.

The blond woman took Kyzyl's hand and placed it on her waist. She took his other hand in hers and led him in a slow, courtly waltz. Kyzyl allowed her to lead him. It was clearly a refined dance, and he assumed she learned it from one of the many nobles that populated the university.

They danced for long enough that Emrys got swept upstairs by one of the orcish woman who turned out to have a rather assertive nature.

"I didn't catch your name, hon."

"Kyzyl. My name is Shenta Kyzyl."

"You go by your last name?"

"Where I come from, people put their family name first. It's a sign of respect for all the people that hold that name."

The woman nodded. "I bet lots of people get it wrong here. Not many people around here think that way."

"Even the Masters say it wrong. It seems disrespectful to correct them, but I feel like I should."

"Does it bother you?"

"Kind of, maybe. I don't know."

"You seem confused." She pressed up against him as they spoke, and Kyzyl suddenly became very conscious of a hand she was spreading over his groin. "Maybe I can do something to relive some of your stress then you can have a clear head to think."

"I don't think that will work." Her lips made a pout and he had to think fast before she was insulted. "I didn't say no, did I?" Her face brightened up and she kissed his cheek.

They finished their dance as the song wound to a close. The woman spent most of the dance teasing him and making his heart pound. By the time they were done and Kyzyl was approaching the bar, his legs felt like they were doing to buckle under his own weight.

Kyzyl was breathing hard and shaking when he

requested a room from Matilda, but he couldn't help but smile. "It's about time. Your friend should be almost finished by now. I know a man by look and he doesn't look like a man who keeps a girl busy for long, not that any of us mind."

Kyzyl blushed, and felt a bit of sympathetic embarrassment on Emrys' behalf. Matilda gave him a once over. "Are you sure you're OK, darlin'? You look about a second from passing out."

Kyzyl nodded. He leaned against the bar for support as he tried to calm his nerves. The day had put a lot of stress on him, but he was, ultimately, excited about what was about to happen.

When he got the key, he came back to retrieve his evening's partner. She half skipped, half ran up the stairs, pulling him along behind her.

He was already kissing her by the time they made it to the door of the room. "I'm sorry, I didn't give you a chance to give me your name."

"Bethany."

"Well Bethany," more kisses, "now that I'm having my first, I'm glad it's with a girl like you."

Bethany stopped kissing him. "This is your first time?" She took a step back.

"Is that OK?" Kyzyl moved toward her but she just backed off again.

"It's just that... I don't feel comfortable taking your virginity for money. Your first time only happens once and should be special. Doing it this way feels... dirty."

"It doesn't have to be dirty." Kyzyl touched her arm. "I've known you for half an hour, and you're by far one of the best things about this place."

"The university you mean."

He smiled and stepped closer to her. "I mean this whole country. What I've seen of it, at least."

Bethany blushed and looked down. She touched a

broach on her collar that Kyzyl hadn't noticed until that moment.

When she looked back up at him, he relented. He said, "if it will make you feel better, we can go in that room and do whatever you want."

She smiled warmly at him. "You really are Donovan's friend."

"What do you mean?"

"Nothing." Bethany grabbed Kyzyl's arm and pulled him into the room. She jumped girlishly onto the bed and turned around to face Kyzyl. "So, mister Shenta, I want to get to know you. I promise, if you are totally honest with me, I'll tell Matilda not to charge you."

"You can do that?"

"Let's just say, the house is paid for. What do you do for fun?"

"I study."

"I said fun."

"Drink?"

"There you go. Do you have a drink of choice?"

"I do, but you can't get it here. It's made from the spring water of a mountain in my homeland. It's brewed with honey made from a rare flower that blooms in the moonlight, and is brewed by men that live in a temple at the mountain's peak. It's said to give a man great fortitude, in all aspects of life." Kyzyl winked at her.

"Is that true?"

"No, of course not. It's alcohol, not medicine. While I'm here though, I drink whatever fine wine I can get my hands on. I'm not big into mead or ale, though Donovan has been known to force it down my throat from time to time."

Bethany giggled "I can understand that. I'm a whiskey girl myself."

Kyzyl raised an eyebrow at her. "You don't strike me as the type to go for the hard stuff. Most girls I've known prefer something sweet and made from fruit."

She giggled again and the sounds floated through the air into Kyzyl's ears. He felt intoxicated by her presence. "You obviously haven't met many women from the Orcish tribes then. Rumor around the parlor is that Gral can drink anyone in the university under the table."

"Which one is Gral?"

"She's the one that took a shine to Emrys. She likes the nervous ones. It makes her feel... I don't know... powerful? Does that make sense?"

Kyzyl raised his eyebrows. "I suspect a woman like that doesn't have to work hard to feel powerful. Either way, as long as her and Emrys enjoy themselves, I suppose that's what matters."

Bethany gave a coy and knowing smile. "Under Matilda's roof, pleasure is the law of the land." She patted the spot beside her on the bed. "Come join me. Watching you stand over me is making me restless."

Kyzyl gave her a questioning look.

"You can keep your pants on. It's just the only spot to sit in here. We didn't exactly design these rooms for friendly conversation."

She beckoned him toward her, and before he knew what was happening, his knees were on the bed and his arm was reaching out to wrap around her shoulders.

"So, how did you meet Donovan?" Bethany asked. She nestled under Kyzyl's arm and rested her head against his chest.

"I met Emrys first. He signed up for one of the same classes I did. We got to chatting and he invited me to a tavern where he introduced me to Donovan."

"I see. Sounds like you have quite the tight knit little band of misfits."

"How do you mean?"

"You have a half elf, a foreigner, and a seventh son. If I didn't know any better, I'd say you were all brought together because you have something to prove."

Kyzyl considered this for a moment. "I didn't realize Donovan was the youngest of seven."

"Technically he's the youngest of thirteen. He also has several sisters." Bethany sighed in a way that made Kyzyl very aware of her chest pressing against his. "Once the eldest inherits his father's title, the rest will likely have a military rank bought for them or join the clergy.

"Between that and the dowries his family will have to put together for his sisters, Donovan will have barely anything to inherit. Except for, perhaps, his tuition money."

"I understand what that's like. Still, I'm surprised he hasn't mentioned it to me yet."

"Would you?"

"No." Kyzyl's tone was flat.

Bethany noticed and looked up at him. "Is everything OK?" she asked.

Kyzyl didn't say anything.

"If you tell me, I promise it will stay between us. I'm very good at keeping secrets."

Kyzyl believed her. More than that, he felt the truth pressing against him from the inside. He didn't know if her natural charisma was making him want to tell her everything, but he merely said, "Donovan isn't the only spare son in our group."

Kyzyl met Bethany's eyes. Their pull tore everything else out in a tumble of confused words. Kyzyl had to swallow to hold back his tears. "I ran away because I couldn't convince them to let me go. My eldest brother will inherit my father's title and the lands around our estate.

"My father's second son," Kyzyl never considered the second eldest his brother, "will more than likely go into the military as an officer. According to family tradition, my duty is to the temples and monks, but those men will get no such servitude from me.

"I couldn't convince them to let me study magic that wasn't wrapped up in fairy tales about spirits and gods. I knew I was never going to become a Kunashi, so I ran away. I came here partly because I knew this place was the best school in the world, but it was mostly so I'd be so far away that they couldn't stop me."

"Shh. It's OK darling. Your family may not want you here, but I'm glad you came. You belong here, and I am certain of that."

Kyzyl got his emotions under control, and Bethany helped wipe the tears from his eyes. He smiled at her and said, "now you know my tragic backstory. What's yours?"

She smiled at him. "Not much tragedy in my story. I came here because I wanted to. Matilda is a really good teacher and most of the women here are the best in the business."

"Have you always wanted to be uh..."

Bethany gave him a plain look. "It's OK. You can say it. I am a prostitute, and there is no shame in it."

Kyzyl remained silent.

Bethany sighed. "I haven't always wanted to be one. My mother had to work from sun up til sundown as a launderer to keep food on our table, and we lived in the city. That meant I spent most of my days walking the streets and playing with whatever children I could meet.

"One day I was playing with a few of my normal friends when this weird man with a scraggly beard came up to us. He started talking about a lost dog, but something about it didn't feel right. I told the other kids to scatter and ducked into the nearest building.

"That building turned out to be the brothel, and all the women there were just so pretty. I watched them flirt with men who seemed to do anything the women asked them to. I was old enough to notice how my mom was treated by her boss, the merchants at the shops, and pretty much everywhere else. But in that room, there wasn't a man in sight who was above these ladies.

"I started coming back and asking questions, you know how kids are. My mom found out and got really mad. I guess she thought I was working there."

"Were you?"

Bethany gave a disgusted look. "By the Nine Hells, no. That was one of the questions I asked the woman who ran the place, but she said fourteen was too young to make that kind of decision. So, I had to wait. When I got old enough, she wrote me a letter of introduction and sent me here to be trained by Matilda."

"And you've been here ever since?"

Bethany nodded. "Matilda is a really good teacher, and being here makes me feel like everything is mine: my body, my money, my choice."

She paused for a moment. "Well, technically we all split the money at the end of the night. It's good money though. I have fun doing what I do and I enjoy how skilled I am at it."

Bethany shifted out from under Kyzyl's arm, and laid her head on his lap. Kyzyl got a full view of her tight blue dress and most of what was in it. Still, his gaze was pulled toward her beautiful sea-foam green eyes. She touched his face and he felt consumed by it.

They stayed in the room for a full hour more before Bethany said their time had been used up. "If I stay here much longer," she explained, "Matilda will have me on the afternoon shift with the new girls for a week."

"Is that her form of punishment?"

"For me it is. I'm terrible at training new girls. Everything I do comes naturally to me, and it's impossible for me to explain it to anyone."

They went downstairs where Donovan and Emrys were waiting for them. "Atta boy," Donovan said, "I was beginning to think you were going to keep Miss Bethany up there all night. How was your first time? Or second or fifth?"

"Still hasn't happened."

Kyzyl explained everything as they walked out the door and back toward the Noble Steed.

Donovan just shook his head in amazement. "How is it that I found the one man in all the university that would spend an hour with a prostitute, and only talk to her."

"I'm sure you are plenty familiar with the concept," Kyzyl said without looking at Donovan.

"What does that mean?" he asked.

"Nothing. Just some gossip I heard from Bethany while we were chatting. Besides, I'm more interested in hearing about our friend and his exploits. How was your first time, Emrys?"

"Gral is a very… assertive woman. It was definitely eye-opening. I thought I was going to get lost in all the muscle and linen." Emrys' wouldn't meet Kyzyl's eye, but it seemed that there was a spark of enjoyment behind his words.

Donovan let out a big laugh. "That's more like it. Sounds like we have divined your type my young, elvish friend." He clapped Emrys on the back. The three friends traded jabs and gentle ribbing all the way back to the Noble Steed

When they made it back to the Noble Steed, Kyzyl bid them both good nights. The sun had just finished setting and he was anxious to get to bed. He wanted to wake-up with the sun tomorrow, so he could study the spell Master Enwin gave him. He was determined to have it mastered sooner rather than later.

The innkeeper's youngest daughter came up to Kyzyl while he was still in the taproom. She was tall for an eight-year-old and had light brown hair tied up in braids that flew back as she ran toward Kyzyl.

He had never met her before; he was always out

until past her bedtime. He crouched down to meet her at eye-level and held out his hand. "My name is Kyzyl. I have heard a lot about you miss."

"Why do your eyes look like that?" she asked after taking his hand.

He smiled. She was referring to the monolid shape and red color that was common among his people.

"Samantha!" her mother chided. "That is not a polite question for a lady to be asking."

The small girl bowed her head and apologized.

"That's quite alright. Something tells me you have never seen a person like me before. I am from a faraway place where everyone looks much more like me than they look like you."

Samantha tilted her head a bit. "That must be a very far place because daddy serves all kinds of people from all over who come to the university to study magic. Are you a wizard?"

"Not yet. I only know one spell, but I'm here to learn more."

"What spell do you know? Can you teach it to me?"

"Unfortunately, as good of a student as I'm sure you'd be, my culture doesn't allow me to teach what I have learned without the permission of my teacher. It's considered very disrespectful, but since he lives so far away, there wouldn't be an easy way for me to contact him."

"You could write him a letter. Mommy has me write letters to all kinds of family members so I can practice writing. I can show you how to do it."

"That would be wonderful, as long as your mommy says it's OK for you to teach me."

Samantha looked at her mother who nodded. "She said yes!"

"Then I will be sure to be back here before dinner tomorrow for my first lesson. For now, I need rest, so I can rise with the sun tomorrow."

"Good night mister Kyzyl. It was nice meeting you. You better be ready to learn tomorrow."

I always am, Kyzyl thought to himself as he ascended into his room.

CHAPTER SEVEN
Studying Spells

The rising sun found Kyzyl on his way to the library. About halfway there he ran into Siradyl, who was talking to someone who looked very nervous and kept bowing low.

Siradyl's eyes locked on Kyzyl as he passed. "Ah, what do we have here? Why, if it isn't the little child from a land so far away. What has you awoken at such an early hour?"

"I was going to the library to see what kind of books I can find on an assignment by the Master Conjurer."

"And how did you get so lucky to be taught by one of the Masters as a first year?"

Kyzyl shrugged. "Perhaps I had impressed him so much during my exam that he wanted to teach my class personally."

This was a lie, of course. Master Enwin was already teaching the class by the time Kyzyl signed up for it, but something about Siradyl's manner made Kyzyl want to put him in his place.

"Really? I suppose with a ten-crown tuition you would indeed have needed to be quite impressive. Let's just hope you are able to maintain your budding reputation. Wouldn't want to embarrass yourself by failing to meet expectations."

Kyzyl kept his face carefully controlled, but he was smoldering with anger on the inside. He knew he'd lash out if he didn't walk away soon. So, without another word, he did so.

As he was turning around, he saw Siradyl give an affronted look. He took a certain joy in leaving that pompous prick feeling offended. He rolled his shoulders back and straightened his back as he walked toward the Divination tower the housed the library. He was beginning to feel comfortable with his place at the university.

Espen was working the front desk of the library, looking as tired as he had last time Kyzyl saw him. When he saw Kyzyl, he smiled, but he still looked dead on his feet.

"Good morning, Espen."

"Is it morning?"

"Another all-nighter?"

"Head Master Herman has me on overnight shifts this term. I'm not sure what made him think I was the man for the job, but at least I have an excuse to take all evening classes."

"Why does Head Master Herman keep someone in the library over night? I thought the library closed at sundown." If that ended up not being the case, perhaps Kyzyl could spend even more time studying the spell Master Enwin gave him.

"It is, but overnights are when we get most of the cleaning and sorting done while there isn't anyone in any of the classrooms or among the shelves. It also gives me plenty of study time since I get most of the cleaning done pretty quick."

"You clean the whole library?"

Espen shook his head. "Just the classrooms mostly." He looked around conspiratorially. "Don't spread it around too much, but I learned a spell in my

Enchantment classes to animate small objects. I have it down well enough that I can get the brooms to do the cleaning on their own while I study. I still tend to stay in the same room though. Don't want them knocking over anything important."

"That's quite inventive of you. You should be proud."

Espen beamed. "My replacement should be here soon. Did you want to go in? I can check you in before I leave."

"That would be helpful. Thank you Espen." Espen nodded and turned the ledger book toward Kyzyl, who signed it and headed in among the shelves.

Kyzyl was equally amazed by the vast reaches of the books as he had been the first time. He was on a mission, though, and he remembered seeing the section he was looking for the last time he was in here.

After looking through four different sections, the last one more poorly organized than the one he tried to fix, he had a stack of books on summoning. He found a reading nook hidden among the shelves. He sat down and began reading one book that had interesting details about the relationship between summoning spells and teleporting spells.

"It would seem," the book explained, "that in most cases, summoning spells and teleporting spells are one in the same. The only noticeable difference is in the subject of the spell and its remoteness to the caster."

He pulled a nub of pencil and a piece of scrap paper out of his pocket and made a note of that point. The next chapter held a glyph similar to the one Master Enwin had drawn for the spell he'd assigned. There were a few modifications in the subject, and Kyzyl realized it was a glyph for a teleportation spell.

His scrap paper was too small for him to copy down the glyph. He went to the front desk and asked for a pen, ink and paper. The student running the desk went pale and explained that, in general, things as messy as ink aren't allowed near the books.

"But I found a glyph I wanted to copy."

"The glyphs in the books are the intellectual property of the author or university. You'll have to get the permission of the Head Master before copying any of them."

That was news to Kyzyl, and he quietly went back to the reading nook and continued studying. He chose a book and examined it.

<u>Advice for the Practical Application of Object Summoning Vol. I</u> was on the cover. He opened to the introduction and read through the first few chapters. This book was much more in line with what he was trying to accomplish. Most of it was advice that was similar to what Master Enwin had told him.

He did find one section that caught his attention. It read, "object summoning is the easiest and most entry level form of summoning. This is because, as objects are inherently inanimate, they will remain in a single place until summoned by the caster.

"Such is not the case for things capable of moving on their own. This makes getting a handle on the sending location of an object a much less monumental task. A wise conjurer will find it prudent to keep objects they intend to summon frequently in a space where they will not be moved by others."

That got Kyzyl thinking about the problems he'd been having. He knew the general location of his sword, but it was possible his father had moved it out of his room and into one of their family vaults to ensure its safety. He decided practicing with objects whose locations where more definitive, like the book suggested, might be better.

He took out the glyph for Master Enwin's spell, grabbed five of the books from his stack, and studied them carefully. He familiarized himself with their weight, texture, and size.

Next, he hid them on random shelves around his reading nook. If any of the scribes or archivists saw what he was doing, they'd likely be furious. Based on what Espen had told him, he guessed shelving books incorrectly was a big part of what made working in the library so difficult.

For now, he needed to do this for practice. He'd shelve them correctly later. He took a deep breath, closed his eyes, and tipped his mind into Wind-Dance.

***

He lets out the breath and begins to chant. He works the sigils out with his hands while he tries to imagine standing, simultaneously, in the reading nook where he was, and the shelves where he had put the book he's summoning. He imagines every slight movement of taking the book off the shelf, and feels a slight tingle when he has to suppress the muscle movement.

***

His concentration broke when he felt the weight of the book in his hand. He curled his fingers around the spine. But when he opened his eyes, there was only air. This went on for several attempts before Kyzyl's concentration had been exhausted.

His muscles were sore. He had been using his own muscle strength to power the spell, and now they were twitching. He went and found the books the manual way and put them back where the belonged. Then he jotted down his check-out time in the ledger and went to his only class for the day: Basic Wards with one of the senior abjuration students.

The student in charge of teaching Kyzyl's class was a long-winded man with hair the color of fertile soil. He seemed to pause for breath less often than Kyzyl would expect. His strong baritone carried through the lecture hall without any hint of a shout.

Even with all his skill in speaking, Kyzyl found his lecture less engaging than the practical assignment Master Enwin had given them during his first class. Even the classroom discussion that Master Jonah had lead was more stimulating.

Despite the lecturer's shortcomings as an educator, Kyzyl made the most out of the class. He kept detailed notes on what the senior student told them about various types of wards. He even went as far as leaving asterisks or other markings near things that were repeated, which seemed to be often.

The lecturer spoke of every type of ward Kyzyl was familiar with and some he hadn't heard of. There were wards for preventing certain types of energy, and usually the mass that carried that energy, from crossing certain thresholds. There were wards that could distort space or time to help prevent scrying and summoning. There were even wards that could brake enchantments by disrupting the physical processes that make the brain function.

The last sounded very dangerous to Kyzyl, and he did not want to learn about what happened when those wards went wrong. The idea of his brain being subject to a poorly done spell and him possibly losing the intelligence he valued so highly made him shiver.

He left the class with a great deal of notes on how wards worked in theory, but he was somewhat disappointed that the student running the class hadn't given him a spell to practice like Master Enwin had. He had hoped his time at the university would be largely spent studying and mastering spells, but he supposed that being taught what the spells did before being given them was a reasonable approach.

He got back to the inn and found Samantha waiting for him in the taproom with several sheets of paper and a set of pens. She waved at him excitedly and beckoned for him to sit across from her. He did so, and she began his schooling on the art of letter writing.

Kyzyl did his best to be an attentive student and decided that he didn't need to tell Samantha that he could probably write a much more eloquent letter than she was capable of understanding at her age.

He did, however, use this time to write a letter home. He apologized to his mother for leaving without a word of explanation. He didn't want her to be worried about where he'd run off to.

He also explained everything that had already happened at the university: his admissions exam, him meeting his new friends, and the beginning of classes. The last he tried to explain as diplomatically as he could. Since he intended to use the new spell Master Enwin had given him to retrieve his sword, he wanted his family to know.

He thought of how his father would react if it went missing. He'd likely march an army into each town on his lands and demand the thief come forward. When no such man would come forward, he likely execute anyone he found suspicious, confiscate their possessions and hold them ransom until the sword was returned.

He and his father had different ideas of what justice looked like. Kyzyl hoped he could spare the men and women that farmed their lands such pains.

When Samantha saw which language he was writing in, she asked what all the "silly pictures" meant. Kyzyl explained what his language was like, that it was syllabic unlike Aragoran which was alphabetical. By the time he was done telling her about it she looked very confused and her mother was calling her for dinner. Samantha told Kyzyl that she would continue his tutelage another time and he agreed.

Kyzyl joined the family for a dinner of vegetable soup and fresh baked bread. It was warm and generously painted with a thick creamy butter. The vegetables had been grown in a neighbor's garden, and tasted earthy. The broth had been rendered from beef bones and added a great amount of flavor to the soup.

After dinner, Kyzyl took a stroll to the brothel Donovan had showed him. He was already missing Bethany's company and wanted to pop in. Matilda greeted him at the door and told him that Donovan had just arrived himself. She led him into the parlor, and he took a seat at the bar. When he didn't see Bethany, he asked Donovan where she was.

"Lad, where do you think she is? She's working of course."

"Oh! Right, of course. How long has she been gone?"

"Not long, and, knowing the guy she's with, not much longer until she's done."

"You know him? Is it Emrys?"

Donovan shook his head. "The way you were making eyes at her when we left, Emrys and I both decided to stay away from her. That way it won't hurt as bad."

"What won't hurt as bad?"

"When you realize she doesn't care about you. She just wants your money. That's why you're here isn't it? Because you think she's your new girlfriend or something."

"Not exactly. I just missed her company is all."

"Yeah, that's how it starts. First you don't mind what she's doing, you just want to be around her. Next thing you know, you want her all to yourself, so you're asking her to leave this life and come away with you.

"Trouble is, these girls aren't here because they have nowhere else to go. They get paid well enough that I'd be willing to bet half of them could afford whatever tuition the Masters gave them and still have plenty of money to fund extravagant living while they study.

"These girls are here because they like the job, and they aren't giving it up for some rich boy promising them the world. When you finally realize that Bethany is no different, you'll be facing a lot of cold winter nights."

"You don't know anything. I'm just here so she has

someone to talk to between, uh, shifts."

Donovan made a dismissive gesture. "You'll change your tone when you see who she's with. They should be just about done, knowing him."

Donovan's estimate turned out to be spot on because a moment later an elf with obnoxiously ornamented ears and a loud, purple cloak walked down the stairs with Bethany on his arm. "Siradyl," Kyzyl said plainly.

"Ah, our young foreigner is playing with the lordling. It seems like quite the pair. A man whose parents are too far away to matter and a man whose parents don't care about him."

"Piss off you knife-eared bastard," Donovan spat.

"Now, now mighty Donovan. I would mind my tongue if I were you. You wouldn't want to get daddy angry at his least favorite son, would you?"

Donovan stood up, and Kyzyl grabbed his arm. "Don't do it." Kyzyl could see the fury in Donovan's eyes, and his hands were beginning to move into a symbol for fire.

Before anything else could happen, Gral, the orcish woman who had taken Emrys to bed their first time at the brothel, set down her mug with a loud thud.

"You both know the rules," she said when everyones attention was on her. "No fighting. Keep a respectful tongue in your head. The clients and the girls don't need people fighting 'round here like this is some seedy dockside tavern."

Siradyl sniffed, but Donovan sat down with his back to the elf. That brought a sneer Siradyl's face. He untangled himself from Bethany and walked out the door without looking back.

"I hate that man." Donovan said evenly.

"You and me both," Kyzyl agreed.

"I know what you mean," Bethany said. She was

wearing a strapless white dress that was held against her by a tight fitting brown leather corset. Her hand was covering a part of her shoulder, and Kyzyl caught Donovan looking at it with disdain in his eyes. "I wish you wouldn't use language like that, Donovan.

"Not only are there better things you could be using to get under that slimeball's skin than racial slurs, but if Emrys heard what you said to him, he'd be crushed."

Donovan nodded once. "That horse's ass just brings out the worst in me I suppose." He rubbed his eyes and stretched out his back. "But you're right. I know enough about him and the company he keeps to write a book or two on the subject."

Donovan took the hand that Bethany was using to cover her shoulder. Without it there, Kyzyl could see the beginnings of an angry welt forming where she'd been keeping it.

She turned to let Donovan have a better look at it, which let her get a full view of Kyzyl's confused look. She smirked at him and said, "I know men like you can't keep their curiosity bottled up for long. You can go ahead and ask."

"What did he do to you?" Kyzyl said. He tried to stay calm, but it came out more like a demand.

Bethany waved him off. "Stop that. I have enough trouble with Donovan worrying about that sort of stuff." When Kyzyl's gaze didn't get less angry, she sighed.

"Look, Matilda's rules on leaving marks are very clear. Firstly, no one does it to anyone who doesn't want them. She has a whole extra week of lessons you have to go over with her about first aid and knowing your limit before she lets you become that kind of whore.

"Secondly, anyone who leaves marks gets to pay what it costs to make them go away. That means that if Matilda has to pay one of Master Telma's students to mend a broken bone, the person responsible covers the medical bill and the time it takes for things to heal."

At the mention of broken bones, Kyzyl perked up and Bethany shook her head again. "It doesn't go that far unless things get really bad. People like Siradyl like to leave bruises and welts. They pay Matilda enough gold to cover the size of the injury for each day that it's visible."

She stepped away as Donovan finished his examination of her. "I'm not some delicate flower the two of you need to protect. I'm a worker under the protection of one of the most well connected women in the kingdom."

"You're right," Kyzyl said. "I just don't like the idea of you getting beat up for money."

Bethany rolled her eyes. "I think it's sweet that you want to make sure I'm not doing anything dangerous, but this is part of my job. I wanted to learn everything Matilda had to teach me, and this is part of that."

She touched Kyzyl's face. "Maybe one day," she whispered into his ear, "I can show you exactly what sorts of things she taught me about leaving marks. Maybe then you wouldn't hate the idea so much." Her breath was hot against his neck and he could barcly keep his legs from shaking.

"Speaking of which," she said, pulling away from him. "I hope you don't think you're here to purchase the services of one of my colleagues. I've already staked my claim on you, and they've all already agreed that you aren't to be touched until you lay with a woman in a bed of roses by candlelight."

"I'm just here for the drinks and the company."

Donovan huffed and Bethany glared at him. "I think it's sweet that you want to keep me company while I work. If you're still around when Matilda releases me from my service for the night, maybe we can go for a walk. I know a lovely little spot with an outdoor garden. The marigolds are in bloom this time of year. I love their fiery color, don't you Kyzyl?"

"Absolutely!"

Bethany giggled and walked away to greet another client. Donovan just shook his head.

"You're playing with fire kid. You don't want to listen to me, fine. Don't come crying when you get burned."

"You're so cynical. Why are you like this?"

"Blame the world. Its cruelty made me this way." Donovan drank the last of his drink and headed upstairs with one of the other girls.

Matilda, then, came and took his seat at the bar, looking up the stairs after Donovan. "Sometimes I worry about that man. To him, all the world is darkness," she said.

"What made him that way?" Kyzyl asked.

"I did, while we were both young and full of hope. Back then he was as bright-eyed as you are now, Kyzyl. Please don't lose that as you age. I'd hate for that cute little face to go to waste." She winked at him and Kyzyl could feel his face get hot.

He looked down at his cup to keep his voice from quivering. "I thought Bethany made you all swear not to take my virginity."

Matilda laughed. "While that's certainly true," she said between chuckles, "we are still working. A little harmless flirting isn't outside my promise to that sweet young girl."

She looked at Bethany who was chatting up a larger gentleman with rings that seemed to be interfering with the circulation to his fingers. "You be careful with her, Kyzyl. I wouldn't want her to turn into a crotchety old gal like me."

Kyzyl looked at her stunned. She couldn't be much older than Donovan, and, while that wasn't youthful by Kyzyl's standards, she was still decades away from greying hair and wrinkling skin.

Matilda giggled again at Kyzyl's expression. "Your look of shock is more a compliment to me than anything I've heard in weeks. Thank you, Kyzyl, you really are a kind young man. You may be a little naïve, but you're still very good at heart."

"I'm not that naïve." Kyzyl downed the last of his drink and beckoned the barmaid for another. He was starting to feel dizzy, and he wasn't sure if it was his nervousness from all the flirtatious looks that he was getting, the alcohol, or both. "Is there anyone in this house who isn't attractive enough to make me feel awkward and confused?"

"That's a matter of perspective. There are many girls here who hardly ever get called pretty."

"Why?"

"Men have certain preferences. Most men have similar preferences." Matilda gestured toward Gral who was still sitting at the other end of the bar. "Gral over there is one of my most skilled girls, but few men will look twice at her because they're terrified of a woman with more muscles than them. Never mind the fact that her hands are quick, light, and can make you tense parts of your body you weren't aware you had."

"Really? She's that good?"

"She has to be. The less attractive men find you, the better you have to perform. How else are any of these girls supposed to make money? Girls like Bethany are cute, so they can pretend to be innocent and sweet. Guys will eat that stuff up if you let them."

"I guess I hadn't noticed."

Matilda chuckled again. "Something tells me at least a part of you noticed." She gave Kyzyl a significant look.

"So, wait. Are you telling me Bethany is just pretending to be nice to get more money out of people?" Maybe Donovan was right about her. Kyzyl suddenly felt very stupid.

"Pretending was the wrong word. I should have said accentuating. Bethany is far from innocent, but her kindness is genuine. When she likes someone, she doesn't let them forget it. For everyone else, the innocent mask keeps her, and me, well compensated."

The barmaid came back with Kyzyl's drink and he took it in one swallow. That's when everything got blurry, and the next thing he knew, Bethany and Donovan were throwing him down on his bed.

"Good night my prince," she whispered so Donovan couldn't hear. "We'll have that walk another night." She giggled and Kyzyl felt her wiggle her hips over his waist before he dozed off. His dreams during that night were filled with the scent of her hair and the sound of her voice.

CHAPTER EIGHT
First Success

Kyzyl woke with a killer hangover the next day to the sound of first bell. The innkeeper, ever the one to help, had already fixed Kyzyl a hearty breakfast when he got downstairs. There were eggs, bacon, warm bread and butter, and a tall cup of something with a deep purple hue.

"Something I picked up from one of the students in the alchemy labs. He said he was working with a couple of the med students on a cure for hangovers. Figured the Masters wouldn't let something like that out into the wild if it wasn't safe."

"Did the student mention what was in it?" Kyzyl asked. It smelled like a compost heap.

"He said something about extracted principals, or something. You know I hardly speak that scholarly dribble you people pass of as speech. Sometimes I think you make up words to keep us laymen from knowing what you're talking about."

Kyzyl finished the cup with a grimace and shook his head. "It's not about keeping secrets. It's about using precise language. When an everyday person says things like 'most people' or 'most of the time,' they could mean any number of things. Scholars have to be specific so that we can better understand each other and refute each other where necessary."

Kyzyl paused when he realized he was beginning to sound like Master Jonah. He thought for a moment. The Master Cleric had spent the first of their classes encouraging his students, particularly Kyzyl, to challenge the arguments he put on the board. It was a much different experience than he'd had with the Kunashi. He still remembered stumbling over his words while the head of his father's temple sneered at him with a self-satisfied grin.

Master Jonah, on the other hand, met challenges to his beliefs with praise. He seemed genuinely interested in inspiring his students to think for themselves and come to their own conclusions. Kyzyl thought about that as he finished his breakfast. When he did, he thanked Seth for the help with the hangover and headed off to class with Master Enwin.

He got to the class early, but not as early as his first day. Some of the other students were already in the lecture hall talking about their progress on the spell they had been assigned. Most of them hadn't put in much time outside class studying it, and they had subsequently not made much progress.

Kyzyl heard one group of students theorizing that Master Enwin had given them a fake spell as some sort of test or cruel joke. That particular group made Kyzyl very proud of the progress he had made in the last two days. He was still far from mastery, but he'd been getting close to the first successful casting. That was, by his estimate, the furthest anyone else in the class had gotten.

When Master Enwin arrived, he began a brief lecture on the mechanics of summoning spells. He explained to the other students what he told Kyzyl after the last class, that summoning spells used energy to briefly cause two different spaces to overlap long enough for the spell's subject to be displaced.

When he finished his lecture, he told them all to get

out their glyphs and keep practicing the spell. Kyzyl still had enough of an ache in his head that he knew practicing was not in the stars for him. He decided, instead, to talk to Master Enwin about what he'd found in the library.

"Master?"

Master Enwin paused in assisting another student. "Yes, Mr. Shenta?"

"I'm sorry to disturb you, but I found something I wanted to ask you about while I was studying the spell you gave us."

"What is it?"

"It was a teleporting spell, I think. It seemed very similar to the spell you had given us, but the book made it seem like it was advanced magic."

"May I see the spell?"

Kyzyl didn't hide his disappointment. "I don't have it, sir. The student at the desk told me I wasn't allowed to copy spells out of the books in the library."

"Ah, yes. Head Master Herman has instilled a very fierce protective instinct in his students over intellectual property rights."

"I don't understand what that means. The student at the desk mentioned intellectual property too, but how can information be property?"

"It mostly goes back to a time when spellcasters were more, for want of a better word, combative with each other. Many wizards spent years, sometimes decades, developing spells to use in their repertoire.

"At that time, we didn't share our secrets, so each wizard would have to develop his spells entirely on his own, but if you could get access to another wizard's spellbook, you could merely copy all the work he'd done and have the same spell with little to no effort.

"Thus, it became taboo, and later actually illegal, to copy a wizard's spell without their permission. Most of those laws have been relaxed now that wizards aren't out there trying to kill each other every other day, but a centuries of laws and traditions aren't ended so easily.

"Head Master Herman is a little bit more relaxed than other Master Diviners, but there is still the matter of the legal precedent set by past Masters. At this point, however, there are few spells in our library you would find difficult to get permission to copy. Do you remember the title of the book?"

"<u>A Summoner's Guide to Teleportation</u>."

Master Enwin nodded. "I'll have a permission slip written for you by the end of class. Present it to any of the archivists, and they will see to it that you are allowed to copy whatever spells you like from that book. Once you have the spell, we can examine it together, and I can assist you in understanding its complexity."

Kyzyl thanked him and went back to his desk. He made some token attempts at summoning. As he suspected, holding his concentration was impossible with his headache. The bell rang out soon after, and he packed his things and headed for Rhetoric and Logic.

Kyzyl sat next to Emrys again. "Logical Fallacies" was written on the slateboard behind Master Jonah. He stood on the dais with his arms out wide. "Can anyone give me an example of a logical fallacy?"

One student raised their hand, apparently feeling bolstered by Kyzyl's exchange with the Master Cleric from the last class. Master Jonah called on him. "Circular logic."

"Very good. What is circular logic?"

"Using your conclusion as a premise. For instance, if I say elves make the best wine because no one makes wine that is better. I am merely restating my original point."

"Excellent. Yes. All arguments must contain a conclusion that is made separate from the premises used to prove it. Are there any other?"

Kyzyl spoke up. "You mentioned straw-man fallacy

in our last class."

"Good Mr. Shenta. What is a straw man argument?"

"When you use an opponent's weakest argument as a representation of their argument as a whole."

"But shouldn't all of my opponent's arguments be defensible? If they present a weak argument, is it not my right as a rhetorician to go after it?"

Kyzyl stuttered a bit when he tried to respond. Master Jonah had the same tone that the Kunashi did when they were leading him into a trap. He fell silent for a moment, and Emrys looked at him with a confused expression.

"That's OK, Mr. Shenta. Take a breath and start over. I'm sure the point you want to make is worth me waiting for you to get your thoughts in order."

Kyzyl wasn't sure if Master Jonah meant to sound condescending, but he followed the Master's instructions. He took in a full breath and let it out the way he would when entering Wind-Dance. His nerves calmed enough for his thoughts to stop spinning.

"You should take any opportunity to point out flaws in your opponent's logic, but that is not the same thing as using the weakest argument as a representation of the whole argument. Doing so is to ignore any valid points your opponent made."

"Very good. Remember students, the goal of this class, and the goal of rhetoric in general, is to come to a better understanding of the world. It is not to defeat our opponents. Thus, it is prudent to consider your opposition's best arguments in conjunction with their weakest."

Kyzyl sat back in his chair. He wasn't sure if it was the lingering anxiety heightening his emotional response, but Master Jonah's praise made him feel exceptionally good about his performance. Emrys must have noticed Kyzyl shaking because he felt a hand on his shoulder from that side of the room. He flinched a bit. He wasn't used to people touching him unexpectedly, but he appreciated that his friend wanted to comfort him.

The class continued to discuss other forms of logical fallacies. Master Jonah wrote a few example arguments on the board a long with a list of the fallacies people had named. For the rest of class, the students would point out which arguments were made of which fallacies. By the end, Master Jonah was using several arguments Kyzyl recognized as common reasoning by the Kunashi.

Once the class was over, Kyzyl's headache was fully gone, so he decided to head to the Noble Steed to catch up on the practice he'd missed in Master Enwin's class.

Kyzyl gathered up a few small objects: pens, books, and an extra pair of boots, and hid them in random places in the inn. He told Seth what he was doing and asked him to keep everything where it was as best as he could. Then he went up to his room and began studying the glyph again. He went over every hand motion, every word, and every sigil until he could do it forward and backward. Then he stood up, took in a breath and tipped himself into Wind-Dance.

***

He decides to try the boots first. They are outside next to the rain barrel. He pictures them in his mind leaning against the wooden barrel, thinking of the way the laces were tied. He thinks of the smooth leather of the soles. Once he has the picture in his mind, he starts chanting and moving his hands. The candle he is using as a light goes out. The energy of its heat is put into bending reality. Kyzyl hears a thump. He opens his eyes and it takes a second for them to adjust, but when they do, he sees his boots sitting between him and his bed.

***

He let out a breath and started laughing. He sat on the bed until the elation he was feeling at his success

118

subsided. He was still missing a few things, and he wanted to make sure the spell wasn't a fluke. He cast the spell several more times, using the mechanical energy in his muscles to power the spell.

By the time he went to bed, his room had many random items, including his dinner which he had summoned when Seth came to tell him it was ready, scattered around it. His muscles were twitching from exhaustion, so he decided cleaning it all up would have to wait until the morning.

\#

Kyzyl woke up to the first light of dawn. His room was a mess and his muscles ached. At first, he had forgotten why. When he did remember, a boyish grin cracked across his face. He mastered the spell in just a handful of days, and he was excited to tell Master Enwin. He put everything back where it belonged and brought the dishes from his dinner downstairs to the kitchen.

"Ay, boy," Seth said when he saw Kyzyl enter the kitchen. "How's that fancy witchcraft coming along from yesterday."

"It's not witchcraft. It's the first spell I mastered here."

Seth chuckled "Ay, I know. Just having a go at you. I be mighty proud of you."

That statement touched Kyzyl. He wasn't used to such open praise, and it filled him with even more excitement. "Thanks Seth. I'm going to tell Master Enwin the great news. I'll be back in time for lunch."

Seth nodded and Kyzyl headed out to the Conjuration Hall. He couldn't contain his excitement, though, and he started to run.

He didn't stop running until he was at the front, arched doorway of the Conjuration Tower. He threw his body weight against the huge mahogany doors, pushing them open slowly. He walked into the entrance hall and flung himself at the front desk. "I need to see Master Enwin immediately."

"The Master is preparing for a class. If you'd like, I can schedule an appointment during his off-period," the tall slender man at the desk said. Compared to Kyzyl's elated tone, his was reserved and steady. He didn't seem at all put off by the overly eager student, and Kyzyl chuckled at the idea that this was a regular occurrence for this man.

Before the front-desk clerk could respond to Kyzyl's odd behavior, Kyzyl ducked past him and into the hallway that was lined with classrooms. Kyzyl had never been to a Master's office, but he suspected that the door at the other end of the hall would be the most logical place to put such a room.

His reasoning proved fruitful. He opened the door without knocking, and Master Enwin looked up at him. If the Master Conjurer was surprised by Kyzyl's intrusion, he didn't show it. He merely looked away from the open book on his desk and toward Kyzyl, who was breathing hard from his sprint and front desk shenanigans.

"I've done it," Kyzyl declared. After he caught his breath, he drew himself up to his full height and awaited the Masters praise.

"What exactly is it you have done Mr. Shenta?" Master Enwin glanced past Kyzyl and gestured for the indignant clerk to return to the front desk.

"I mastered the spell you gave us."

The Master's face did not change. He waited for further explanation, but when none came he nodded. "You have completed the summoning of the object you wished?"

"Well, no, Master. I uh— thought it best to try and practice on things that were closer to where I am. You see, you had mentioned a clear picture of the sending location would make the spell easier, and I'm not sure if what I was trying to summon had been moved."

"I don't believe I have mentioned the effect clarity

of the sending location has on casting. I remember mentioning the dangers of being nonspecific about the receiving location."

"Oh. I— well, maybe I read it in one of the books I was studying in the library."

"Which books were you studying?"

"Anything I thought might help, sir. I found a few books that went over some advice, theories about the mechanics, and what those theories mean for practical application."

"You seem to have been dedicated to your mastery," Master Enwin said. His tone was devoid of emotion, and Kyzyl was growing disappointed. As far as he could tell, what he had done was exceptional. He knew this was the fastest he'd ever mastered a spell, and, by his estimation, everyone else in the class was weeks away from being able to summon something.

Master Enwin stood and took a few steps toward his bookcase. "If you think you are ready to be tested on your mastery of the spell, then we will conduct your practical exam tomorrow during class." He began scanning the books on their shelves. "I hadn't expected anyone to try for another week or so. I'll need to prepare a few things."

He took a book from the shelf and turned back toward Kyzyl. "What was it you were trying to summon originally?"

"Well," Kyzyl said. He wasn't sure how the Masters would feel about him trying to summon a weapon on their campus. In Hanra, Kyzyl had studied and mastered dueling, and that gave him a professional license to wear a sword. He didn't know if such a thing existed in Strophe.

Master Enwin sensed his hesitation and took the wrong meaning. "If you don't believe in your mastery of the spell, Mr. Shenta, you do not have to take the exam tomorrow."

"It's not that, Master. It's that what I was hoping to

summon was a dueling sword. It's a family heirloom that I've been practicing with since I could hold it. I had to leave it behind because my family would've worried that I'd lose it.

"I'm sure it sounds odd to you, but I've been feeling kind of vulnerable without it on my hip. I'm sure the other Masters would object if I started wearing a sword again, but if I can summon it, I wouldn't have to wear it."

"That's fine. As long as you assure me that, after it is summoned, you leave it locked in your chest at the bunkhouse, you may summon your sword."

Kyzyl nodded vigorously and didn't bother mentioning to Master Enwin that he hadn't taken a room at the bunkhouse. The sword would be safer behind the locked door of the Noble Steed anyway. As long as he kept his promise not to wear it, why did it's exact location matter?

Kyzyl turned to walk out of the office, but the Master's voice called him back. "In the future, Mr. Shenta, you will make an appointment if you wish to speak with me."

Kyzyl hung his head, thoroughly chastised by the Master's carefully controlled tone. "My apologies Master. I —"

Master Enwin raised his hand for silence. "You are not the first student to forget propriety in the heat of excitement. Nor, do I suspect, will you be the last. It is the job, however, of all those who wish to master the arcane forces of the world to exercise control."

"First you master yourself, then you master the world, then you master your opponent." Kyzyl recited something one of his dueling tutors had taught him.

Master Enwin nodded and waved a hand to dismiss Kyzyl. Before he closed the door, Kyzyl heard Master Enwin say, "this is exceptional. If you pass the exam tomorrow, you will undoubtedly be the quickest student to master their first spell-assignment."

Kyzyl walked out, feeling a bit embarrassed at how he'd acted. That embarrassment was quickly overshadowed by pride when he realized the Master Conjurer had just called Kyzyl's feat "exceptional". He had a spring in his step for the rest of the day and even found himself greeting Master Jonah when they passed each other in the street.

When Kyzyl got to class the next day, he stayed quiet about what he'd accomplished. However, he couldn't keep himself from grinning so wide that people around him were giving him odd looks. When Master Enwin walked in, everyone snapped to attention as he called Kyzyl up onto the dais.

Kyzyl didn't respond right away. He hadn't realized his exam would be in front of the whole class, and the idea of it froze him in his seat. When Master Enwin held out his hand as if to help Kyzyl out of his seat, despite the fact that he was easily ten feet from the man and toward the back of the gathered students, he stood.

Kyzyl spent the entire walk up to the dais at the front of the room trying to convince himself that it would be fine. No, this man was not trying to embarrass him. No he would not forget how to preform the spell. No, he was not going to mess this up. He was ready.

"Kyzyl, you have claimed to have mastered the spell I assigned to you in only five days, is that correct?" The Master asked when Kyzyl finally was standing beside him. His tone was ritualistic. Kyzyl didn't know how he was meant to respond, so he tried to match the Master's tone.

"Yes, sir. You told us to decide on a specific object we wished to summon, and I chose the sword I had left in my homeland."

"And you have done this?"

"Not yet sir. I am going to do it now."

"Proceed."

It was time to summon the thing he most regretted leaving behind. His sword was much more to him than a blade. He'd earned the right to hold it through a decade of work and determination. To him, it was a symbol of both his heritage as a noble and his skill as a duelist. He took a breath and tipped his mind into Wind-Dance.

***

As he starts to chant and make the sigils with his hands, his concentration goes fully into the sword. He remembers the weight and balance of it in his hand. He thinks of the ruby set in its pommel and the flowing steel that acted as its cross guard.

He puts his right hand, his sword hand, to the side. He imagines it as part of the final flourish of the duelist's salute. When he closes his hand, it wraps around a cold steel handle. He opens his eyes to see the sword, his soul and heritage made manifest, by his side once again. He draws the blade from its scabbard and lifts it in the air, triumph flooding his heart.

***

"You were successful in summoning it then?" Master Enwin asks from behind him.

"Yes." Kyzyl put the sword back in its scabbard. The lingering effects of being in Wind-Dance made it easy to forget that he was still on stage. Instead, it was like he had stepped back to when his dueling instructor had given him his first silk belt as a student duelist. It was just him, his teacher, and the skills he had mastered.

"This sword is a family heirloom. There is no other sword like it in the world, and, when you had given us this spell to master, it was in my family's estate. Now, it is in my hands."

Kyzyl let the moment come back to him as he looked out over a stunned crowd. He thought the formality of the situation had passed and whatever ritual he was performing was over. Then Master Enwin spoke again.

124

"That's all well and good," he said. "Now it's time to show all of us how well you truly have mastered this spell. I have hidden an item in this room. I want you to find it and summon it here."

Kyzyl waited but no further information was forthcoming. "Are you going to tell me what I'm looking for?"

"No. I am testing more than your mastery of the spell. A conjurer must be able to see things in his mind he's never seen with his eyes."

This was unexpected. "But, Master..." Kyzyl was confused. "How can the spell work if I don't know my subject?"

"Kyzyl, do you trust me?"

Kyzyl thought for a moment about the things he'd seen from the Master Conjurer in the two classes he'd attended. He'd watched the Master assist students in deciphering glyphs, offered advice and encouragement to students who were struggling.

Nothing Kyzyl had seen so far suggested he was the type to embarrass a student in front of an entire class. "I trust you Master." He tipped his mind back into Wind-Dance.

***

He starts to shape his hands into the sigils necessary to bind the heat of the air to his spell, but once it comes time for him to define the subject, he stumbles. He feels something stir inside him.

A small voice he doesn't recognize starts chanting the spell. He follows it as best as he can. He follows the words carefully, and a picture begins to form in his mind. Whose voice was that? Was it even a person?

The picture in his mind becomes clearer, and he makes more sigils with his hand. It's a book. It's bound in soft leather and has a brass lock on it. His chant continues as the voice inside his head continues to guide him.

At this point, he can't tell if it's a real voice, or if it's in his head. Still, he follows along until he starts to feel an unfamiliar weight in his hand. He holds his concentration until the spell is finished, and he opens his eyes.

***

In Kyzyl's hand was the book he had imagined. The same brown leather and brass lock. Master Enwin handed him a key and he unlocked the book to find it completely blank.

There was no writing in the book save an inscription on the first page. It read,

Kyzyl,

I know you will be exceptional. From this point onward, I expect great things from you.

-Master Enwin

"Congratulations Kyzyl, you just summoned your very own spellbook," Master Enwin said with a wide grin. Kyzyl gaped at the book in his hands. "You will do well here. I am sure of it."

"Yes sir," Kyzyl said in a single, shaky breath. This went beyond anything he'd imagined. A spellbook was the first sign of recognition within the university. Normally, a student would have to take at least two to three years worth of introductory classes before they were given their own spellbook. This went beyond exceptional and pushed the boundaries of what was considered proper.

"Sir, I— I don't know about this. Are you sure I am ready?"

"I have great confidence in you, my student," Master Enwin said. All the pride Kyzyl had expected when he was in the Master Conjurer's office was now on full display.

There was a moment of stunned silence from the other students before they all started talking at once. Many were complaining to the Master Conjurer about how unfair it was that Kyzyl had received his spellbook so quickly.

126

Others walked up to Kyzyl and congratulated him. He noticed one common detail between those that were congratulating him versus those who weren't. It seemed each of the students that objected had a leather-bound book similar to Kyzyl's.

Kyzyl hadn't noticed it before, but it seemed that there were many older students in this introductory class. It wasn't uncommon for wizards to take introductory classes of all subjects to ensure a complete education in the arcane arts. It also explained why Master Enwin expected those who took this class to be adept at deciphering glyphs.

The rest of the class period was given over to practice time. Kyzyl helped Master Enwin offer advice and corrections to the other students. He helped one of the first-term girls with deciphering her glyph.

Spellcasting was subject to a number of different factors, including the season of the year and the movement of stars. It was the reason that the university used complex glyphs to keep track of a spell's casting components. It also meant that deciphering a glyph had limited use beyond the original context of its deciphering.

After class, Master Enwin approached Kyzyl. "I'm not used to students taking charge like that after they master a spell. Most of them want to move on to the next lesson as quickly as possible, and they don't concern themselves with leaving their fellow students behind."

"What's the point of mastering a spell if I can't share what I learned?"

"That's a good philosophy. Hold to it as you progress." The Master Conjurer walked away. Kyzyl decided that it was a good time for a celebratory lunch, and headed to the Noble Steed.

On his way back to the Noble Steed, Kyzyl saw Siradyl speaking animatedly with the Master Artificer. He couldn't make out what the two were saying, but the stocky dwarf had a grim expression on his face, and Siradyl's face was red.

When Siradyl saw Kyzyl, he looked right at the spellbook Kyzyl had hung from his silk belt. His eyes went wide and he began screaming like a petulant child.

"Who gave this filthy little foreigner a spellbook? He hasn't been here a full term. This is an absolute injustice. Where is the Head Master? I want a word with him."

The muscular Master Artificer looked in Kyzyl's direction. "Master Enwin mentioned to me that he was going to be doing something unconventional. I'm guessing he and Master Jonah have taken a shine to you."

"Yes Master. It seems I am proving to be a worthwhile student. Although, I do wish I had more hours in the day to learn from the rest of you."

The Master Artificer chuckled. "Yes, well, you'll have to leave the study of time magic to the storybooks in the library. A day has twenty-four hours and that doesn't change for any of us it seems."

Kyzyl nodded. "Head Master Herman did mention to me that divination magic is a useful tool to those who wish to maximize the efficacy of their studies. Perhaps that will be my next area of pursuit." Once he could get his finances in order to ensure his tuition was paid.

"Excuse me," Siradyl demanded. "I am still here, and I will not be ignored. If you and the other Masters see fit to give some first-termer a spellbook, then I see no reason I shouldn't be allowed access to the advanced alchemical labs."

The Master Artificer gave Siradyl a dark look. "Kyzyl is not my student and I hold no dominion over his advancement. You, on the other hand, have shown me no patience since you became my student, and I will hold you back from those labs until I see fit to do otherwise. And if you have a problem with that, you may go learn from a Master who will put up with your petty complaints."

Kyzyl left before Siradyl could mutter out a

response. He had to hide his look of satisfaction at the sight of that pompous jerk not getting his way. He made it back to the Noble Steed, and told Seth about his accomplishment.

Seth opened a bottle of his best wine that he had been saving "for just such a thing." He poured two cups and cheered Kyzyl.

"Sounds like ya've earned a special lunch. What can I make for our young prodigy?"

"Do you have any more potatoes?"

"Ay, yer wantin' them mashed no doubt. And some fresh baked bread and a leg of mutton too I bet."

"Sounds like just the thing," Kyzyl said with a smile.

CHAPTER NINE
Figures and Finance

"Eighth of Summerfell," the registry declared when Kyzyl gave his name. "Noon."

He had spent the remaining days of the three month term progressing rapidly in his summoning skills. Soon after he'd mastered the third version of the object summoning spell, Master Enwin wrote him an exemption from further classes in Basics of Conjuration and began teaching him directly during their mutual free time.

Kyzyl's progression in summoning made leaps and bounds in that term, but he kept up with his other school work. Master Jonah's patient tutelage and constructive critique had helped Kyzyl get comfortable with speaking in class.

Kyzyl had begun to enjoy challenging the Master Clerics arguments with his own rebuttals, which the Master Cleric actively encouraged. By the end of term, Kyzyl felt a vague melancholy at the idea of their class coming to end and their discussions being over.

It made him consider taking another class with the Master Cleric. He'd never take one of the Religious Studies classes, but there were other classes Master Jonah and his students taught that focused logic and building arguments.

Perhaps he could convince Emrys to take one of those with him.

That would have to come after the next exam, however. As was tradition at the university, before any new students were accepted, each returning student would be tested again by the nine Masters to decide what their tuition would be for the next term.

Eighth of Summerfell was one of the latest slots that were normally assigned to returning students, and that gave Kyzyl enough time to refresh his knowledge in the library. For now, however, he felt his time was best spent in good company.

Kyzyl met up with Emrys and Donovan at the Burning Forge. Both had gotten their slots before Kyzyl, and both looked rather disappointed. "What's wrong you two? Didn't get the slots you were hoping for?"

"I have my exams later this afternoon," Emrys exclaimed. "What am I going to do? I'm barely ready for Master Jonah's questions and I studied Rhetoric hard enough last term that I lost sleep over it. I can't imagine what the other Masters will put me up against."

"I'm sure you'll be fine Emrys," Donovan consoled. "I've seen the kind of wizard you are, and I know for a fact there isn't anything those Masters can ask you that you won't know the answer to. That's a fact."

"And what about you Donovan? You look like your favorite horse kicked you in the head," Kyzyl said.

Donovan gave Kyzyl a confused look, but Kyzyl just shrugged. "I guess that expression works better in my language."

"I got a pretty good slot, but I got a letter from my father this morning. Turns out he's having some tough times and decided he can't afford me anymore. Not sure how I'm going to be paying my tuition, whatever it might be."

"That's horrible. What are you going to do?" Kyzyl

asked, astounded.

"I don't know. I guess I can find a well-paying job. Maybe one of the Masters could use a lackey of some kind. Something to get me able to pay for myself."

"Well," Kyzyl said, "maybe the answer lies at the bottom of a cup of ale. Come on, since mine seems to be the only good luck of the day, I'll buy the first round."

"Sounds like a deal to me," Emrys declared.

Kyzyl waved the over the serving girl, Serena. She came over to them looking a little red in her cheeks. The Burning Forge wasn't busy, but Kyzyl did notice she was the only person running the taproom. He wondered where the bartender was.

She took their orders and Kyzyl watched her pour them and bring them over to the table while fielding expressions of impatience from other patrons.

"There you are gents," she said, setting the wood tankards on the table. "Our finest white for our young prodigy, a honey ale almost as sweet as yours truly for our elvish friend, and a hard rye whiskey for your elder mentor."

Serena gave a cheerful smile despite her tired appearance. Donovan thanked her with a kiss on the hand and Kyzyl gave her a generous tip to apologize. She sauntered off, leaving the men to their drinks.

"You sure you don't want something harder?" Donovan asked Emrys. "It might calm your nerves."

"Or it might make me vomit in front of the Masters. I'm not taking my chances. I have two hours before I have to be in line for admissions, and I want to be ready."

"He's right. There will be plenty of time to drink after he gets a five-crown tuition," Kyzyl said over his glass.

"For someone who doesn't believe in the gods, you sure do expect a miracle," Emrys said somberly.

"The secret, my dear friend, is confidence. If you

say your answer with absolute conviction, they won't have a choice but to except it."

"Is that how you got your first tuition to be ten crowns?" Emrys asked.

Donovan practically choked on his drink at that. While Donovan got a hold of himself, and Serena grabbed a towel, Kyzyl explained how his first term's tuition came to be so low.

"Based on how quickly you earned your spellbook, it seems they were right to give you such a low tuition. I'd be surprised if they charged you half that this time around," Donovan said after getting a breath or two in him.

"I don't think so," Emrys said. "From what I've heard, once you start advancing, your tuition goes up not down."

"Which is why I'm totally screwed," Donovan complained. He started coughing up more whiskey.

"You're not screwed Donovan," Emrys insisted. "We will figure something out for you, right Kyzyl?"

"Absolutely! We're the merry band of misfits. We won't leave one of our own behind." Kyzyl put a consoling hand on Donovan's shoulder, and Emrys gave him an encouraging smile before standing.

"It was fun drinking with you gentlemen, but I must go. I'm going to go do some recon before my entire future is to be decided."

"Spying on other students during exams is an expellable offense," Kyzyl reminded him.

"Only if you get caught. Besides, I don't need to go quite that far." Emrys left, and Kyzyl looked at Donovan as he finished coughing.

"I need some company of a more feminine variety. Come Kyzyl, we're going to Matilda's." Donovan stood and Kyzyl followed him down to the brothel.

There, Matilda greeted them at the door like always, except that she had concern in her eyes when she looked at Donovan sulking. He looked back at her and waved her unspoken question away.

When they got into the parlor, Donovan didn't give any of his normal banter. He just chose a girl and went upstairs. Kyzyl went to the bar and was surprised to find Bethany there looking sad.

"Hey. Copper penny for your thoughts."

"That's the only service I'll let you buy from me," she said with a half-hearted wink. She took the penny and looked into Kyzyl's eyes. "I heard about Donovan."

"That was fast. I only found out myself earlier today."

"This brothel is the center of news in the university. Nothing happens without one of the girls here catching wind. What's going to happen to him?"

"I don't know. What I do know is that we're going to be there for him whatever it is. Right?" She nodded her head vigorously.

"Shouldn't you be working?" Kyzyl asked, looking around the parlor at all the men. They all seemed to be waiting for something while all the girls stood around chatting.

"I'm not on right now. Matilda saves most of us for the evening crowd. Most of the girls that are on duty right now are new, girls that still need to get used to the business."

"Which is why everyone looks like they're at a ball waiting for the music to start. The men don't want someone who doesn't know what they're doing, and the women don't know how to start a conversation."

Bethany's eyes were distant. She chewed on the inside of her cheek until she spoke again. "It's different when you're trying to talk to a potential client. You don't know how to gracefully approach the idea of having sex with them. Most of the time, it's girls that get propositioned."

"By boys."

"Sure. Most of the time. Anyway, when the script is flipped, and you have to be the one to approach someone, that's when you realize you're a full adult who has never had to ask anyone if they're interested in you."

"I get the sense we aren't talking about the current new girls any more."

Bethany looked at Kyzyl and her eyes focused on him. She looked like she had just remembered that she was talking to him. "Hm? Oh, of course. Anyway, it's hard to know what to do when it's your first time doing something like this.

The only way to get better at this sort of thing is with practice, and that takes time. Most girls go a year or more before they get repeat customers. I went a whole three years before people started asking for me by name."

"Is that why you all pool your earnings at the end of the night?"

Another nod. "We all remember what it's like being new. You're nervous about approaching a guy because you've never done it before. You have all manner of anxieties about what he'll want and if you'll be good enough.

"I remember when I started. I was horrible at approaching anyone. On my first day, I actually threw up on the first client I tried to speak to."

"That must've been embarrassing. Did you ever see him again?"

Bethany nodded. "He's actually one of my regulars now. He thinks it's the funniest story, but I'd just like to forget it, if I could."

"What about the others? Can't the other women give the new girls advice?"

"Some, but you also have to find your own brand. Some of us are straightforward and upfront, and a lot of guys appreciate that. Others want to feel like they're being seduced, or like they're seducing you. Different girls are good at different games, and you have to find where you fit."

Kyzyl thought about that for a moment before realizing his curiosity had distracted him. "If you're not working, does that mean you're free?"

Bethany nodded.

"If memory serves, you still owe me a walk, and I could use a meal. You in?"

"What about Donovan?"

Kyzyl looked up the stairs toward his friend. "He's in good company, right? He should be fine. We'll be back before he's done."

Kyzyl brought Bethany to a small stand that sold toasted nuts. He asked for two, and the man running the stand handed him two corn husks filled to the brim with chestnuts. Bethany took in a deep breath off hers and sighed dreamily.

"I love the smell of cinnamon. It reminds me of my hometown during the Winter Festival."

"Winter Festival?"

"You don't have them in Techarae? The way our calendar works, there are a bunch of extra days at the end of the year that don't make up a full month, so we just spend that time having a two-week long party."

"Your calendar has two weeks just tacked on at the end? Why?"

Bethany shrugged. "I don't know. I suppose it has something to do with how long a year is, but I haven't really questioned it. If it means we get to spend the end of the year having fun with the people that we love, I'll accept our calendar doesn't make a whole lot of sense."

"We have something similar. At least, we have an end-of-year holiday, but it isn't because of some odd extra days or anything. We just set aside the last month for self-reflection and spending time with extended family."

"It sounds so... serious."

"There are parties as well, not to mention drinking like you wouldn't believe."

"Oh? Self-reflection requires you to be intoxicated?"

"No, but having to be with our families for an entire month does."

Bethany laughed at that. "So, your family is eccentric I take it."

"That's a nice way of putting it. Most of my family has a field to till with someone so most of it is just back handed compliments. You know the type. 'Oh, cousin, I absolutely love that dress. I remember having one just like it, last year.'"

She giggled again. "I see. Does that mean you'll be happy to be among friends this time around?"

"I absolutely can't wait. I may even show you three some of the games my family plays when they get particularly... under the table."

She laughed again. "That sounds fun, but I can't wait until winter for something like that. What do you say we make it happen earlier?"

"What do you mean?"

"Donovan is really upset about his father. I was thinking we could have a day where it's just us, ya know? No clients or other people coming into the brothel. Just the girls, and you three boys."

"Would Matilda be OK with losing a whole day of business like that?"

"She wouldn't mind if it's for Donovan. She and him... well she... I don't think she'd mind."

"Something is going on that you aren't telling me."

"Remember what I told you about Donovan when we first met?"

Kyzyl remembered the conversation, but they had touched on so many different topics that it was hard to keep it all straight. "Remind me."

Bethany looked around at the people passing by in the street. "OK, but not here. There's a garden down that road. It's pretty private, so other than the stray pair of lovers, it will be empty."

Kyzyl let her lead him down the street and through a gate that was flanked by a hedge that was easily ten feet high. Inside there were all manner of trees, flowers, and wooden benches. All of it was set around a large fountain in the center of the greenery. It gurgled and splashed sending mist into the air to form a rainbow.

"OK," Bethany began. Her voice had dropped to a low whisper. The gurgling of the fountain ensured no one outside of their close circle would be able to hear anything she was saying, but there was already no one around.

Kyzyl was startled by the gravity in her voice. He hadn't realized their conversation had taken such a heavy turn. "You remember that I told you Donovan never sleeps with any of the girls he brings upstairs, right?"

"Right," Kyzyl whispered back. "You said he pays for services, but when you all go upstairs with him, he just asks about your other clients. Are you guys selling him secrets or something?"

Bethany made a gesture with her hand. "Yes and no. That's what it has turned into. It's almost like a front for what's really going on."

"Wait. Pretending to have sex with all of you isn't the front?"

Bethany sighed. "Yes but there's a secondary front. You're from a noble house. You know how people like Donovan get raised. Everything is about appearances.

"Anyone coming into the brothel thinks Donovan is just another patron. The girls think he's buying secrets instead of sex. Think about it, though. Why wouldn't he want both? You can talk during sex, right?"

"I still don't understand. If he can have both, why

doesn't he?"

"That's what I started wondering when I had thought about it like that. Then I started watching how he and Matilda interact."

"I can't seem to remember anything significant."

"Exactly. The two of them could be strangers for as much as they talk to each other."

"So?"

"So, strangers don't buy each other mansions near the university."

"What? Donovan bought Matilda a mansion?"

"He bought the brothel. The brothel was being leased to Matilda by a landlord who would come in every other week and demand to see one of the girls without payment. He called it 'part of the rental agreement' and Matilda couldn't do anything without risking us getting kicked out."

"That's horrible. Isn't that extortion? Why didn't she tell someone?"

"She tried to go to the Masters, but they kept giving her the runaround. Property crimes between a landlord and tenant aren't exactly their strong suit. Their too focused on keeping their school orderly, and the closest other court is all the way in the capital."

"So, wait, how does this relate to Donovan?"

"That's the real reason Donovan's father cut him off. Last term, Donovan bought the brothel from its previous landlord and signed the whole thing over to Matilda."

"Why? So his favorite brothel wouldn't go anywhere?"

"So Matilda wouldn't go anywhere. Matilda has been trying to keep me from... I mean... she's been talking to me about you ever since we met. I assume Donovan's been doing the same to you."

Kyzyl thought back to all the comments Donovan

made about him and Bethany. It never occurred to him that it was anything more than bitterness, but Bethany had a point. He was too specific at times for it to not be personal for him.

"You mean... Donovan and Matilda are..."

"Not anymore. She probably didn't want to give up her job for him, and he didn't like that."

"So why does he still come around the brothel? Why buy it and just give it to her?"

"Because love doesn't just go away because you're mad at someone. Donovan still wants to support Matilda. He just can't be with her while she's sleeping with other people for money.

"Instead, they have this... sort of... dance they do around each other. Donovan comes around the brothel to be close to her. He has to pay for services to keep up appearances, but he can't bring himself to have sex with any of us because he still loves Matilda.

"So, instead, he and whatever girl he picks stay in a room for an appropriate amount of time. In the meantime, he makes conversation with us and we tell him things we hear from other clients. Nobody ever thinks about the things they let slip to their whores, but we hear a lot." Bethany smiled playfully.

"And when you hear something, Donovan will hear about it soon."

Bethany tapped her nose and winked. "As long as it's interesting, of course. He's especially interested in things about people like Siradyl."

"Is that why you endure all his beatings? So you can hear his secrets and give them to Donovan?"

Bethany became very serious again. "No. I told you both already. I am choosing to do those things because I want to and not because anyone is making me. I may get hurt sometimes, but I understand that going in."

Kyzyl nodded once. "I understand."

They shared a moment of silence, and Kyzyl couldn't tell if she thought it was awkward or not. He felt uncomfortable, but that wasn't abnormal for him.

When nothing more was forth coming, he turned toward the gate that let them into the garden, but Bethany held hi back. "Kyzyl," she asked. "Do you like me?"

"Of course I like you. I'm not going out of my way to hang out at a brothel where the working girls have all promised not to sleep with me because Donovan is there."

"What do you like about me?"

"I like that you make me happy. You're a really sweet girl and it's hard not to smile around you."

"Do you ever think about me when I'm not around?"

Kyzyl stammered a bit. Where was this coming from? She took his hesitation the wrong way, and she sighed.

"It's OK if the answer is no. I understand."

She turned to leave and it was his turn to stop her.

"All my life, I have never done anything halfway. When I wanted to learn how to duel, I made sure that a day didn't pass without me picking up my family's sword. When I heard about the University Arcanum and the nine Masters who were the most powerful mages in the world, I knew I was going to do everything it took to learn from them.

"I have studied everything I can about any topic that caught my attention. I never once stopped to wonder why I was doing it until Head Master Herman asked me the one question on my entrance exam that I couldn't answer."

"Why you came to the University. Donovan told me about that but..." Kyzyl put a finger to her lips. She looked a him and he held her gaze.

"I told Donovan that they asked me why I chose the University, but Head Master Herman also asked me why I wanted to become a wizard at all. It was the one question I hadn't prepared for, and I've been working on my answer ever since."

"Do you have one now?" she asked. He had her whole attention. He wondered if what he was about to say would be the answer she was looking for, but he decided that it was the truth either way.

"I have done all this studying throughout my entire life because I wanted to understand the world around me. If I could understand it, then I could, on some level, control it. At least, I could control how I respond to it because I understood what was going on.

"That's what I want most out of all of this. I want to feel in control of something. Being able to master magic is probably the biggest piece of that, but the way I try and master things is the whole.

"But with you... I've never felt less in control in my entire life. What's terrifying is that I don't hate it. I feel like a puppet on a string when I hear you laugh or sigh. It feels like you can tug at me and get me to do anything, and I always want more. I..."

She pressed her finger to his lips. "Don't say it. Not yet. You've said more than enough. Thank you."

She turned toward the gate again and she let him lead her back out of the garden and onto the busy street. Kyzyl wasn't sure if what he'd said had somehow offended her, but he figured it was best to follow her lead.

The two of them munched on roasted nuts, talked, and laughed as they made their way back to Matilda's house. They had just entered the main parlor area when Donovan came down the stairs.

"What good timing, we just got back. How was it?"

"I'm not nearly drunk enough to tell you about my sexual exploits, Kyzyl."

"Are you drunk at all?"

"No, that's my point." Donovan nodded to Bethany. Kyzyl poured the rest of his chestnuts into his mouth and kissed Bethany on the cheek. She walked away with a spring in her step toward a throng of girls. Donovan and Kyzyl left to look for Emrys.

They found him chatting with Master Jonah about something. As they approached, Emrys waved at Kyzyl and beckoned him over.

"Your timing couldn't be better Kyzyl; I was just telling the Master Cleric that you and he should absolutely participate in a friendly debate during the upcoming Harvest Festival."

"You were? Why?" Kyzyl realized too late that his tone was overly combative. If Master Jonah noticed, he didn't make an issue of it.

"Young Mr. Emrys pointed out to me that it would be an effective way to showcase the importance of Rhetoric. I was just thinking it was a rather clever idea. After all, you were one of my most improved students this last term."

"There aren't other students who are closer to your level, sir?" Kyzyl asked. He tried to sound more polite.

"Don't be so modest, Kyzyl. You practically dominated the discussions during the final days of our class. I've never seen someone argue like you," Emrys said enthusiastically.

"Your friend is right, Kyzyl. While there are students under my tutelage that have advanced further than you in classes, you seem to have a natural gift for putting together arguments." Master Jonah paused for a moment. "That is, when you can avoid becoming frustrated or anxious."

"In that case, I suppose I have no choice but to agree with you Master."

The Master Cleric smiled. "You always have a choice, but I'm glad to hear you'll accept. I look forward to our on-stage coming to blows, as it were." With that, the Master Cleric walked away. Kyzyl turned and gave Emrys a blank look.

Emrys smiled encouragingly. "Don't look at me like that," he said. "You're going to do great. I've seen Master Jonah take on students before. He's not going to try and embarrass you. What was it he always said in class? 'The point of rhetoric is not to defeat your opponent but for everyone to get a step closer to a deeper truth.'"

"What is the resolution of the debate?" Donovan asked.

"Hasn't been decided yet. The resolution will be announced at the beginning of the festival, so each of you has equal time to prepare. That's how we keep things fair," Emrys said.

"And you decided that the best time for this is the second largest celebration in your part of the world?" Kyzyl said. He was already feeling the pressure of all the people watching him while he tried to form arguments and debate the Master Cleric on the fly.

"How else are we going to promote Rhetoric and Logic to the people?"

"I'm going up against one of the Masters in his own subject, and you think this is just some sort of promotional stunt?"

"What do you think is going to happen, Kyzyl?" Donovan said. Kyzyl could tell he was coming around to Emrys' side. Neither of them seemed to understand how Kyzyl felt about this event.

Kyzyl thought about it for a moment. It was true that Master Jonah had spent their class time encouraging his students to speak their minds. No matter what the argument, it seemed the Master Cleric would give it the most favorable light, even when attempting to defeat it.

Kyzyl realized there was no good reason to say no to the debate. He sighed. "What is this meant to do?"

"It's meant to demonstrate the idea that magic isn't the only thing worth learning here."

"And you really want me to do this, don't you?"

"I think it will really help."

Kyzyl felt defeated. He nodded his ascent, and Emrys hugged him out of excitement. Kyzyl tensed under Emrys' arms, but Emrys didn't seem to notice.

They separated in time to watch Donovan wave down the street at Kahente. She noticed him greeting her, paused, and walked the other direction. Donovan shrugged in an attempt to seem nonchalant. Kyzyl and Emrys looked at each other and just laughed, earning them a glare from their elder friend.

Kyzyl suggested they make their way over to the Noble Steed for a round, and both his friends agreed. When they arrived, Seth greeted them at the door, and they chose their normal table near the fireplace.

"How'd your interview go, by the way, Emrys?" Kyzyl asked as they sat down.

"Not terrible. I got out with only a seventy-five-crown tuition."

"That's high," Kyzyl commented. He meant for it to sound consoling, but Emrys just shook his head.

"We can't all be the prodigal son who masters spells in two days, can we?"

Kyzyl bit his lip. He forgotten how abnormal his first tuition was. Emrys just laughed.

The next day Kyzyl went to the dwarvish bank, which he had learned was called the Bank of Dalthor after the clan that ran it. The branch they set up near the university was even larger than the one he'd gone to in Tamerrel, the port city where he'd arrived in Strophe.

When he walked in, the first thing he saw was a huge mural covering the back wall. It depicted a dwarf, no doubt the clan's patriarch and namesake, wielding a smithing hammer and standing on a mountain peak.

The bank's set up was wildly different from the one in Tamerrel as well. Instead of one long counter toward the back that was reinforced with iron and wards, there were several smaller desks that appeared to each belong to a singular clerk.

The entire room was still warded, and now that Kyzyl was trained in what to look out for, he saw the displacement wards that made scrying and summoning impossible among the other wards. His original plan was looking less and less likely with each new revelation, and he was feeling desperate.

Kyzyl approached one of the desks, and the clerk sitting on the other side looked at him, but said nothing. Kyzyl didn't immediately sit down or start speaking. Instead, he examined the runes that had been etched into the mahogany desk. Among the wards from the other bank, the displacement wards, and a few he didn't recognize, Kyzyl spotted a ward the would prevent anyone who was outside a particular lineage from opening many of the desk's drawers.

"What can I do for you?" the clerk behind the desk asked in an annoyed tone. It wasn't until she spoke that Kyzyl realized she was a woman. The only other dwarvish women he'd seen were at Matilda's, and their outfits didn't leave much room for speculation.

"My apologies ma'am. I have an account with your clan, and I was hoping to open up a line of credit for my tuition at the university."

"Oh?" She looked him up and down slowly. Kyzyl had put on his best silk robe, and he hoped it gave him a more noble bearing. Otherwise, this would be a difficult task. "Do you have a letter of pedigree from your house?"

"Ah, well, you see," Kyzyl began, pitching his voice between regretful traveler and putout noble. "I lost my letter on my way to these fine lands, so the only thing I have left is this."

He produced a signet ring he had summoned during his studies with Master Enwin. Since his had been stolen, he had to borrow it from his eldest brother, but he wasn't likely to need it for anything. Besides, they still had his father's ring, and he needed a way to pay his tuition.

The clerk took the ring and examined it. "I'm not familiar with this insignia. What house are you from?"

"I'm from Techarae. My name is Shenta Kyzyl of House Shenta in the Chenshu providence of Hanra."

"Well, that certainly was long enough to be a noble title. Unfortunately, if what you say is true, there would be no way for me to verify quickly if you truly are a noble, nor would I be able to transport your credit balance to your house for them to pay it should the need arise."

Kyzyl looked dejected. He had been pinning his hopes of paying tuition on being able to open a line of credit with the bank. Without that, he didn't know how he'd pay a tuition measured in crowns.

"There isn't anything you can offer me?"

The clerk looked him up and down. "If you got as much tied up in your wardrobe as you want me to think you do, I can probably offer you a fifty-crown line of credit, but it would come due at the end of every month."

Kyzyl looked down at his clothes. He was confused, but he tried his best not to show it. Finding a way to get fifty crowns within a month of tuition being due wouldn't be much easier, but he might not need the full fifty crowns. He juggled numbers in his head, paused, then nodded to the clerk. She took down his name and account information, and he left having solved one problem, but taking on a new burden.

\#

"Please demonstrate your mastery of rhetoric by convincing us why you believe this previous term has been successful for you," Master Jonah said.

Kyzyl was taking his interview and he had already demonstrated a few of the more complicated spells he had learned from Master Enwin and answered questions of the other Masters. Master Jonah was the second to last person to question him, the last being Head Master Herman.

Kyzyl paused for a moment to gather his thoughts. One of the most important things he had learned from Master Jonah was how to avoid filler words like um, er, and uh.

"Well, Master, as you have pointed out, I have proven myself a very capable rhetorician. So much so, in fact, that you seem to believe that I am ready to go up against you in the upcoming Harvest Festival.

"I believe I have already demonstrated what I learned from Master Enwin, but to reiterate, I have mastered a number of spells under his instruction. I have moved on from summoning merely objects to summoning pieces of whole objects. I summoned a leaf off a tree branch without summoning the whole tree. Lastly, Master Enwin mentioned that he will be allowing me to advance to summoning living creatures.

"I have also completed the introductory course taught by one of Master Alec's assistant abjurers, and have begun on my path to master warding spells. I have learned a few basic concepts, and I am close to mastering the anti-kinetic ward I was assigned at the end of the term. I would have it mastered by now, but Master Enwin and I have been using a great deal of free time to advance my study of summoning magic.

"I have not yet had the pleasure of learning under any of the other Masters, but I think I have given ample evidence by answering your questions that I am a capable autodidact and studious learner. In short, Master Cleric, I consider last term a success because I learned what I set out to learn, and now it's time for me to learn more."

The Master Cleric nodded in agreement, pride plain on his face. "Thank you, Mister Shenta, that is my only question."

"Master Diviner," The Head Master introduced himself. "Kyzyl, my scribes and clerks inform me that you spend a great deal of time at the library. Is all of this time consumed by study for your classes?”

"No, sir, I must admit some is to satisfy my own curiosity about the world. There's so much to learn from your library. I don't have enough slots available in my normal schedule to take classes to satisfy these curiosities, so I must make due with my own research for now."

The Master nodded. "Curiosity can lead to great discovery, Kyzyl. I will not fault you for that. There are, however, rumors concerning the other places you frequent. Need I remind you that teaching others what you learn here is expressly forbidden without the permission of all nine Masters?"

"No Head Master, I wasn't even aware there were such rumors. May I ask about specifics?"

"According to my cursory investigation into these rumors, there is a small girl who is a resident of one or the local inns. She and you have taken to spending a great deal of time together with a great deal of books and notes. Others have been suspecting that you are tutoring her in our arcane secrets. There is also the matter of the brothel you seem to spend a lot of time in."

"Who would I be teaching at the brothel, sir?"

"If you say the rumors are untrue that is all that matters. Please step back as we confer."

Kyzyl did so, and, as before, he couldn't tell what any of them were saying. His mind tried to work out who could've been spreading such rumors about him. No one he knew would want to get him in trouble as far as he could see.

The Head Master turned back to Kyzyl and spoke, "tuition is set at thirty-five crowns. Please settle your accounts with Bernard in the Accounts Office."

Kyzyl hopped off the platform and went to Bernard in the antechamber. He wondered why the Head Master seemed to specify the Accounts Office when Bernard seemed to always be right outside the door.

"How bad is it this year? Still being treated like a prodigy?"

"Thirty-five."

Bernard snorted. "With all the talk around your spell mastery this last term, I'm surprised it's even that high."

"A friend of mine mentioned that tuition gets more expensive as you progress. Why is that?"

"Mostly a numbers issue. As you advance you have fewer and fewer peers being taught by more and more advanced students. Eventually the only people left who can teach you anything worthwhile are the ones who have already become fully realized wizards, like the Masters or their deputies. People whose time is worth a king's ransom to most students."

"Their deputies are the people who are next in line for their role as Master, right?"

Bernard nodded. "They also serve as a substitute when the Master has something to attend to or is ill. Bottom line, the cost of teaching you goes up, and the number of people we can divide that cost amongst goes down."

"Meaning I'm left with a tuition getting inflated on both ends."

"And now you know why you're sucking up. Get one or two Masters to like you, and stay out of the way of the rest of them, and you'll keep your tuition within the realm of possible, if not always reasonable."

"I'm not sucking up."

Bernard laughed. "It's nothing to be ashamed of, lad. We all do it. We have to keep our tuitions low somehow, right? Anyway, am I taking this out of your account at the bank?"

Kyzyl nodded. Bernard made a few notes as Kyzyl headed to the Noble Steed.

When he got there, Emrys and Donovan were

already sitting at a table, waiting for him. He sat down with them and announced his tuition. They both rolled their eyes at him.

"What exactly do you do in the admissions interview? Do you have some way to threaten the Masters or something?" Emrys asked.

"There's no way a little runt like our Kyzyl could threaten the nine most powerful wizards in Lukor. You must be bribing them. Is that why you live here instead of at the Gold Coin? Are you spending all your money on bribing the Masters?" Donovan suggested.

"That wouldn't make any sense," Emrys said. "Think about how much money it would take for the Masters to even hear of such a thing. Even the most dubious Master is more concerned with making sure the school looks good than he is with money.

"They hold on to the school's prestige like it was a matter of life and death. In short, my wise yet foolish friend, it would cost more for Kyzyl to bribe them than he would likely spend in normal tuition."

"If you two are done with your debate, I'd like to know where you got the idea that I had so much money just lying around," Kyzyl interjected.

"We don't think it's just lying around," Donovan began. "It's quite clear that it's tied up in your wardrobe." He gestured toward Kyzyl's silk robe.

"What in the Nine Hells are you talking about?"

"Look at what you're wearing."

Kyzyl looked down at himself. He was wearing his blue silk robes. He had been wearing one of his best for the exam and gaining a line of credit at the bank. It was the best formal wear he had, and the end-of-term exam seemed like a formal event. "What? It's just silk."

Donovan scoffed. "'Just silk' he says." He paused, looking at Kyzyl's confused expression. "You don't know do you?"

"Know what? Surely this kind of thing isn't that expensive." Kyzyl said. Emrys looked at him as if he were a simpleton. "What?"

"How did you get this far into Strophe without realizing what you're wearing?"

"I mean, the captain of the last ship I was on told me they were expensive, but any tailored clothes are expensive to a sailor. Surely plenty of people here can afford..." Kyzyl trailed off as Emrys shook his head.

"The clothes you're wearing could pay each of our tuitions for a year. By the Nine Hells, we'd probably still have some left over to keep us cozy through the winter too."

"That's ridiculous. I don't think we spent more than," Kyzyl juggled numbers in his head, "maybe thirteen crowns for my entire wardrobe. And most of that either got sold to a pawn shop or is still in my father's estate."

Emrys sighed. "You're not seeing it. Think about it. How long did it take you to get here?"

"Six months, maybe a little more."

"And think back to all the... adventures you had along the way. How many merchants do you suppose want to brave that journey regularly?"

"I suppose a few might be deterred by the pirates, a few more by the long journey, but there has to be some that are willing to make it out here."

"Not a whole lot. Don't get me wrong, silk makes its way here no problem. The way it generally does is through the Pirate Isles, passing from one hand to another. The price gets bumped up just a little bit each time, so each merchant can make a profit to feed his family and each pirate can pay for his drinks. Pretty soon a single arm's length of silk is going for twice its weight in gold."

Kyzyl stared at him, dumbfounded. "You mean... my clothes..."

"Are probably worth the entire king's treasury,

maybe a little more to someone like Siradyl who has money to spare."

Kyzyl paused for a moment to take in what his friends were saying. After a bit, a thought occurred to him. "If silk is so difficult to get across the Pirate Isles, why doesn't a wizard just summon a great deal of it and sell it?"

Donovan shrugged and set his drink down. "Most wizards are from noble families. Nobles are the only ones that can afford tuition here. Among nobles there are few who are so concerned about money that they'd accept the embarrassment that generally comes with becoming a merchant.

"Fewer still have any knowledge about where, specifically, the silk actually comes from. They know its Techarian, but you need more than that for a summon, as I'm sure our new conjurer adept knows."

"Wait, why would nobles be embarrassed by having to become merchants?" Kyzyl asked.

"Status. It's all about status among those of us that can afford not to care about money. The idea of having to work for something that you were raised to believe was yours by birthright is appalling to most nobles. That's how you get such petulant men like Siradyl."

Kyzyl sat in his chair for a long moment, thinking. He sold a great deal of his wardrobe when he first landed, and he had asked only for what it was worth in his homeland. He began to wonder just how much money that pawn shop owner made off that purchase. He started to chuckle.

When Emrys and Donovan gave him a worried look, he shook his head and began to speak. "If what you're telling me is true, I made that pawn broker's whole career. I sold him my wardrobe for what it was worth in Hanra. If he can flip it for five times that much..." Kyzyl stopped.

Numbers were rolling around in his head. He felt waves of relief wash over him and he could barely keep from laughing. Donovan raised an eyebrow at Kyzyl as he covered his mouth to hold in the giddy laughter. Emrys put a hand on his friend's shoulder.

When Kyzyl could finally look at them again without seeming like a madman, he said, "they may not know where to get silk, but I do." That was all the explanation he offered that night, but as the night wore on, Kyzyl, having solved his financial needs, bought his friends drinks in response to their questions.

CHAPTER TEN
Gifts Given and Gifts Received

Kyzyl got up the next morning at the first light of dawn. Knowing none of the shops he was going to would be open, he spent some time summoning the rest of the wardrobe he'd left at his father's estate. When he was done, the wardrobe Seth had built for him was over stuffed with silk and Kyzyl's arm muscles were twitching from the strain of the castings.

After he ate breakfast with Seth and his family and finished telling Samantha another story about his homeland, he went from shop to shop, trading, negotiating and selling everything he'd summoned.

In the end, he had four sets of linen dyed deep royal colors, three warmer sets made from thick wool, and a fur cloak for the coming winter. His last stop was at the bank where he settled his credit and deposited half of the money he had left over. It was a tidy sum roughly equivalent to what he'd arrived in Tamerrel with before it was stolen.

Finally, he met up with Donovan and Emrys. Both of them made comments about his new lack of silk dressings. They were used to seeing him in the local fashion, but this was the first time they'd seen Kyzyl without a hint of silk on him: no sash, belt, or anything.

"I'll explain later," he said in response to their questions. "Donovan, did you ever figure out what you were going to do for tuition this term?"

"I might have to skip and work in a shop or something. I'm sure Matilda might be able to help." His face was a mask of despair, but Kyzyl was all smiles.

"Good god man," Emrys said, "You're not going to whore yourself out for tuition money, are you?"

Donovan shrugged. "It might be my only choice." He looked at Kyzyl. "My misery funny to you?"

Kyzyl shook his head. "Follow me gentlemen. We are going to a party." Kyzyl led them to Matilda's and Donovan just looked at him. When they went inside, however, Donovan's face lit up. All the girls were waiting in the parlor for them, and there wasn't a client in sight.

They all ran up and hugged Donovan like they hadn't seen him in years and he quickly became confused. "Bethany may have let it slip where all your money went. She and I planned this party to cheer you up."

Bethany skipped over to them. "What you did was really thoughtful, and the girls and I have been meaning to thank you properly for it."

Donovan backed off a bit, giving Bethany a look of concern.

Bethany shook her head and giggled. "Nothing like that. We are all well aware of how you feel on that front. Still, we thought you deserved a day without clients and all the rest."

"Not to mention the day off it gives the rest of us," Gral said while raising her cup to him.

"I'm confused," Emrys proclaimed. "What did Donovan do that's so special?"

"Haven't you ever stopped to consider why Donovan's father cut him off?" Kyzyl asked.

"Because Donovan's father is a cold-hearted

bastard," Emrys said.

"True, but that's not the only reason. Donovan's father felt his son was spending too much time in brothels and not enough time on books. Donovan, would you like to explain to our nice young friend here where all that money went?"

Donovan looked like a kid caught in a lie. He looked from Kyzyl to Bethany to Emrys. Finally, he sighed, defeated.

"I bought Matilda's house from her previous landlord. I thought if she and her girls didn't have to pay rent, they would have more freedom to deny less... savory clientele. I just didn't want them to be held by the purse strings and forced to do something they don't like because they needed the money."

Emrys looked astonished. "Is that why Matilda never kicks us out for loitering? You own this brothel?"

"No," Donovan said quickly. "I just bought it. I signed the deed over to Matilda almost immediately."

"And me and my girls never forgot the generosity." Matilda said from the bar. All the girls raised a glass to her statement.

"There's more," Kyzyl said. "I've been up since the crack of dawn running from place to place to get this. I'm not taking no for an answer." He threw a bag at Donovan, who almost dropped it.

"What's in this thing? Stones? It's heavier than a fat cat." He opened it. The bag was full to bursting with gold crowns.

"You're not the only one who can give away a fortune."

Tears welled up in Donovan's eyes as he looked from the bag to Kyzyl. "Is this why you're wearing linen?"

Kyzyl nodded.

"It makes you look like a barbarian." Kyzyl gave him a mock sneer. Then they both laughed and Emrys joined in. Bethany just gave them all a confused look.

Donovan and Emrys headed to the bar, but before Kyzyl could follow them, he felt a tug on his arm. Turning around, he saw Bethany standing there, blushing and grinning. Before he could say anything, she pulled him upstairs and into one of the bedrooms.

"What you did for Donovan was really sweet. I'm really impressed and proud of you."

"I just didn't want him to have to leave the school."

"You and I both know Matilda would never let that happen. Be honest, you just wanted to do something nice for your friend." Before he could respond, she kissed him. He was so surprised he almost forgot to kiss her back.

When she began to pull back, he wrapped his arms around her, pulled her close and kissed her softly. Her lips were full, nimble, and sweet. He could feel her body pressing against his. She parted her lips, and he felt her tongue slide into his mouth and begin dancing with his own. Their teeth knocked together and they both pulled back, holding their mouths. Bethany laughed and Kyzyl turned a bright red.

"Sorry. I don't have any…" He trailed off as Bethany put a finger to his lips.

"I know. It's OK. Just relax." He nodded vigorously. She ran her fingers through his hair and kissed him again. He felt his muscles relax at her touch, and his mind went to the feeling of soft clay in a potter's hand.

Her mouth was so warm and inviting. This time, it was his tongue that slipped into her mouth, but he was so focused on his teeth he forgot to move it until he felt her tongue pressing against it. He felt her lips tighten into a smile.

He closed his mouth and pressed his lips against hers as he unlaced her dress. The skin of her back was hot against his fingers as she arched it, pressing her breasts against his chest. She turned around and let the dress fall as she pulled his arms around her waist. Her butt grazed his crotch and he quickly became aware of his own arousal. His heart was pounding and his limbs were shaking, but Bethany held him still.

"I'm here," she whispered, "there's no need to be nervous." She rubbed her butt against his crotch again. "Or are you just excited?"

She wiggled and Kyzyl drew a shaky breath. She giggled and tilted her head to expose her neck. Not wanting to miss the invitation, he began kissing her on every inch of bare skin he could reach while she still held his hands around her waist.

He pulled his hands up and began massaging her breasts and playing with her nipples. She let out a soft moan and let her head fall back against his shoulder. His hands were careful and dexterous from years of practicing hand signs. His fingers moved independently of each other. Bethany let out a soft squeak as he pinched one of her nipples.

"I'm sorry, did I hurt you."

"No," she breathed, "keep going." His fingers glided across her skin, and he felt the goosebumps rise as his hand descended. Her parted her lips and let his two middle fingers slide inside her. She let out a small moan of pleasure.

Her hands clenched and her knees buckled, but he wasn't ready for her weight and they both fell onto the floor. She laughed again. Kyzyl's face got hot with embarrassment, but Bethany pulled him close. "Perhaps we should move to the bed now."

She stood up and pulled him to his feet. Then she pulled off his tunic and playfully pushed him onto the bed. She started to unlace his trousers as he laid back. Soon he felt the warm wetness of her mouth again, but it wasn't on his mouth.

He gasped, and she let out a giggle around his cock.

He didn't last long against her deft hands and nimble tongue. He threw himself up to try and warn her, but she was already prepared. His cock went past her throat and she swallowed.

Then she looked at him and smiled. "I didn't want to make a mess." She winked. "At least, not yet."

She hopped into his arms and soon his tongue was in her mouth. They were rolling and grinding and moaning together on the bed. The warmth of their skin pressing against each other made Kyzyl's heart beat faster. The muscles he'd used to summon his silks were twitching, but whether from excitement or exertion, he didn't know.

After he had pinned her, he smiled at her surprised face. "I'm stronger than I look." He began kissing her neck. He felt her hands on his back as he got lower and lower. He stopped to massage her breasts again and kiss the space between them.

He only continued after tickling her nipples with the tip of his tongue. He began to descend again. Getting lower and lower, he could hear her breathing getting heavy. As he passed her navel, he heard her let out a soft, little sound. He parted her legs and kissed his way up her inner thigh.

When he moved over to her other thigh and start to descend, he heard her whisper "not fair." He continued his little tease, moving up one thigh and down the other, then up and down, until she moved her hips and said "please, stop being so mean."

He smiled. He had been thinking about this for a long time. He moved his way up her thigh one last time, savoring every small moment and every inch of her skin. When kissed her lips, and let the tip of his tongue tickle her clitoris her breath caught.

She let out a shaky moan as his tongue moved from the bottom edges of her lips all the way up to her clit, once, twice. Then her fingers spread them apart and he let his tongue slide inside her, massaging the inside walls of her vagina. His fingers continued to massage and tickle her lips and clitoris, making her twitch with pleasure.

Her back arched and she said his name before another wave of muscle spasm hit her. He only realized it was meant as a warning when the flood of fluids filled his mouth. It was a unique taste, and he wasn't sure if he liked it. One thing he was sure he liked was the look of satisfaction on Bethany's face when he came up to meet her.

She wrapped her arms around him and began kissing him vigorously. He pressed his cock against her and started rubbing, making them both moan. He tried to get the angle right, but he missed. He tried again and missed again.

Bethany took his cock in her hand, whispered, "let me," and set it against the right spot. He looked into her eyes. They were filled with love and gentleness. He watched her close them and bite her lip as he slid inside her. His arms began to shake, but his thrusts were firm. She wrapped her legs around him. She pulled him down to her and held him thigh against her chest.

With his arms no longer supporting him, he focused on thrusting harder and faster. He slipped out, but his hand was quick, and he didn't lose the rhythm. Harder and faster. She was moaning now. Harder and faster. He started to grunt. Harder and faster. They both felt the pleasure building. Harder. Her nails dug into the flesh on his back. Faster. He felt it now. Her moans were getting so loud there was no way everyone downstairs couldn't hear them. Harder. He didn't care. Faster. Their pleasure mounted and he felt it release.

Bethany let out a similar sound to her first orgasm, and her tense muscles told Kyzyl he hadn't been the only one to finish a second time. Her limbs held him tight for the space of three rapid breaths before she released him.

Kyzyl rolled over onto the bed next to Bethany and she snuggled up next to him. He kissed her forehead and she nestled against his chest. "That was the best I've ever had," she told him.

"Really? I didn't think I was all that great."

"It wasn't perfect, and we both stumbled a bit, but knowing that you were all mine, even just for the moment, I think that's what made it special." Kyzyl sniffed, trying to keep the tears inside. Bethany noticed and sat up, looking in his eyes. "What's wrong? Is it something I did? Did I offend you?"

Kyzyl placed his hand on the side of her head. She leaned her head into it. I have never felt this way about anything," he explained. "I love you, Bethany."

"Oh. My mighty mage. My fearless warrior." She took his face in her hands and brought his eyes to hers. "I love you too, Kyzyl." She kissed him again with a passion gentler and more relaxed than the mad scrambling they were doing before.

Kyzyl and Bethany lay in each other's arms for a while, enjoying each other's nudity, before Bethany suggested they go back downstairs. Kyzyl agreed, and they both got dressed.

When they got to the stairs, however, Matilda was at the bottom looking very stern. She gestured toward Kyzyl and he followed her to a room he had not seen before. It looked like an office, with a large oak desk and three stuffed armchairs. Matilda took the one behind the desk. There was a large window behind her that made it hard for Kyzyl to see her face. Eventually his eyes adjusted, mostly.

"So, I see you and Bethany finally conquered your virginity," she said plainly.

"Honestly ma'am, it was more like a release," he said, not sure how to feel. Matilda was clearly upset, but he didn't fully understand why.

Kyzyl looked up and saw Matilda fighting back a smile. "Kyzyl," she said exasperated, "I know the two of

you think you love each other, but the fact is, you're just
too young."

"What does age have to do with it?"

"Nothing, save for the fact that you two live in
entirely separate worlds. Whatever else she might be,
Kyzyl, Bethany is literally a whore."

Kyzyl opened his mouth, but Matilda raised her
hand.

"What I mean is, are you ready to accept the fact
that Bethany's job requires her to be unfaithful to you? I've
seen too many girls have their hearts broken when some
man comes in here and 'falls in love with them' only to
disappear when the girl won't give up her job for him. Are
you going to be one of those men, Kyzyl? Because I won't
let you hurt Bethany like that." She paused. "And I don't
want her hurting you either."

Kyzyl cocked his head for a moment, thinking.
Certain puzzle pieces were beginning to fall into place.
"Bethany told me Donovan never sleeps with the women he
takes to any of the rooms. She told me it was because he
was paying them for the information they gave him, but
that never made any sense to me.

Donovan isn't interested in court politics or
subterfuge. He doesn't care about the rumors or the sex.
He spends all his time here for a different reason doesn't
he?"

Matilda didn't respond, so Kyzyl continued.

"Donovan didn't give you this house just to be nice,
did he? There's a reason he pays for services here, but
never sleeps with any of the girls. You're that reason. What
happened between you two?"

"Kyzyl, I... I hurt that man. I hurt him in a way that
I can't take back, but I can keep you and Bethany from
making similar mistakes."

"I understand what I'm getting into, but I love
Bethany."

"Kyzyl, do you even know what that word means?"

"You're not my mother. I came here to be free of people making decisions for me." He stood and walked to the door. He only paused when he heard Matilda standing as well.

"I'm not trying to control you. I'm trying to help you. Please don't be so egotistical as to think this is anything else."

"I know what I'm doing." He walked back to the party and joined Bethany at the bar.

"What did Matilda have to say?" she asked him.

"It was nothing. She just wanted to congratulate us." He wasn't feeling up to telling Bethany her boss, who she loved like a mother or a protective aunt, disagreed with their relationship.

Bethany touched Kyzyl's cheek. "Kyzyl, you look a little angry. Did I do something wrong?"

He took her hand and kissed it. "You're perfect my love." She giggled. They spent the rest of the night laughing and joking with Donovan and Emrys. Kyzyl didn't get back to the Noble Steed until the moon was high in the sky. He stumbled drunkenly into his room and tripped onto his bed.

CHAPTER ELEVEN
Harvest Festival

The next morning was the first day of the harvest festival. Kyzyl woke up with his head pounding and walked down to the bar to ask Seth for a hangover cure. Seth made him a plate of eggs, crisp bacon, bread still warm enough to melt butter, and a cup of the strange purple concoction from the alchemy labs.

"You didn't have any bad side effects last time, did you? The boys who sold it to me came by and asked."

"Not that I could remember, but the effects did take a while to... umm... take effect. Five spirits of the earth, my head hurts."

"I mentioned that to them. I hope what they're doing is safe."

"If it wasn't, Master Telma likely would've confiscated their notes and put a stop to their experiments before it was let out to the public. The Masters take the reputation of the university very seriously. At least, according to Emrys."

"That half-elf that has the hots for you?" Kyzyl gave the innkeeper a confused look. "You mean ya haven't noticed? The first time you brought him here I thought the two of you were gonna start something soon. Then last night you came in here talking about some girl, and I figured I had you wrong."

"Emrys is... he's never mentioned it to me before."

Seth shrugged. "It was none of my business. I'm sorry I said something."

Before Kyzyl could respond, Emrys burst in the door and grabbed him by the arm.

"Dude! You're late, what are you doing?" He started pulling Kyzyl toward the door.

"Late for what?"

"The debate. You have to go. I have to announce the resolution to the both of you at the same time, or the whole thing won't be fair. C'mon!"

"Alright, alright. I'm coming." Kyzyl shoved the last bit of his breakfast into his mouth before Emrys pulled him off the stool.

They walked together toward the courtyard. Emrys kept catching Kyzyl staring at him. Eventually, he finally asked, "are you going to tell me why you keep looking at me like I have horns?"

"Something Seth said before you showed up. I'll ask later."

They arrived at the courtyard where a makeshift stage had been set up. Head Master Herman and Master Jonah were already standing center stage.

"Kyzyl," Head Master Herman said, "how nice of you to join us. Please come up on to the stage." Kyzyl and Emrys pushed through the crowd with difficulty and stepped onto the stage. "Now that both of our contenders are here, it is time to announce the resolution. As this debate was his idea, young mister Emrys will announce the resolution."

Head Master Herman stepped down from the stage, giving the floor to Emrys. "The resolution is this: The Universal Law of Balance should, always, be considered by all magic users. Kyzyl, as the student, you have the privilege of choosing to affirm or negate this resolution."

Kyzyl paused for a moment. What kind of nonsense was Master Jonah trying to pull?

"I will choose to affirm," he said finally to even his surprise.

Master Jonah nodded once. "I suppose that means I will be going second. I look forward to it," he said, looking at Kyzyl.

"Very well," Emrys said. "Both of you have until the end of the Harvest Festival to prepare your cases. Good luck to you both."

Kyzyl watched as the crowd dispersed. What was Master Jonah up to? The resolution had to be his idea. Did Kyzyl play into his trap by deciding to affirm it?

Emrys and Master Jonah approached him as he hopped off the stage. Emrys got a look at the confused look on his face. "You OK, Kyzyl?"

"Did you pick that resolution to embarrass me?" Kyzyl asked, directing the question at the Master Cleric. A few of the remaining students paused at the sharpness in his voice.

"Kyzyl, we went over this. Master Jonah isn't trying to embarrass you. I picked the resolution. I wanted to give you two a chance to show the rest of the university the discussion you two had during our first R&L class."

"If I had chosen the resolution, Mister Shenta, it wouldn't have been fair to you. I would've had time before the announcement to prepare."

Kyzyl felt his face get hot. "Master Jonah I am so sorry. I thought—" The Master Cleric cut him off with a raise of his hand. He gave a stern look to the students who were unapologetically eavesdropping. Each of them looked away hurriedly and walked out of earshot.

"You really ought to learn to control your temper around the faithful, Kyzyl. We're not all out to get you, you know. Such an outburst like that from you again will result in my hand being forced. I pride myself on my patience, but continuing to indulge you would undermine my authority, and the authority of the other Masters."

Kyzyl hung his head. "Yes Master."

The Master Cleric nodded and walked away from the stage, leaving Kyzyl looking at Emrys who raised his eyebrows and smirked. "Looks like you have some research to do. Want to go to the library?"

Kyzyl mirrored the smirk and nodded. Then he jumped off the platform, and he and Emrys walked to the library.

On the way, Emrys asked, "what was it you wanted to ask me, Kyzyl?"

Kyzyl thought for a moment, choosing his next move carefully. "What do you think of Bethany?"

"She's a nice girl. She seems to really like you. I'm glad you guys found each other."

Kyzyl wasn't good at reading other people's emotions, but he thought he heard a hint of regret in Emrys' voice. Emrys waited for more from Kyzyl, but he was quiet the rest of the way to the library.

When they got to the library, they found that Donovan and Bethany were already waiting outside for them. Kyzyl began to ask them what they were doing, but stopped, looking at Emrys.

"What?" Emrys said. He put his hands up in mock defensiveness. "I thought you could use some help finding books. You don't have much time to waste walking through the shelves. That's our job," he indicated Kyzyl's three friends, "and, since I study here under Head Master Herman, I will guide these two know-nothings to the right sections. All you have to do is tell us what you need."

"Know-nothings?" Donovan asked, giving Emrys a pretend glare.

Emrys painted a look of innocence on his face and the four friends laughed as they walked into the reception room of the towering library. There, a familiar face stopped them.

"She can't be here. This place is for students only," Espen said, indicating Bethany.

"Relax Esp, I already talked to Head Master Herman about it. Kyzyl needs extra hands to research for the debate, and she was available."

Espen didn't look convinced.

"Do you want me to go find him and ask? I think he's somewhere on the fair grounds."

Espen sighed. "No. It's fine. But if he comes asking why there's a non-student in the library, I'm sending him straight to you."

"Deal."

Espen let the three students sign in. Bethany wrote her name on the line next to Kyzyl's. It was an improvised way of indicating she was not a student, but a guest. They walked through the doors into the vast library. After a long moment of searching, they found a reading nook, and Kyzyl's three friends turned to him, awaiting his instructions.

"I'm going to need to familiarize myself with this 'Universal Law' before I can build my arguments. Emrys, do you know where the books on philosophy and ethics are?"

"I can do you one better. I know where the books on the law you want are. C'mon you two. Kyzyl needs books."

"Master Jonah didn't go over the Universal Law with you in class?" Bethany asked. "Seems like a bit of an oversight considering that is the main topic of the debate."

Kyzyl shrugged. "We had a bit of a discussion about it during our first class, but since then his focus has been argumentation itself. We weren't really there to discuss the finer details of philosophy."

"But," Emrys interrupted, "we are here now. Our

studious friend needs to read his weight in moral philosophy to prepare for the debate. He has a Universal Law to affirm."

Kyzyl and his friends spent the mornings of the festival in the library. He studied as much as he could, and, under Emrys' guidance, his friends brought him the books he asked for. He devoured books on the energies used in spellcasting and how they interacted with the natural world. However, the books on moral philosophy and the Universal Law took him a great deal more effort to work through.

After a few hours, Bethany would sigh or lean against Kyzyl's arm. He'd put his arm around her, and that would appease her for a moment. He'd go back to studying a passage on the morality of interrupting "the natural flow of energy with spells and enchantments" from some long dead philosopher that clearly had a problem with wizards as a whole. It wouldn't be long, however before she was kissing his neck.

By the time the noon bell rang, she was always sitting in his lap, tousling his hair, and encouraging him to finish studying for the day and go enjoy the festival with her and his two friends. His face would turn red, and she'd giggle at his embarrassment. If he tried to go back to reading, she'd "lose her balance," and he'd have to catch her.

Donovan and Emrys would feign disgust at her "shameless display." They would, however, also express their agreement with her by insisting Kyzyl had read enough about the "interplay between magic and the natural rhythms of the world." Kyzyl would relent, and they would go buy lunch at one of the stalls or see a puppet show.

When the big day came, Kyzyl couldn't help but feel incredibly nervous. He was about to go head-to-head with one of the Masters, and he had no doubt there would be a large crowd. Merely the idea of public speaking would've filled him with nervous energy, but Master Jonah, whatever else he was, had proven himself to be a valuable teacher. He'd instilled Kyzyl with enough confidence to speak in front of a crowd without wanting to throw up. Whether or not he enjoyed the experience was a different matter.

Kyzyl took a deep breath and let it out slowly. He allowed his mind to stand squarely on the edge of Wind-Dance. If his anxiety began to get the better of him, he knew it wouldn't take much effort to tip into it. He went over everything Master Jonah had taught him in class: speak from your gut, take time to gather your thoughts, and, most importantly, stand tall. The Master Cleric had reiterated time and again that confidence could be projected without being felt.

Kyzyl reminded himself of all the time spent doing his research. He'd studied not only a number of texts in support of Master Jonah's Universal Law of Balance, but had studied the most popular arguments against it. He'd found several of them quite compelling. Still, his job today was to successfully refute those arguments, and he had put together as many of his own ideas and evidence as he could to prepare.

Kyzyl looked out the window to judge the time. The light of the sun was just beginning to reach over the horizon. He only had a few hours before he had to meet Master Jonah and Head Master Herman on the temporary stage they'd set up in the courtyard where the resolution was announced. He spent those hours pouring over his notes and practicing different deliveries for his arguments.

In those moments, he thought of nothing else until a knock came from the other side of the door. Emrys' voice came through the door, "Kyzyl, are you ready? It's time." Kyzyl looked out the window. The sun had fully risen, which meant he'd spent his few remaining hours practicing, and now it was showtime.

Kyzyl gathered his courage and mentally prepared

himself. As he opened the door to see Emrys' shinning face, the tension in his shoulders eased noticeably. Whether he succeeded or failed, he found solace in the fact that his friends would be in the audience to support him. He returned Emrys' slight grin and nodded. The two men walked out of the inn and toward the waiting spotlight.

"You kept one of your silk robes?" Emrys asked on their way to the stage.

He was wearing one of his nicest crimson robes. It had a slim cut around his midriff and flared out as it reached down his legs, creating a silhouette he enjoyed. "I kept a couple. I couldn't part with my favorites and I had sold enough to keep Donovan and me in the university."

"I'm glad you were able to keep a few. You look good in silk. It suits you."

"Thanks." Was Emrys trying to flirt with him, or was he just being nice? Seth's comments rolled around in Kyzyl's head.

Donovan and Bethany were waiting for them when Kyzyl and Emrys arrived at the side of the stage. They were standing next to Head Master Herman, who was going to be the moderator. "Mister Shenta, are you prepared for the day's debate?" he asked formally.

"Yes, Head Master. I have done as much research as my friends would allow me." The Master Diviner raised an eyebrow at this, prompting Kyzyl to explain. "My friends didn't want me to spend the entire festival in the library, sir."

"They sound like rather good friends then. The point of this festival and the break we give between each term in general is to give our students a chance to live their lives rather than studying continuously. I'm glad your friends prevented you from missing that opportunity." Emrys and Bethany smiled at the compliment while Donovan simply nodded.

The Head Master gestured for Kyzyl to follow him

and they both stepped on to the platform where Master Jonah was waiting. The crowd was bigger than Kyzyl had anticipated. It seemed that not only were students of the university interested in the debate, but many of the surrounding townsfolk and shopkeepers as well.

Kyzyl looked out at the sea of faces and saw Seth and his family toward the back. He saw a man with a slight paunch that ran one of the apothecaries in town. He counted three of the nine Masters, and with the two standing with him on stage, that meant half the men running the university were about to watch Kyzyl go up against one of their own. Kyzyl's throat felt dry as Head Master Herman introduced them, and the two debaters shook hands.

"We decided at the beginning of the week that Kyzyl will open this debate with his affirmation of the resolution 'The Universal Law of Balance should, always, be considered by all magic users', Kyzyl?" Master Herman announced.

Kyzyl stepped up to the center of the stage and greeted his audience with a formal raise of his hand. "Thank you, Head Master Herman. My fellow students and citizens of the university, I will begin by first explaining the Universal Law of Balance. The Universal Law of Balance, or the Law of Magic as it is colloquially known, states that the world is in a state of equilibrium and us, as magic users, must be charged with maintaining this equilibrium with each use of magic, each spell, enchantment, and artifact we create. It also states that failure to do so will have dire consequences.

"The truth of this Law is plainly obvious to anyone who has stopped to consider the natural world around them. In nature, things flow in cycles, cycles of energy, of life, and even of gases. These cycles have been constructed to maintain balance. If anyone were to, let's say, add a substantial amount of energy to a natural system, the system could degrade or even out right break under the strain. That is why we must maintain the balance that nature has spent so long creating."

Kyzyl stepped back, and Master Jonah stepped forward. "That's a fair point, Kyzyl. However, you did overlook one thing. The simple fact is, if the natural order were so perfect, we would still be living in the woods.

"Granted, many people do live in the woods, but most of us recognize that civilized society is beneficial to humanity. Not to mention the fact that nature contains cycles due to limited resources. If we, as magic users, are able to construct a system of limitless resources, there is no evidence that it would be harmful to the world at large.

"If you were to provide evidence for the rest of us that this equilibrium is useful beyond those limited resources, you could better prove your point."

Master Jonah stepped back, and Kyzyl stepped forward for his response. "My opponent has pointed out that the natural world is limited by its resources. However, the Law of Conservation, that all matter and energy in the world is fixed and can merely be transformed from one state to another, simultaneously supports and refutes that argument. What I mean to say is, when you use a resource, it is not destroyed. Merely its matter and energy are converted. Nature has found cycles that allow it to transform energy and matter back and forth between states.

"This has, in effect, given the natural world a limitless supply of those resources by allowing it to reuse the resources it has already used. Thus, it is the equilibrium itself that maintains these cycles and should, itself, be maintain by magic users.

"An example, if you'll indulge me Master Jonah." Kyzyl looked back to the Master Cleric. He was asking to take up his opponent's remaining time to explain his example, and the rules of the debate required their permission.

Master Jonah nodded, indicating he'd like Kyzyl to

continue. "I would like to direct everyone's attention to the fall of the Akyani Empire. Several factors went into the fall of such a mighty force in history, but one was the tendency for Emperor Ganyi the Second to use magic to solve the Empire's problems. During their reign, there was a famine that caused many of their citizens to starve. No matter, they had Transmutist at their disposal, so they could turn stone and other substances into bread.

"This did not address the underlying structural problem the Empire was facing. Their infrastructure had been built on a system of government sponsored agriculture that didn't take into account the various climates of their satellites states. Because the farming practices they had been forcing on people weren't fitted to the environment, soon they ran out of other resources because of the growing need for food and, later, energy to fuel the transmutation of other matter into food.

"In the end, peasant revolts and border skirmishes caused the Empire to collapse. All of this could've been avoided if Ganyi had taken the time to fit their systems into those the natural world had already created. The agriculture would've been made stable, and we'd all be speaking Akyani instead of Lukoran."

As Kyzyl stepped back again, he noticed Master Jonah was smiling at him, and he wondered what the man was getting out of all this. He seemed very pleased, but Kyzyl couldn't tell if he was about to reveal a huge flaw in Kyzyl's argument, or if he was enjoying watching Kyzyl speak.

"That's a very interesting story," the Master began. "However, I feel I must point out that there were many other factors that lead to the decline of the Akyani Empire, such as the destabilizing military policy and the economic inflation they were facing due to a large influx of slaves. Making it seem like the entire Empire was brought down by one person's failure is a bit narcissistic, don't you think?" The Master stepped back and winked at Kyzyl as Head

Master Herman walked on to the stage and stood in the middle.

"As appointed judge of this intellectual debate, I am charged with declaring a winner," The Master declared. He looked down at a sheet of paper and Kyzyl could see that he had been taking notes. "By my count, it was close. The clear winner however, with just one point over his opponent," Kyzyl took half a step back as he waited for the Head Master to call on his colleague. "Kyzyl Shenta."

Kyzyl paused for a moment. He had won? But how? Then he felt someone nudge him forward and he stepped up next to Head Master Herman and bowed to a roaring crowd. Master Jonah stepped up to him and shook his hand. "You were great. I haven't had such a satisfying debate with someone in a long time," he told Kyzyl.

Kyzyl was still too stunned for words, so he just nodded. When they both stepped down from the stage, they were greeted first by Emrys and Donovan. Bethany was not far behind and they all had words of congratulations for Kyzyl. Most of the students he knew from the university, and even some he didn't, walked up to him to shake his hand, absolutely amazed that he beat a Master on their own subject.

Master Jonah listened to it all with a wide smile on his face. Was there pride in that smile? Kyzyl began to wonder if he'd earned this victory, or if Master Jonah had handed it to him to make himself look better as a teacher. Kyzyl continued to thank each person for their praise, but all the while he felt his victory growing tainted. "Would Master Jonah do something like that? Throw a debate for pride or prestige?"

Kyzyl felt someone touch his arm and he saw Bethany looking at him. She was beaming. "You were amazing Kyzyl. I'm so proud of you. It looks like all the work you put in paid off."

"The Head Master told me you had put in a great deal of hours in the library studying," Master Jonah said.

He put a hand on Kyzyl's shoulder. That made Kyzyl tense, but he said nothing. "It's no wonder you've become such a prodigy with such a work ethic."

"Thank you, Master," Kyzyl said respectfully, hoping Master Jonah didn't notice the tension in his shoulders. Master Jonah nodded and left with Head Master Herman. Kyzyl looked at Bethany, and then to Donovan and Emrys. "I guess there's nothing left to do now but enjoy our last day of freedom before the next term starts," he said.

The merry band of misfits enjoyed all the festival had to offer until the sun sank in the sky and everyone gathered at the square for a giant bonfire. Master Enwin and Master Sendrin had worked together the whole day to build the biggest, brightest, hottest fire Kyzyl had ever seen. Some of the flames danced higher than the top of the Pyramid-shaped Evocation building. There was a little music and a lot of drinking, and Kyzyl knew there wasn't anywhere else he'd rather be.

CHAPTER TWELVE
A New Term

Kyzyl went to sign up for classes during this term. Now that his finances were secure, he was looking forward to possibly studying under Head Master Herman and learning divination magic.

He was stopped at the registry by one of the clerks. The clerk pointed out a notice. It said, "Kyzyl Shenta is not to register for any classes before he speaks with Enwin Geraltson, Master of Conjuration and Head Master Herman D'Argentum."

Kyzyl's heart stopped. He hadn't done anything wrong as far as he knew. He wasn't even aware students could be barred from signing up for classes after their tuition was paid. He asked the clerk where the Masters were. She pointed him toward Head Master Herman's office in the library. Kyzyl became more nervous with each step closer. Was Master Enwin upset with him? Did Master Jonah have something to do with this?

He knocked on the door to Head Master Herman's office and was invited in. He entered into a room that was lined with bookshelves. Head Master Herman was sitting behind his desk and Master Enwin was leaning against it. Both of them were wearing a dark blue version of their

Master's robes.

Kyzyl felt a wave of relief when they both smiled at him openly. Whatever they had called him here for, they weren't angry with him. At least, they didn't seem to be.

"Mister Shenta, please have a seat. I'm glad you could join us. I presume you saw my notice at the registry," Head Master Herman said.

Kyzyl took a seat in one of the available armchairs. "Yes, Head Master. Have I done something inappropriate? Whatever it was, I assure you I can fix it. Please don't make me miss this term."

Head Master Herman raised a hand and Kyzyl went quiet. "You have done nothing wrong. My notice was not meant to be seen as a punishment, and I apologize if it came off that way."

He gestured toward Master Enwin. "Master Enwin and I have been discussing your research habits here in the library. He has spoken to me at length about your dedication under his tutelage, and as I have mentioned to you previously, I have been made aware of the great deal of time you spend in this very library."

Master Enwin didn't hide his look of pride, but far from putting Kyzyl at ease, that and the Head Master's words made Kyzyl confused about what was happening.

Head Master Herman continued, "it is clear to both of us that you neither require assistance to learn the things you desire, nor do you benefit from any structural environment you do not already create for yourself. With that in mind, we will both be signing off on you taking this term for independent study.

"If, after the end of the term, any of the three of us, you included, feel that you should return to a more traditional teaching method, you will be allowed to do so. Until then, your time is yours to do with as you please. I have no doubt you will use it to learn more than anyone could've ever taught you in a single term.

"Myself, Master Enwin, and Master Jonah will still be available to you if you get stuck or have questions. However, I suspect you will be answering many of them for yourself."

Kyzyl couldn't find the words to express how he felt. In fairness, he wasn't sure how he felt. This was a great deal of freedom that the Masters were entrusting him with, but it came with a lot of expectations. Could he maintain his status as a prodigy and fulfill the expectations of his teachers without anyone to guide him? It was all so much at once. He looked at Master Enwin, a thousand questions boiling up in him.

Master Enwin must've seen one or two because he spoke up. "I am of the opinion that there are some students that thrive better when given freedom. You have proven yourself to be a capable student and self-teacher Kyzyl. I look forward to seeing what things you might learn when given room to grow."

It should've been the furthest thing from his mind at that time, but his recent brush with financial issues brought another question to mind. "Will I still have to pay full tuition if I'm not in classes?"

He realized how improper the question was as it left his lips. His face tightened into a cringe when he finished the words. Rather than expressing offense at the notion, Master Enwin just chuckled.

"Frugality is a virtue few have at this university," Head Master Herman said. "Yes, you will still pay your tuition, though being known as an adept autodidact will likely earn you a reputation that would serve you in that regard.

"Still," Head Master Herman continued, "we do acknowledge that, as someone who is not taking up class time to learn, tuitions like yours are best used to improve self-teaching facilities. Rest assured, Kyzyl, there is a system in place to ensure your tuition goes to things you will be using as well."

Kyzyl was dismissed by the Masters, and he left not knowing what to do. He walked into the entrance hall that served as the gateway to the library on one side of the building and the classrooms and offices he'd just left on the other. Without any other ideas, he decided he'd spend his time in the library.

Kyzyl nodded to the student at the front desk and signed in. He walked through the double doors and started looking through shelves of books. As it always did, the size of the Library of Arcane Theory overwhelmed Kyzyl somewhat.

Having no direction to take his inquisition, Kyzyl was left wandering around the shelves with a sense of decision paralysis. He'd learned so much about summoning and wards during his last term, and between his class and the debate, he was certain he'd had enough of argumentation for a while. Should he continue down the path he was already on, or should he take the lessons he'd learned about spellcasting and apply them to a new area of study?

Divination magic seemed like an obvious choice. According to both Head Master Herman and Emrys, divination magic allowed a wizard to learn a great deal in a much smaller time frame than would normally be possible. Kyzyl's entire life was filled with a curiosity about the world around him, and the idea of being able to explore it further using magic was tantalizing.

Finding books that served as a primer for divination magic, however, proved to be an elusive challenge to conquer. Kyzyl searched through several different shelves and even asked a few of the scripturi, students who worked in the library organizing and documenting the collection.

According to them, it was difficult to get books that outlined the basics of just about any of the major subjects. The Masters tended to put a great deal of emphasis on basic skills, and thus the books covering those topics were always assigned in multiple classes. One scripturon who was also studying Enchantment magic told Kyzyl that the wait-list for many of those books filled before the class sign-ups did.

With that idea thoroughly shattered, Kyzyl went back to looking for any sort of book that caught his attention. He found one that was entitled <u>A Study on the Myth and Legend of Demons</u> that looked intriguing. The cover was blue and made of a soft, velvety material. The spine said "Volume 1," but Kyzyl couldn't spot another piece of the set anywhere near the book. He shrugged and picked it up.

Paging through the introduction revealed that it was a five volume set that explored everything the author could discover about the beliefs people had surrounding demons. Deciding it would be as good of a read as anything else, Kyzyl took it to a nearby reading nook.

He read through the whole book. The author was careful not to make any claims on the existence or non-existence of the supernatural. As the intro made clear, the entire book, and presumably the four volumes after, were a catalog of what people claimed about demons. The author made no attempt to investigate the claims they'd gathered. Kyzyl felt the scholarly work left some to be desired, but it was a good starting place for an idea that began forming in his mind.

After finishing the book, Kyzyl's eyes were getting heavy and he realized that he had read the last paragraph a half dozen times and still didn't know what it said. He attributed it to a little mental exhaustion, and got up to peruse the aisles once more.

After an hours or so, he found a spellbook that was filled with wards and containment fields he'd learned about in class. They seemed to be designed by a summoner who wanted to contain the creatures he summoned for studying. He decided the book was worth his perusal, so he brought it back to the reading nook and laid it down on the table.

He paged trough it until he found one that appeared to be simple enough based on his limited knowledge of wards. It was a simple barrier that absorbed kinetic energy. That meant the only power the caster needed to provide was to construct the initial threshold for the spell.

Like most spells, this one left the source of power up to the caster, and Kyzyl had been meaning to try something as a source of power for a spell. He decided this new spell seemed easy enough that it was a good place to experiment, and memorized the components with relative ease. He tipped his mind into Wind-Dance and began casting the spell.

***

He begins to chant while his hands make the necessary sigils. The sigils reflect on the floor. He tosses a pen from his pocket and binds the kinetic energy from it falling to the spell as the sigils start to glow and spin. The pen slows its fall and Kyzyl feels the galvanic energy of gravity flow into his body.

The muscles in his neck start to twitch. He feels like his limbs are being pulled in different directions. He tries to hold the spell, but his concentration breaks as the pain overwhelms him.

***

Kyzyl exhaled. He hadn't even realized he was holding his breath. He took a few more breaths to calm his beating heart.

"You're lucky. The last student who thought to use gravity as a source of energy had his left arm torn off completely."

Kyzyl turned to see Head Master Herman standing behind him. "Master! I'm sorry. I didn't mean... I know we aren't supposed to practice spells in the library sir. I'm sorry."

Master Herman raised a hand. "Wards are not the concern that rule was made for. I merely want my books free from summoned animals rampaging through the shelves or lightning from an evocation spell. Still, it is best for you to know that some wards work by making the air solid. When such wards break, they tend to shatter like glass. Best be mindful of such things as you experiment."

"Yes, Head Master. Again, I am sorry." Kyzyl bowed. Something occurred to him just then. "Sir? Would it be possible for me to copy a few spells from this book? They would be very helpful in my research."

"You have found a project for your independent study already, have you?"

"Not yet, sir, but if I am going to pursue conjuration beyond what I have learned, I suspect I will be summoning living creatures soon, and I'd prefer they be behind a protective barrier."

"A wise decision. I have no doubt Master Jonah will be sad to see such a bright student not attend his classes this term."

"I'm sure he will survive."

"That he will. I will inform the student at the front desk that you have my permission to copy spells from the books in the library. Ask them for a pen and a bottle of ink, but do be careful. Even with magic, getting ink stains out of books is a headache."

"You have my word Head Master."

The Head Master nodded, and Kyzyl went with him out to the front desk. The Head Master told the student at the front desk what they'd discussed. The student gave a questioning look to Kyzyl, but brought out four sheets of parchment, a bottle of red ink, and a pen made from a raven quill.

He brought the writing materials back to the nook he was reading in. He paused for a moment, considering the space he'd created for himself. He grabbed the book he'd been reading and the papers and ink, and he went in search of something more private. There were a number of small rooms built off the main floors of the library. Many students used them to study together with friends or classmates. Kyzyl and his friends had even made use of a few when he was studying for the debate.

He spent hours in there, copying every detail of three spells: the anti-kinetic barrier, a heat-absorbing energy field he thought would be useful for a multitude of things, and a complex containment barrier that created an air-tight space between ten and a hundred steps in diameter.

All three of these spells got him thinking of the many things he could contain within them. He started to wonder, which lead him wandering through the shelves of the library once more. When he finally found what he was looking for, it was in a book labeled <u>The Grimoire of Demonic Invocation</u>. A little dramatic. Its red leather binding cracked with age as he opened it, checked the contents, and brought it back to his study. He copied the necessary formula onto his last sheet of parchment and made notes on the back of it.

"Yes." Kyzyl heard the word whispered from somewhere behind him. When he turned around, however, there was no one there. It was probably a trick of his tired mind. He'd been studying in here for most of the day. He set down the quill after he finished the last note and stretched the muscles in his hand.

Perhaps he just needed some sun. He got up, put his books back, gathered his papers, and returned the ink and quill to the front desk. As he started to walk out the door, he thought he heard someone say something. He turned back to the student at the front desk.

"What?" the student said.

"Did you say something?"

"No."

Kyzyl nodded and left to go find Donovan and Emrys. He had a lot to catch them up on.

When he found his friends, they were loitering around Matilda's brothel, drinking and hitting on all the girls. When Kyzyl sat down, Bethany skipped over to him and he told them all about the events of that morning.

"Independent study? That's bull! I've been dogging Head Master Herman for two terms to get that kind of freedom!"

"Prolly doesn't help old Ky here hasn't even been here that long," Donovan said.

"You're drunk and trying to get a rise out of me. The fact that you wouldn't point that out otherwise is the only reason I'm going to let it slide," Emrys told him. The two exchanged friendly grins. Kyzyl was often confused how much of their banter was for the joke and how much was genuine.

"Even if you did try something, you'd lose. My body alteration magic can't be beat in a hand to hand, even if I am drunk." Body alteration was a subset of transmutation magic and Donovan's preferred focus.

"What's so great about body alteration magic? I bet I can summon anything to do the job as well," Kyzyl said. "At least in theory. Ya know, if you didn't have a decade of experience on me."

"Nice save kid. However, you also pointed out your biggest weakness. You have to summon something to take me on. I am self-reliant. That's why alteration magic is better than summoning."

"I'm still being self-reliant. I'm the one summoning the thing."

"Still gotta be able to come up with something to summon. You might've gone up against a Master, but there's no way you're winning this debate."

"I don't want to talk about the debate," Kyzyl said.

"Why not?" Bethany asked. "You were amazing,

right guys?" The other two nodded enthusiastically.

"I was amazing at defending a stance I don't believe in. How could I stand up there and try and prove something when I don't agree with it? What would people think of me if they heard me bouncing between opinions like that?"

"Have you heard anything Master Jonah told us in class last term? Debates aren't about winning or being right. It's about everyone coming to a more realistic truth. Even if you don't agree with the statements you're making, there's value in knowing the arguments. Even if it happens to be that you can easily defeat them, at least then you know," Emrys said.

Emrys had a point. Even Kyzyl had to concede that Master Jonah spent more time in their classes encouraging students to defend their beliefs regardless of his opinion on the subject. It was a surprising contrast to the religious leaders Kyzyl was used to: always making him feel small or foolish.

Bethany sat in Kyzyl's lap and touched his face with the tips of her fingers. "You're not with me," she said. "Is everything OK?"

Kyzyl still wasn't used to how easily she could read his thoughts, and it took him a moment to think of what to say to her. "Everything is perfect, my love. I am only now realizing how different Master Jonah is from the people I'm used to defending my skepticism from."

He felt her kiss him and he kissed back, pulling his mind back to the present. Kyzyl smiled as Bethany seduced his attention back to her. They didn't break apart from each other until Kyzyl heard Emrys clear his throat.

"You know I hate it when you two do that," he told them.

"You're just jealous," Bethany said. "If you had your own girl to sit in your lap you wouldn't have nearly as much objection to it." As Bethany spoke, Kyzyl tried to read Emrys' reaction, but the man simply wore his everyday playful smirk.

"Maybe," Kyzyl said to Bethany, "we should save all the physical stuff for when we have alone time." He glanced at Emrys. Emrys' smirk faded into a confused smile. He tilted his head at Kyzyl and gave him a puzzled look.

His puzzlement was reflected in Bethany's face as well, but she stood and moved to her own chair. Kyzyl felt a bit awkward by the whole situation, but he didn't want to make his friend uncomfortable.

Donovan spoke up with a bit of slur in his speech. "If it's alone time you want with your girl, we can find a few of our own and leave you two to have your fun."

"If I spend any more time alone with Gral, she promised to put some kind of enchantment on me. I don't know if she's serious, but I don't want to know what kind of mystical bindings that woman is familiar with," Emrys said.

Bethany giggled behind her hand. "Gral isn't the only one who has taken some classes while she's been here," she said conspiratorially. "Many of us have been hoping that we'll find the right class to teach us something for our more... tight lipped clients." Bethany gave a hopeful look to Emrys.

"If you're speaking of hypnosis, I'll remind you that I merely dabble in enchantment spells for my own benefit. Autohypnosis comes in handy during the overnight shift at the library.

"If it is mind reading that you're after, I doubt you'll find that kind of thing in anyone's spellbook at this university."

"Oh? It isn't possible?" Bethany asked with a curious tone.

"No, it's merely dangerous and complex. It takes a lifetime to master even with dedicated study, and that's assuming you can get the Master Diviner to sign off on giving you the spells to practice. Head Master Herman is very against it."

"Why is that?" Bethany asked.

"The Head Master is very protective of his students and the reputation of the school," Donovan said after finishing his drink.

Emrys nodded. "Mind-reading spells work by essentially merging your mind with that of the other persons. First you have to put a lot of concentration into keeping it one way, so they don't read your mind as well. Then you have to focus on which pieces are part of you and which ones are theirs. That's not even going into the difficulty of trying to not project your own expectations on to their mind. That's an entirely different spell."

Emrys' description made Kyzyl's head spin. He thought there was a lot to concentrate on for summoning spells, but this sounded like it was on an entirely different level.

Bethany also looked as if she was taking in the scale of what Emrys was saying. "What would happen if any of that went wrong?" Bethany asked.

"Depends on which part went wrong. If you don't focus on making it one way, the worst that will happen is that they will get as much of your thoughts as you get of theirs. It wouldn't necessarily be a problem. It just wouldn't be the desired effect.

"If, on the other hand, you fail to keep the pieces of your mind from mixing with theirs, you could end up coming out an entirely different person than you went in. In a sense, you could accidentally steal parts of their mind from them."

"Wow. Sounds very difficult. No wonder you haven't mastered it yet," Bethany said. She winked at Kyzyl, but he didn't understand why.

"I haven't been working on it. I got all that from a lecture Master Herman did on the dangers of misused

Divination. I, personally, would rather master spells that help me learn faster: speed-reading spells, scrying spells to help me see things from across the world, that sort of thing."

"Wait," Kyzyl said. "Is that how you know so much about my culture? Have you been spying on my people?"

"Not spying, *scrying,* I would never invade someone's privacy. I only scry on people while they're in public anyway."

"And yet, they are still unaware of your presence at the time," Donovan pointed out. "Meaning you aren't necessarily in the clear, privacy wise."

"Could you scry on anyone? At any time?" Kyzyl asked, not wanting to get pulled into another debate.

"Mostly. There are spells, mostly wards, that can protect against scrying. The Head Master regularly renews the wards around the Masters' offices to make sure no student has access to them without permission."

Kyzyl remembered being taught about these wards in his abjuration lessons, but he couldn't remember a single time any of his previous tutors had mentioned such a thing. Now that he thought about it, Emrys was the first person he remembered saying anything about scrying. Did his people know wizards were capable of this? Was their secret already exposed to a diviner like Head Master Herman?

Bethany took his face in her hands and pulled his eyes to hers. "My love, you have left me again. Tell me what's wrong."

"I'm just realizing what kind of power diviners have at their command."

"I'm glad you appreciate my work," Emrys said with a wink. He looked at Kyzyl's face. Kyzyl's eyebrows were knit together and his anxiety was clear in his eyes. "Are you worried about something?"

"My people's secret."

"The weapon we talked about when we first met?"
Kyzyl nodded.

"Don't worry about that. I asked Head Master
Herman after you mentioned it. The same thing occurred
to me. There aren't many secrets that a diviner somewhere
doesn't know. As it happens, that seems to be a well-
guarded secret."

"What do you mean?"

"I don't want to offend you or anything, we're
friends, and I respect the fact that you have your secrets.
But it turns out diviners have been trying to get the secret
your people have been holding back for centuries now. To
this day, the most we know about it comes from the pirate
journals I mentioned.

"No one can figure out how to scry on someone
while they're creating it. No one whose seen it can
remember any useful details beyond that it's a ranged
weapon that makes a loud noise. Not exactly helpful if
you're trying to design one of your own."

"Wait, what? Really?" Kyzyl's eyebrows knit
together again, but for a different reason. What magic
could be so powerful that no diviner in centuries could
break through it? Had he been wrong to assume his
people's magic was inferior?

"Yeah. That secret is well under lock and key. I
don't know what sort of wards you can put around an idea
like that, but I'd love to learn more about it. Alas, to do so
would weaken the defense itself more than likely. Secrets
inside secrets seems to be the way your people's weapon
stays safe."

The four friends spoke idly for the next couple
hours until Bethany announced that she had to work and
kicked the other three out, giving Kyzyl a passion-filled
good-bye kiss before he left. They each decided to attend
to their individual studies, and Kyzyl walked back to the
Noble Steed alone.

On his way back, he heard several incomprehensible whispers, and each time he checked behind himself to see if anyone was around. The sliver of moon that shone down on the street created more shadows than it illuminated, but Kyzyl was sure the street was empty except for him.

"I must have drunk too much," he thought. He tried not to let the thought disturb him as he opened the door. The inn was quiet. Seth was wiping down the bar and Samantha was by the fire trying to stay warm. She shivered when the wind blew through the open door. Kyzyl shut it quickly, knowing not to incur the wrath of the little girl.

"Ay, have you been spending all your time at the library again, lad?" Seth said.

"No sir, I've been drinking with my friends."

"Ay, that's a good lad. Sometimes you spend too much of your time in those dusty old halls."

"Yes sir."

"Come and have a bite then. Don't want you passing out on an empty stomach."

Kyzyl sat at the bar and the innkeeper brought him out a side of venison and bowl of potato soup. Kyzyl felt himself sober up a bit as he ate and told Seth and Samantha all about Master Enwin giving him free reign this term.

"That's a great deal for you, my boy. What will you be spending your time on? Maybe you could summon me up a prettier wife."

The innkeeper winked as a voice from the kitchen shouted, "I heard that." He laughed, but Samantha looked at him sternly.

"You shouldn't talk about mommy like that. It could hurt her feelings," she scolded.

"Ay, my little bunny, you're right." He turned his head and shouted over his shoulder. "I love you, my dove."

"Go to the seventh layer of hell," came the reply,

but there was a smile in the tone.

Kyzyl smiled as he watched the small family interact with each other. Even with insults and sternness, there was a depth of affection between the three he'd hardly known with his family.

Eventually, Seth shuffled Samantha upstairs to her bed, and Kyzyl was left alone with a mostly empty bowl of soup and a bone stripped of all its meat. "What is it you desire?" he heard over his shoulder. He turned, but no one was there.

"What?" Kyzyl asked to the empty room. There was no reply. "I need sleep. Right now." He walked up to his room.

Along the way he listened carefully and started to identify every sound. A creak, his foot on the floor boards. A flutter, a bird returning to its nest for the night. A giggle, Samantha listening to her dad tell a story. Kyzyl got an uneasy feeling as he climbed the last flight of stairs to his room in the attic.

He didn't want to believe he was going crazy, but maybe the mental strain of spellcasting was beginning to take its toll. He certainly wouldn't have been the first student that cracked under the strain of it all. He laid down on his bed, and sleep met him the moment he closed his eyes.

CHAPTER THIRTEEN
A Spark of Insight

Kyzyl awoke later than usual. The sun was already fully in the sky, and he could smell bacon from down stairs. He walked down into the main bar area to Seth's greeting.

"Ay, boy. I was beginning to think you weren't going to come out of that room of yours. You been sleeping all this time?"

Kyzyl nodded.

"That's a good thing. With how late you've been stayin' with your friends and how early you get up each morning you haven't been getting the sleep a body need."

"There aren't enough hours in the day, Seth. I want to spend time with my friends, but there's so much for me to learn here. Not to mention Bethany."

Seth chuckled. "Poor boy. The lady been keeping you up with tending her needs. I remember those days. Enjoy it while it's lasting. Soon you'll both be tired from just getting through the day, and you won't have the energy for such things. 'Course, she'll still be wigglin' her butt on you to try and provoke you if she's anythin' like my little pixie."

Kyzyl heard a voice from the kitchen say something vulgar and Seth simply smiled and winked.

Kyzyl chuckled a bit and shook his head.

"Breakfast is coming out soon. Will you be staying since you don't have a class to get to?"

"I'd love some. Smells like you have bacon in the pan."

"Ay, and a fresh baked loaf too. Plenty of eggs and milk to go with it if you want."

"If you're selling, I'm buying." Kyzyl winked. All his meals had been paid for when he and Seth renewed their deal at the beginning of the term. The middle-aged innkeeper seemed to be happy to take Kyzyl's offer, and Kyzyl was beginning to see why. Other than Donovan and Emrys, the Noble steed saw very few regulars.

Two crowns, while a pittance to the noble families that sent their children to the university to study, were plenty to keep the inn stocked and the doors open, but Seth and his family didn't seem to be growing rich with all the competition they had to deal with. Kyzyl was glad he could help.

Kyzyl finished his breakfast and told Seth he was heading to the library to get more work done on his new project. He didn't mention to him that he still wasn't wholly sure what that project was going to be.

Kyzyl saw Siradyl in the courtyard on his way to the library. He started to walk toward the other side. However, Siradyl walked briskly over to meet him, holding up his hand in greeting. Kyzyl groaned internally, but tried to keep his face friendly. Whatever else Siradyl was, he was a powerful noble, and Kyzyl knew how to deal with nobles.

"Ah, foreigner, good. I'm glad I caught up with you. I wanted to congratulate you on your defeat of the Master Cleric during the Harvest Festival. You were able to show a great deal of restraint and deftness by avoiding an embarrassing defeat."

"Thank you... I think."

Siradyl nodded. "I was surprised to see such a close

victory. With the Masters, they usually find ways to keep themselves from looking foolish. I was expecting either a victory so complete it looked handed to you, or a total defeat."

"What do you mean?"

"Why do you think Head Master Herman was judging the event? The Masters are always very controlling over their image, and I heard the two of them discussing the scoring beforehand. I suspected they were coming up with a plan to make you look foolish, but it seems you moved through their laid trap with a charismatic grace."

Several questions started to rise into Kyzyl's mind at that moment. Why was Siradyl telling him this? Were Master Jonah and Head Master Herman really trying to make him look foolish? Perhaps Master Jonah was much more like the sages in Hanra after all.

He felt a rage well up in him that he'd never felt before. Here this man was, pretending to be open-minded, while in the background, manipulating everyone he could to make himself look like the person with all the answers. The anger formed a small lump in his gut that felt foreign to him.

He was reminded of Siradyl's presence when the elf made a curt bow to him and said, "I shall not underestimate you like that in the future." He walked off after that, leaving Kyzyl to his angry thoughts.

"I see," came a voice from nowhere. "You wish to expose this 'Master Jonah' for the fool he is. Yes. Help me, and I will help you."

Kyzyl didn't know where the voice was coming from, but he knew what he was going to do now. If Master Jonah wanted to scare people with stories of gods, angels, and demons, then Kyzyl would show everyone what a demon really looked like.

A plan started to form in his thoughts. He knew there were books in the library that proposed that legends and myths about demons came from exaggerated stories of natural creatures. He also knew the library contained a vast collection of spells, including summoning spells. He'd already found one that claimed to summon a demon.

After he proved that demons were nothing but mythologized animals, he'd be in a prime position to expose clerics, sages, and all of the faith-based charlatans for the frauds they were.

When he got to the library, he approached the student at the front desk and asked for the sign-up sheet for practice rooms. Each building had a number of rooms built specifically for practicing new spells, and most were built to accommodate the specialties of each type of magic. Divination spells weren't likely to cause a huge explosion and trying to build around that need for such spells would be a waste of resources.

"What spells are you going to be practicing?"

"For now, a couple of wards and abjuration spells."

The student took out a thick leather ledger book that contained the date and time slots for each of the abjuration practice rooms. Kyzyl signed up for three of the open slots in the upcoming week. The rest of his time he could spend researching the subject of his summoning spell.

The student put the ledger away and Kyzyl signed into the library to do further research. He went to the part of the library where he found the first book on the fables and mythology of demons. There, he found other books by the same author, but none of them where a follow up on their original study on the subject.

Kyzyl sighed. He was in the largest archive of knowledge on this side of the world. Many of the shelves were barely organized at all, and many of those were organized in different ways. He couldn't begin to know how to find the books he needed.

Something occurred to him as the scale of his

problem unfolded itself before him. Emrys knew a great deal about how to find books on the right subjects. A great deal of that came from working in the library under Head Master Herman, but not all of it.

Emrys also used divination spells to memorize and locate the books he needed. It was one of the things the young half elf couldn't help but show off during their time studying for the debate. He boasted about how Bethany and Donovan always came back with one or two books each while he found a half dozen or more.

Kyzyl didn't know the first thing about divination magic, but he had summoned something before without knowing what it was. He found a part of the library that was off the main paths and closed his eyes. He imagined the sort of book he wanted: a simple leather-bound tome. He thought of the pages of parchment and the information they might have on them. He held tight to the one word the book would need to contain: "demon."

Going through the motions of the object summoning spell was so ingrained into Kyzyl's mind that he didn't need to be in Wind-Dance to perform it. He moved through the motions the way you pick up a spoon or take a step. Within moments his hands closed around a tome of soft brown leather with no title on the front.

Kyzyl opened the book and glanced at a few of the pages. It seemed to be a fictionalized guide through the lower planes of existence. Chapter by chapter, the author brought "you," Kyzyl was not used to books being written in second person, through the many tiers of the three main places where souls could be damned for all eternity.

It was an interesting bit of trivia, but barely mentioned anything about the demons that were meant to be the planes' primary inhabitants. Kyzyl also realized that, because he didn't know what part of the library this book had come from, he didn't know where it was meant to go. He resigned himself to finding more information about demons the old fashioned way.

It took Kyzyl about a month to master the three wards individually. When he couldn't get slots in the practice chambers in the Abjuration Hall, which still struck him as more of a military fort than a proper university campus, he spent time studying in the library.

Most of the hours were spent trying to find the pockets of organization that contained information about the creature he intended to summon, but some amount of it was on trying to unpack the summoning itself. The spell had been designed in a very strange way, and it seemed to Kyzyl not to have a source of power.

In the first week he'd spent in the library, he'd discovered the name of the spell's author, and it seemed he'd cultivated quite the reputation for himself. There were a number of treatises and essays, no doubt written by clerics, that colored the man as some kind of mad cultist. A number of people accused him of worshiping some kind of demonic exarch, but Kyzyl suspected that a great deal of those accusations arose from the man attempting to do the same as Kyzyl.

Kyzyl wondered how people would think of him once his project was finished. Would clerics like Master Jonah try to discredit him with similar accusations?

He hoped that he would at least have the backing of other arcane practitioners like the other Masters and the students here. What he found about this man told a different story, however. Kyzyl couldn't find a single contemporary scholar that seemed to have anything but hatred for this wizard.

Kyzyl felt the welt of anger move in his stomach again. This was no doubt the influence of the Lukoran church at work. Kyzyl was getting tired of theocracy getting in the way of true scholarship.

Still, the vitriol that people seemed to have for this man made Kyzyl want to step more carefully with his project. If the wrong people got the wrong idea before he could complete his work and put together his own findings, things would probably go very wrong for him. The Masters were reasonable people, but Kyzyl had no doubt they'd punish him to protect the reputation of the school.

\#

It was an especially frigid winter morning when Kyzyl was able to master holding all three spells in his mind at once. He'd moved to a conjuration practice room under the pretext of being ready to summon his new subject.

He summoned small pebbles from a nearby stream and threw them, one at a time, at the barrier to ensure it would hold. Next, he used a spell he'd learned under Master Enwin to summon a bull from a nearby farm, had it charge the barrier, and the barriers held. He dismissed the bull back where it came from, not wanting to be accused of stealing anything.

Kyzyl released the barriers and felt a cold gush of wind as the air moved to equalize the pressure differential his summoning spells had caused. He was ready to get to work on the last spell he wanted to learn.

Kyzyl practiced the incantation until he had it memorized. Then he moved on to the hand motions. He continued to practice until he was confident that each of the spell's pieces had been memorized flawlessly.

Practicing the pieces apart from one another proved to be rather easy, suspiciously easy. All the formulae and glyphs seemed odd, but real. Still, Kyzyl wondered if the spell he was studying was authentic. Real spells were complicated and it was easy to simplify them to the point they could pass for a real spell without really doing anything.

Kyzyl continued studying the glyph, trying to determine its authenticity as he exited the practice room and walked out into the street. There, he found Master Jonah exiting the university temple where exams were held. Master Jonah greeted Kyzyl with a wave of his hand, and Kyzyl felt the welt of hot anger stir deep in his gut. It felt foreign, like it wasn't his, and he was trying to figure out where it was coming from when Master Jonah spoke.

"Mister Shenta, I've heard you've been studying rather diligently since you've been put on independent study. I have no doubt that this has proven to everyone here that Master Enwin was right to recommend it for you. Although, I must admit, I do miss our classroom discussions."

"I'm sure Emrys and the others are able to fill the void my absence has left in your life." Kyzyl did his best to keep the venom out of his voice as he continued to struggle with this rage he didn't understand.

Kyzyl's tone did not escape Master Jonah's notice. He adopted a very stern expression and began, "I trust you remember our discussion about your attitude and showing me..." Master Jonah trailed off as he looked closer at Kyzyl's face.

Kyzyl. Look at me." Master Jonah's tone was harder than stone, and Kyzyl rose his face toward Master Jonah before realizing what he was doing. Master Jonah took Kyzyl's chin in his hand with a gentle force. Master Jonah's gaze bore into Kyzyl's eyes. It made Kyzyl feel uncomfortably exposed, and he started trying to think of a way to excuse himself.

Before he could, Master Jonah spoke, "if something is bothering you, or it begins to at any moment, you can come to me Kyzyl. I know I am not your favorite Master, but the safety of each of my students is my... rather it is our... the Masters' greatest priority. I wish to be a resource to you, if you'll allow me."

Kyzyl couldn't help but hear the distress in the Master's voice. He started to feel appreciative of the Master Cleric before his anger reasserted itself. It was as if it had a will of its own.

Kyzyl decided he didn't want to risk blurting out something offensive as he struggled to keep the rage under control. He muttered out an apology and left Master Jonah standing in the street confused.

Kyzyl walked to the Noble Steed, taking stock of his emotions along the way. Master Jonah was being kind to him and, regardless of what happened at the debate, was always willing to help his students learn. So, why was Kyzyl feeling more enmity for him? It simply wasn't reasonable.

As Kyzyl walked through the door to the main floor of the inn, Seth looked up at him and gestured for Kyzyl to come to the bar.

"Your lady friend came in asking after you. I told her you were likely out and about practicing whatever odd witchcraft you were working on this semester."

Seth smirked a bit. When Kyzyl started living at the Noble Steed, it was hard to tell if Seth was comfortable with all the magic that was around him constantly. Now it seemed that, while the man might have his reservations about it, he was perfectly willing to settle into a joking descent.

Kyzyl wondered what the average person must see when a wizard comes to them able to do so many difficult to explain things. Seth and his family had the luxury of being exposed to the university and its many students. Bad things happened here on occasion, and every student heard at least a dozen stories about what happens when magic goes awry. But if all you have is legends of mighty heroes and sorcerers that make pacts with demons, it would be easy to get the wrong idea, like Baerûn's father.

"Did she mention if she was free tonight?" Kyzyl asked after he realized what Seth had said.

"She may have. I told her you'd be back for dinner if nothing else. No one under my roof skips a meal, and you know that well enough."

Kyzyl nodded. "Sounds like I might be having a guest for dinner. I hope you don't mind."

"Thing about running an inn is that there is always room at the table for another person."

Kyzyl smiled at the warmth in the man's voice. He

still wasn't used to the easy hospitality Seth and his family were ready to give to anyone who walked through their door. Kyzyl looked around the empty taproom and couldn't help but feel they deserved better than a struggling inn.

Kyzyl had a few drinks while Seth and his wife finished getting dinner ready. Kyzyl was two drinks in when Bethany walked through the door and nearly tackled him with an excited embrace. He buried his face in her forearm and let her flowery scent fill his senses.

Seth greeted Bethany warmly and Samantha ran up and hugged her shins. When Bethany knelt down to introduce herself, Samantha pointed at a braid in her hair.

"Can you do mine like that?" she asked with amazement.

"Of course, but I think your dad wants to get dinner started. How about after we eat?"

Samantha nodded, and everyone chose a spot at the bar to sit. Bethany filled Joanne in on the gossip she gleamed from her work while Seth and Kyzyl listened to Samantha tell a story about an interesting rock she found in the woods.

The evening went by pleasantly, and it wasn't long before Bethany was pulling Kyzyl away from the bar for another stroll through the starry night. The night air was cold enough that breathing at the wrong time made Kyzyl think of icy daggers scratching his lungs.

He was thankful for the woolen cloak he'd traded for and doubly thankful Bethany had thought to bring one herself. He'd have given her his, but he would've been miserable without it. A night like this was a night meant for forethought not chivalry.

"Have you ever thought about the moon?" There was no preamble to Bethany's question, and Kyzyl wasn't sure what to make of it.

"Every once in a while, I'll see it hanging in the sky.

Why do you ask?"

"It just occurs to me that, if you don't believe in any gods or anything, what do you think the moon is. According to the clerics in Calcut, the moon is the King of the Night, and he moves between the Fey Realm and here. That's why the moon changes phases. But you don't believe in gods or fairies, so what makes the moon change?"

"I... I never thought of that. I guess it would largely depend on what the moon is. It could be something transient. For instance, if it was a ball of sand or dirt that kept crumbling and reforming, that would explain why it seems to change."

"So, the moon is a ball of sand?"

"Possibly. Again, it depends. It could be another round object like our world, but really far away. Sort of like how a giant oak tree can look like a sapling if you're far enough away."

"Can anything be that far away? Isn't there a limit to how high up you can go before you hit something?" Bethany stared up at the night sky, as if trying to see what she might hit if she kept going up.

"Like what?"

"I don't know. The sky perhaps. Maybe the edge of reality."

Kyzyl thought about that for a long time. Bethany's question about the moon sparked a number of other questions in his head. He thought about how to approach the idea of asking her a few, but wanted to do it carefully. "Suppose, for a moment, you are skeptical of the existence of gods like me."

"That's an interesting opening."

"Go with me on this journey. You don't believe in gods or the afterlife or any of that. The moon, for all you know, is a ball of sand somebody hung from the sky on a string."

"What an odd world this is. Is this what life's like for

you every day? I can see why you want to study so much."

Kyzyl looked at her, confusion written on his face. "What do you mean?"

"I mean, without the gods to help explain things, you have to resort to calling the moon a ball of sand. Without an afterlife, you have to wonder what happens when we die or where our lives come from in the first place. There are so many questions you have to answer all on your own. It's interesting, but seems like it could get overwhelming. Do you ever feel lonely in this confusing world of yours?"

"Not since I met you."

That made her smile. "You had a question, and I interrupted. I'm sorry. Please, continue."

"I..." Kyzyl stammered. He realized that the fluting sound of her voice as she wondered out loud had drained him of all of his questions. "I have completely forgotten where I was going with my thoughts."

"Does this happen often? Forgetting where you're going?"

"More often now that there's someone to distract me."

She made a show of looking hurt, and he took her hand in both of his.

"However, one of my teachers once told me that a destination is not a requirement for a good journey."

Bethany pulled Kyzyl into a warm embrace. His skin became covered in goose-flesh and he couldn't tell if it was the cold, the closeness, or something else. Bethany seemed to be the only person Kyzyl enjoyed being physically close to.

They continued to talk idly until the evening turned into late night. The chill got deeper and Kyzyl walked Bethany back to the brothel, which doubled as a boarding house for some of the women who worked there.

She made a comment about how nice it was to have

a wizard as her body guard, and Kyzyl didn't mention that
he just wanted to spend as much time with her as possible.
She gave him a long, deep kiss goodnight that involved just
enough tongue that, when she pulled away, Kyzyl had to
wait a moment before walking was comfortable again.

CHAPTER FOURTEEN
The Summoning

Kyzyl awoke and went straight to studying his notes on the demon summoning. He didn't realize how long he had been up until Seth came upstairs to fetch him for breakfast. He asked Seth to bring it to his room because he was fitting pieces of the spell together in his mind and didn't want to stop while the inspiration was flowing.

He studied the gestures and words and realized it was much more like a prayer than an arcane chant. He recognized some of the sigils he had written down from some of the religious texts he read in preparation for the debate. These symbols were older, however, and seemed to bear a striking resemblance to the conjuration sigils he was familiar with.

If this spell truly worked to summon something that people could be convinced was a demon, the symbols and chants of this spell could be incorporated into religious rites as a way of fending off demons. Without the practiced mind of a spell caster, the chants and symbols wouldn't do much, but they would sound like magic.

Kyzyl's mind began to flood with ideas. He started taking down notes in a form of short hand he developed as a way to allow his hands to keep up with his racing mind.

Once he mastered the spell and summoned the creature that served as its subject, he could use both the spell and creature as evidence that modern religious doctrine was derived from misunderstandings of arcane theory. That revelation would blow a huge hole in the entire idea of the supernatural and Master Jonah would...

Kyzyl paused in his writing. Master Jonah would what? Resign in disgrace? Did Kyzyl really want to take away a man's livelihood just because they disagreed on something? He thought for a moment.

If Master Jonah maintained his position under false pretenses, it would be reasonable to reveal them as false and let whatever happens take its course. Master Jonah would understand that Kyzyl was merely trying to do what he was encouraging him to do: come to a more complete truth about the world. Still, the idea that Kyzyl might be responsible for making someone leave the university made him sad. This was such a wonderful place, and he couldn't imagine a better one for any scholar to be.

He decided, whatever the result, the truth should be sought for its own sake. Kyzyl picked up his pen and continued writing.

\#

When Kyzyl finally did go downstairs for lunch, Seth was wiping down the bar.

"Ay, there he is. Finally emerged from your study-cave, eh?"

"Yes sir. I had a question. Is there somewhere I could get a lamb or some kind of small animal?"

"Can't you just summon one up with your fancy magic?"

Kyzyl shook his head. "It has to come from somewhere, and I intend on keeping it. I doubt the Masters would be pleased if I used their lessons for stealing."

"Ay, they would not be. I remember a couple years back, maybe five or so, they strung up a student who made a habit out of taking gold from the banks. Not sure how he managed to undo their wards, and no one else has been able to figure it out. Guess that secret died with him."

Kyzyl tried not to look as terrified as he was. He had been mere days away from trying something similar when he found out how much his wardrobe was worth. Then something else occurred to him. "The Masters have the right to execute people?"

Seth nodded. "The nine Masters of the university have the ability to act as a court appointed by the crown. At least, that's what the magistrate said that oversaw the execution. He stopped in for a drink afterward and we got to talkin'."

"What else did you two talk about?"

"Not much. He went on and on about the crown, and Strophe's unique legal system. I remember a bit of it, but not enough to be useful to anyone. You'd be better off going to the library and asking for a copy of the <u>Codex Arcanum</u>. I remember the magistrate saying that's the university's law book. So, a wise student would familiarize himself with it." Seth gave Kyzyl a wink and a friendly smile.

"We got off track," he continued, "you said you're looking for a small animal? I think one of the farmers has a nanny goat whose kids are just about ready to be weaned. You could ask to buy one off him. What do you need it for anyway?"

Kyzyl didn't want to tell him the truth, that the spell he planned to cast called for "blood of an innocent." He assumed the author of the spell was merely being dramatic, but blood was filled with trace elements and compounds that make a good source of chemical energy until it congeals.

Kyzyl settled on a simple lie. "I'm thinking of taking anatomy with Master Telma, but I want to see what I can come up with on my own. I have a reputation of being an exceptional student I have to maintain."

"You're going to dissect it?" Seth looked very uncomfortable. "I wouldn't tell the farmers that. Not everyone is quite as used to you, wizardly types, as I am." His face didn't seem to suggest he was used to the idea of someone poking and prodding a carcass.

Kyzyl thanked him for the advice and finished his lunch. Then he took a midday stroll to some of the farms, asking about their livestock. Winter was well on its way and Kyzyl's warm and well-tailored clothes made it clear he'd pay good money for the animal he was asking for. Still, most families insisted that they needed to keep their livestock at least until the planting season.

Eventually, Kyzyl came across the farm Seth had mentioned. The nanny goat was sitting with her kid outside the farmhouse. When Kyzyl knocked on the door, a slim man with hollow eyes opened it and greeted him with a smile. Kyzyl made a slight bow, which he'd learned was the customary greeting for nobles of equal rank in Strophe. The farmer gave him an odd look as his eyes went to Kyzyl's woolen cloak and thick fur boots.

"I'm sorry to disturb you on this chilly afternoon, sir. I heard you had a kid that was about ready to be weaned off its mother's milk, and I was hoping to buy it off you." Kyzyl presented the man with two round silver nobles.

The farmers eyes widened. Kyzyl could see the wheels in his head spinning. Two silver nobles meant a warm winter for a family that was struggling. It meant a safety net and money to buy seed grain when the weather warmed.

The farmer looked up at Kyzyl. "She ain't got much meat on her yet. She wouldn't be any good for a feast."

Kyzyl shook his head. "I have a lady friend that's been missing her life on the farm. I thought a pet goat would make her feel less homesick."

The farmer relaxed a little. He nodded and Kyzyl gave him the money. The farmer showed Kyzyl how to carry the kid so she wouldn't squirm. Kyzyl gave him a warm thanks and farewell. The farmer bowed low as Kyzyl began to walk away.

Kyzyl took the kid the to a secluded part of the woods by the university. He summoned a knife, a flask, large mixing bowl, and wooden funnel from the Nobel Steed. Seth was used to him borrowing things from the inn. He'd make sure to replace them before they were missed.

Kyzyl stabbed the knife through the goat's jugular. It spasmed as blood poured out the over side into the bowl. He had to kneel with his knee on the goat's side to keep it from moving too much. His arm shook both from the force needed to bury the knife in the goat's neck and from the emotional strain of watching the light leave the poor beast's eyes.

He felt a tear run down his cheek, and, since he was alone, he didn't fight back. He let out a single strained sob for the loss of life and quietly hoped that it wouldn't be for nothing. If his plan worked, the world would be a more enlightened place, and this small, innocent creature, would not have died in vain.

\#

"What are we doing here Kyzyl?" Emrys asked. Kyzyl had brought him, Donovan, and Bethany to the Conjuration Building to witness the culmination of his independent project. The term was coming to a close and winter's first snow fall was beginning to cover the streets.

"I'm going to show the three of you what I've been working on since I was given free reign by the Masters. Ever since the debate, I've been wanting to do something like this." Kyzyl stepped in front of the circle he'd prepared with the three wards he'd been studying.

The room itself was large and mostly featureless. Their side, which was closest to the only door, had a simple stone bench and a table Kyzyl had moved to the far corner of the room.

The rest of the floor was taken up by the prepared circle. Donovan looked closely at the air above the circle, and Kyzyl spotted him looking up at the ceiling.

"Are you still worried about what happened at the debate? Look, I thought we decided that Master Jonah just wanted you to get a feel for his side of the argument," Emrys said.

"We did. This has little to do with the debate itself. This has more to do with dispelling a myth that is still common among your people.

"Donovan, I see you've noticed the enclosure I've prepared. It reaches all the way up to the ceiling and nothing can penetrate it from either side."

"Looks like you learned a lot from your class on wards," the older man commented. "Are you sure they'll hold whatever it is you'll be summoning?"

"I've tested under the most strain I can place upon it. I even summoned a bull from one of the nearby farms to ensure it is structurally sound."

Donovan nodded. "Sounds like you've done your homework. What are we here to see you summon? You said a bull?"

Kyzyl shook his head. "The bull was just a test run. Although, I do have to say, summoning living creatures is way more complicated than I originally anticipated.

"No, I'm summoning something much more noteworthy. After all, I have a reputation to maintain. I'm going to let the three of you be the first to watch me summon a real, living, breathing, demon."

"What?" Donovan said, jumping up and grabbing Kyzyl's shoulders. "Have the books and spells gotten to you that bad man? Do you know what the Masters would do to you if you tried to summon something like that? Forget expulsion, they'd turn you over to the courts and have you tried for... something, I'm sure!"

"Relax. I'm not actually summoning a demon."

Everyone let out a great sigh of relief.

"I'm going to summon one of the creatures everyone mistakes for a demon. I found a spell that summons what the author claims is a demon, but when I studied it, I realized it had to be an offshoot of an older spell, and confusion and years of legends made everyone believe that creature was a demon. I plan to write a paper explaining everything after I have the creature as proof."

"My love," Bethany said. "If what you're saying is true, then whatever you do summon is likely to be dangerous. Are you sure this is a good idea?"

"That's what the barriers are for," Kyzyl explained. He summoned a pebble and threw it. Before it crossed the threshold of the circle he'd drawn in chalk, it stopped and bounced back at him with equal force.

"I've been testing them all term with everything I can throw at them. They won't budge as long as I keep my concentration."

"Even if you can prove that what you summon isn't something supernatural, that would merely prove that spells cast by first-year university students don't have the power to call on the demonic. Not exactly compelling evidence for its nonexistence. Maybe you just found a bunk spell," Emrys pointed out.

"I don't think the grimoire I found has any bunk spells in it."

"Hold that thought," Donovan said, raising his hand, "you said grimoire? Was this a red book with ink that could pass for blood?"

"The <u>Grimoire of Demonic Invocation</u>. Honestly, I'm surprised that a wizard would be so dramatic, but I guess some of us do enjoy our fanfare."

Everyone but Kyzyl went ashen. "Do you know whose spellbook that was?" Emrys asked.

"Does it matter? The spell is what matters." Kyzyl turned toward the space he'd prepared for the creature's arrival. "Whatever I summon will be locked behind three containment spells I learned just for this experiment: the anti-kinetic one you already saw, there's also an anti-thermal, and a general sealing barrier to attach the others to. Nothing will be able to move through that system of wards. It will be safe in there, and we will be safe out here."

His three friends gave Kyzyl an uneasy look, but they sat down and let him finish his spells. When he brought out the ingredients for the summoning spell; salt, sulfur, and the goat's blood, Bethany grabbed Donovan's wrist and held on until her knuckles turned white.

"Our boy knows what he's doing," Donovan assured her. His face told her he was trying to convince himself as well as her. Still, she swallowed and nodded, but her eyes were wide and fixed, unblinking on the magic circle in the middle of the room. The arcane sigils began dancing and spinning around until they were nothing but a blur.

Soon the air above the circle began to shift as Kyzyl's chanting reached a crescendo and the blood in the bowl evaporated. A hideous laugh began to bellow out of the circle as a dark, muscular form began to take shape. It was vaguely humanoid, save for the bat wings that were forming on its back and the claws appearing on the end of its fingers.

"Impudent fool!" a familiar voice called. Kyzyl faltered for just a moment, but it was all the creature needed. With a sweep of its claws, the barriers Kyzyl had worked tirelessly to master shattered like glass. A shard of hardened air flew past and cut Kyzyl's cheek.

The demon beat its massive wings and punched through the wooden ceiling leading to the floors above. Soon the walls began to tremble, Emrys and Donovan lunged toward Kyzyl, and the building began to crumble.

CHAPTER FIFTEEN
The Fallen

Kyzyl pushed against the heavy stones that were weighing him and his two friends down. They wouldn't budge. There was barely enough room for the three of them and they would run out of air soon. His heart started to pound as he tried again, in vain, to lift the impossibly large chunk of wall.

He considered himself lucky. Buildings, especially ones designed to hold practicing mages, were designed to stand. Which meant that when they fell, they created pockets as material falls into a new structure.

He heard Donovan begin to chant and he wondered what sort of spell he knew to get them out of this situation. Then, he heard a grunt and the rubble on top of them began to shift. He looked. Donovan was pushing the rubble off them, so they could dig their way out.

When they were free of their rubble prison, Donovan looked down at him. "That's why alteration magic is best. There's no way you would've been able to summon something to lift this stuff up when we could barely fit under it."

Kyzyl looked around at the destruction he'd caused. Where the Conjuration Building once stood there was now only rubble and dust. He watched, unblinking, as older students with more magical prowess sprang to action to help Master Enwin save as many people caught in the collapse as possible. Kyzyl just stood there. He couldn't register what he had done. Then something occurred to him. "Bethany," he said. "Where's Bethany?"

"There," someone said. Kyzyl couldn't tell if it was Emrys or Donovan. He looked to see a small feminine hand poking out of a pile of rubble. Kyzyl ran. He knelt and started digging out the woman he loved. He broke when he saw what had happened to her, what he had done to her. The rubble had crushed her torso, so it caved in on itself. Her face, however, was untouched. It was still painted with the fear and anxiety of watching her beloved summon a creature of pure evil. Kyzyl's hands shook as he brushed the hair from her face. Her skin was still warm, but not nearly as warm as it had once been.

"No." Kyzyl could feel tears welling up inside him. He'd come to this cornerstone of civilization to learn how to master himself and the world around him. He'd met someone who made him feel like giving up control didn't always have to be scary. Now she was dead, and it was his fault.

He felt a hand touch his shoulder and he flinched. Then he heard Master Enwin's voice. "Kyzyl? Kyzyl what happened?"

Kyzyl didn't answer. He just sat there, trying to come to terms with what he had done. How many more people were crushed under the weight of his mistake? He heard Master Enwin talking with Emrys and Donovan, but it seemed so far away. He just stared blankly at Bethany's fearful expression.

Donovan tugged at his arm and said something about taking Kyzyl somewhere. He tore his eyes away from Bethany's broken body, not wanting to look at her any more. He felt sick. His stomach lurched, and he vomited. Donovan yelled, and Kyzyl felt something hard hit the back of his head. Then all he saw was darkness.

\#

Kyzyl woke up in a soft, clean bed. He was naked, but covered with a white sheet. One of Master Telma's students was taking notes on a clip board. "What..." that was all that would come out of Kyzyl's mouth. He felt groggy, like he was on the verge of slipping back into unconsciousness.

"A clay roof tile fell off some of the rubble while it was being moved. It struck you in the back of the head. You're lucky you weren't paralyzed."

Kyzyl didn't feel lucky. He remembered now. He had summoned a demon, a real one, and it had knocked down the Conjuration Building. Suddenly unconsciousness didn't seem so bad and he fell back asleep.

The next time he woke up, he was surrounded by Donovan, Matilda, Emrys, and both Master Jonah and Master Enwin.

"Hey, how do you feel?" Emrys asked.

Kyzyl didn't answer right away. He just looked at Matilda. Her back was straight, and her face didn't betray any emotion. "I'm sorry," he said finally. It was mostly directed at Matilda who just looked down.

"I'm not going to pretend like I knew this would happen, but I tried to tell the two of you it would end badly."

"Kyzyl, your friends have told us that the reason the building fell was that you had summoned a demon and let it loose. Is that true?" Master Jonah asked. His voice betrayed no emotion, which was unusual for him. The Master was always filled with an encouraging energy that Kyzyl didn't appreciate until now when it was gone.

"That's not exactly true. I had sought out a spell that was meant to summon a demon because I wanted to prove that they were just a myth. I studied spells meant to contain it, but it wasn't enough. I faltered on my concentration when I heard its voice, and it broke free."

"Why Kyzyl? Why would you do something like this?" Master Enwin's voice was a mixture of lament and surprise.

"I just wanted to prove that... I... I don't know."

"You wanted to discredit me. Didn't you Kyzyl?" Master Jonah said.

"I'm so sorry, Master. You told me to let go of my resentment, but I didn't listen. Now people are dead, and their blood is on my hands." Kyzyl broke down into tears. Between his great heaving sobs, he could only let out one word. "Bethany."

Later, the student in charge of Kyzyl's care made it clear that he wouldn't be released for at least two weeks. The Masters had canceled classes, citing a time of mourning for the lost. This allowed Emrys and Donovan to spend a great deal of time visiting with their friend.

"I'm so glad you guys are here. They're making me stay in this bed, and there's nothing to do but think about everyone I hurt."

"About that," Emrys said, "the Masters are waiting for you to be well enough to stand trial."

Kyzyl nodded. "Seth had mentioned to me that the Masters had been given the right by the crown to act as a court."

"The university is older than the crown itself. Generations of Masters have guarded their authority over university matters. That's why the Masters are so, uh, judicious with their punishments," Emrys said. He shifted uncomfortably from foot to foot.

Kyzyl nodded. "Whatever punishment they decide is what I deserve. It's going to take a lifetime for me to make this up to Master Enwin. He trusted me, and I let him down."

Donovan shook his head. "Kid, you don't get it. They're talking about executing you."

"Executing? Is there anything I can do?"

"Only Master Jonah seems against it," Emrys said. "He wants you to have the chance to make things right."

"What does that mean?"

"He wants you to send the demon back where it came from," Donovan said.

"Great, my only ally and it's because he expects me to do the impossible."

"I brought you this." Emrys handed him a book. The cover read <u>Codex Arcanum</u>. It was the main book of the university's laws. "We have to go. Read up on this and see if you can craft a defense." The two left and Kyzyl started reading.

It was only after he had studied the Codex that he understood what a huge crime he'd committed. Some of the very first laws written by the university's founders were specifically about dealing with the demonic and it was very clear that it was expressly forbidden under any circumstances.

Kyzyl suspected that was the influence of the Church at work, but it didn't matter now. Kyzyl had broken a law that had formed the bedrock of the university's legal code. Was there a way to defend against such a basic trespass?

The day came when Master Telma declared Kyzyl to be in perfect health, and Kyzyl suspected that Master Telma wouldn't bother waiting to tell the other Masters of his recovery. He had a day at most before he was brought before them. He made his way straight to Emrys. Kyzyl knocked furiously on the door that the innkeeper indicated as his.

When Emrys opened he started talking rapidly. "Emrys," he said, "I don't have a whole lot of time before I have to face them. I need help. What's the fastest way out of the university?"

"Whoa! Hey, what are you talking about?"

"They're going to execute me. They're going to hang me from the gallows in the busiest courtyard they can find. I have to get out of here. I'm going to need supplies but I can get them in the next town over, right? I'm sure there's plenty of merchants there that can—"

Emrys smacked Kyzyl with such force it made him almost bit his tongue. Kyzyl's first thought was, "good idea. They can't prosecute me if I'm still in the infirmary." Then he looked at Emrys' face. It was more serious and somber than Kyzyl had ever seen with none of the usual jovial undertones.

"Think about what you're saying Kyzyl. You're talking about trying to run away from the nine most powerful wizards in the known world. Head Master Herman has been studying divination for decades, Master Enwin can summon anything from anywhere, and Master Telma has your blood. What makes you think you can hide from them?"

Kyzyl dropped on to the floor as the weight of what Emrys was saying crashed on top of him. "You're right. I'm doomed. No matter what I do I'm doomed."

"You're not doomed," Emrys sighed. "Look, while you were recovering in the infirmary, I was getting a handle on just how much trouble you're in. The Masters' quarters have all kinds of enchantments and wards against divination and practically any other kind of method of magical spying, but they don't have those things everywhere. I was able to listen in on some of the Masters while they were talking about you."

"Yeah? What did they say? Anything hopeful?"

"They're all furious with you. You're right that most of them want to string you up. Master Enwin seemed especially disappointed."

"Is there anyone on my side?"

"Like I said, most of them want to string you up as an example to the other students. You broke some serious laws, Kyzyl."

"I know."

"Remember, Master Jonah is still as on your side as anyone can be in this."

"That hardly seems hopeful."

"You don't understand. The other Masters, Enwin included, are talking about you like you're a criminal. Master Jonah is speaking like this was some sort of lesson you needed to learn. I'm pretty sure he thinks you can make this right if you're given the chance."

"I don't think I can."

"Honestly, I don't know either. What I'm telling you is this: The other Masters respect Master Jonah a great deal. Between that and the fact that he literally teaches us how to persuade people, I'm willing to bet he's going to make sure you get to walk away in one piece. You'll still be expelled, there's no avoiding that, but you probably won't be executed."

"Forgive me if I don't jump with joy."

Just then, there was a knock on Emrys' door. When he opened it, a young boy of about ten shoved his way past and jogged over to Kyzyl. "I'm supposed to give this to you. You're expected in the Master's Hall immediately."

Kyzyl's heart sped up. He opened the message and saw that the Masters were able to organize a trial much faster than he'd expected. The message was specific that there was to be no delay, and Kyzyl suspected Head Master Herman would know if he did.

"Emrys, come with me. We need to work out my defense on the way there."

"OK, but I should warn you, Donovan and I already gave our testimonies, so lying to the Masters won't work. Sorry."

"Something tells me it wouldn't work regardless. I'm thinking I go with what you said about learning a lesson."

"What?"

"You said Master Jonah was talking like I needed to learn a lesson. What if I demonstrate to them that I have learned a lesson and I need to stay here to keep up with that lesson?"

"And what lesson is that exactly?"

"That summoning a demon is bad, obviously."

Emrys rolled his eyes. "Kyzyl, is that all you're getting out of this?"

"What do you mean?"

"Really? After all that time in the hospital? After we mourned Bethany together? All you have is 'summoning demons is bad'?"

Kyzyl paused and tried to think. What did Master Jonah want him to learn from all this? Emrys obviously knew, so why couldn't he just say it?

He was under a lot of pressure and facing the end of his life. Even if he wasn't executed, though Emrys' assessment wasn't all that reassuring, he was going to be forced to leave the one place he had dreamed about for as long as he wanted to be a mage.

"You killed Bethany. Because of your short-sighted, selfish actions, she's dead."

Kyzyl hung his head. "I know. It was a stupid, selfish, irresponsible decision brought about by my own over inflated ego."

Emrys nodded as he pushed open his door. "Good. I'm glad you understand that. Now go tell the Masters that, and they might just let you keep your head." Kyzyl swallowed as his hand went to his throat. He walked out the door to meet his fate.

The walk to the Masters' Hall took longer than normal. Between his heart beating and his legs nearly giving out from anxiety, Kyzyl had to concentrate on every step. By the time he got to the front door of the Hall, he was trying to push himself into the state of mind he used for spellcasting.

He walked down the long hallway to the last door at the end. He knocked on it.

"Enter," came the deep voice of Head Master Herman.

CHAPTER SIXTEEN
Fate Decided

The hall Kyzyl entered was lit by the glowing orbs he had come to associate with the buildings of the university. The room itself stretched so high that the light from the orbs didn't reach the ceiling, creating a sense that the room stretched into infinity.

Each of the nine Masters were dressed in black formal robes. They each wore their own grim expression with piercing gazes locked on Kyzyl that left him feeling completely exposed. His throat tightened and his limbs began to quiver as he looked around.

The nine Masters sitting at their raised table reminded Kyzyl of a painting he once saw in a high noble's house. It was called "Condemned" and had several dark figures looking down at a very small man cowering in the foreground.

Kyzyl looked to Master Jonah, but his face was a stone mask that revealed nothing. Head Master Herman spoke with a firm, ceremonial tone. "Kyzyl Shenta, you stand accused of reckless magical experimentation, demon worship, and several counts of reckless manslaughter. How do you plead?"

Kyzyl took a deep breath to calm his thundering

heart. He ignored the annoyance he felt at the Masters continuing to put his names in the wrong order. He opened his mouth once, but no sound came out. He breathed again and focused his mind the way practicing magic taught him.

"Head Master," he said. His voice held more conviction than he felt, and he hoped it would prove to be a boon. "I plead guilty on the accounts of experimentation and manslaughter, but I plead innocent on the count of demon worship."

"What say you in your defense?"

"Masters, I do not worship demons. In point of fact, as some of you may have heard, I don't worship anything. Until the recent tragedy happened, for which I take full responsibility, I did not believe in the supernatural.

"My intention, as misguided and foolish as it was, was not to worship the thing I summoned, but to prove it wasn't a demon. I discovered a spell in a reputable spellbook in the library that claimed to summon a demon.

"Upon further inspection, I realized the spell used sigils and chants that were reminiscent of prayers and religious iconography. That meant, if I could prove the spell itself summoned a creature devoid of supernatural powers, I could provide evidence that demonic superstition came from a misunderstanding of arcane practices."

"What was this reputable source you found in our library?"

"It was called the Grimoire of Demonic Invocation. It seemed a bit dramatic, but the spells appeared to be legitimate."

"Legitimate? Bah! That book is filled with dark things. I thought we destroyed all the copies we have." The outburst came from the Master Evoker.

Head Master Herman rapped his knuckles on the table for silence. "Mister Shenta, that book was written by a man most consider to be…" he paused, looking for a word, "unjustifiably cruel."

"I understand Head Master. I read a number of accounts by other people concerning the author of that book. However, since most of the texts came from clerics and other religious people, I assumed they had a vested interest in discrediting his work."

"It is always important to consider the source of your information, Kyzyl," Master Jonah said. "However, if several people describe a man as a monster, and the only source you have against such claims is the man himself, it would seem prudent to take the side of the former."

"Master Jonah, you were the one who warned us in class against groupthink. I realize now, of course, that I had my own biases to contend with in making a choice in who to believe, but I thought a fellow scholar deserved the benefit of the doubt."

Head Master Herman rapped his knuckles on the table again. "We are getting off track. Kyzyl, you said that your intention was to disprove the existence of the supernatural."

Kyzyl nodded.

"You assumed that a journeyman wizard's failure to summon a powerful force of evil and chaos would be sufficient?"

"I was not thinking straight, sir. I have been hearing voices and feeling overwhelmingly angry since the beginning of term. Such mental strain led me to believe that, through this experiment, I could satisfy my immature vendetta against Master Jonah."

"You thought your failure to produce a creature of supernatural evil would be enough to discredit one of the nine Masters?"

"Honestly Head Master, yes and no. I understood that proving nonexistence takes a great deal more than one failed summoning. Still, as I stated, I was not in my right mind and too sure of my own cleverness."

"Then you see now why what you did was foolish?"

"Yes, sir. With the benefit of hindsight, I see how my ego should've been set aside to ensure the safety of my peers."

There was a slight movement from one side of the table. Head Master Herman announced, "Master Conjurer, you have the floor."

"Kyzyl," Master Enwin said, "you were made aware of the dangers of summoning creatures you could not control from the very beginning of your training."

"Yes, Master Enwin. As I have already mentioned, my desire to prove myself clouded my judgment. I wanted to prove to you, the other Masters, and everyone at the university that I knew better than the Master Cleric. I thought I was more enlightened when, in reality, I was blind to all the things I didn't know."

Another movement came from the opposite side of the table. "Master Cleric. You have the floor," Head Master Herman announced.

"Thank you, Head Master," Master Jonah said. "Kyzyl, it takes a great deal of courage to stand here and admit to your short comings. That level of bravery is something I would see more of in the world. I heard that Head Master Herman has been allowing you to read up on the law code of this university."

Kyzyl nodded.

"So, you understand the seriousness of the crimes you have admitted to?"

Another nod.

The Master Cleric sat back and Head Master Herman took the floor again. "Would any Master like to speak on behalf of the accused?"

Master Enwin was first. "Kyzyl has shown a great deal of short sightedness in his most recent actions. However, that being said, I know him to be a dedicated and capable student. In our investigation, I have made myself familiar with the things Kyzyl did to prepare for his summoning.

"Firstly, the summoning itself took a great deal of preparation and mastery. This is not the type of spell one masters as a passing fancy. This took a level of time and dedication that I know the accused to be capable of.

"Secondly, the accused did also take the necessary precautions in erecting three separate barrier spells to contain the summoned creature. As any Master present can attest, holding concentration on up to four spells at one time is something few people accomplish while here at the university.

"Lastly, there is the issue of what went wrong. As I have stated, the concentration required for four different spells is no minor feat. It seems the accused faltered for a moment, which is all the beast needed to escape. In seeking a way out to the world at large, the demon damaged enough of the structural integrity of the Conjuration tower to have it fall.

"In summary, this was a tragedy to be sure. However, the accused is not without his redeeming qualities. He was willing to be responsible enough to break the rules while doing his best to maintain the spirit of them. He failed, and deserves to be punished for that failure. That is the situation as far as I can see it."

It was far from a ringing endorsement, but Kyzyl could hear a lot of conflict in the speech Master Enwin gave. He was clearly proud of everything his student had accomplished so far, but was vastly disappointed in the application of such talent.

Master Jonah spoke up next. "I have spent much of the time while Mister Shenta was in the hospital expressing my concern at the idea of putting him to death. As my colleague has pointed out, Mister Shenta is an exceptional student with a great deal of intelligence and knowledge. With the history of the Church, of which I am a representative, I am well aware of the dangers of destroying knowledge.

"I have made it clear that I fundamentally disagree with putting people to death, but in this case, I really must insist that we consider what is in front of us. Mister Shenta has admitted to his guilt, and I believe he has shown himself to be repentant. There is only one reasonable response: mercy."

There was a slight pause as the Head Master waited for any other inputs. "Seeing no other Master wishing to come forward, I hereby move us to the vote. All those in favor of pronouncing the accused guilty of the charges of reckless experimentation."

All nine masters raised their hands.

"The vote is unanimous. All those in favor of finding the accused guilty of demon worship."

Master Telma as well as the Master Artificer and Master Enchanter raised their hands.

"The count is three for, six and a half against. The accused is pronounced innocent of demon worship. All in favor of finding the accused guilty of manslaughter."

Only Master Jonah did not raise his hand.

"The count is eight and a half to one. The accused is found guilty of the charges of reckless magical experimentation and manslaughter. Kyzyl Shenta, do you have anything to declare before a punishment is pronounced?"

Kyzyl shook his head.

"As the Head Master I pronounce your punishment to be five single lashes and expulsion from the university. The punishment shall be carried out tomorrow at noon."

Kyzyl's heart sank. Being expelled from the university was as good as being executed. All the dreams he had of studying and becoming a great magician were dead. He felt empty as he walked out the door where Emrys was waiting.

"What's the verdict?"

"I'm to be whipped and expelled."

Emrys didn't hide the look of relief on his face. "So, you get to keep your head?"

Kyzyl looked down at his feet. "Yeah, but what's life worth if I'm not here? This was my dream. Where do I go? What do I do?"

Emrys considered the question, but before he could answer, Master Jonah approached them and put a comforting hand on Kyzyl's shoulder. "I know it's hard to be facing a life away from this place."

"Thank you, Master Jonah. If it weren't for you and Master Enwin, I would probably be getting executed tomorrow instead of whipped."

Master Jonah nodded. "It was not easy to convince Master Enwin to spare you. He takes these sorts of things very seriously, and he was very angry with you. Still, convincing him to merely give a recount of the events, as far as his investigation could tell, helped. I think once he said them out loud, even he had to recognize that what you did was not out of malice or evil desires."

"Yes, sir. I still don't know what I'm going to do now that I can't be here."

"The Masters have been discussing that as well. Once I got them to entertain the idea of not executing you, most of them agreed that you would be expected to set things right."

"Are you saying the Masters expect me to defeat a demon?"

"No. Most of them expect you to perish in the attempt. They think it is more likely that, after you die, the Church will dispatch a demon hunter to take care of the issue."

"The church has demon hunters?"

"It's more of an honorary title. I don't expect even the head demon hunter has ever truly faced a demon, but

230

what else are they supposed to do?"

"Do you think I can defeat it?"

"Master Enwin studied the spells you used to contain the demon. They weren't just any simple barrier spells. If you put your mind to it Kyzyl, you may be our best hope for banishing this creature of darkness. Still, it will not be easy, and the attempt will likely bring you within a hair's breadth of your own demise."

"What if I choose not to fight it?"

Master Jonah suddenly looked very serious. "Is that what Bethany deserves? Would you dishonor her memory in such a way?"

Kyzyl looked down at his feet again. "I'm sorry, Master."

Master Jonah nodded. "This is your responsibility Kyzyl, and accepting your responsibilities is not only part of being a great wizard. It is part of being a great man."

Kyzyl nodded. When Master Jonah left, Kyzyl looked at Emrys. "Would you like to relieve me of my worldly possessions?"

"I'm sorry?"

"Since I'm going to be traveling the countryside hunting a demon, I can't exactly take an entire personal library and full wardrobe on my back. The least I could do is offer it to you and Donovan.

"There might be some books in there that you won't find in the library. Come to think of it, Head Master Herman might be willing to take them off your hands. You could sell the clothes to keep yourselves in the university and keep Matilda's girls happy."

Emrys blushed at that. "Won't you need them now that you can't study here?"

Kyzyl shrugged. "I probably know enough to parley my skills into a spot in a noble's estate somewhere. With a respectable retainer and some time, I'll find a way to continue my studies."

"If that's what you really want."

"I want nothing more. My friends deserve better than what I've given them so far."

Emrys put a hand on Kyzyl's arm. The two shared a silent moment before Kyzyl went to check on his account status with the dwarves.

After juggling a few numbers in his head, he noticed he had more than he should've. When he questioned this, the dwarf at the counter told him that some "old twig" of a woman had come in a few months ago and added money to his account.

"Are you sure you didn't get the ledgers mixed up?" Kyzyl asked.

The dwarf glared at him before saying, "we don't mix up ledgers, boy."

Kyzyl put his hands up in resignation. "Fine. If that's the case, I'm going to need a letter of credit for my account balance."

"To which bank should I make it out?"

"I'm not sure honestly."

"Well, ye daft boy, where are ye going?"

"That's just it. I'm going to be doing a lot of traveling in the foreseeable future. I'm not sure where I'm going to be stopping or for how long. Is there a way for you to draw up a basic letter of credit that's redeemable at any bank?"

"Neh. Too many clans with too many different systems. For a small fee, though, I can put it in the master ledger for ye."

"The master ledger?"

"Something we've had for millennia. Only the oldest banks have copies. They're a network of connected tomes. If I put your account in it, all ye gotta do is find a bank with another tome and they will be able to honor your account."

"And this works across clans?"

"Aye, the network is tuned to each bank's specific

cipher, so there won't be any issues there."

"How much?"

"Two silver nobles."

Kyzyl laughed. "For that kind of money, I'd expect you to let me summon my money from anywhere in the world."

"Maybe your precious Masters can teach you a spell that can get through our defenses. Until then, the price is two silver nobles, and you can do your banking anywhere in Lukor."

Kyzyl thought for a moment, then he relented. "Very well. Will you be taking it out of my account then?"

"Aye. That can be arranged." The dwarf took down some information and gave Kyzyl a receipt that had his account information on it. He carefully folded it up and placed it in a pouch he had strapped to his forearm under his sleeve.

With the business of his finances taken care of, Kyzyl decided it was time to face the person he had been avoiding. As he made his way to the brothel, he thought about Bethany. He thought of her bright, smiling face and her gentle touch. With each step he could feel another crack form in his heart. He wondered how many other people had been affected like this, how many other people lost someone like Bethany because of his arrogance?

He stopped at the door to the brothel. He clenched his fist and bit his lip, but a tear still forced its way on to his cheek. He opened the door and walked into the room with the bar. He looked down at his feet and asked, "Where's Matilda?"

"She's in her office. Do you know where that is?" An unfamiliar voice told him. He was still looking at his own feet, so he couldn't tell who it was.

He didn't respond. His heart was pounding now and he couldn't put his thoughts together. He just walked quickly to through the parlor to the door of Matilda's office. He hesitated for the space of a single breath, then two. He swallowed and clenched his fist until his knuckles turned white. He knocked, harder than he intended. Donovan opened the door and gave Kyzyl a somber look.

When Kyzyl didn't immediately move out of the way, Donovan pushed past him and went over to the bar. Kyzyl stepped in and closed the door. He stood there with his head down for a long time.

When he finally did speak it was with a shaky breath that cracked often. "I know I'm the last person you probably want to see right now. I screwed up and got someone you loved killed. I murdered her just the same as if I put a knife to her throat, and I will never forgive myself. I just wanted you to know, I'm sorry."

There was a long moment of silence, in which Kyzyl found the courage to look up, only to see that Matilda was facing the window behind her desk. One of the artificers must have added a joint to her chair so she could turn it.

All he saw was the back of her chair when she said, "Kyzyl, ever since you came into my brothel, I knew you were different from the regular patrons here. I saw you with Donovan and I knew what was coming, so I tried to keep you from making the same mistakes as your elders, as Donovan and me. I still want that for you. Please, learn from my mistakes."

Kyzyl tilted his head. He wasn't sure what he expected, but this wasn't it. Matilda's voice sounded so defeated. He opened his mouth to speak, but no words came out. He just stared at the back of her chair. After a while, he opened the door again and walked out.

Kyzyl walked back to the Noble Steed, hearing, but not listening to the rumors he heard about him as he walked. He was wrapped up in processing the events of the day and wondering about what was to happen to him at noon tomorrow.

When he walked into the Noble Steed, Seth nodded curtly at him. He'd never received such a cold greeting from the man. That change hurt as much as being expelled. Now he'd truly lost everything: the place he'd come to think of as home, his friends, and even the family that had treated him as one of their own.

Kyzyl sat at the bar. Seth gave him a bowl of cold potato stew, and Kyzyl ate it silently. He wanted to apologize, but he didn't know what to say or how to say it. The man had given him a home and a better family than the one he'd left back home, and Kyzyl repaid him by making himself a criminal. Whatever struggles the inn was facing, they were going to get worse for being the place the murder lived while at the university.

His mind moved to the whipping scheduled for noon tomorrow. He'd never been whipped before and he never thought about how it might feel. Would it sting? Would there be throbbing?

He finished his stew and silently walked up to his attic room. He wondered if Master Telma would have him stitched up or if he would be expected to find someone outside the university to do that. If he had confidence in his ability to avoid flinching, he'd be able to do it himself.

Stitches always hurt, however, and an anesthetic would dull his senses and prevent him from doing a good job. These and so many other thoughts kept him awake late into the night. It wasn't until the moon was finishing its arc in the sky that sleep finally took him.

CHAPTER SEVENTEEN
Leaving

Kyzyl woke up several times but didn't get out of bed. His dreams were filled with Bethany's cold, dead stare and the feeling of sticky blood covering his hands and chest. When he woke, however, he had to remind himself that it wasn't all a dream. He'd killed the woman he loved and destroyed the one chance he had to become a great wizard.

His anxiety about the coming day made his stomach turn over at least a dozen times. The whipping filled him with a fear of pain, but the fact that by midday today, he would no longer be allowed in the university put a lump in his throat. When he finally did get out of bed, he packed a single bag with everything he could think might be useful on the road and headed down stairs. There, he saw Donovan, Emrys, and Matilda waiting for him.

"We came to see you off. You didn't think we'd let you face your fate alone, did you?" Emrys said in answer to Kyzyl's surprised expression. Matilda gave him a sad smile, and Donovan stayed stoic.

Kyzyl didn't know what the man was thinking, but he was glad that he could face this whole thing with his friends by his side. "Thank you. All of you. A man like me doesn't deserve friends like you."

"If you're about to tell us we're too good for you, save it. We're all part of the merry band of misfits," Matilda said. Kyzyl smiled and hugged each of them in turn. Then shared a round of drinks and stories until the noon bell chimed, and the four friends left the Noble Steed for the last time.

Kyzyl felt like the walk to the square took forever. He could feel his head and heart pounding. About halfway through, Matilda took his arm and Donovan put a hand on his shoulder. The gestures made him feel more solid. By the time the square and the crowd were in sight, those were the only things keeping Kyzyl from running in the exact opposite direction.

Donovan nudged him forward and he began a slow walk to the pole. He focused on his steps: one foot, then the next. Half-way through, he straightened his back and lifted his head. Kyzyl was a man of noble blood, he was willing to concede his mistakes, but not his pride.

When he reached the pole, he took off his shirt and allowed his hands to be bound to the iron ring set in the top. Though he was determined not to pass out, he also knew they would insist, to keep him from running. With his back turned to the gathered crowd, Kyzyl heard Head Master Herman give his speech about Kyzyl's charges and the punishment. His voice was pious and stately, as if he were giving a sermon.

Next, he heard the crack of a whip. A whoosh, a crack, and a stinging sensation scrapped across his back. It burned briefly before the whoosh and crack came again and another stinging, burning sensation slashed against his shoulders. He had to bite his lip to keep from crying out, but he stood straight, even as the third and fourth lashes hit. The fifth, however, wrenched a yelp from his mouth as he felt warm, wet blood trickle down his back.

When the whipping was over, all Kyzyl felt was a burning sensation across his back, and streams of warm, sticky blood dripping onto the ground. He focused his mind on the pain, as he would focus on a spell. He let the burning and bleeding sensation fill up his entire being. To him, this was his penance for what he had done, and there was still more to come.

He was untied from the post and the magistrate pushed him to the hospital where Master Telma would have a student of his stitch Kyzyl's wounds. After that, he would be asked to gather his things and leave the University forever.

His trek to the hospital was fairly uneventful. The magistrate that had carried out his punishment was also his escort, and the large man wasn't much for conversation, so Kyzyl occupied himself with taking in everything he could about the place he was leaving. He focused on the smells coming from the Workshops, metallic and smoky, where the artificers designed and built wondrous things. He locked on to the sight of students having animated discussions about who knows what. Too soon they had reached the hospital and one of Master Telma's older students checked him in.

"Right this way Mr. Shenta." The student was a gnome and very tall by gnome standards. He had long, careful fingers and a bright playful smile. Kyzyl wished he had a reason to smile like that again.

He brought Kyzyl to a small room that smelled distinctly like alcohol-based anti-septic. There, he was left alone to take off his shirt and sit on a stool that was placed in the middle of the room. While he sat alone, he looked around the room. There was a basin in the corner with a jug, no doubt filled with water. A cabinet he suspected held the most commonly used ointments, creams, and tonics.

Other than that, the room was bare. It did have a large, glass window overlooking one of the university's many courtyards. This one had a hickory tree growing in the middle. Kyzyl watched the leaves on it dance lightly in the wind until he heard the door open. A stout, stern looking woman walked in. She held a hook needle in one hand and her other was wrapped with a generous amount of gut.

"So, you're the arrogant little twit that knocked down the conjuration tower, hmm?" So, this woman wasn't shy with her disdain. She was the first person whom Kyzyl met that was openly angry with him, but he appreciated the authenticity.

"Yes ma'am. After you finish stitching me, I will be leaving the university."

"Good. Gods know we don't need more of your reckless kind around here. I've been having to work doubles ever since the accident to keep up with all the pain you've caused."

"Yes ma'am, I'm sorry." Kyzyl turned his back to her and hung his head.

"Don't tell me sorry," she said as she spread a numbing ointment over his back, "say sorry to the people who still can't get out of their beds. Goodness I hope Master Telma and Master Jonah can find a way to make them walk again."

He hadn't received an exact count of the number of lives he'd destroyed, but he had been mostly occupied by the ones he'd cut short. He didn't even consider the number that would be permanently damaged by what he'd done.

"The Masters at the university are the best in the world ma'am. I know that, if there is a way to help the people I hurt; they will find it."

The woman started to stitch up Kyzyl's cuts and he winced a bit at the dulled pain she was inflicting on him. She made quick work of his stitches and moved on to bandaging him with a practiced efficiency. Kyzyl wondered if she was one of Master Telma's assistant physicians. She was well old enough to have completed her courses at the university, and her hands were as skilled as anyone Kyzyl had ever met.

"There," she said after she was finished bandaging the stitches, "now you are free to go."

"I would hardly call what is happening being freed." He said it without thinking, but she didn't respond as he dressed and prepared to leave.

When he made it to the door, he turned to face her. His head had been hanging for most of their time, so this was the first time he saw her sharp green eyes. They bore into him like daggers, but he knew he had to do this.

He bowed low to her and reached out a shaky hand. In it was his signet ring. "In my culture, these are given as tokens of favor, but they can also be used to convey a debt. With this, I declare to you and the people I have harmed that you are owed more than I can give. Do with it as you please, but know that, whatever else it is, it is a symbol that I am deeply and truly sorry for the pain I caused."

He dared a look at her face. It had softened a bit as she looked at the ring. Her eyes rolled and she took it. "I'll make sure Master Telma puts it somewhere safe," she said.

When Kyzyl got back to the Noble Steed, Seth had already put together his things. He supposed the man was looking forward to having such a controversial guest leave his establishment. Kyzyl couldn't blame the man. He knew there were going to be few places within a hundred miles of the university where he would be allowed to stay.

He gathered up his backpack and put on his warmest clothes. Frostfall was giving way to the proper winter months, and snow was beginning to cover the streets. Kyzyl was thankful that he'd taken the time to buy local clothing. His homeland never dropped below a mild chill, so nothing in his home wardrobe would've stood up to snow. He put on his fur boots and headed to the gates at the boundary of the university complex.

On the way there, he started thinking back to the first time he laid eyes on the university and all the things he dreamed of studying here. That was no longer possible, and he felt his stomach turn sour at the idea of such a wasted opportunity.

When the gates came into view, Kyzyl saw two figures standing in front of them. As he got closer, he recognized Emrys and Master Jonah, conversing quietly and animatedly. When they noticed him, Master Jonah waved Kyzyl toward them.

"Mister Shenta. I'm glad we didn't miss you. Emrys and I have a few things we'd like to give you for your journey." He held out a brown paper package.

"I took the liberty of studying the spell you used to set the demon loose. I had hoped you could do it again to summon the demon to a place where you could conquer it. Alas, the spell you used merely undid the bindings that held it in the lower planes, and its appearance was largely accomplished by its own power it would seem."

Kyzyl hadn't realized that about the spell. It seemed like a normal conjuration spell to him, but he was done questioning the wisdom of the Nine Masters. If Master Jonah said it wasn't a normal summoning, then Kyzyl would believe him until he had substantial proof otherwise.

"I've allowed myself to get distracted from my point. My point is, I studied the spell, and found a way to make you something that would aid you in finding the demon."

At the Master's beckoning, Kyzyl opened the package. It was a flat jewelry box. Inside was a pendant in the shape of a crescent moon and a note that had something like a prayer on it.

"It's an amulet. When you speak the chant I gave you, it will glow. The brighter it glows, the closer you are to your target."

Kyzyl closed the box and placed it in his backpack. "I'm not sure if I'm ready to face the demon yet. I don't even know how I'd banish it. Usually, I can do whatever spell I use to summon something a second time to send it back where it came from, but if you're telling me that I didn't summon the demon in the first place, I don't know if I can force it back."

"That's where I come in," Emrys said. He handed Kyzyl a thick creamy envelope. "This is a letter of introduction to my patron, the man who raised me. I've already told him he'll be receiving a friend of mine as a guest for the rest of winter. He has plenty of material you can study from to figure out how to banish that cursed thing."

Kyzyl put the letter in the pouch strapped to his forearm. Then he took one last look around the university, taking in as much as he could about the home he'd lost because of his arrogance. He landed and the two encouraging faces of Master Jonah and Emrys. He smiled despite the growing feelings of anxiety and regret inside him. "You are both wonderful, and I am so glad to have people willing to stick by me after all the mistakes I've made."

Emrys hugged him tight, and Master Jonah shook his hand. After that, he walked through the gate, and they close behind him for the last time.

CHAPTER EIGHTEEN
Confronting Your Demons

As Kyzyl walked down the road leading away from the university, it was hard to shake the feeling that, just beyond the tree line on either side of the road, there was something moving. It was as if it was following him. He thought about going to investigate, but thought it best to stick to the road where it was safe.

Even after several minutes though, he couldn't shake the feeling he was being watched. More than once, he stopped and looked behind him, only to see nothing but an empty road. He told himself he just wasn't used to being alone. He was probably hearing the animals moving around in the underbrush.

Kyzyl looked toward the setting sun and saw that all but a sliver of the disc had set below the horizon. The sky around it was a dark red that reminded him of blood. If it was going to be dark soon, it wouldn't likely be safe on the road.

He found a nearby tree with a branch low enough to hang his backpack on, but high enough that most people would have to reach for it. He set his back against the tree and pulled his cloak over himself. He was asleep before he realized he had forgotten to eat.

After a full day of walking, Kyzyl reached a crossroads. It was then that he realized he hadn't looked at where Emrys' patron lived. He pulled out the note Emrys had sent with him and read the address:

Kingdom of Strophe
Riverstone Barony
Milltown
Riverstone Estate

Kyzyl didn't know where Milltown was, but he knew he was closest to the Ironkeep Barony, as the university wasn't technically part of any of the King's fiefdoms. He wasn't sure which way to go, and the signs pointing to the closest towns and cities didn't help. While he was pondering how to solve his quandary, a troupe of Wanderers playing a folk song came down one of the forks in the road.

"Hail traveler. What brings you on your way?" the piper said. He held out his hand with his index and fourth fingers tucked and the rest extended. He presented the back of his hand so the two tucked fingers looked like they had been severed.

"I seem to be in need of guidance if you would be so kind." Kyzyl had heard of Wanderers at the university. They were nomadic performers who, if you believed the legends, collectively knew all the stories of the world.

Kyzyl showed the piper the address on Emrys' letter. The piper perked up a bit at the sight of it.

"Going to Riverstone Estate? You will most certainly do well for yourself. There is no place safer or more generous to travelers in all of Strophe than Milltown. We are, in fact, heading about that way if you'd like to join us. Safety in numbers and all that."

"Would you require payment for my traveling with you?" Kyzyl raised an eyebrow and gave a half smile.

The piper laughed. "I see you've been privy to some of our customs. I'm not used to foreigners like yourself knowing the Wanderer ways."

"I lived at the university for a time and was warned about your kind." Kyzyl winked to indicated the humor in his comment.

The piper laughed. "Well, then you'll know our payment is something every person, especially travelers, have plenty of. You will come with us, and we would hear your story."

Kyzyl followed them down the opposite road in the fork. He began with stories of his homeland. The troupe was an attentive and reactive audience. Kyzyl got the impression that Wanderers had a lot of practice being good audience members.

It was late into the evening after their meal when Kyzyl ran out of things to tell them. He had run out of stories about himself, and started telling them all legends he'd heard a thousand times growing up. They were eager to hear stories, fanciful or otherwise, from such a faraway land.

"I'm glad I ran into all of you on the road," Kyzyl said while they were sitting around the fire digesting a particularly well-done stew the juggler and his wife put together. "It gets lonely on the road all by myself." He didn't mention the dark places his mind seemed to wander when he was left to his own thoughts. He often thought of the looming threat of the demon, Bethany's glassy stare, or the way Seth had treated him in the end.

"Ay. It's dangerous as well. There are bandits and bears aplenty in these trees. Safety in numbers is best these days," the flutist agreed.

The piper, who seemed to be the closest thing the group had to a leader, got up and stretched. "Yes, well, it's even more dangerous to be on the road while tired. We should try to get some sleep."

The rest of them agreed and each of the Wanderers rolled out a bedroll. Kyzyl, however, rested his head on his backpack and covered himself with his cloak. It wasn't comfortable, but it allowed him to keep his head out of the snow.

After a week of traveling, the Wanderers told Kyzyl they were going a different way. As thanks for his stories, though, they taught him their customary greeting. It was the one he saw the piper use when they first met, with thumb, middle finger, and pinky extended and the other two tucked to look like they had been severed.

"It's a callback to when kings and lords used to hunt us down," the piper explained. "They would maim or kill us to keep us from singing our songs. The Wanderers sing only truths, you see, and no one fears the truth more than those in power." He grinned at Kyzyl and gave him a fond farewell.

Kyzyl looked up at the sign that read "Milltown, two days." It had a number two and half circle with a curve under it that looked like a rising sun. Kyzyl suspected that was for people who couldn't read, but wondered how they'd know which town it was referring to.

He started walking west toward where the sign was pointing. The snow was starting to pile up and Kyzyl's shins were half buried in it through most of his walk. More than once, the wind blew a new drift from the trees on top of his head, so when he stopped for the night and tried to pack snow into a serviceable campsite, he was already cold and wet.

As Kyzyl was gathering wood, he remembered a story the Wanderers had told him about trees being sentient. Kyzyl remembered a journal he'd read in the university's library that was written by a naturalist that posed the idea that trees could feel pain, and therefore were sapient. He'd never heard anything resembling the idea that they could also be sentient.

He stopped at an oak that was thicker than he was shoulder to shoulder. He placed his hand on it and thought about how two months ago he would've dismissed that story as nothing but fantasy. Now that he'd summoned a demon, not just a creature that looked like a demon, but a real-life in-the-flesh demon, he was ready to believe that trees might have their own way of communicating.

"I hope I'm not intruding by touching your trunk," Kyzyl said to the tree. He didn't expect a response, and, as far as he could tell, he didn't receive one. Still, even without its leaves and only a single cardinal perched on its branches, the tree seemed like it was emanating life. He could almost convince himself that this tree had a certain level of awareness, similar to that of a sleeping person. Could trees sleep? Was that how they thought of winter? As just a full season of napping?

He thought of what it would be like to leave behind the waking world for an entire season. To seek refuge within blissful unconsciousness, but then he remembered the nightmares he'd been having on nights where he was alone. He thought it best if those were limited to a few hours every night rather than an entire winter. Otherwise, his mind may not come back from those dark places.

Kyzyl finished gathering wood and returned to the spot where he had packed the snow. When he got back, there was an old man sitting by a roaring fire. Kyzyl couldn't guess where he'd gotten the wood, his own bundle was hardly more than pathetic and took him most of the evening to gather.

"Ho traveler. Where you headed?"

"Hail! I'm headed to the Riverstone Estate. What about you sir?"

"Here to there, there to here."

"Are you a Wanderer then?"

"Of sorts, but not the sort you'd be thinking of most likely."

Kyzyl nodded.

"I was just about to have my dinner before turning in for the night. Care to join me?"

"Of course, but I don't have much to share." Kyzyl tried to ignore the fact that this was supposed to be his campsite.

"Nonsense. I have plenty for the both of us."

"That's very kind of you."

The old man waved a hand in dismissal. "Think nothing of it. Come, sit and eat with me."

Kyzyl sat on the packed snow next to the old man who tore a piece of trail bread and handed it to him. Kyzyl took it and started to chew it as the man asked, "so what brings you out on the road?"

"I'm looking for something."

"No doubt a girl, by the look on your face."

Kyzyl swallowed. "What makes you think that?"

The old man laughed. "Now don't go getting defensive about it me-boy. It's nothing to be ashamed of."

Kyzyl went silent. The old man didn't push the subject, so they ate without speaking. When Kyzyl was done, he stood and opened his mouth to thank the old man, but the old man cut him off.

"I hope you don't think I'm going to let you leave. I have to thank you properly for releasing me into this world."

It took a moment for Kyzyl to realize what the old man was saying, which was just enough time for him to turn into a huge mass of rippling muscles and giant bat-like wings. That form Kyzyl recognized immediately.

He jumped back as far as he could to get out of the reach of the demon, then started to chant while drawing symbols in the air. As soon as he did, flashes of the tower and Bethany's face crossed his mind and he lost his concentration. He looked up just in time to see the demon's claws slash across his chest and send him spinning into the snow.

Kyzyl crawled as quickly as he could away, trying to get his own mind under control. He tried chanting again, but the flashes came back and he lost another spell. The demon pinned him to the ground with a foot, forcing the air out of his lungs. He tried to reach for his sword on his waist, but the demon tore it from his belt. He unsheathed the sword. It glimmered in the light of the roaring fire behind them.

The demon's laugh was so deep as it lifted the sword, it sounded like it came from the furthest depths of the Nine Hells. "You think this puny thing can harm me?" the demon chuckled. He placed one hand on the blade of the sword and snapped it, sending a ringing through the trees.

The demon dropped the broken sword, and Kyzyl watched as the last thing that meant anything to him fall to the ground, broken. He felt his will break under the weight of that loss. He relaxed his muscles as he felt the demon's foot come off his back. He was lighter than air. He felt cold seep into him from the wound on his chest. He knew the blood loss would soon be fatal, but he couldn't muster the will to care. Perhaps dying was simply what was meant to happen now. What else was there to do? And with that, darkness over took him.

CHAPTER NINETEEN
A Safe Place to Rest

Kyzyl awoke for the second time in as many months in a clean soft bed. This one had curtains and the sheets were dyed a forest green instead of the bleach white of the Physician's building at the university.

Kyzyl heard people talking from the other side of the bed curtains, but when he tried to sit up, a searing pain blossomed across his chest and he fell back onto the pillows. He must have let out a shout of pain, because the next thing he knew, the curtains were being pulled back to reveal a man with kind green eyes and a touch of age around his mouth. They were the sort of wrinkles you get after a lifetime of smiling and laughter, and that joy was reflected in the comforting smile he gave Kyzyl.

"I'm glad to see you are awake," the man said. "I am Baron Robert Galthos of Riverstone Keep, Ruler of the Torish Marshes, Defender of the Eastern Gate, and Protector of the Realm. Although, to my guests and friends, I am merely Robert. Baron Galthos to those who insist on being polite."

Kyzyl waited for the pain to subside before he spoke. "My name is Shenta Kyzyl. I am a friend of Emrys who you once allowed to live here and who you are currently patronizing at the University Arcanum."

The man nodded. "I know. Emrys no doubt mentioned he was sending a letter ahead of you. Even if he hadn't, my Emrys is no fool. He wrote you a letter of introduction that was enchanted to fall into my hands the moment I came within a certain range of you. He's such a clever young man."

The pride in the Baron's voice was surprisingly fatherly. Emrys always spoke of him as being kind, but Kyzyl never got the impression that the two were particularly close. "My question, if you'll excuse me, is why you had a demon attack you on your way here?"

Kyzyl faltered for a moment. He couldn't think of what to say. Should he lie to this man who was giving him such generous hospitality? "I don't know, sir. I'm sorry. It just all happened so fast."

"If I may, Robert," a new voice said. When the man stepped into view, Kyzyl saw the telltale holy symbol and outerwear of a cleric. He stifled a groan as the man stepped closer to the Baron. "Our guest no doubt needs his rest. If you give me another day to close his wounds and apply a healing tonic, he should be well enough to answer our questions. Until then, I would advise against anything that might be stressful."

The Baron nodded. The two closed the curtains and left Kyzyl to his thoughts for a few moments until the cleric came back alone. He held a handful of herbs in one hand and he uncovered Kyzyl's chest and touched it with the other.

He spoke a chant that was like a rhythmic prayer. As he did so, the herbs in his hand withered and turned to dust and Kyzyl could feel a warmth spread across his chest. Muscles Kyzyl hadn't realized were tensed relaxed and he felt a small amount of the burning pain subside.

"That's very impressive. How does it work?" Kyzyl asked.

"The herbs have healing properties that come from their natural chemical make-up. I use the powers granted to me by the Night Watcher to siphon off those properties all at once to heal you more quickly. That way I can do in a few hours or days what your body would take weeks or sometimes months to do on its own."

Kyzyl wasn't expecting such a... scientific answer. He was used to faith-based magic users being all about spirituality and divine will. He expected this man to give a vague answer about miracles and blessings, but this man was direct about how his magic worked and what it could do. "Can all clerics heal so quickly?"

"Some can do it more quickly, others less. A cleric's powers are based on their devotion to their patron god. The deeper your devotion runs, the easier the magic flows. Plus, it helps to have the right medicines on hand. The Baron is a good resource in that regard. His lands a very fertile, and there are many medicinal plants within his Barony."

"Do all clerics need medicinal plants to heal people?"

"If you have a particularly powerful devotion, such as the high clerics in Calcut, you can rely on your own power alone. Generally, that works by flooding one's body with life-giving energy so the body heals quickly because of the abundance of energy it has access to in that moment."

Kyzyl had many more questions he wanted to ask, but he suddenly felt very tired. He lay back on the bed and the cleric stood. "Some of the herbs I used have sedative properties, so they are making your body tired. That coupled with the energy we expended to heal you so quickly means you should take time to rest. I will be back later tonight, and we can discuss further after your next treatment."

Kyzyl slept. He couldn't tell how long he'd slept, but the light shining through the curtains had sunk, telling him it had been hours. He was thankful that the sedatives seemed to silence his dreams for the time being.

He didn't see the Baron for the rest of the day, but the cleric brought him dinner. He brought more herbs as well as a stone platter that he warned was hot. It was laden with silver plates with venison, fruits that were totally out of season, and a loaf of bread.

As Kyzyl took the plates from the cleric, his fingers brushed up against something on the underside of the plates. He ate as quickly as he could without being rude or making himself sick. The food was clearly well made, but something about it didn't compare to Seth's cooking. Kyzyl pinned that fact to his attitude these days being much darker and things in general being harder to enjoy.

When he'd cleared the plates of their food, he flipped one over and examined it. He saw sigils of abjuration and some used for heat transfer that were the same as the fire spell he learned before ever coming to the university.

"You have a careful eye," the cleric commented. "What do you see?"

"The sigils allow the plate to act as a focus for an abjuration spell with the heat from the stone platter as a power source."

The cleric nodded. "Do you know what the spell does?"

Kyzyl shook his head. "I only got to study the introductory classes on wards before I had to leave the university." He was careful not to mention why he had to leave.

"It's a kind of stasis field. It keeps the food locked in its current state as it leaves the kitchen. That way, it doesn't lose heat and no chemical reactions occur. As long as the stone stays hot, the food tastes like it just came out of the oven, no matter where in the keep you have to take it." The cleric smiled. "Robert hates cold food. I can't tell you how long it took him to work out that little trick. He practically lived next to the kitchens while he was working on it."

That made Kyzyl smile. He remembered what it was like in his father's estates. He never loved the idea of eating in the dining hall with his father, but if he asked for his dinner to be brought to his room, it was always cold. It always seemed like a lose-lose situation.

Kyzyl realized something as the cleric pulled out another bundle of herbs. "We never made proper introductions. I assume you were within earshot when I introduced myself to the Baron, but just in case, I am Shenta Kyzyl of the Chenshu providence of Hanra. Kyzyl is my personal name. I have learned since I've been in this kingdom that I need to specify that."

The cleric smiled. "I am Luthor of the Temple of the Moon, Cleric Second Class and Spiritual Advisor to Baron Robert Galthos. Luthor to my patients."

"Good to meet you Luthor. I'm glad I am under the care of someone capable."

Luthor gently pushed Kyzyl down onto the bed. He began his rhythmic prayer and Kyzyl felt the warmth fill him up again. His muscles relaxed and he felt a slight tingle this time that made him want to scratch at his chest. He resisted the urge, suspecting that Luthor would stop him. The wave of fatigue hit him soon after Luthor was done, and, since he was already lying down, Kyzyl merely fell back asleep.

CHAPTER TWENTY
Truths Revealed

Kyzyl awoke to a book landing on his bed. It was his spellbook. When he looked up, he saw the Baron with a very stern look on his face. After the kind and jovial man that he'd witnessed the previous day, this face sent chills down Kyzyl's back.

"The demon attacked you because you were the one who summoned it," the Baron said. It wasn't a question, nor an accusation. It was merely a statement of fact.

"You read my spellbook." Kyzyl knew that reading another wizard's spellbook without permission was strictly taboo.

"You talk in your sleep. Some of the things you said made me suspicious of what Emrys left out of your letter of introduction. I have contacts at the university who filled in the pieces I was missing."

Kyzyl could tell by his tone that there was no getting out of this. "It's true. I summoned the demon as a way of trying to prove I was cleverer than the Master Cleric."

"Master Jonah?" Kyzyl hadn't noticed Luthor enter the room, but most of his bed curtains were drawn, so that wasn't surprising. "I'm surprised anyone would hold such enmity for that man. He always seemed unfailingly polite and kind as far as I could tell."

"It wasn't anything he had done. I have a particular distaste for religious men. I've been trying to be more tolerant lately, but…"

"But that is only after you unleashed a hell-beast on the mortal plane. What could you have possibly proven by doing that?" The Baron's voiced held barely restrained fury. Emrys described this as one of the kindest men he'd ever known. Either Emrys had a terrible memory, or Kyzyl had truly angered him.

"I was going to study it to prove it was merely a natural creature."

"The Masters mentioned something about this, but I didn't fully understand what they meant. What sort of natural creature has the ability to power its own summoning?"

"I… What? What do you mean?"

"Did you read the spell you used? Its power source is the demon itself. It acts as an invitation for it to use you as a focus to escape its bindings in the Nine Hells."

Pieces were starting to fit together in Kyzyl's head. The reason the spell was simple was that the demon, as well as being the subject for the spell, was, in a way, doing its own casting. Two wizards concentrating on the same spell in tandem can lend a great deal better focus for a spell and can make casting easier on both. Another question arose in Kyzyl's mind.

"You mentioned bindings. I don't remember any countermagic components to the spell. Did the demon undo its own bindings?"

The Baron shook his head. "Luthor can explain it better than I can. Honestly, I don't think I fully understand it myself."

He nodded to the cleric, who stepped forward.

"Right," he began. "The demonic powers are bound to the Nine Hells by ancient magic that mortals lost the secret to a long time ago. These bindings are woven into the very fabric of the Nine Hells' existence and are maintained by siphoning off power from the demons trapped there. When you cast the spell, inviting the demon to the mortal plane, you essentially transferred the bindings on it to yourself.

This allowed the demon to enter our world and gives him certain freedoms while he's here. That's how he was able to topple the Conjuration Tower."

Kyzyl hung his head. They really did know about everything he had done. Luthor continued, "the demon is not allowed to cause direct harm to any sentient being other than you. He can't, for instance, grab hold of anyone and choke them to death. He can burn crop fields, spoil food, or cause plagues however.

Really what it does depends on the type of demon we're dealing with. Some like to watch people grow sicker and die painfully and slowly. Others like to watch a mother choose between feeding herself and her children. We can't know at this point."

"You said he can't cause direct harm to anyone but me. What happens if he manages to kill me? Will he be sent back to the Nine Hells?"

Luthor shook his head solemnly. "This is why we are lucky you weren't executed. As long as you live, these bindings are in place until we can find a way to send the demon back. Once it's back in the Nine Hells, the original bindings will take hold. However, if you die, it will be freed of all its restraint, and the world will fall into abject chaos."

"That must be the reason Master Jonah didn't want me to be executed."

"I don't think so," Luthor said. "I don't think Master Jonah knows that much about demonlore. I do know he is largely against executions on principle."

Kyzyl sat up in bed and looked at his hands,

thinking. "If the demon is going to try and kill me, then staying here puts the two of you in danger as well. I feel well enough to be on—"

The Baron cut him off with a sharp, rebuking gesture. "Firstly, you are in no shape to be going anywhere. That demon did a number on your ribs as well as the slash across your chest. You're going to need Luthor's help to be able to walk out of this room in a week.

"Secondly, if you think I don't have layers of protection on this place, you're a fool. Riverstone Estate is protected by a unique mix of arcane and divine magic that keeps all enemies at bay." He gave a prideful grin that made Kyzyl think of Emrys. "The stone walls and machicolations are mostly just for show at this point. There is nowhere else in Strophe where you would be safer."

Kyzyl looked from Luthor to the Baron. The Baron's words had to be hubris. There was no way they could have set up defenses to combat a demon before they knew one would be unleashed on the world.

"There are things in this world that pose as great or greater threat to the citizens under the Baron's protection. He takes his job as a Protector of the Realm very seriously," Luthor explained. "Now that we know the demon will likely comeback, we can set up more specific wards against it. Once we do that, you and the rest of the servants that live here will be safe."

"You will stay here through the winter," the Baron added. "That will give us time to train you in combat magic and banishments. With any luck, you'll come out of this victorious and the demon will be back where it belongs.

"But first, you need to get well. I'll have some of my staff bring up a few books from my personal library so you can familiarize yourself with demonlore. For now, you must rest. Luthor will be by later for treatment."

The Baron closed the curtains on Kyzyl's bed and left him to lie on the bed, thinking of everything he had learned. The demon wanted him dead, but it didn't kill him when it had the chance. What happened? Did it get scared off? These questions kept tumbling around in his head as sleep took him under once more.

When he awoke again, Luthor was back with another tray of food and his satchel filled with herbs. He helped Kyzyl sit up and lean forward so the cleric could work on reknitting some of his ribs from the back.

Kyzyl ate while he was leaned forward. He asked Luthor how long he'd known the Baron.

"Quite some time yet. We met at the university actually. I was originally studying botany under Head Master Herman while he was still the deputy to the previous Master Diviner. The Baron was a bit rowdier back then, and he'd get into some... heated debates with the other student archivists. I was the only one of his friends with the herblore and physician training to patch him up afterward."

"If you were going into botany and physic, how did you become a cleric?"

"That's a story all its own. Suffice to say, there was a time in my life that was filled with dark thoughts and bad decisions. Around that time, Master Jonah, who was still an acolyte at the University Temple, asked me to attend one of his first sermons. He was nervous and he thought having someone like me in the audience would motivate him."

"You two were friends?"

"Quite the opposite. I had no need for gods or religion at the time. He suspected having someone in the audience he knew would challenge him would inspire him to speak more fluently and carefully. He always seems to enjoy seeking out opposition."

Kyzyl agreed with a nod, but Luthor told him to stop moving. "He once told my class that rhetoric was not about defeating your opponent. It was about everyone coming closer to the truth."

"That sounds like him. Never one to run from a defeated argument."

"So, he gave his sermon, and then what, you decided to switch all at once?"

"Good gracious no. If that was the case, I would be a part of the Temple of the Knower."

Kyzyl tried to turn and give him a confused look, but Luthor caught his head and held him still. "I suppose as a Techarian you aren't familiar with the Lukorian pantheon. The patron god, the Night Watcher, is the father of the other gods. The university is dedicated to his son, the god of knowledge and enlightenment. He is generally worshiped there as the Knower."

"Those are strange names for gods."

"Not names. Epithets. You don't say a god's name out of respect."

"I understand. We have a similar tradition surrounding our ancestors. We use titles to refer to them. Some people worry that if you use a dead person's name, they'll try to take you to the land of the dead with them. Others just do it out of a sense of respect."

"And what about you?"

"It's considered rude. I don't do it because it makes other people uncomfortable. I'm not afraid of a ghost coming for my soul in the night, but I don't want to scare someone else because of their beliefs. We got off track, though. You said you had gone to his sermon. Then what?"

"Then I listened. I heard about what he believed the gods wanted for us. He believed that each god, though they embody something different and can help with different things, they made this world to be a home for us. They want us to be happy.

"Before that sermon, most of what I'd heard of the gods involved not invoking their wrath. So many people I knew walked on eggshells out of fear of being smote, and it didn't sit well with me.

"But Master Jonah saw something else. He saw powerful things that could, without a second thought, wipe us all off the face of the world, but didn't. He saw that as the only evidence he needed to believe that they loved us.

"After the sermon, I asked if he had time to discuss with me. He invited me to dinner with some of the other acolytes, and I went. I asked questions. They answered. By the end of the dinner I had a lot of things to think about. By the end of the term, I was on my way to Tamerrel to join the temple of the Night Watcher there and be ordained into their ranks."

"What did the Baron think of that?"

"He was excited to have a cleric in his inner circle. The baron has always been curious about how the underlying mechanics of all the different magics in the world work. He encouraged me to go and write him constantly about what they were teaching me. By the time he had inherited his land and title, he already knew who his Spiritual Advisor was going to be. I've been responsible for his family's spiritual well-being ever since."

"That's amazing. They were able to convince you the gods were real? That must've been quite the experience for you."

Luthor chuckled. "That's one way to look at it. Another is that I decided that, if the gods are real, they must want what is best for us in a similar way our parents once did when we were children. If they aren't real, I lose very little by devoting myself to taking care of the people around me in their name."

"I thought you had to be devoted to the god to use faith magic. How can you be devoted to something you aren't sure exists?"

"I am devoted to the ideals the Night Watcher embodies: Life, Freedom, and Nature. As far as my devotion to the Night Watcher himself, if he came and told me to do something, I would do it. However, I am a man with my own mind and will not follow someone because they claim to be from him. I am devoted to my god, but I do not follow blindly."

These were not words Kyzyl ever expected to hear out of the mouth of a religious leader. Kyzyl could definitely tell this man started life as a scholar. "The Baron mentioned protections on his estate. Is that part of your job as his Spiritual Advisor?"

"Not exactly. My charge as his Spiritual Advisor is to ensure he doesn't do anything to lose the divine favor that has allowed his family to be the stewards of this corner of civilization. The protections are something he and I did together. He studied some abjuration magic when he was in the university, and, as you will no doubt see when you are well again, has made a sort of miniature university out of one of the studies this keep holds.

"One of the first things he wanted to do when he inherited his father's lands was make the estate that he grew up on a safe place for anyone who needed it. He and I spent about a year pouring over every ward that would be useful to us. The next three years were spent finding ways to ensure the wards and protections had a source of power to draw from. That was tricky, but we were able to manage. Now, as Robert mentioned, the estate is protected by a unique blending of divine and arcane magic."

"And that's what is going to keep the demon at bay?"

Luthor nodded. "Robert has already begun his research into spells we can use to handle that issue. I have been in contact with a few higher-level clerics from my church that can help recommend divine protections. Wards against creatures of the Nine Hells are some of the magic that is common in every temple regardless of its patron."

"Why is it common? I thought this was the first demon summoned in a while by the way Master Jonah spoke of it."

"You misunderstand. I meant this is an area of

overlap between the temples. The magic itself is... not difficult necessarily, but it is something that is underdeveloped. The reasons being obvious I'd hope."

Kyzyl nodded. Luthor finished his casting, but Kyzyl didn't feel as tired. When he didn't immediately lie back on the bed, Luthor smiled and nodded. "You are taking to the healing very well. I am able to stop using the sedative herbs, it seems. I'll have books sent up to you. You will be awake for most of the day from now on. It would be wise to spend your time getting more familiar with your foe."

For the next few days, in between Luthor's healing sessions, Kyzyl read every book on demonlore the Baron had in his library. He learned about the different types of demons and their preferred method of causing catastrophe.

There were Imps that liked to follow a single person and fill their life with minor inconveniences until the weight of each small difficulty or failure drove them to madness or suicide. Devils seemed to prefer using natural forces like tornadoes, wildfires, and storms to cause destruction on a massive scale. Neither of these compared to the Archfiends that used plagues, famine, and war to cause death on a massive scale.

There was a book that went into more detail with sub-classifications and made the argument that these types were less about fundamental nature and more about preference in style. Kyzyl read that book several times. The author explained things in a way it was easy for him to understand.

CHAPTER TWENTY-ONE
Training

The day after Luthor pronounced Kyzyl fully
healed, Kyzyl received a request from the Baron the he be
met in the library. Kyzyl asked where the library was, and
the servant who delivered the message showed him to a
room that was much like a miniature university.

The room was lit by a soft yellow magelight. Its
walls were covered from floor to the twenty-foot ceiling
with books. There was a still and several glass vials set on a
mahogany table. There was a desk that had folding panels
that seemed to be designed to hold open four books at
once.

The Baron himself was standing in the middle of a
large circle that seemed to outline the range of most of the
containment wards Kyzyl was familiar with. His eyes were
joyful and bright and his smile reached so far back that it
made his ears wiggle. Whatever dark emotions Kyzyl had
inspired in the man were gone, and he was left with a man
that radiated positive energy.

The Baron crossed the threshold of the circle and
spoke to Kyzyl in a friendly tone. "Ah, Kyzyl. You are
looking well. Are your rooms to your liking?"

The Baron had given Kyzyl an entire suite of rooms,

including a bedroom bigger than the taproom at the Noble Steed, a sitting and drawing room, and a dining chamber. This was not the real meaning of the question, however.

Kyzyl had learned a great deal about Lukorian manners from Donovan and his friends while they were together at the university. In polite society, if someone has been bed ridden by sickness or injury, you do not mention it. That seemed to be a commonality between his culture and this one.

"They suit me very well. My host is quite generous, and I am in his debt because of it." Speaking indirectly about a higher ranked noble was a new custom for Kyzyl. In his culture, one thanks his superiors directly for gifts and other shows of favor. Here, however, even if you happen to be speaking to your host, it's as if the *real* host is someone who could walk in at any moment.

"That is good. I trust my messenger informed you of what I invited you here for."

"Yes sir. You plan on teaching me more about combat magic and how to defend myself against the demon. I must inform you, when I fought the demon last, I was unable to cast any of my spells. I fear they may be gone forever."

"I see. Unfortunately, we only have the latter half of a season before it is spring and I must send you on your way. In that time, I don't think I would be able to teach you a proper suite of combat spells if you could cast them. Even if we tried, if the Masters catch wind of me teaching such things, there would be trouble.

"Instead, I want to see what spells you already have at your disposal. That way, we can get you used to thinking about how to use them for combat purposes."

"I know a heat-transfer spell I used to great effect against a swarm of giant spiders. Unfortunately, from what I've read, demons are largely immune to damage from both ends of the temperature extremes. But again, I don't know if I could cast even that."

"You are correct with your assessment of the nature of demons. The fires of the Nine Hells ensure they are used to heat, and it would seem they take a piece of that flame with them when they are allowed to leave. Thus, rendering cold temperatures not a problem for them."

The Baron gestured for Kyzyl to join him in the circle. Kyzyl stepped in and felt a distortion in the air. When he gave the Baron a confused look, the Baron smirked. "Something I studied during my time at the university. It's a ward that protects casters from serious injury when practicing new spells. I find it is also useful when applied to practicing new applications for old spells. You mentioned a heat transfer spell?"

Kyzyl nodded. He wasn't sure what the Baron was planning. They had just agreed it would be useless against the demon.

"Show me. Use the light emanating from my magelight."

Kyzyl slipped into Wind-Dance and braced himself for the flashbacks. They didn't come and he was able to rattle off the spell with ease, creating a burst of flame that flew toward one of the bookshelves. Before it crossed the outer boundary of the circle, however, the spell dissipated.

Kyzyl breathed a sigh of relief. On the other side of the barrier was one of the Baron's many shelves and Kyzyl couldn't imagine the disastrous loss of knowledge had it erupted into flames.

"Did you learn that at the university?"

"No sir. I learned that from one of my tutors back home. He knew I had an interest in magic and wanted a spell that could help me develop the proper mindset for casting." The flashbacks didn't seem to be asserting themselves at the moment.

"Mindset? It's not merely a matter of concentration for you?"

"Not exactly. I don't know what it's like for other

casters, but for me it's a state of mindfulness. I tip my thoughts to the here and now. That allows me to put all of the conscious mind behind my castings."

At least that's how it used to be. When he'd fought the demon, he couldn't bring himself into that mindset without flashbacks to the tower collapsing. That hadn't happened with the spell he'd just cast, but that spell was almost reflex by now.

"Interesting. That explains why you pick things up so easily, I suspect. A properly focused mind can accomplish more than most people realize. If you have mastered this state of mind, we may be able to use it."

The Baron gestured for Kyzyl to stand at the center of the circle. He walked outside of it. When he crossed the threshold, the Baron's voice was suddenly in Kyzyl's head and he jumped a solid foot off the ground.

"My apologies. Sound can't cross the threshold of the ward because it is designed to contain and absorb all forms of energy. This is the only way I can communicate with you while we are on opposite sides of it."

"It's fine. Just don't probe too deep. I like my privacy."

"You have my word. Surface level thoughts, and only if I hear my name in them."

"So, I should avoid bad mouthing you by name while we are training?" Kyzyl regretted that thought. It was too familiar, but the Baron reminded him so much of Emrys that he had let himself slip.

The Baron merely laughed. "I am not in possession of an ego so fragile that I can't bear a little criticism. But if you are concerned about your thoughts, I will try to keep in mind that something thought is not necessarily something said."

The Baron's tone shifted to something more tutorial. "Can you put yourself in the state of mind you described?"

Kyzyl took in a breath and let it out in a slow, controlled stream. He focused on everything he was feeling in that moment and let all other thoughts fall away. At first, he felt the fear that it wouldn't work, and it almost pulled him out of it. His training took hold, and he was able to slip into it after some recalibrating.

***

"Are you there?" the Baron asks in Kyzyl's mind.

"Yes," he responds.

"I can feel a shift in your thoughts. This is very interesting. What are you thinking now?"

"I am processing the information from my senses. It is the best way for me to stay in the present. Right now, I'm thinking of the temperature of the room, how the books make the whole room smell like old parchment, and how odd it feels to be speaking without moving my mouth."

"That's good. Being aware of your surroundings it always important when you are in a fight."

Kyzyl nods. Maintaining the mindset with an outside intrusion, even if it is from the Baron, adds a layer of difficulty. Kyzyl thinks he can keep it up, but it becomes harder as the Baron continues to ask questions in his mind. He takes another long slow breath and the Baron senses his discomfort.

"My apologies. My distraction is probably not helping."

"I was trained to shut out distractions while in this state of mind. Having those distraction effectively come from my own mind does make it more difficult. More difficult still is that fact that I don't have a spell to draw my attention. So far, your questions are both my greatest distraction, and the thing that is holding my attention to the here and now."

The Baron's questions cease for the time being and Kyzyl's attention goes to his breathing. In and out. He notices the Baron shuffling around and hears papers being gathered. With no other prompting to guide his focus, Kyzyl relaxes into a fighting stance and begins to practice the sword forms he was taught as a duelist.

He moves from the graceful motions of flowing river to the stable footing of mountain stone. He is just moving from flying dagger into spinning leaf when the Baron's voice returned to his mind.

"What are you doing? Those look like sword forms, but I've never seen someone move between them as if dancing."

"Being able to move between them with fluency is a mark of an expert duelist where I come from."

"Which providence of Hanra are you from?"

"I am surprised you are familiar with my people's dueling traditions. I am from Chenshu. My father is a second ranked Nok-Jang to the head of the providence." Kyzyl steps into falling rain.

"I am unfamiliar with your people's ranking system. What is a Nok-Jang?"

"Very basically it is a person who is given a parcel of land and is responsible for seeing that it is cultivated properly. As a second rank, my father is one of five estate holders that oversee all the food grown in the providence."

"Sounds like an important task. I take it your father is highly respected."

Kyzyl's head tilts back and forth in a "yes and no" gesture. "He is important to the providence, and by extension the nation as a whole. However, agriculture is traditionally seen as brutish work. Not many people realize how much administrative work goes into it, so they assume my father is too dumb to do anything 'more important.'"

Kyzyl suppresses the stirring anger and feeling of inadequacy he'd become so familiar with in his childhood. He knows that such emotions would break his concentration, and he wants to maintain it. It has been so long since he's maintained Wind-Dance for so long and it feels calming.

"If the people who grow your country's food are not deemed important, who makes up the respected class? Scholars?"

Kyzyl gives a sarcastic chuckle. "I wish. At least most scholars are practical enough to know how a country is run. No, the people who command the most deference, apart from the royal family, are the sages in the temples. Unfortunately, that also means they're the ones with the biggest egos."

"Thus explains your distaste for religious leaders."

***

Kyzyl's concentration shattered at the comment the Baron made. He had never considered that how he felt toward people like Master Jonah and Luthor was because of his experiences with the sages. Sure, Master Jonah and Luthor might fill a similar role in this society that his sages did, but they had been kind to Kyzyl where the sages merely talked down to him and his family.

"Your concentration broke. Did I say something offensive?"

"No sir. I'm sorry. I just never considered that idea before now."

"Which one?"

"Master Jonah was kind to me, and I treated him like he was the same as those pompous sages just because he appeared similar. I can't believe how blind I was."

"We are often blind to our own habits. It is difficult to take a wider view on one's own life."

The Baron had Kyzyl reenter his mindfulness state, and for the rest of the day they tested how well Kyzyl could hold it. The Baron asked Kyzyl to resist his mental intrusions. After a while, they realized they had to set up a hand signal, so Kyzyl would know when to stop.

The rest of the month was spent preparing Kyzyl to fight the demon. He learned how to dodge spells, guess at which spells were being cast based on the words and sigils, and how to gain advantages based on his surroundings. His training as a duelist helped in many ways, and by the end of the month, the Baron declared him the finest combat mage that knew only one combat spell. Kyzyl grinned at the joke.

Luthor sat in on more than one training session. That gave Kyzyl the opportunity to apologize for holding such disdain for his kind. He explained the breakthrough he'd had and Luthor nodded and chuckled.

"I had my suspicions it was something like that. I've been in contact with Master Jonah, and, while he spoke forgivingly of how you conducted yourself around him, he made it clear that you weren't adept at restraining your hostilities toward him. I've known many skeptics in my life, both as a skeptic myself and as a leader of the faith. There are few in this world as openly hostile as you apparently have been.

"Those that are, they usually have something in their past to explain it. The burden is not entirely yours to bare. There are too many among our kind who are the way you describe your sages, and not nearly enough like our Jonah. Still, I'm glad you are able to unravel this disdain you have for us."

CHAPTER TWENTY-TWO
Winter Gives Way

After a month of training, a servant came to Kyzyl's rooms and informed him that, as today began the Winter Festival, training would be postponed until further notice. Something about the Winter Festival tickled at the back of his brain. He tried to figure out what it was as he dressed and ate his breakfast.

When the servant came for his breakfast dishes, her scent reminded him of Bethany and the memories came flooding back. She had been excited to spend the Winter Festival showing Kyzyl how they'd celebrated in her home town. Kyzyl was suddenly reminded of all the plans he hadn't even remembered he'd been making about his and Bethany's future.

He sat in one of the overstuffed chairs in his sitting room. He very suddenly didn't feel like joining whatever festivities the Baron had in store for him and the people of the estate. He thought of Bethany's blank face when she had been crushed by debris. He thought of how her hands felt as the warmth of her smile leeched out of her flesh.

Somewhere, off in the distance, the demon he'd unleashed on the world was forcing others to feel that same pain and tragedy. Here he was, practicing spells and feasting with a baron while other people suffered for his mistake. He felt like he should cry, but he couldn't muster up the energy to force the tears from his eyes. He just sat, looking into the fire.

He didn't realize how long he'd been sitting there until a servant came with a plate for lunch. She told him the Baron had missed him at the ceremony to begin the festival, but Kyzyl simply nodded and told her to leave the food on the side table. He chose a piece of bread, put jam on it, and took a bite. The jam was slimy and the bread was… just bread. A piece of him could feel the pillowy texture of it and taste the sweet aromas of the jam. To the rest of him, it was just bread and jam. Merely a source of nutrients that he forced down his throat so that he could continue to survive.

It took so long for him to take a second piece that the stone the plate sat on had gone cold. Luckily it was merely bread and jam on top, so it merely meant the bread no longer taste like it was fresh out of the oven. Still, Kyzyl looked at the stone, guessing it was granite.

With a heat-binding ratio of 790/1000, it would take at least a day for it to have cooled naturally. The stasis enchantment had to siphon off heat a great deal more quickly than Kyzyl had realized. Otherwise, it being cool would mean he'd been sitting in the same chair for a dozen hours.

Kyzyl tried to use his heat transfer spell to bring the stone back to the proper temperature, but the moment he did it happened again. The tower falling, Bethany screaming, and a laugh that seemed to emanate from the depths of the Nine Hells. It all came flooding back in a rush.

He tried to stand, and felt his legs immediately give way beneath him. "Pour circulation due to restraint and very little movement," a piece of him thought. "Subject should stretch and massage muscles until they regain feeling. Then, make use of them to avoid further complications."

After he rubbed some feeling back into his legs, he walked over to his spellbook and started to page through it. He found the spells he'd learned under Master Enwin and the barrier spells he'd taught himself. He knew what began on the next page, and decided that further study of that spell would not be helpful for him at the moment.

Looking out the window, he saw that it had gotten dark a lot earlier than he'd expected. He went to his bedroom and dressed down for sleep. When he got to his bed however, he simply lay awake for many moments recounting all the things he'd done wrong to lead him to a situation as dire as this one. If he died, the demon would sow chaos throughout Lukor. If he refused to fight it, people would continue to suffer because of him. The only way out was to send it back where it came from, and Kyzyl had no idea how to begin to do that.

The rest of the festival passed in a blur of dark thoughts and days spent doing little besides eating and paging through books without really reading them. Kyzyl mustered up enough energy to answer Luthor and the Baron's questions when they came to visit him. The rest of the time was spent watching the flames in his fireplace dance around.

He often thought what it would be like to use his heat transfer spell to absorb the fire's radiance. Sometimes, he could almost convince himself that it would help thaw the growing feeling of coldness in his chest before his training in medicine told him, "No, it would merely cause severe burns to the inside of your body and you would likely die."

"Is dying such a bad thing? If the sages are right, at least then I'd be with Bethany wherever she is."

"And the demon would be let loose. Jonah, Emrys, and the Baron would be in danger. Do you want to let your friends down?"

That would inevitably bring tears of shame to his eyes. Of course, he didn't want to abandon his friends, but he already felt so alone.

Near the end of the festival, the Baron came to visit Kyzyl. Kyzyl got up and bowed to him as was customary in Hanra. The Baron nodded in acknowledgment, but when Kyzyl went to sit, the Baron stopped him.

"We are not staying in your rooms today. I want to show you the forest that grows in my south field."

Kyzyl wanted to object, but he couldn't find a polite way to do so. He felt very tired, despite the fact he'd only been sitting in a chair for the entire day. Still, he followed the Baron out of the room and down a few flights of stairs until they were at the ground level of the Baron's keep.

At the front entrance was a pair of blond horses with saddle and bridle. They were being held by one of the stable hands who bowed his head toward the Baron. Technically, a more submissive gesture was the correct way to greet one's own noble and head of estate, but the stable hand couldn't do anything else without letting go of the horses, and the Baron didn't seem to mind.

"Do you know how to ride, Kyzyl?"

"My father saw to that piece of my education personally. He didn't want me to embarrass him if I was ever invited to a mock battle with one of the providence's leaders."

"Very well, you shall take Sterling then. He is a gentle horse if one knows how to treat him. Be careful though, he doesn't spook often, but he doesn't do it lightly either."

Kyzyl nodded and made his introductions to the horse by offering it his hand to sniff. It bowed its head, allowing him to pet it. Once that was out of the way, he stepped up into the saddle and allowed the Baron to lead him to the south fields.

"Fields" was a misleading term. It seemed the Baron had allowed his south fields to remain in an uncultivated, wild state. The trees around them seemed young by forest standards, and Kyzyl guessed the Baron planted them when he'd inherited the estate. Still, there was plenty of underbrush that would have been swept away if this had been a garden of some kind.

The animals in this forest stayed quiet, but, other than moving out of the way of the horses, they did not scurry away at the sight of humans. If this place had ever been cultivated land, that time was past, and the wilds of it had spared no time in reasserting their dominance over it.

"It's getting warmer," the Baron said. Kyzyl knew where he was going with this opening. Their agreement was that Kyzyl would spend the rest of winter with the Baron, but once the sowing season began, Kyzyl would be sent back into the world to finish the job he'd started.

"I'm sure your people are looking forward to the beginning of a new year. As winter loses its grip on the land, they will be able to plant food and watch their lives return to prosperity."

"I prefer to see to it that prosperity is not a seasonal enjoyment. When I began to insist that summer was a time for storing and preparing for the colder seasons, my people felt I was stealing away their right to celebrate things. Then when the first winter under my care came, and none of them feared starvation, they began to understand."

"That is a very wise thing to do. Many leaders would've given in to the will of the masses for fear of revolt."

"Many leaders think their people are something to fear. I believe they are merely in need of guidance. I was never going to outlaw feasts if it came to that, but I wanted them to try it a different way just once. Not everyone agreed at first, but I set an example with Milltown, and others saw the value in what I had shown them."

"That is an interesting tactic. I never would've thought of using my own town as an example to others."

"Being a leader isn't about forcing others into

compliance. The best leaders are ones who can stand as an example to the people around them."

"I don't know what I am supposed to do." The words came out before Kyzyl could consider them. "How do I kill a demon? I barely know how I summoned it. Is there anything on this plane of existence that can help me?"

"I don't know, Kyzyl. There is a lot about this that is uncertain." The Baron turned to the trees around them. "Do you know what it is like to be a father, Kyzyl?"

The question took him off guard. "No, sir. I've never had a child before."

The Baron nodded. "Most people think you must have a child before you can become a parent. This is not the case. It is merely the most obvious way to become a parent.

"When I planted this forest, I could've made it into an orchard. I could've set it up as a garden for me and other noblemen to walk through and enjoy. I could've done many things with it that would've been easier and more traditional than give it back to the natural world. Do you know why I made the choice I did?"

"No, sir."

"I knew that an orchard might give me fruit, a farm could give me wheat, but a forest could give a home to many creatures that would otherwise be pushed out of spaces we have decided belong to us. What right do I have in taking that from them merely because I can?

"Being a parent is very much the same. It is the same as being a leader, and gardener, and a baron. In all of these things, your choices will affect more than just your life. They will affect the lives of so many other people, places, and things you might not ever see. That is why all of these people, and in fact every person with a mind to do so, must take responsibility for their actions.

"You say you don't know how you can kill the

demon. I don't know either, but I didn't know what this forest would look like when I planted those trees so many years ago. I didn't know if a storm would come to uproot them and blow them away. When I told my people to save their food for winter, it could have been eaten by rats. None of us know what the future holds, but we still have to make our choices anyway.

"You and I will be judged by those that come after us. They will judge us with information we don't have. It is up to us to make the best choice we can with the information we have. For me, it is letting my south fields be wild so that creatures that are not humans have a place to live. For you, the choice is to face the consequences of your actions. After that, all you can do is hope you have the tools you need to succeed."

During the next few days, the Baron brought Kyzyl on many riding trips through the south forest. They discussed everything to from what makes a memorable leader to the nature of power. By the end of the first week of this, Kyzyl found himself looking forward to these trips.

Unfortunately, they would not last. Two weeks after he had become used to the riding trips, Kyzyl was greeted by an invitation from the Baron to join him for breakfast. It was the first official day of the sowing season on the Lukorian calendar, and Kyzyl suspected this would end up being a farewell breakfast feast.

The dining hall was covered on one wall, floor to ceiling, in a huge mural that seemed to depict and number of figures landing on a shore Kyzyl couldn't identify. The figures were riding what appeared to be a massive storm cloud. The opposite wall was adorned with tapestries that depicted a massive tree encircling nine figures, two bands of warriors clashing, and an archer with their bow drawn standing on a wooden house.

The Baron sat at the head of the table under a large family crest. Kyzyl wondered if above your head of estate was the best place to keep two hanging swords and a massive shield, but the Baron didn't seem to think he was in any danger. To the Baron's right was Luthor, and to his left was an empty space meant for Kyzyl. The rest of the table had high ranking staff members who all stood and bowed to Kyzyl in the custom of Hanra.

Kyzyl greeted them and sat in his appointed spot. The Baron stood and lifted his goblet. "It is my pleasure to welcome you all to the feast celebrating the beginning of sowing season, and the end of another winter with you all. We all worked very hard to put on a festival to remember for the people of Milltown and the surrounding farms, and I can't thank you all enough for your dedication to them and to your service.

"This winter was also a time when we had the pleasure of having a guest from the continent of Techarae. Kyzyl, is there anything you'd like to say?"

Kyzyl's heart dropped into his stomach and his throat became suddenly dry. The Baron must have seen the look of panic on his face, because he merely waved the question aside.

"No matter. I'm sure you prefer more personal expressions of gratitude. You'll have plenty of time to thank my servants in the coming days as you prepare for your departure."

He lifted his goblet again. "To another glorious year. And may we have many more ahead of us." The Baron drank deeply from his goblet and the servants each raised theirs and took a drink. Luthor raised his goblet but set it down because he was still chewing.

Kyzyl looked down at his plate. The walk through the forest had helped his mood, but his appetite wasn't yet back to what it used to be. The eggs did smell excellent, rich with spices and giving off a complex aroma. He took a bite, and for the first time since the festival began, he was able to taste the expertise with which the meal was prepared.

The eggs had a blend of spices in them that made

Kyzyl's tongue tingle a bit with their savory flavor. The bacon was cooked to the point that it broke apart like a dried leaf, leaving salty fragments on Kyzyl's tongue that enhanced the flavor of everything else he ate. The jams were as sweet as anything he'd ever tasted, and he wondered if they had somehow gotten a hold of molasses from the pirate isles to add to it.

  Kyzyl couldn't help but think of Seth and his family. The cooking was more expert, but the atmosphere wasn't the same. It filled him with a bittersweet feeling that pushed tears out of his eyes. He felt the Baron's hand on his shoulder, but he merely smiled down at his plate. For once, though the emotions were complicated to explain, they weren't wholly negative.

CHAPTER TWENTY-THREE
The Quest Begins

After the breakfast feast, the Baron took Kyzyl and
Luthor into a private study. Much like the library, this
place had books lining every wall. However, the mahogany
table at the center of the study held maps of the Baron's
holdings with several notes written in some kind of cipher.
There were arcane glyphs at each of the four corners, but
Kyzyl didn't recognize any of the sigils used in the spells.

"The time has come for you to face your destiny,
Kyzyl," the Baron said without preamble. "I'm of course
not going to kick you out of my estate without giving you
time to make what arrangements you need. Luthor will
provide you with everything you require before you head
out. Just remember, the longer you delay, the more
destruction this demon will cause."

"Yes sir," Kyzyl said. "I will make my arrangements
as quickly as I may. I have very little to pack and fewer
people to contact. I suspect I will be ready to leave by
tomorrow morning."

The Baron nodded his dismissal, and Luthor went
with Kyzyl back to his rooms. The two of them spent the
rest of the day packing and gathering things Kyzyl would
need for his journey: food, a waterskin, a bedroll so he

didn't have to continue sleeping in the dirt, and a salt box.

Luthor also brought Kyzyl a satchel filled with various plants and chemicals sealed in glass vials. When Kyzyl questioned this, Luthor explained that pouches like these were carried by spellcasters of all kinds. The vials were filled with potent, complex ingredients that held a great deal of chemical energy. A scholar who knew enough about alchemy to combine them in the right way would have all the energy he'd need for any spell he could wish to cast.

After he ate the next morning, the only thing left for Kyzyl to pack were his clothes he'd put in his bedroom's wardrobe. He opened the wardrobe as a knock came from the outer doors. Kyzyl told the person to come in, expecting a servant with a message from the Baron. Instead, Luthor entered his bedchamber and made note of his packing choices.

"The Baron meant for all of those clothes to belong to you. It would be a terrible slight for you to not accept at least some of them," Luthor said, indicating the clothes the Baron had tailored for Kyzyl during his stay. He paused for a moment, thinking. "I don't think the Baron would mind, but the staff would talk."

Kyzyl considered for a moment. Propriety seemed like such a low priority at the moment, but he knew far too well how quickly rumors could spread. If he was to get a position as a court wizard at an estate like this one, he should be considerate of the Baron's generosity. He went back to the wardrobe.

There were two sets of clothes he hadn't noticed before. They were linen. The shirts were both dyed a sky blue while the pants were a metallic grey. They were the Baron's colors, and very clearly road clothes despite being tailored.

"I don't think these were meant for me to wear during the festival," Kyzyl said as he pulled them out to show Luthor.

Luthor nodded. "This is the Baron's way of ensuring people know you have his favor. If you ever find yourself in the court of another noble, and you aren't seeking their patronage, wearing the Baron's colors will make it clear that you are someone of high standing politically speaking."

Kyzyl took the two sets, folded them and placed them in his backpack. Then he noticed what was missing from his personal items.

"Luthor?"

"Hm?"

"I had a package that was in my backpack. It was from the university. Do you know what happened to it?"

Luthor nodded and moved to the desk Kyzyl had used to study several of the books the Baron had sent him. He opened a drawer and took out the package Master Jonah had given him. "This was quite the interesting find when we saved you from the demon."

This was news to Kyzyl. He had wondered why the demon hadn't killed him, but assumed that Luthor and Baron Galthos wouldn't have an answer. "*You* saved me from the demon? How?"

"As Robert mentioned when we discovered your... uh... secret, we have access to a unique blend of arcane and divine magic. Using both the magic he and I had access to, we were able to temporarily censure the demon and send it elsewhere long enough to get you behind the barrier where you'd be safe."

Kyzyl was impressed, but when he remembered all the books on magic theorem in the Baron's possession, he decided he shouldn't have been. Still, the idea that these men were capable of forcing a demon away from a particular place, even temporarily, eased a tension Kyzyl hadn't realized he'd been carrying. With people like the Baron and Luthor, the world would not be completely defenseless against the demon should Kyzyl fail.

Luthor seemed to read these thoughts on Kyzyl's face, or merely see a fear of death in his eyes, because he placed a hand on the young man's shoulder. "I know how terrifying this must be for you. Before you came here, you probably thought demons were mere superstition made up to scare the faithful into compliance. Remember this, if nothing else: believe in them or not, the gods want you to succeed. Do not be afraid to ask for help."

"No god or man will bear this responsibility for me. I have made enough people pay for my sins. I am going to do this on my own. If I fail, tell the Baron I'm sorry."

Kyzyl could tell Luthor wanted to say more, but the man stayed silent. He led Kyzyl through the entrance hall of the Baron's keep, which was decorated with another mural depicting a great battle between an army of humans, or possibly elves, and three giant figures that towered over the whole army. Kyzyl began to wonder if Lukor had giants or if these figures were meant to represent something else entirely.

Luthor brought Kyzyl to the outer gate for the estate where the Baron was waiting for them. He opened his arms, and Kyzyl leaned in for a quick embrace. His muscles tensed slightly as he did. Physical contact, even from people who had been kind to him, made Kyzyl uneasy.

"I am sad to see you go. It has been wonderful getting to know one of Emrys' friends. Tell him I miss him the next time you get the chance, and take care of yourself Kyzyl. You are a good man, and I know you are destined for great things."

The Baron placed a coin purse in Kyzyl's hands. "This is to make sure you are well fed while you're traveling. My servants told me how little you were eating while you were here. We can't have you going hungry while you're out hunting, do you understand?"

"Yes, sir. Thank you for all that you have done for me. Your generosity knows no boundaries."

The Baron waved the comment aside and clasped

Kyzyl's hands in a firm grip. Kyzyl gave him and Luthor a different bow than he had previously. This one was used among his people to represent a personal relationship like one between a child and their parents. The two men had given Kyzyl so much, he wanted to at least give them that honor.

Kyzyl turned toward the horizon and the still rising sun. With his cloak on his shoulders, pack on his back, and a satchel filled with strange chemicals. He set out on his quest to kill a demon.

It took about a week for Kyzyl to get to the next thing that he'd call a town. There were a few collections of farmhouses between that and Milltown, but he didn't feel comfortable asking a stranger for a bed in their own home.

Just outside the town, Kyzyl got his first hint that he was on the right track. He'd used the amulet and chant Master Jonah had given him every night to check his progress, the amulet seemed to glow brighter as he got closer to the demon he hunted, and every morning to orient the day's travel. However, it wasn't until he saw the burned out, collapsed grain silo that he was certain the demon had been through here.

From the research he had done, Kyzyl guessed the demon he summoned was an Archfiend of Famines, so it made sense that, while he was unable to cause direct harm to people, he would burn down silos of seed grain during the sowing season. The more he could disrupt the planting of Strophe's crops, the worse their harvest would be and the leaner their winter.

Kyzyl walked into the town proper and noticed that it was eerily quiet. It was late in the evening and any townsfolk that went to help in the fields would've been back by now. However, there were no lanterns or candles flickering in any windows, no sign of families sitting down to dinner, nothing. The only light seemed to be streaming out of the small inn and tavern at the end of the main road.

Kyzyl entered to a vacuum of silence that seemed

to deaden the echoing sounds of murmured conversation that had recently ceased. He looked around the room to find glaring eyes looking at him from over shoulders and the tops of mugs. If this town had a functioning inn, it was not unaccustomed to strangers, but these people looked like they expected him to be the demon.

"What're ya drinkin' tonight stranger?" the barman said as Kyzyl approached.

"Any kind of ale you have will be fine." The bar man nodded and turned toward a large barrel set atop a shelf behind the bar. He filled a clay mug and handed it to Kyzyl.

"Ya 'ere fer tha festival?"

"Just passing through actually." Spirits and ghosts, did these people have a festival for every season. "Which festival are you celebrating? I would've thought the Winter Festival would've been over by now."

"We usually enjoy an early and quiet Winter Festival since most folk are down to the last of the winter stores. However, once the seed grain starts goin' in tha ground, we start up the Towns-founding Festival. It's a bit a local fare we do to celebrate surviving winter. Still, this year it'll probably be quiet too if it ain't canceled all together."

"Why? What happened?"

"Ne'er ya mind. I shouldn't a said nothin'. You go on and enjoy yer ale."

"Please sir. I saw the burned silo on my way in. I don't know much about farms, but the university has been getting strange reports all winter, and one of those reports came from a village near my home. As soon as the roads cleared of snow, I had to investigate."

Kyzyl let a bit of panic slip into his voice. He suspected when he saw the hostile glares that these people weren't going to open up to anyone. However, a fellow victim who is trying to understand their own tragedy would be someone they could relate to.

The barman nodded. "The silo burned down just yesterday. We ain't sure what caused it yet—"

"I told ya! It was a demon. Seth seen it with him own eyes."

"Quiet down there, Jay! Old, crazy Seth ain't see nothin' but a bat."

"Ta ain't no bat. Ting was twice as tall as a man. What bat you know whats twice as tall as a man?"

"What did the demon look like? Do you know?" Kyzyl was glad to see that someone was willing to talk about it.

"I didn't see nothin'. Old Seth's what saw it. Said it flew off into the night. The next mornin', bam!" he slammed his hand on the table, "livestock's dying, silos are burnin' and the rain ain't come yet. We under a demon's curse now."

"Do you know which way it went?"

"Flew up northward, then veered southwest."

"That's enough," the barman interjected. "Son, why are you so interested in a demon?"

Kyzyl took a moment before he answered. Surely the truth would get him thrown out or laughed out depending on if they took him seriously.

"Like I said, the university has been getting similar rumors from towns since the middle of winter. One of those reports came from a town I grew up in. I knew the baron that protected it, and I still have family in the area.

"The Masters at the university allowed me to go out and investigate once it was safe to do so. I want to know what happened here because it might help me stop it from happening elsewhere."

It was a believable enough lie. It had enough truth mixed in that, if you squinted hard enough, you could almost convince yourself of its validity. Regardless, it did the trick. Kyzyl felt a tension ease in the room, though it could just be his own anxiety about talking in front of so many people giving way to Master Jonah's training.

"Well, you're not doing it tonight. I have an extra room upstairs. It's not much, but the bed is warm."

"I would like that very much." Kyzyl gave a quick bow to the barman as he took a key out from behind the bar. The two of them walked upstairs and down a hallway to a small room with a slanted ceiling.

"Here she is. You're welcome to join the town in the bar for a bit and gather more information about the 'demon.'"

"I think I'm going to get some sleep first. Hopefully I'll be able to talk to a few people in the morning. While I do, would it be possible for you to put together some good road food and fill my waterskin for me? I'm running a bit low on supplies."

"Not a problem, apples and hard sausage OK for you?"

"Sounds excellent. Thank you." The barman nodded and walked out the door, leaving the key on a nightstand next to the bed. Kyzyl lied on the bed. It was the first soft thing he had felt in weeks, and he fell asleep almost instantly.

That night his dreams were filled with a familiar chilling voice and the dead glassy stare of Bethany's corpse. More than once he woke up in a cold sweat. After the third nightmare, he turned to look at the amulet which he had hung on one of the posts at the foot of his bed. The faint silver light filled the room with shadows. However, rather than making the shadows seeming looming and intimidating, the silver light made Kyzyl feel safer.

He fell back asleep thinking of what Luthor said about the gods wanting what is best for all of us. "If anything is out there listening," he thought as he started to drift into sleep, "I could use some of that protective spirit your clerics keep talking about."

His dreams after that were bittersweet. He dreamed

of Bethany, but she wasn't screaming or crumbling into dust the way she often did in his dreams. This time, they were enjoying a picnic on a hill that bordered his father's estate. She was wearing the traditional dress of a new bride and they were watching the sunset behind his father's cherry blossom orchard.

When Kyzyl awoke after that dream, it was hard not to feel a mix of delight and longing. He'd never get to have that life in the real world, but at least his dreams could make him happy for a few moments during the night.

The sky was beginning to pale, but the sun wasn't up yet. Kyzyl knew he wouldn't have another dream as pleasant as that one, so he took out his spellbook and tried to think of how to use the few spells he had in it to his advantage against the demon.

He stopped on the page that contained the notes on the Extraplanar Summoning he had used to call the demon. He saw the pieces Luthor and Master Jonah had spotted. The simplicity of the spell that he had originally taken to mean it was a fake was due to its apparent lacking in specified power sources. The glyph of a spell was often taken over by the subtle changes you needed to make to it to account for different power sources. This one, since it only had one power source, was much simpler.

He noticed that the spell also only had the one subject, which appeared to be the exact demon Kyzyl summoned. He wondered what sort of modifications he'd need to make to change the subject to something else. Was there an angel out there waiting to be invited to the material plane for the chance to slay a demon?

He stopped his thoughts in their tracks. This kind of recklessness was what lead him to make this horrible mistake in the first place. This sort of experimentation killed his beloved Bethany, and he was thinking on how to do it again. He let the weight of the things he had done pour over him as one of his father's sayings came back to him. "Bottle up too many emotions, and the bottle gets too heavy to hold," and tears ran down his face.

When he was done crying, he felt a bit lighter. He thought it must've been because he had let out at least a stoan of tears and snot, but he felt a bit better all the same. There was a basin and a jug on a table near the bed. He didn't remember seeing it last night, but figured he was too tired to notice things. He got up, grabbed a cloth towel from a chest of drawers next to the table and washed his face of his sadness. Then he went down to the tavern to see if anyone was cooking breakfast.

He found that the barman was nowhere to be seen, but there was a stout looking woman whistling to herself in the kitchen. When Kyzyl cleared his throat, she jumped and spun around. "Oh," she said, "good to see you up, young sir. Would you like some breakfast?"

"I would love some. What are you making?"

"Oatmeal and bacon are on the menu today."

Kyzyl had to keep his face from turning up. Instead, he tilted his head a bit. He always thought of oats as something you give a horse, but he didn't want to be rude. He sat down at the bar and she set the bowl in front of him. When he took a bite, he was pleasantly surprised. She had mixed it with something, he wasn't sure what, but it tasted just like the cinnamon his father's chef used at home mixed with the molasses he had tried on the merchant ship. "What's in this?" Kyzyl asked amazed.

"Just oats, a little milk, butter, oh and a secret ingredient of mine. Sometimes I boil a bit of my husband's rum and put a dollop of honey in it for sweetness. Do you like it?"

"It's one of the best breakfasts I've had in my life." Coming off the back of a season of forcing himself to eat to avoid being rude, despite eating in general losing its pleasure, having a meal that reminded him of Seth's family made Kyzyl smile.

The woman giggled girlishly. "Thank you, sir.

You're quite the charmer."

Kyzyl ate voraciously. He hadn't realized while he was on the road how much he missed a warm cooked meal from a kitchen. The innkeeper's wife offered him a second helping and smiled when he nodded. "My goodness. Here I thought my husband was the only one who enjoyed my cooking."

Kyzyl smiled when he was finished. "Thank you very much. I appreciate all the hospitality you and your husband have offered me." Kyzyl retrieved his backpack from his room and headed out the door, leaving two silver nobles from his purse on the bar. It was ludicrously generous for a night's stay and a meal, but Kyzyl had his money, the Baron's money, and was certain that, whatever happened with the demon, worldly goods wouldn't mean much to him soon.

On his way out of town to the farms, he started wondering again if the townsfolk would trust him. He started to worry he would say the wrong thing and let loose that he had summoned the demon by accident. He clutched at the strap of his backpack as his anxieties grew. When he found the first farm, he stopped. He couldn't make his feet walk toward that farm or those people. He just stood there, staring down the road. He thought about walking straight out of town. He had the charm that would lead him to the demon. Did he really need the accounts of some townspeople?

He checked his backpack. There wasn't much food left. If he went back to the inn, the innkeeper would wonder why he wasn't investigating, or, worse, he'd try and have Kyzyl stay and wait for the town to gather in the bar and have him talk to them all at once. He went over all the edible roots and plants he knew in his head. He thought of using his magic to hunt. In the end, he found his resolve and, without a word to anyone, walked directly out of town.

CHAPTER TWENTY-FOUR
Luck on the Road

Kyzyl spent the next several days walking, eating, and paging through his spellbook looking for something to help him defeat the demon. Every night he came up empty. Besides, his magic already failed him once against it. Since then, even during the training sessions, he hadn't tried to cast a spell other than his heat transfer spell. He was able to maintain his mindfulness state in most other circumstances, but he remembered the flashbacks. He worried that putting his focus on anything more complex would result in him panicking like he did during his last fight with the demon.

He was considering these things while the sun went down and he spotted the glow of a fire on the side of the road. Moving quietly through the trees as he approached, he spotted an elderly man stirring a pot on the fire.

Kyzyl stood there for a moment before deciding that it was probably the demon trying to lure him in again. He turned to walked into the tree line where he could hide for the night while the demon got bored and moved on.

"You aren't afraid of an old traveler are you boy? I'm certainly no bandit."

From where he had moved, Kyzyl could hear the

man's voice, but he couldn't see him. That was fine. If Kyzyl couldn't see him through the shadow of the trees, the demon probably couldn't see him in their shadows. He thought about running, when he felt a hand on his shoulder. He jumped and spun around, ready to die fighting, but the old man was standing behind him, still an old man. If the demon wanted to kill him, could he do it in the body of an old man?

"I say boy, you look mighty tired."

Kyzyl looked down at the forest floor. It was covered in underbrush. Nothing he knew of could move quickly and silently enough to have snuck up on him like that. Whoever this man was, he wasn't human. "I just wanted to make sure no one was accidentally burning down the forest," Kyzyl lied.

"And what would you have done if they were? If I remember correctly, you lost your magic. Or have you found it again?"

That's it, this man has to be--

"Boy if I was that demon, you'd be dead already."

Kyzyl looked at the man, surprised, then looked at his feet. They were pointed toward the road and set wide. Anyone with eyes and a piece of a brain could tell he was ready to run. He put his feet together, but he kept his head down.

"What do you say to taking a load off next to the fire? I can even offer you some of my stew if you'd like."

Kyzyl nodded. He followed the man back to his fire and sat down while the man stirred the pot. In the firelight, Kyzyl saw a mottled green cloak covering a pointed shape. "The name's Luck by the way. 'Least that's what most people seem to call me these days." Kyzyl nodded again. There was a long pause between them. Then, Kyzyl began to wonder something.

It took him a moment to summon his voice. He was still uncertain of who, or what, this old man was. The only way Kyzyl saw to start figuring it out was to get some answers out of him. "How did you know I was a mage... or, at least, how did you know I was having trouble with my spells?"

The mysterious man ladled a serving of stew into a bowl and handed it to Kyzyl. "Aye, I was wonderin' when you'd ask me that. A friend of mine that you met a while back asked me to keep an eye on you. He thought I'd be able to help you."

"How, who--"

"Luthor."

"You know him?"

"Aye, but that isn't important right now. What is important is what you plan to do about that demon."

Kyzyl shifted uneasily. "What can I do? I've lost my spellcasting abilities. I broke my family's sword. I have nothing left.

"'Nothing left' he says. Boy, who were you before you picked up that sword? Who were you before you cast your first spell?"

Kyzyl stared at the man. "I... I don't..."

"You were you. And that core of who you are is what's going to pull you out of this mental beating you've been giving yourself. You gotta go back to your roots and answer some important questions, kid. Most importantly, who are you and what do you want?"

"I am Shenta Kyzyl and I want to kill a demon."

"That's good. That's a good start. Why do you want to kill it?"

"Because..."

"Because it dropped a building on your girl?"

"Yes... and no."

The old man gestured, prompting Kyzyl to continue. "This isn't about revenge. This is about stopping a creature of pure evil from sending an entire kingdom spiraling into famine and hardship."

The old man gave a hearty laugh and slapped his knee. "That's it exactly."

"But..." Kyzyl deflated. He hadn't realized he was standing until fell back to the ground on his ass. "How?"

"Give me your spellbook." Kyzyl looked at the old man, but he simply held out his hand expectantly. After a moment of hesitation, Kyzyl rummaged in his backpack and pulled it out. "You were trained at the university, correct?"

Kyzyl nodded.

"Right then, glyph-style. When you need help in your fight against the demon, use this spell. Help will come."

"I don't want anyone else to have to suffer for my mistake. I will find a way to do this on my own."

The old man slammed the spellbook shut with one hand. "There's that pride that got you into this mess trying to reassert itself again. If you go into this fight with that kind of attitude, you'll be killed, and this world will become a demon's playground. Is that what you want?"

"I... of course not but..."

The old man handed Kyzyl his spellbook back. Kyzyl looked at it. On the page opposite his Extraplanar Summoning spell was a different spell of a very similar style. The only problem was, "this spell has no subject. How am I..." Kyzyl trailed off as he looked up to see the old man had disappeared. He'd left his tripod and cookpot.

With nothing better to do, Kyzyl finished the stew. It was a bit gamy, but seasoned to perfection. He wondered idly where an old man who looked like a traveling beggar got the money for such an array of flavorings.

After he finished the stew, he laid down his bedroll and fell asleep. In his dreams, Bethany visited him again. Altogether, it was a pleasant night.

CHAPTER TWENTY-FIVE
Demonic Destruction

After he woke up, Kyzyl found a version of Master
Jonah's chant in his spellbook as well. It seemed to be
geared toward a moon god of some sort, which Kyzyl
suspected would work better with the amulet considering it
was in the shape of a crescent moon.

When he used the new chant, he felt a chill run
from the pendent near his chest all the way up to his eyes,
and a dark spot appeared in his vision when he looked
toward the southern horizon. He took a breath and started
walking, sensing the demon wasn't very far away.

While he chased the dark spot over the horizon, he
studied the other spell he was given by the curious man. It
still bothered him that the spell didn't have a subject.
Every summoning spell has a subject and a calling, but this
one seemed to only send a call through the aether to
whomever happened to hear it. It was truly bizarre. He
flipped through a few of his other spells. There weren't a lot
that would be useful in a fight. Whatever else the university
was, it definitely didn't train you to slay demons.

He was so absorbed in his contemplations he didn't
realize he was coming close to the farm where the demon
was wreaking havoc. He nearly walked past it until he

heard the laugh. It struck him to his very core. He started to shake. He clenched his fist and took a deep breath. He looked down the dirt path to the house where the demon was. He saw it standing over a woman and a boy. There was only one thing he could do. He slipped his mind into its focused state and braced for the oncoming flashbacks.

When they came, he took a breath and used a trick he learned during his practice with the Baron. He counted five things he could see: the demon, a mother huddling over a child, a red barn, a collapsed silo, and an ox. Next, he listened for four things: the demon's laugh, the crackling of a fire, the woman's sobs, and the flapping wings of birds fleeing the tragic scene. Then touch: his cloak was soft, the sun was warm against his skin, and the leather of his boots was pliable. Smell: blood and burning wood. Taste: His own saliva.

***

He is in Wind-Dance now. The scene spread out before him takes on new context. The boy is bleeding and the farmhouse behind them has caught on fire.

Kyzyl thinks of approaching the group, but knows the demon would attack if he did. The only thing he can do is summon the boy and his mother to him. He starts the casting, binding the heat of the fire to his spell to bend reality. His limbs shake and he starts to hear screaming, but he throws his whole consciousness behind the spell to escape it.

The spell works and the pair are laid out before him. The woman is still spread out over the boy. He's pale-faced and covered in blood. Kyzyl takes off his cloak and nudges the women's shoulder with it. She holds the boy tighter and sobs louder.

"Ma'am, I can buy this boy some time, but you have to move," Kyzyl says. His voice is calm and reassuring.

She looks up with a surprised expression on her

297

face. She moves to the side and Kyzyl presses the cloak up against the boy's wounds. "Hold this and keep pressure on it. That will slow the bleeding. I'm going to draw the demon away from you two. Start praying to whatever gods may be listening to send a healer."

Kyzyl sees a lot of questions in her eyes, but she nods and obeys. The bleeding slows, but Kyzyl isn't sure if it will stop on its own. The boy needs time and a miracle, and since Kyzyl is no god, there's only one thing he can give him.

He stands and looks straight at the mass of rippling muscles powerful enough to tear down a tower. An idea begins to form in the back of Kyzyl's mind. An observation he read at the university and some advice Master Enwin had given him starts to fit together.

He puts one foot in front of the other, then again, and again. Soon, he's walking toward the demon with a resolve on his face. This was a dangerous gambit, but beating the demon at all is a long shot no matter what he tries.

The demon smiles as Kyzyl starts to charge. He brakes eye contact with the demon, locks his eyes on a spot just behind him and starts to concentrate on a spell for summoning living matter.

He feels a tight squeeze as he is pulled through the aether. The spot he'd locked on to grows bigger until his feet find the ground. He stands and turns his head to the demon, who is now behind him. Kyzyl has just performed his first self-summoning, or teleportation, and it had worked.

He doesn't let his triumph last long. The demon still needs to be drawn away from the other two. Somewhere in his mind, a piece of Kyzyl wonders how the demon was able to hurt the boy, but it doesn't matter. For Kyzyl and the demon, this all ends here. Kyzyl starts to run in the opposite direction of the bleeding boy and his mother.

He doesn't know where he was running to, he still

had no plan, but the demon was chasing him. Better him than a farmer and her son.

Kyzyl looks at the ox in the pin next to the barn. It was a desperate gambit. He races inside the barn and bars the door.

The barn is dark and piled with hay. The demon will burst through the closed doors any second. He needs to work fast. He'd used his own muscle energy to perform the teleportation spell, so his arms move slowly through his heat transfer spell. He feels his body heat leech away as the hay catches fire.

The doors fly off their hinges and hit the roof as Kyzyl binds the heat of the fire to a new summoning spell. The ox appears in front of him, confused. With the fire behind it, it charges toward the open doorway and straight into the demon. Before it hits the demon, the barn doors that had been spinning in the air fall on top of Kyzyl pinning him to the ground.

Kyzyl is barely holding on to consciousness when the demon slams the bull on the ground twice and throws it to the side. He grits his teeth, summons all his will and magical might. He chants Luck's spell like a prayer and makes the few hand gestures to send two words echoing through the field of aether that permeates all of existence.

"Help me!" He feels a warm glow on his face and sees a soft yellow light begin to grow. Then darkness over takes him.

#

Kyzyl awoke next to the boy, still bloody, but the color had returned to his face. The sun was setting, even though it had just passed its zenith when he had gotten to the farmhouse. He sat up.

His legs tingled like they had fallen asleep, but he was able to move his toes. The woman was talking to a strange winged man wearing armor and a sword on his belt.

She started crying fresh tears, and the man gestured her toward her son. They both walked over to where the boy and Kyzyl were and the man held a hand out to Kyzyl. Kyzyl took it, stood, and they walked away from the boy and his mother.

"The boy will be fine," the man said without preamble. "Closing wounds is the first thing one is able to do when studying healing magic. You, however, were more difficult. You had been paralyzed by the fall of the door, so I had to regenerate a small piece of your spine and spinal cord."

"And what of the demon?"

"Sent to where he belongs. He will be bound to the deepest shadows of the Nine Hells for a century. After that, the old bindings will reassert themselves."

"Thank you... for coming to help me."

"I do not answer summons from mortals. My kind cannot be compelled in such a way. We also don't, generally, answer calls of people who allow forces of destruction to run rampant through the mortal realms. Had I been here on my own business, I would have let you die when the demon was securely sequestered."

Kyzyl just stared at the ground. He had many questions for this strange man, but shame kept him silent.

"Luck, however, was on your side. I was not here on my own business. Instead, I was sent here by someone who has been thoroughly convinced of your growth."

Kyzyl looked up, but the man did not explain further. Kyzyl opened his mouth to ask some of the questions he'd been thinking of, but the man held up his hand.

"Which leaves one last thing."

Kyzyl looked up at the man with a questioning tilt to his head.

"That sash on your waist. It means you're a master duelist from Techarae. Am I correct?"

Kyzyl nodded.

"It does not do to see such a master without a sword." He pulled his sword out of its scabbard and handed it to Kyzyl. It was perfectly balanced. The metal of the blade looked like swirling wind or crashing waves. It was a work of art. The man handed Kyzyl the scabbard and Kyzyl sheathed the weapon.

"Thank you, sir." The man bowed and a soft glow sprang up around him. The light grew until Kyzyl had to blink away spots in his eyes. When he could see again, the man was gone.

CHAPTER TWENTY-SIX
The Road Back

Kyzyl spent the next week helping the boy, whose name he found out was Jason, and his mother, Laurie, rebuild the barn and fix the roof of their farmhouse. He used the last of the Baron's money to ensure they had all the necessary materials, and was even able to help haul them with his summoning magic. It seemed to be the least he could do, especially since he had gotten their ox killed.

"Better it than my son," Laurie had said.

Right around the time they were finishing up the roof, a raven perched near the farmhouse. It had a roll of paper tied to its back, which Kyzyl took. Afterward, the raven flew away and Kyzyl read the note.

Dear Sir,

It has come to my attention that you displayed exceptional magical prowess by banishing a demon from this plane of existence. I am a Master at the University Arcanum, where we make a study of such things, and we would be honored to have your talents at our school. If you wish to study here, we will be holding admissions interviews during the final week of this month. I hope to see you there.

Sincerely,

Master Jonah Kalero

Cleric of the Knower, third class

Kyzyl crumpled the letter and threw it to the ground. Where did he get off? Inviting Kyzyl to the one place he could never go again. He had half a mind to— in fact, he just might.

"Where is the nearest town?"

"A half day to the west," Laurie said. "I can pack you a meal if you need one."

"That would be a very good help, thank you. Does it have an Inn?"

She grimaced. "It's more like a tavern with an extra room."

"It'll do. I'll need food good for the road."

"We have some vegetables, dried meat, and I can bake you some bread if you wait until the morning."

Kyzyl nodded absently as he began to think. Looking back on his travels, he realized he had no idea which direction the university was in. Perhaps he could find a map or guide in the next town. "Are we still in the Riverstone Barony?"

"No, that's at least a week of hard walking north of here. You're in Whettfel Barony."

Kyzyl hadn't a clue where that was. He'd need to find a map or a caravan that was going toward the university. In a large enough city, that wouldn't be too hard. The university was almost a center of power unto itself, and it held all sorts of things prized by merchants. It was just a matter of finding someone who knew where to go.

"What do you say to staying tonight and leaving in the morning? I still haven't thanked you properly for saving my boy. Besides, it's been far too long since I got to cook a full feast. Of course, it wouldn't be like the feasts a man like you is used to, but I can hold my own."

"I would love to stay for your feast. Then I will certainly need some rest."

"I'll get started then."

Jason and Kyzyl spent the rest of the day finishing the repairs to the barn. By then, the sun was going down. Jason started to walk toward the house, but turned around when he realized Kyzyl wasn't with him.

"Go on. Tell your mom I'll be in soon. I just need a moment." He stood there as Jason walked the rest of the way back into the house. Kyzyl just kept looking at the setting sun. "Bethany would've loved it here," he thought. He felt a twinge in his chest. He smiled as the memory of her brought a small pain to his heart.

Kyzyl spent his last day with Jason and Laurie telling them all the stories he'd left out while helping them repair their farm. He admitted to them that he'd been the one to summon the demon in a vain attempt at proving the Master Cleric wrong. Jason seemed initially upset by this revelation, but his mother said something about the other entity Kyzyl summoned. He didn't catch what it was, but it seemed to pacify her son.

The next morning, Laurie made them each a grain cake. She had a dish of honey-sweetened butter in the middle of the table. There was no meat or jam, but Kyzyl was able to have three glasses of fresh milk. All-in-all, it was a good way to start a journey.

Kyzyl's anger at the Master Cleric burned down to a bed of smoldering coals as he walked the road into the nearest town. Soon, it was overpowered by his realization that, if he did make it on to the university complex, he'd likely be executed.

He touched the hilt of his new sword. It was tied to his waist with the silk sash he'd earned when he became a master duelist, the last remaining remnant of his homeland. He had summoned all the silk robes he had put in his rooms at his father's estate, and he wasn't familiar enough with any other place where silk would be to summon it from there. Besides, the silk robes he sold were his, any other silk he'd summon would belong to someone else, and whatever else Shenta Kyzyl was, he was no thief.

He stopped to rest and eat a midday snack out of his backpack. He drew the blade out of its scabbard. It was an arming sword the length of his arm. Its swirling pattern again reminded him of blowing winds. He rotated his wrist to get a feel for the weight. The steel felt almost impossibly light.

He stood and got into the stance for falling petal. He flowed like water from one sword stance to another and the blade seemed to anticipate his movements. He couldn't tell if it was guiding him, or if it was merely so light that it felt like he was merely moving a part of his own body.

He sheathed the sword, picked up his pack and continued walking. When he got to the town Laurie had mentioned, he saw that how she'd described it was perfectly accurate. The only thing that made this collection of houses and shops worthy of the word town was a large temple in the square. Its plaster walls were a contrast to the tiled roof and sturdy oak beams that held it up. It seemed whoever constructed it considered the walls an afterthought.

The tavern was small and cozy. When Kyzyl walked in, he experienced none of the cold reception he'd gotten from the other small town that had experienced a demon attack. That made Kyzyl suspect Laurie and Jason were they only people here who saw it.

Instead, the shouts of greeting that everyone gave him as he entered a room filled with patrons made Kyzyl jump back out of the door way. He tripped on the step and fell flat on his butt. Not the entrance a nobleman's son generally hopes for, but at least these people were happy to see him.

He approached the barman and asked for a cup of his best wine.

"I got some mead in the basement I was fixing to crack open soon. It's a strawberry melomel and she's been waiting all winter for me to break 'er out."

"Mead does sound good right about now."

The barman tapped his nose and went around back to the cellar doors. While he was gone, a few people came up to Kyzyl and asked him what he was doing in town. He explained that he was helping Laurie and Jason fix a few things around the farm, leaving out how they had broken in the first place. If these people didn't know about the demon, and it was gone now, there was no point in scaring them.

The barman came back with a cup of amber colored liquid with a pungent aroma. Kyzyl took a sip and let it settle onto his tongue. It was sweet with a few earthy tones that reminded him of a deep forest.

"Were the strawberries in the mead wild?" he asked.

"Right you are. I bought them off a ranger that had come into town just as I was racking the mead. Decided to cut them in half and let the juices mingle with the mead as it started to settle down."

"Your instincts for brewing are impressive." Kyzyl turned to the man with whom he was speaking. "Where was I? Right, I'm heading to the University Arcanum. The Master Cleric sent me an invitation to take their admission exams."

"That's quite the journey for such a young pup. Are ya up fer it?"

"I think so. I've been doing a lot of traveling lately. Although," he directed his next statement at the barman, "I could use some help with directions. I got turned around on my way through your barony and I need to get to the closest city. Really any place that has frequent visits by caravan merchants will do."

"A caravan just came through on their way to Tamerrel. They may be going inland toward the university after that. That was two days ago, but caravans tend to go slow and stop in any town with money. If you hurry, you could catch them before they make it to Tamerrel."

Even if he didn't, Tamerrel was the city he'd docked in when he first came to Strophe. It was the largest trading hub in the entire kingdom. There would be plenty of people there going where he needed to be. "Which way is Tamerrel?"

"It's on the coast. Follow the road northwest out of town and follow the signs for Crownrel. It'll take you about five days if you don't catch up with the caravan in that time."

"That's perfect. I was told you had an extra room in this tavern?"

The barman nodded and brought a key out from behind the bar. "It ain't no suite like I'm guessing you're used to." He nodded to Kyzyl's silk sash.

"Is it an attic room?" Kyzyl said, letting a bit of excitement touch his voice.

The barman nodded slowly.

"Then it'll feel just like home." Kyzyl smiled and took the key, leaving a copper penny on the counter. For a drink and an attic room, it was a bit steep, but it was his last coin. He had his account with the dwarvish banks, but he didn't expect one of those to be within convenient travel for the barman.

In the morning, Kyzyl packed and started to make his way out the door when the barman caught up to him. He handed Kyzyl a rolled-up piece of parchment.

"One of the King's mages left this with me a few seasons back. It was his only method of payment, but I don't have any use for it. Since you were so generous a tipper last night, I figured maybe you could take it to the university for me. It might be useful to someone there."

Kyzyl unrolled the scroll to discover it was a spell scroll. It contained a glyph that outlined a simple scrying spell. It would be of use to very few people at the university since it was one of the first spells any divination wizard learned. Still, it was the first divination spell Kyzyl had ever had access to.

He thanked the barman and tucked the scroll between the pages of his spellbook. When he got to a place where he could withdraw money for ink, he'd copy it. For now, he'd have to practice from the scroll.

On his way to Tamerrel, Kyzyl met up with a band of Wanderers that were making a living doing stunts and stage combat. When he gave the traditional Wanderer greeting; first, third, and fifth fingers extended while bending the second and fourth like they were cut off, they cheered and greeted him like family. He asked them which way they were going, and they told him they were headed to their patron's estate in Ironkeep.

"Are you passing by the university?" he asked, more than willing to change his plans if it meant traveling with their band.

"Alas," declared the sword-master, "we are headed to the other side of the barony. If you're looking for a group to travel with, Tamerrel tends to have a great many merchants who are on their way to the university. Most of them are smalltime men who fancy themselves Caravaners."

"Aren't all traveling merchants Caravaners?"

"Are all traveling performers Wanderers?"

Kyzyl didn't know the answer, but he suspected there was only one. "No?"

"No, of course not. Caravaners and Wanderers are a special kind of people. Each of us train, in our own way, from birth til the time we can no longer walk the roads. Every day for us is a new adventure and the road is our only true home. Our fellows are our true family."

"So, Caravaners and Wanderers are races of people? Like elves and humans?"

The sword-master gave a hesitant "yes and no" wobble. "Humans can be both. Elves, halflings and dwarves too. It's not about where you were born or what your bloodline is. It's about the spirit. If one is truly a Wanderer, they will feel caged being in one place all the time. I suspect the same is true for Caravaners. Both seek treasures from far away places. Although their treasures are more... merchant-ish."

"Merchant-ish?"

"Caravaners seek treasure worth coin more than anything else."

"What treasures do you seek then?"

"The treasure of a well told story, of course. Nothing is more precious to a Wanderer than a story they don't know. Even a new telling of a story we already know has value in our circles."

"I thought that Wanderers knew all the stories in the world already."

The sword master gave a conspiratorial grin, leaned in, and switched to a stage whisper. "Don't spread it around too far, but the truth is, Wanderers are people like any other.

"We know stories because we grow up with tons of them, but the fact is, everyone probably has at least one story that's be new to us. Most times it's their story, but sometimes it's a different one."

Kyzyl enjoyed his time with the Wanderer troupe as they traveled together. He learned a great deal more about Lukor. The Wanderers told him stories about an upstart in the orc tribes that was trying to unite the entire unclaimed hills under his banner. They also told him stories of the deserts of Maskohma and the diversity of cultures that had sprung up around its various city-states.

He gave them stories in return about his homeland. He told them of the Storm Giants that were said to live at the tops of mountains and bottoms of deep lakes, of the underworld where dark and monstrous creatures were locked away by the earth spirits.

They had many questions when he told them of the

gods that sacrificed themselves to create the world, and Kyzyl answered them as best he could. He wished he could answer them, but he'd actively avoided his people's belief structure. The sages weaponizing their knowledge to make him feel like an inadequate intellectual still made him want to avoid the subject.

Kyzyl parted ways with the Wanderers on the last fork in the road before he went to Tamerrel. He bid they good-bye, and then stood looking up at the sign that bore the name of the first city in Lukor he'd ever encountered. It had various scratches and graffiti on it. Even the name was almost completely obscured by something that looked like a sideways eye.

Kyzyl looked down the road toward the city. It still wasn't visible over the horizon, but the wind carried the smell of tar and coal smoke. He remembered the breeze off the ocean pushing the dockside smell deeper into the city, the look of dockhands in homespun, and the sounds of men yelling and women making sultry invitations to passing sailors.

He touched his coin purse where it was strapped to his chest. Easily accessible, but safe from the wandering hands of pickpockets. He took a breath and walked toward the city, knowing it was one step closer to confronting Master Jonah.

Kyzyl's anger at the Master Cleric had long since died, and his sense of immediacy toward getting to the university had gone with it. He was still determined to tell Master Jonah exactly who'd defeated the demon, but he didn't let that stop him from enjoying a nice lunch at a familiar tavern after he withdrew a bit of coin from the bank.

The server who'd brought him his food recognized him almost instantly. She pulled him playfully to a table in the back with a bench seat. Afterward, she brought him a plate of venison, a hard cheese, and a bowl of steaming stew. She sat very close to him and he could feel her hand on his arm. This was a much warmer reception than she gave him the first time, but the attention made him quiver with anxious energy.

"I was hoping you'd come back so I could apologize for my cold treatment of you, my lord." Her hand moved to his knee, and he felt his heart beating inside his chest. Her hand started to move up his thigh, but he stopped her.

He pushed himself in his mindfulness state to stay calm. Once he had his anxiety under control, he turned to her and said, "I appreciate and accept your apology. However, if it's all the same to you, I would prefer to eat alone. Thank you for the meal."

He waited for her to huff at him and walk away angry, but she just looked at him. When she looked down at the hand that was still holding her wrist, he followed her gaze. His grip was firm but gentle. The hand itself was still shaking, but it was steadier than it had been a moment ago.

"I'm sorry. I didn't..." she trailed off. Then she began again, "I didn't mean to make you uncomfortable. I'll let you eat in peace." She got up and went back to the bar.

Kyzyl felt he should apologize, but couldn't think of anything he should apologize for. Deciding that it was better to just leave it be, he began eating.

The food was as tasty as it was the first time. The venison was dripping with some kind of brine solution, making in tender and juicy. The stew was made from chicken broth and thickened with flour and butter to make it creamy. The cheese had a bite to it that made Kyzyl want to try something.

He took a piece of venison and soaked it in the stew long enough for it to pick up a bit of the flavor. Then he broke off a piece of the cheese and placed it on the venison. When he popped the concoction in his mouth, it was creamy, tangy, and tender.

After he finished his meal, he made his way to the

bar where the server was polishing bottles. He placed a copper penny on the counter, and she looked at it.

"Need something for the road again?" she asked.

"Not this time. The rest is yours. Thanks for remembering me." Kyzyl smiled at her guilty expression. She was sweet, he decided, if a little forward for his taste. The only woman who could get away with being that fast out of the gate was Bethany.

His heart gave a little twinge of sadness at the memory. Thinking about her still hurt a little, but it was a lot like the pain he felt when trying to use a leg that had fallen asleep. The pain was a feeling, and feeling meant that his heart was working again.

Kyzyl found a caravan going inland toward the university. It resembled the one lead by Baerûn, though none of the faces were familiar. The dwarf he spoken to seemed yet more abrasive than him.

"One silver noble. Takes care of your food and shelter while you're with us. You pull your weight while we load and unload carts. Sithy, the little woman over there," the dwarvish Caravan Master pointed to a stout halfling woman organizing crates, "she'll be making your dinner each night. You ever had a halfling cook for you?"

"Not recently," Kyzyl said. He remembered most of this from Baerûn's caravan, but the Caravan Master seemed to enjoy explaining things in a slightly threatening tone. Kyzyl decided it was best for both of them if he got it off his chest.

"Even with the increased quality of food, though, a whole silver noble seems a bit steep for as far as I'm going. After all, I could buy any food I'd need for a couple of iron mills and still have plenty left over for a stay at an inn every night."

"Aye, but ya won't have an inn to stay in e'ery night. Not to mention what dangers might be on these 'ere roads."

"Aren't these the king's roads?"

"Ay. Ye didn't 'ere about the demon running around these lands, I'm guessing. Clerics all over are talking about this being the end times. Reckon they'll take any excuse to get butts in their seats, but the point remains."

"I heard the demon had been taken care of. Probably a powerful spellcaster from the university."

The dwarf gave a quick huff. "Sooner trust the church to take care of the problem. The university prolly the one that summoned the cursed thing in the first place."

"Tell you what," Kyzyl said, changing the subject back to the matter at hand. He untied his silk master-duelist sash from his waist where it had been keeping his sword, "you're a merchant by trade, what will you give me for this?" It was the last thing he had from his homeland, but, after everything he had been through, he wanted to put as much of his past as he could behind him.

The dwarf took it and ran it through his fingers. "Is this silk? Where did you get this?"

"I brought it with me when I came here." It seemed so long ago. Had it really only been a year?

"Something like this? I might be inclined to give you a full gold royal for it."

"That'd be nice considering it's probably worth at least five. Anyway, that, less my silver noble, leaves you nine nobles in my debt. I'll expect to be repaid by the time we reach the university." Kyzyl winked at the flustered dwarf. For all he'd learned in the past year, he was still the son of a noble.

The dwarf heaved a great sigh and walked off muttering something about lousy nobility and thinking they're better than everyone. Kyzyl chuckled at the half-heard comments. He learned through his dealing at the university that, even if the dwarf felt swindled, the opportunity to sell any amount of silk was a great symbol of status among merchants on this side of the world.

CHAPTER TWENTY-SEVEN
A Magical Protector

After a week of traveling with the caravan, Kyzyl
started to get an odd feeling. While they were walking, he
kept turning around, certain that they were being watched.
By this point, he'd used the scrying spell he'd been given by
the innkeeper to locate a remote piece of the woods on
Baron Galthos' estate. He had familiarized himself with it
through the spell such that he could send his new sword to
that part of the forest where it'd be safe.

Now he could use the first spell he'd learned at the
university to summon the sword any time he needed it. He
moved his hands through the needed sigils and ran through
the chant in his head. Without the concentration or a
power source, the spell wouldn't work, but repeating it in
his head made him feel ready to cast it at a moment's
notice.

Kyzyl heard a rustle in the underbrush by the trail.
He stopped and stared at the source, heart pounding and
teeth clenched. The caravan passed by him, some of the
merchants looked at the trees where he was staring, but
none stopped save for him.

Kyzyl thought he could see shadows moving in the
underbrush beside the road. He strained his eyes and ears

and wished he had the extra-sensory spells Emrys once mentioned to him. The last wagon passed him, the driver looking at him confused, and he decided that it was just the breeze moving the underbrush making rustling sounds.

Moments later, however, he saw the shadows between the trees again. They started to grow larger. He saw glowing yellow eyes peer at him through the shadows the underbrush made. Then, a massive grey wolf bounded out of the tree line and landed half a dozen steps from Kyzyl.

It looked at him for a single moment before two more wolves joined it on the road. Kyzyl had never seen a wolf up close. He'd always assumed they were much like wild dogs, but the beasts that stood in front of him were larger than any dog he'd ever seen. Their powerful jaws could easily fit a clenched fist inside them and, probably just as easily, bite it clean off.

The wolves ran across the road into the underbrush on the other side. Kyzyl listened to them rustling through the underbrush as they continued on whatever journey they'd been on when they came across his path.

Kyzyl let out a sigh and continued walking, but there was a new rustling on the side of the road where to wolves had jumped out at him. He had a single heart beat to turn toward it before and arrow sprung from the trees and landed in the dirt behind him.

"Bandits!" he cried before diving behind the nearest cart for cover. He summoned his sword, then looked up. Six men were attacking the merchants, brandishing clubs and, in one case, a longsword. He couldn't face six men on his own, and the caravan guards were nowhere to be seen. No doubt having their own bandits to deal with.

Kyzyl only had one choice. He took in a deep breath and let it fill his lungs. He pushed his mind into its concentrated state. It took a few heartbeats for him to be certain, but when it came, he was ready.

***

Kyzyl stands and takes out two vials from the pouch Luthor had given him. These had been meant for his fight with the demon, but that is over. He needs them now. He breaks one of the vials under his boot, sending yellowish goo spreading through the dirt. He uncorks the second vial and spills white salts over the goo, and a bright white flare burns where they meet.

Kyzyl binds the light energy from the flare and begins a summoning as the men around him try to blink away their blindness. They aren't quick enough, and Kyzyl's summoning calls three massive figures to appear between him and the bandits.

The wolves chase off four of the bandits, but the man with the longsword rallies another to continue their assault on the wagons. The flare is gone, and the wolves have chased the bandits into the forest, nipping at their heels.

Kyzyl spots a drop of blood where one of the felling bandits was standing. A dark thought occurs to him. Something one of his tutors once said to him comes to mind, "once together, always together." This sort of thing was never done by an upstanding wielder of the arcane arts, but these men were bandits. They had chosen their path, and now Kyzyl chooses his.

He binds the drop of blood to the person it came from. He doesn't know which one, but it doesn't matter. He pulls heat from the blood left in that bandit's body, probably leaving him wracked with sudden chills somewhere while wolves tear him apart.

He transfers the heat using the first spell he'd ever learned. However, it doesn't transform into a bolt of fire. Instead, he uses it to warm the handle of the longsword. The man screams and drops the sword like he'd been bitten by a snake.

Kyzyl approaches him. He sees the burns on the man's hands where he was holding the sword. The man looks up at him. Kyzyl knows the punishment for banditry. If this man is turned over to the crown's law, he'll be hanged. Instead, Kyzyl cuts his throat, leaving him bleeding out in the dirt. The other man runs into the trees without looking back, giving the fight to Kyzyl. Except...

Kyzyl turns and throws another handful of salts across the road, muttering the chant for an anti-kinetic barrier. An arrow stops mid-flight and falls to the ground in front of the barrier. Kyzyl waits for the second arrow. When it doesn't come, he shouts into the tree line, "you're going to have to come down here and face me."

There is no response. After a few more moments, the chemical energy locked within the salts is used up and the barrier dissipates. Kyzyl waits another moment to be sure, then rejoins the caravan to help the wounded.

***

CHAPTER TWENTY-EIGHT
Reunion and Redemption

Kyzyl stood before the gate to the university. His heart was racing, his whole body was shaking and sweaty, and his jaw was clenched. He wanted to throw open the gates and scream for Master Jonah until the entire Kingdom of Strophe heard him, but he was also certain just being this close to the university was likely to get him executed. He was firmly planted, not wanting to move forward, not wanting to run.

That's where Emrys found him. Emrys' eyes went wide. He shouted "What, in the Nine Hells, are you doing here?"

He turned red and looked around, which gave Kyzyl just enough time to be surprised. Emrys rushed over to the gate and whispered, "you were banished. You know that if you step through this gate, they'll execute you right?"

In that moment, anger won out in Kyzyl's gut. "Where's Jonah?"

"He's teaching. Why?"

Kyzyl handed him the crumpled letter he received. Emrys smoothed it out and read it quickly.

"What is this? Did you steal it from--?"

"I would never! He sent this to me!"

"He... but, wait," Emrys read the note a second time. "That means you..." Emrys trailed off as he read the letter again. "You killed that... thing?"

He ducked his head and looked around once he realized he was yelling again. He spotted Master Jonah. His eyes went wide and he looked at Kyzyl, but Master Jonah just smiled at him.

"Master Jonah. I thought you were teaching. I would've come..." Emrys trailed off as Master Jonah raised a hand for him to be quiet.

"How are you doing Mr. Shenta?" Master Jonah asked.

"How am I doing? You sent me a letter inviting me back here. You called me back to the one place I want to be and the one place I can never be again. How do you think I am doing?"

"Yes, I do admit that letter is not my best work, but it did the job."

"Did the job?"

"I can explain, but I'd rather do it with both of us on this side of the gate, if you please."

Kyzyl hesitated.

"I can promise you won't be executed. After all, you have written evidence that one of the nine Masters invited you back." Master Jonah pushed open the gate and waved Kyzyl through.

When Kyzyl stepped through the gate, his heart was still pounding in his ears. He heard the chatting of students around him, smelled the coal smoke coming out of the artificing workshops. He couldn't keep his body from shaking, but the sights and sounds of the place he loved filled his senses. Emrys put his arm around Kyzyl when the shaking came close to keeping him from walking. Master Jonah smiled and lead the two back to his office.

"I sent that letter because I believe I am on the

verge of getting your banishment recused, but I will need you to testify concerning your most recent conquest," he explained while they were still on the way.

"You mean the demon I killed."

Master Jonah nodded. "Ever since your sentencing, I've been speaking with the other Masters and combing through the legal codes of the university trying to find your best legal recourse."

"Why?"

"I'm sorry?"

"Why do you want me back at the university?"

"Because I believe it's where you belong."

Kyzyl gave a surprised smile.

"As I was saying, the legal codes allow few avenues for reintegration. Un-banishment seems to largely not exist within the Codex. Apparently, the forefathers of the University Arcanum didn't expect we would be forced to banish an ultimately virtuous, however misguided, wizard.

"There is, technically, always the possibility that the other Masters will agree to setting a new legal precedent. However, given their concerns for the university and its independence, they will likely be very protective of the current set of legal precedence."

"Were you able to find anyway that we can get Kyzyl back in without such a major change?" Emrys asked.

"No. Nothing that applies in this situation. Most of the avenues for reintegration involve new evidence that exonerates the person in question. I doubt the current set of Masters is willing to set such a large and sweeping legal precedent. To put it bluntly, since you are still guilty of your crimes, we're stuck."

"Thanks for being honest," Kyzyl said. "You said you've been talking to the other Masters?"

The three reached the door to the Master's Hall. Master Jonah hesitated. "We should find another door," Master Jonah said.

"No need. Do you still have the same office?" Kyzyl asked.

"Yes, wh--" before Master Jonah finished, the three were pulled through the aether and arrived inside his office. Master Jonah's eyes where wide and he stumbled a bit as they landed. "Did you just preform a triple teleportation of a place you couldn't see?"

"Yes, teleporting was something I learned during the... fight." Emrys was looking at Kyzyl like he grew an extra set of limbs. Kyzyl looked at him and shifted uneasily. "I had to do some dodging before..."

"How did you defeat the demon?" Emrys asked.

"I... I had help. I learned an odd spell from an old man that summoned, I honestly don't know who it was, I was passed out for most of it. He did give me this though."

Kyzyl summoned his new sword. Master Jonah and Emrys gasped as Kyzyl drew it from its sheath and allowed them to see the swirling pattern of its steel. "It's just a sword."

"No, Mr. Shenta, that's not just a sword. That is celestial steel. May I?" Kyzyl handed Master Jonah the sword. He took it, reverently, and brought it to his desk and sat down to examine it.

"This metal is... legend says this is the metal from which the Calisi Emperi was made. You said that the person who gave you this was the one who helped you banish the demon?"

"Kill him, yes. What is the Calisi Emperi?"

Master Jonah shook his head. "Demons can't be killed while on the material plane. In fact, most of them can't be killed by anything less powerful than a celestial entity."

"Master. What's the Calisi Emperi?"

"The lost sword of the Lukorian Emperor. Legend says that whoever wields it is crowned High King of Lukor."

"Lukor has a high king?"

"Not for at least two hundred years. The man who gave you this, you said he answered a summons from you?"

"More like a request. An old man gave me a new spell that only had a call, not a subject. The man just answered the call."

"I don't think he was a man."

"He didn't strike me as particularly feminine but..."

"No, I mean I believe the thing that answered your call was an angel. One of the gods sent you a celestial servant of theirs to help you defeat a demon. Which means you have been deemed worthy by a god. If I can use that to get a letter of recommendation from a high-ranking priest in Calcut..."

"Will the Masters really listen to a priest about a legal decision that is ultimately theirs to make?" Emrys asked.

"No." Master Jonah sat down, deflating a bit. "They would much rather hear what one of their own has to say. Even the most religious of them would rather make a decision themselves than bowing to the whims of anyone, even a god."

"You almost sound resentful of your fellow Masters," Emrys pointed out.

"I sometimes find scholars and their tendencies frustrating. Even if you think it's obvious why you're right, everything needs proof."

"How else do you expect us to pursue truth, Master?" Emrys asked.

Master Jonah smiled at his student. "Too true. Sometimes, it seems, my impulse to be frustrated goes against my own best interest. Still, it seems that my peers will expect a full case with facts and reason, without subjective opinion, before they consider overturning their decision."

"You are the Master of Rhetorician here at the

university," Kyzyl said.

Master Jonah stood from his desk and walked toward the door. "I am going to ask the Head Master to call the Masters together. We will discuss whether you will be welcomed back to the university. I suggest that the two of you work on your arguments for being allowed back in. Oh!"

His head popped back into the doorway. "It'd be best if you weren't seen on the premise until the Masters call you, Mr. Shenta. While you technically have my permission to be here, proving that would be an event on its own, and my time is better spent speaking with my colleagues. You understand?"

Kyzyl nodded as the Master closed the door behind him. He turned to Emrys. "Up for another jump? I was hoping to find Donovan."

"Oh... yeah." Emrys looked out the window behind Master Jonah's desk.

"What's wrong?"

"Well... him and Matilda... I mean..." Emrys looked down at his feet. "We didn't agree about what happened to you, so... Donovan and I haven't talked since you left."

"Ah," Kyzyl said. He saw a lot of pain and regret on what little he could see of Emrys' face.

"Well, like Master Jonah said, I am best left somewhere people won't find me until I am called. So, you're going to have to be the one to go and find them."

"I... Kyzyl... I can't. What we said to each other, it's more complicated than you realize."

A memory pushed itself forward as Kyzyl started putting pieces together in his mind. The real reason Emrys supported him, even when his other friends didn't.

"Because you're in love with me." Kyzyl hadn't meant for it to be said out loud, but Emrys just looked up with a surprised expression.

Emrys relaxed into a pose Kyzyl often saw on

people who felt caught or guilty. "Yeah. It wasn't all at once, but when I saw you on your first day, I thought you were cute. Then we got to know each other and things kept progressing."

"Why didn't you say anything?"

"I was going to. Donovan and I were even talking about how best to word it. Then there was that night we got drunk and you said you weren't..." Emrys trailed off. The word seemed hard for him to say, and Kyzyl suddenly felt awful.

"Oh, Emrys. I'm so sorry. I didn't mean it like that. I just..."

Emrys waved his hand. "It's fine. To be honest, that is one of the tamer words I've heard for what I am. I just wish there were fewer slang words and more words that sounded... I don't know... academic?"

Kyzyl chuckled. "I don't think this is a subject the Masters intend on offering at the university."

That got a smile out of Emrys. "That's fair. I guess I'll just have to make up my own words for what I am. How about..." he paused thinking. "Ambisextrous. Like ambidextrous, but—"

"Yeah, I get the joke. If that's what you want to be called, then I'm OK with it. You are Emrys, the Ambisextrous Diviner. Do you still stay at the Broken Bridle?"

Emrys nodded, smiling at his friend.

Kyzyl created a clear picture of Emrys' room in his mind, spoke a few words, and they were both pulled through the aether, and suddenly standing next to his bed. Kyzyl looked around at the messy desk and narrow bed. Emrys had done a lot with his room to utilize as much space as possible. Books were piled on top of the dresser, spell scrolls and research notes were scattered around the desk and pinned up on the walls. Most of them were for divination spells, but Kyzyl noticed a few noted on the university's legal code and several decisions made by past Masters acting in their roles as the university's judges.

"Looks like Master Jonah has had some help in trying to get me back in," Kyzyl said.

Emrys shifted his weight from foot to foot. "I told you most of the magic I'm studying is to gain new information. I figured, what better way to put it to use than to help a friend?"

"I appreciate that, but four minds are better than two. I know this is going to be hard, but I would really like to see Donovan and Matilda again. Especially if this is going to be my last chance."

Emrys nodded and, with a deep breath to calm his nerves, walked out of the room.

It took hours before he returned. Kyzyl was reading a book on advanced divination techniques when he walked in with Donovan and Matilda following behind him.

"Emrys, are you aware that you could be prosecuted by the Masters for harboring a fugitive?" Donovan asked.

"Have any of the Masters seen you?" Matilda asked Kyzyl, and he could see the emotions churning inside her. Neither of them looked happy to see him, but he could sense something else behind their stoic expressions. Perhaps it was something Emrys had said to get them here, or maybe they really didn't know how to feel about Kyzyl. Either way, it wasn't just anger or spite behind their eyes.

"Just one. Master Jonah seems bent on seeing me back at the university now that I have banished my demons, both literally and otherwise."

Matilda's eyes went wide. Her mouth opened and closed several times while Kyzyl saw questions form and dissipate on her face.

"He's trying to get you back into the university? Is that even possible?" Donovan asked. The anger seemed to have subsided. Now he was just confused.

"It's definitely a long shot," Emrys said. "But Master Jonah seems to think Kyzyl has a chance if we can all come up with a sufficiently compelling case. I've been reading up on a decision written by the ninth Head Master a few centuries back and—"

"Wait! We're all just going to skip over the fact that someone with barely a year of university training took down a creature powerful enough to knock down a tower built by ancient Masters?" Matilda demanded.

"I'll give you the full story over the victory feast after I'm back in the university. In the meantime, what is going to convince the Masters to let me back in here?"

"Actually," Matilda said, "I think the story might be important. If you found a new way to banish demons, the Masters are going to want to have that kind of magic in their library. They'd be willing to do a lot for it." Donovan sat in the chair by Emrys' desk.

"There's truth in that," Emrys said. "You mentioned you got help from an angel, but the spell you used didn't have a subject. How is that possible?"

Kyzyl opened his spellbook to the page with the strange man's version of the Extraplanar Summoning. Donovan had to stop Matilda from looking over Kyzyl's shoulder, and she looked embarrassed as he quietly shook his head at her.

Kyzyl, for his part, turned it around to show them. Donovan and Emrys gave surprised expressions, but Kyzyl just shrugged. So many people had looked at his spellbook, with and without his permission, lately that it felt less like an issue if his friends did as well.

"As far as I can tell, the spell is designed in a similar way as the spell that summoned the demon. It works by sending an open invitation through the aether to all of creation. It doesn't have any of the unbinding components that the demon's spell did, so anything that is bound to a certain plane would still be trapped. Other than that, anything with sufficient power to move between worlds would be able to answer the call."

"And it just so happened that an angel answered your call?" Donovan asked. He seemed a bit skeptical of the whole thing.

"I suppose if a god had an angel on retainer during the fight, it would stand that the call could easily be answered by that angel," Matilda said.

"Master Jonah seems to think something similar," Emrys responded. "He mentioned that the fact an angel appeared is a sign that Kyzyl has earned the favor of a god of some sort."

"To be honest, I don't really know who, or what, sent the... whatever it was, to me. It said something about me convincing a lot of people of my growth and that's why it came. There seems to be a lot going on in the world that I am unaware of, but I don't know that I'm ready to accept all of this demons, gods and angels stuff without understanding more."

Donovan nodded. "For now, we ought to focus on the task at hand. No doubt Master Jonah is on your side now. He probably thinks you've been blessed by the Ten Divines."

"At least he has an ally this time," Matilda said.

"He's been an ally to Kyzyl throughout this process," Donovan countered. "Just in ways that didn't always give Kyzyl what he wanted. Still, we've gotten off track. One new spell isn't going to be enough to convince the other eight Masters to set a new legal precedent for reintegration. As far as anyone is concerned, the only way Kyzyl gets back into the university is if he is somehow exonerated."

"That's going to be hard," Matilda said. "You are, ultimately, still guilty of the crimes they charged you with. If I thought we could convince Master Enwin to our side, I'd suggest using the spell. As it stands, he is still very disappointed in how things turned out with you. According to every rumor I've heard, he was very proud of you before all this."

That cut Kyzyl to his core. He hadn't realized the Master Conjurer had favored him so much. He was so focused on his vendetta against the Master Cleric, he hadn't noticed Master Enwin's support of him.

"Still," Emrys began, "having the spell as a persuasive tool could be helpful. You should make sure to have your spellbook with you when you face the Masters. Is there anything else in there that might persuade them?"

"Only an entry level divination spell I got off an innkeeper. I doubt that's going to be terribly valuable to them."

"New spells aren't going to convince the entire Master's council that he should be forgiven for killing a score of students and injuring two dozen more," Matilda repeated.

"Even if one of those spells was powerful enough to summon an angel?" Emrys asked.

Matilda shook her head. "You have to convince all of them that you have learned how to be responsible with magic."

"Is there any way to prove that in a single interview session? It seems the only way he can earn back their trust is with a bit of that trust up front," Donovan said.

"There's wisdom in that. Maybe you could point that out to them." Emrys looked at Kyzyl. He was looking out a window to the square. When Emrys moved to stand next to him, he saw that he was looking at the post where he had been whipped. "Do you think they'll execute you if you fail to convince them?"

"I don't know. I'm trying to decide if it's worth it."

"Master Jonah believes you belong here. Is there anywhere else you might belong?"

"I don't know. Do I deserve to live with all the

blood on my hands?"

"Stop it. That kind of talk will not help you." Matilda's voice was firm. She took Kyzyl by the chin and pulled his face toward hers. "That question will prove irrelevant. You WILL convince them you've become responsible." Her eyes were intense. Kyzyl couldn't figure out what emotion he was seeing, but he felt like her gaze was going to bore a hole right through him.

There was a knock at the door, and Master Jonah entered the room. "Mr. Shenta, it's time."

CHAPTER TWENTY-NINE
The Final Judgement

Kyzyl followed Master Jonah to the Master's Hall and into the Examination Chamber. The Chamber was lit with the same glowing orbs of blue light. The light shone across the Masters' stone faces. Kyzyl looked to Master Enwin, but his face betrayed nothing.

"Kyzyl Shenta," declared Head Master Herman, "Jonah Kalero, Master Cleric has asked us to reexamine your banishment. He claims that you have atoned for your sins."

"That is--"

"You will have your chance to speak. First, we will review the charges brought against you. You were originally convicted of reckless experimentation of magic and heinous manslaughter."

Kyzyl didn't look at any of the Masters. He just stared straight ahead, trying to maintain his composure. Even after facing a beast from the depths of the Nine Hells, he was still far more afraid of the nine Masters. "Has anyone found new evidence that would absolve Mr. Shenta of his crimes?"

Silence.

"Master Jonah."

"Thank you Head Master. Gentlemen, each of us was present the day we decided to expel and banish Mr. Shenta from our university. I argued then, as I do now, that such a decision was better than the execution many of my colleagues advocated for. Kyzyl had come face-to-face with a mistake that ended in tragedy and to deny him the opportunity to learn would have reflected poorly on each of us as an educator."

"More poorly than not seeking justice for the bereaved parents and friends who lost loved ones?" Master Telma demanded.

The Head Master spoke up before Master Jonah could answer. "You will get a chance to speak Master Physician. Please allow your colleague to finish his point."

"Thank you Head Master," Master Jonah said before continuing. "As I was saying, our duty as educators then was to send Kyzyl away to face what he had done and overcome his demons, both real and metaphorical. Now, seeing this young man stand before us with new insight and a better understanding of his actions and their consequences, it is our duty to ensure these lessons are reinforced by our firm and diligent guidance.

"What does it say about us as teachers, or by extension our university, if we do not prioritize personal growth as well as academic. This university's purpose is not merely to create new knowledge through study and practical application, nor is it merely to create better students of the arcane. This university's primary purpose is to help our students grow into upstanding and well-rounded people. If we cannot do this for someone who has fallen so low as Mr. Shenta, we might as well each give up our robes to those who would come after us. I yield the floor back to the Head Master."

"Thank you, Master Cleric. Master Physician, you had a comment?"

"Thank you, Head Master. Gentlemen, I had to treat at least sixty of our students, students we have a duty to protect, after the fall of the tower. Then, I had to prepare twenty funerals and contact twenty families and tell them that someone they loved would not be coming home. I had to explain to them that a student under our watch found a way to invite a demon on to our campus and allowed it to kill.

"Those people, the ones mangled and killed by this negligence deserve justice. Now you are asking this council to revoke that justice because of your misguided ideas of salvation. I will not stand for it." The Master Physician sat back in his wooden throne with his arms crossed.

"The Master Physician makes a good argument. Master Jonah, my first duty as Head Master is to this school and the preserving of its integrity. How do you suggest this proposal of yours to further that goal?"

"Master Telma is right in stating that our duty is to uphold justice in the face of such a tragedy. However, Head Master, what he fails to realize is that continuing to punish someone after their lesson has been learned is not justice. Master Telma is not advocating for the continued punishment of the young man before us out of a belief that it will continue to reinforce his growth and understanding of right and wrong.

"Instead, what Master Telma is advocating is for the feelings of the public to be considered above the needs of this individual. That is not justice, but merely vengeance. I do not believe this council, nor the Head Master of this university, should be swayed by emotions and vengeance when our duty is to our students and their growth."

A movement from the far side of the table caught Kyzyl's eye. "Master Conjurer, do you have something to add?" Head Master Herman asked.

"Yes. Thank you, Head Master. As the person who had taken Mr. Shenta on as his student, I feel it is my responsibility to weigh in on this discussion. Master Telma and Master Jonah have made a great many points about the idea of justice and our responsibilities in general, but it is important not to get lost in the philosophy when there is a very real issue of importance here.

"Kyzyl was my student, and one of the brightest I've had in a while. He chose to use that brilliance to feed his own hubris rather than to focus it on bettering himself and the world around him. There was a great deal of potential in him as a student, but how can we be certain that continuing his training will not yield another act of foolishness in the future?"

Kyzyl swallowed back the tears, but the pain in his chest didn't subside. "The Master Conjurer's concerns are valid. Mr. Shenta, how can this council be sure you will not attempt something like this again?"

"I..." Kyzyl took a deep breath. His limbs were still shaking, but he made his voice firm. "My ego got the better of me." He looked at Master Jonah. "I was convinced that I knew better than one of the Masters at the university where I came to study. In a way, I thought I knew better than all of you. I should've realized that if each of you was willing to treat Master Jonah as a colleague, then I should trust him as a Master."

Kyzyl wasn't sure if it was his imagination, but it seemed like the Masters' faces softened a bit. "Mr. Shenta, admission of your mistakes doesn't answer my question. How can this council trust you to wield the secrets we hold responsibly?"

"Honestly, Head Master, you can't. At least, there isn't anything I can say that will reassure you. All of you have been made aware by Master Jonah that there isn't anywhere I'd rather be than at this university.

"That means, no matter what I say, you'll have to consider it in the context that I would say anything to reenter your good graces. In short, the only thing this council can trust is that I wouldn't risk getting banished, or worse, again."

One of the Masters shifted in his seat. "Master

Enchanter, you have a comment?"

"Yes, thank you Head Master. As a man who's devoted his life to deception, I can honestly say that what this young man says is true. If his only desire is to be here, the only thing we can do is trust that he knows the consequences of doing something that foolish again. Maybe he will be able to regain our trust beyond that. Today is not that day. Today is the day we decide whether we can trust that he has learned his lesson."

"Then let us decide that. All in favor of overturning the banishment of Kyzyl Shenta and declaring him innocent, raise your hands."

Master Jonah, Master Enwin, and the Master Enchanter all raised their hands. There was a moment of silence. Then Head Master Herman declared, "three to six and a half. Banishment stands."

"Head Master?" Kyzyl had just thought of something. It was a thin, desperate hope, but it was all he had."

"I'm sorry Kyzyl—"

"I don't mean to be rude Head Master, but you just asked the Masters to declare me innocent."

"Unfortunately, that is the only avenue for re-entry into this university. There is no legal precedent for someone who remains guilty begin absolved of their punishment."

"I understand that Head Master, and it would be a large new precedent to set for this council. One I am sure many of the Masters here are not yet ready to make, but precedent is based on the records we have of proceedings."

"Correct."

"What if the record showed you admitting a new student. Rather than readmitting me. That would preserve the precedent while allowing me to re-admit."

The Head Master shook his head. "I would not let the record be tarnished by falsehoods. I understand that you want to be here Kyzyl, but admitting you under a name that is not your own—"

"Again, sir, I'm sorry to interrupt, but you didn't admit me under my name to begin with. You see, the first time I attended this university, I did so as Kyzyl Shenta."

"That is your name, isn't it?"

Kyzyl shook his head. "According to the traditions of my homeland, the family name is given first. To admit me properly, my name would be recorded as..."

"Shenta Kyzyl," Master Jonah finished. "Herman. I do think the man has a point. You and I have read the same histories. You know how important names can be."

The Head Master paused for a long time. Kyzyl felt his whole body go ice cold as he waited for this single man to decide the trajectory of the rest of his life. He looked at each of the other Masters in turn. He gave a desperate look to Master Telma, pleaded to Master Enwin with nothing but his gaze.

When the Head Master was finished deliberating, he said, "You understand what this means. You understand that you will be admitted as a new student and that all the progress you made until this point will be lost to you."

Kyzyl nodded.

"Do you also understand that Master Telma will not be the only one who will object to you being allowed to study here. Many of your fellow students are going to be justifiably furious at seeing you again. A simple change of the record will not change their minds."

"Yes, Head Master," Kyzyl said. "Their anger and objections are the consequences of the mistakes I made. I will not shy away from them, and I will do whatever it takes to prove to each of you and my fellow students that I can be better. If it takes the rest of my life, I will rebuild the trust I failed to uphold."

"All those in favor of allowing Shenta Kyzyl to take the admissions exam." Master Jonah, Master Enwin, Head

Master Herman, and the Masters of Enchantment and Artificing raised their hands. "Five and a half to four. Shenta Kyzyl, are you ready to take the exam to join the University Arcanum?"

"Yes, Head Master. I am ready."

The End

Acknowledgments

I have a ton of people to whom I owe this publication. Friends and family are, of course a cliché for this situation for a reason. No man is an island, as they say, and I am no exception. Not only has my family been the loudest supporters and the first people to promise to buy my books, but many of them were the people I looked to for help when I was stuck on certain scenes and concepts.

Still, there are a ton of professionals that deserve thanks for there excellent work on this project. Firstly, there are my wonderful editor and sensitivity readers. Susan Gaigher of Influunt Publishing Service was a great help in making my book make sense to everyone who is not me. Her help with consistent grammar and style as well as helping me cut dropped plot lines or flesh them out better was an invaluable service.

I owe a great deal to both my sensitivity readers as well: Georgina Kamsika and Nathaniel Glanzman (of Helm & Anchor Editing, LLC). Allowing me to borrow their experience and perspective was a major part of making sure this book addressed certain difficult topics with grace and humility. Getting to hear their voice helped me understand the perspective of my characters better than I could've ever done alone.

Finally there is the artistic talent behind my covers. You are, statistically speaking, more than likely enjoying the paperback version of this book with cover art courtesy of Andrei Bat. He did a wonderful job capturing my description of the University Arcanum.

If you were lucky enough to get the hardcover convention edition, you're looking at the stunning artwork of Mirela Barbu. Her cover art is instantly recognizable and I look forward to working with her again on future projects.

Thank you to everyone who came with me on this

journey. It still doesn't feel wholly real to me that this book is about to be published. I've done everything from setting up my LLC to sending final documents to Ingram Spark, and still this feels like a dream I might soon wake up from. Thank you all for making it real, and I hope I get the pleasure of working with you again on a future project.